La Conquistadora

La Conquistadora

Sharron S. Davidson

Chris Greer Press LLC
Rio Rancho, NM

ISBN 978-1-972194-05-8 (hardcover)
ISBN 978-1-972194-06-5 (trade paperback)
ISBN 978-1-972194-07-2 (ebook-PDF)
ISBN 978-1-972194-08-9 (ebook-EPUB)

First Edition
Printed in the United States of America

10 9 8 7 6 5 4 3 2 1

For my family, and for the country that raised us all.

In meteorology, a perfect storm is the rare convergence of ordinary forces into something none of them could have produced alone.

CONTENTS

BOOK ONE

BOOK TWO

BOOK ONE

Chapter 1 — La Conquistadora, Summer 1946

THE SKY WAS STILL. La Conquistadora knew better.

Sophie Louisa Degarrin, named quite properly for a grandmother and her own mother, woke on a May morning in 1946 to the smell of coffee and bacon drifting through the thick adobe walls of Casa Blanca. For a moment she lay still. She was home. After a whole year in Virginia, she was home, and through the open window the New Mexico sky was already that high, clean, heartbreaking blue that she had missed every single day she'd been gone.

Her room was exactly as she'd left it, but a year away made everything visible again: the child's lariat coiled on its hook by the door, the faded ribbon from a barrel race she'd won at thirteen on a horse that had since gone to pasture, and on the windowsill the jar of arrowheads she'd spent whole summers collecting across the mesas, chipped from flint by Comanche and Kiowa hunters who had tracked buffalo over this same land centuries before anyone called it La Conquistadora. Things she'd stopped seeing long before she left. She saw them now.

A letter lay on her bureau, propped against the mirror. She recognized the handwriting, a boy from a spring dance in Lexington, pleasant enough, forgettable. The envelope had been opened. Sophie pulled the page out and scanned it. Something about hoping she'd had a safe journey, hoping she'd write, hoping to see her again in the fall. A lot of hoping. She folded it back into the envelope and set it down.

Her mother had opened her mail. That was new. Or not new, exactly. Maybe just the first time she'd noticed.

Sophie dressed quickly: stiff new Levi's, her father's hand-tooled belt, and a light blue cotton blouse scattered with tiny white flowers that she'd brought back from a shop in Richmond. She hadn't thought much about it when she bought it. She just liked it. She tucked the tail in neatly and left the collar loose, a couple of buttons undone against the warmth of the morning. Her grandmother's small gold locket glinted at her throat, where it always was. She'd worn it since she was ten and never thought to take it off. She pulled on her boots and headed for the door.

Casa Blanca was an old rambling Spanish adobe whose rooms opened one onto the other at different levels, a hodgepodge that some people found completely charming and others deemed an appalling mishmash. Sophie loved every crack and creak of it.

She went out along the portal, the long covered porch that served as the house's true hallway, canopied by ancient trumpet vines, their green leaves and orange blossoms vivid against the old whitewashed adobe. The morning air carried that thin, dry sweetness she had ached for all winter: sage and sun-warmed earth and the faint clean bite of piñon. She let the screen door bang behind her.

"It's good to have you home." Michael Degarrin smiled at his daughter.

"It's even better to be home," Sophie told him.

Her mother, Louisa, gave a mock sigh. "I'd hoped my old home state would have been more to your liking." Her gaze touched the open collar of Sophie's blouse, the scattered flowers, the small gold locket catching the light against her daughter's skin, something quick and guarded that came and went before Sophie could place it. "I love your home state, Mamma," Sophie assured her. "I just love mine more." "Actually," her mother said with a laugh, "so do I." "It was silly that you made me leave New Mexico, you know," Sophie said.

"We have been over this many times, as you very well know," Louisa said. "Your father and I were not about to consider sending you to a co-ed school with the war just ending and the G.I.s returning in droves. Besides, it didn't hurt you one bit to spend a year at my old Randolph Macon, now did it?" "No, ma'am, it didn't," Sophie said. "In fact it buffed up my social graces so I can just be a proper belle for all those G.I.s at the University in Albuquerque this fall." "I'd still feel better if you were going back to Virginia," her father said.

"Now, Daddy, you just said you were glad I'm home from there," Sophie reminded him, "and besides, a deal's a deal." "I know." Degarrin sighed. "But we were hoping you would change your mind when we agreed you could finish up at the University of New Mexico if you went back east to a girl's school for your freshman year." "South, Michael, South. Not East." Louisa, whose people had been Virginians since before the Revolution, and who had never quite forgiven herself for falling in love with New Mexico, chimed in to defend her abandoned homeland. "Besides, I can't really say I blame Sophie for wanting to come home. This place really does grow on you. And, as she says a deal is a deal." "Hear, hear." Sophie raised her glass of orange juice. "I'll drink to that." The three Degarrins clinked their glasses and downed their juice.

Sophie sat back and smiled at her parents.

"I can hardly wait for things to get started," she said. "I lived all winter for this, the wagon, the riding, being out there under those skies. You know what I mean." Sophie paused, suddenly hit with a new thought. "Daddy, you two are still going to let me ride with the crew, aren't you? Just because the boys are back from the War won't change anything, will it?" Sophie's flood of anxious enquiries was stanched momentarily by a bite of bacon and biscuit.

Degarrin's and Louisa's eyes met and locked fleetingly over their child's head.

Sophie had no intention of staying at headquarters and missing anything. Still, parental approval always made for smoother sailing, so she promptly fell back on childhood charm.

"Well, I'm still your best hand, aren't I, Papa?"

"I guess so, Punkin, I guess so." Degarrin sighed a little, unconsciously falling back on his childhood name for her. He carefully avoided looking at his wife. Degarrin cleared his throat and continued with an attempt at parental firmness and authority. "But I'll tell you what, Sophie, your Mamma is getting a little worried about you spending too much time on a horse and not enough at the piano and in the kitchen. It might be about time you started learning how to act like a lady. Besides, hanging around those cowboys can be a bad business. They're just drifters, most of them. They've got no future, won't any of them amount to much." "Oh, good lord, Mamma!" Sophie turned disgusted eyes on her mother. "I'm not going to run off with some saddle tramp." Then, eyeing her mother, "Besides, like I've always told you, I intend to settle for nothing less than the governor's son or a prince or something — I just never can decide which. So you don't have to worry about that..." "Now, Sophie..." "Now, Mamma, don't try to act so astonished and innocent. I know that is exactly what you are fretting about, and without any reason whatsoever. All I want to do is laugh and ride and have a good time, just like I always have. All right? As for acting like a lady — I am a lady. How could I be anything else with you two for parents? Besides, when forced, I can make a cake, heavenly light biscuits, and play a waltz as well as anyone. Now, isn't that right?" Sophie tipped her head and twinkled, first at her mother and then at her father, "Well, isn't it?" Charmed, as ever, by their only offspring, Degarrin laughed. After a moment Louisa did too, though her smile arrived a beat late, and Sophie might have noticed if she hadn't been so pleased with herself. "Yes, yes it is true," Louisa acknowledged.

Degarrin smiled at Sophie. "You remind me of my cousin, Laura. Laura was the prettiest girl in town, and everyone knew it." "Well, Missy, as for you and the ever mythic 'Cousin Laura,' just remember, pretty is as pretty does," Louisa interjected tartly.

"Now, Louisa." Degarrin smoothed his wife's ruffled feathers with a sly wink. "Laura was just lucky you weren't in the same town." "So who would have been prettiest?" Sophie asked.

Degarrin turned an innocent gaze on his daughter. "Your Mamma, of course," he said with another wink and a sidelong glance to check his wife's response.

Louisa just rolled her eyes.

Through with food and teasing for the moment, the little family rose from the breakfast table. As they made their way along the portal, the early morning sun lit their world with a hint of gold and the promise of a beautiful day.

All in all, Sophie felt breakfast had been a success. In spite of her mother's considerable misgivings, she was going to be allowed to ride with the crew one more time. If there was one thing Sophie had learned in her nineteen years, it was to never rush her fences, and to choose her battles carefully, particularly where her mother was concerned.

Her parents turned in to the sitting room. Sophie slipped through the screen door and back onto the portal, catching it before it banged, something she'd forgotten while away but quickly remembered. She knew her mother's habit. Louisa would stand at the sitting room window after breakfast, gazing out across the hill-rimmed meadow to the dirt tank, water filled for once this spring, catching the sky so that from here it looked like a pretty pond of blue, fringed with new grass. Up close it was just brown muddied water in a scraped-out hollow. But Louisa had always had a gift for standing at exactly the right distance from things. So as Sophie neared the open casement she moved quietly, keeping to the far edge of the porch.

Her father's voice carried through first.

"Louisa, if you really object just say so. If it's really not proper, I won't let her do it."

Sophie stopped.

"She would never forgive you," her mother said.

"After a while she would. It's up to you, yea or nay. Either way I'll back you up."

A silence. When her mother spoke again her voice had gone soft, the way it only did when she called him Mike. Nobody else on the ranch called him that. Sophie sometimes wondered if anyone else even knew his name.

"I know you would, Mike, and I thank you."

"Well? It needs to be settled."

Her mother sighed. "Oh, let her ride. It means so much to her. But I don't like it. Kitten and Christine are hardly the type of girls she needs for bosom buddies. As for her close association with the cowboys, don't like that at all. They and their lifestyle can appear very romantic to a girl like Sophie. Putting a young girl, a young woman really I suppose..." A pause. "...in their midst can be very dangerous."

"Now, Louisa, no one on the Conquistadora crew would dare hurt Sophie, or even want to."

"Mike, that is not what I mean, as you very well know."

Sophie's face went warm. She should have kept walking.

"I know, dear, I know. You are right, though. Sophie isn't a little girl anymore. She really is a young woman, whether we are ready for her to be one or not. She's a smart girl, Louisa. She knows what she's about. Besides, we'll keep a close eye on her. Everything will be all right."

One more sigh, quieter than the others. "I suppose you're right. I worry about her too much. Anyway, she will be going to Albuquerque and the University in the fall. Maybe this will be the last summer of this nonsense. Hopefully by this time next year she will have outgrown all of it."

Sophie moved then, quickly and quietly. Out across the meadow, a cow and her calf were meandering toward the pond of blue for a drink.

Back in her bedroom she stood before the full-length mirror on her closet door. Her eyes went to the belt at her waist, the flowing, twining pattern of rosebuds and blossoms her father had carved for her last February. La Conquistadora was a country unto itself. A single pasture could swallow most ranches whole, and there were dozens of them. Her father's days were long, their hours crammed with the many duties, great and petty, that came with the captaining of such a vast endeavor. That he had found the time to sit somewhere quiet and carve flowers into leather for his daughter's birthday, she didn't know when he had done it, couldn't imagine when. It touched her more deeply than she had ever told him. She cherished the belt and wore it on every possible occasion.

A young woman, her mother had said. Not a girl.

Sophie studied her reflection. Over the years her baby-fine platinum cap had thickened and darkened to become the dark blonde cascade now caught back, unceremoniously, into a single fat ponytail. In the last year or so her face had changed, leaner, more defined, the soft roundness of girlhood giving way to something she wasn't quite sure of yet. She looked at herself through pure blue eyes and for a moment she saw what her mother saw, not the tomboy scamp who had ridden these hills since she could stay in a saddle, but someone new. Her grandmother's locket hung on its thin gold chain between her breasts, the same locket that had once lain flat against a little girl's chest. It didn't lie flat anymore.

Her boots were looking pretty ratty. Maybe she should polish them sometime. Not today though, not just now.

Sophie stepped out onto the portal and headed for the bunkhouse to tell Old Toby he was once again to be saddled with a petticoat crew. The trumpet vines hummed with early bees above her, the morning warming around her. Out past the corrals the land opened up, the mesas standing blue in the distance under a sky so big it could break your heart or fill it, depending on the day.

Sophie Degarrin knew exactly what this summer would be.

Chapter 2 — Getting Started

TOBY HAD MADE THE string assignments the night before, designating ten to twelve horses to each rider, divvied up so that every man would have a few good outside horses for the rough canyons and rolling plains, steady mounts for cutting and holding herd, and a few broncs and green horses whose educations needed continuing over the summer. At the end of six weeks he'd know their prospects, outstanding or merely serviceable.

For the most part, he was content with the way things were shaping up. There were still a couple of question marks as to who would be on the crew this year, and there might still be a last-minute bail out or two, but all in all, Toby felt confident about the makeup of his hands. It would be the first time since the fall of '41 that he would have a crew of able-bodied young men. He had been helping Degarrin run the huge show that was La Conquistadora with a bunch of old-timers and kids, the ones the War didn't want because they were either too old or too young. They had even had to let the girls ride, they were that short-handed. Toby had to admit that Miss Sophie, Christine, and his own daughter, Kitten, had made fine hands. But he didn't like it. It went against the grain to have girls out there whooping and hollering, acting like boys. It looked like he was going to be stuck with the girls for another season if last night was any gauge. At supper he had mentioned that with the War over and the men home from foreign parts, he guessed they could scrape by without Kitten's help this year. Of course there had been a major explosion. An outraged Kitten was damned near impossible for a naturally quiet man to handle. He had just barely been able to hold his own, in his own house, against his own daughter. If Miss Sophie was as set on the summer work as Kitten had been, he wasn't going to have any choice. He was going to be stuck with the girls.

It was early morning and cool yet, the sun still streaming over the hills to the east, lighting the canyons and painting the mesas. Toby liked this time of day the best, when everything was fresh and the day's face was still clean and bright. It was a peaceful time and he breathed it in, taking advantage of the calm. There was no telling how long it would last.

It didn't last long.

"Good morning, Toby!" Sophie sang out as she came across the graveled driveway toward him. "What a great day." She turned slowly around, arms outstretched, as though trying to soak the perfection of the morning into the pores of her skin. Completing her pirouette, Sophie bent her steady gaze on Toby, letting it rest there. It disconcerted him, just as it always did. Most people regarded Toby kind of casual-like; it wasn't often someone really looked him right in the eye and kept on looking. Miss Sophie was one of the few who did. She could lock about a hundred and twenty percent of her attention on you when she felt like sitting up and taking notice. It half irritated Toby to have a dab of a girl fluster him so.

"You oughtn't to be so dramatic, Missy. It's just another morning, like all the others."

"No, it isn't, Toby. This morning is perfect. Toby, life doesn't get any better than right here, right now, does it?"

Toby stopped being flustered by her earnest gaze and felt the old familiar affection tugging at him.

"Well, no, Miss Sophie. I don't suppose it does. Not for me, anyway."

"Not for me either, Toby." They grinned at each other. "We're lucky to be here, aren't we, Toby?"

"Yes, we are. Listen, do you hear it?"

"I hear it. The remuda is coming in."

Even though they had witnessed the scene hundreds, if not thousands, of times, both felt a surge of excitement as they eagerly watched for the leaders. Every morning the wrangler for the day rounded up the remuda and brought it in to headquarters so that the day's work could get started. The wrangler liked to be out there galloping in the crisp early light, and the horses did too. They knew the routine as well as he did and could have moseyed along to the corral and saddle shed in their sleep. But the herd liked a little fun, too. So every morning as the rider approached, a few of the leaders would feign amazement, throw up their heads and tails, and stand all aquiver for a moment or two. Then, snorting, they would pound away in a reckless escape from their herder and indulge in a thundering romp toward the headquarters, a mile or so away. The rest of the two-hundred-head remuda would spread out behind the leaders across the flats and the little rolls of hill, like a great spill of sorrel paint. The headlong dash to captivity was on. It happened every morning, and every morning it was like it had never happened before.

This morning's wrangler let out a howl as he crested the rise behind the herd, pure abandon, pure joy. Connor, back from the war. It had been close to four and a half years since the man had been part of this morning ritual, and from the sound of that howl he'd missed every day of it. Toby watched him spur his horse and settle into a hard run after the retreating remuda. It was hard to say who was having more fun, horses or rider. Connor was a good hand. Toby was glad to have him back.

• • •

The next two days were controlled chaos, and Toby was in the middle of all of it.

Getting the wagon out was a concerted effort, every hand on the place working sunup to sundown toward a single goal. The cowboys spent the days getting the last of the remuda shod and the chuck wagon loaded down with the host of paraphernalia that six weeks on the range required. The saddle shed rang from first light to last, men bent over horses, driving nails and filing hooves, while final repairs were made on everything that rolled or swung on a hinge, whether they were needed or not.

Toby moved through it all, checking and rechecking, because that was how things got done right and stayed done right.

He had Connor working steady at the far end of the shed, quiet, efficient, hadn't lost a step in four and a half years away. Junior Allen talked enough for both of them, which suited everybody fine. A quiet hand was worth two loud ones, in Toby's estimation.

Danny Parks was next to them, bent over a colt's forehoof. The boy had come up from Tennessee the winter before. Just showed up, hat in hand, asking if there was work. Toby had put him on a green colt that first day, just to see, and the colt had gentled under his hands like it had been waiting for him. Parks had a gift with horses that you couldn't teach a man if you had a hundred years. Toby had given him a strong string this summer, stronger than a hand his age and tenure usually drew. He'd earned it. If things went the way Toby hoped, he'd talk to Degarrin about keeping the boy on year-round.

Sophie showed up at the saddle shed before the dew was off the grass, dressed for work and looking to be useful. She fell in beside Kitten and Christine as naturally as if she'd never been away to Virginia at all, and the three of them set to work on their own strings with an ease that Toby, in his private heart, had to admit was impressive. Miss Sophie could handle a rasp and a hoof pick nearly as well as any man on the crew, and she didn't make a fuss about it; she just did it. Her mother would not have approved of the sight: her daughter's hands black with hoof oil, her blouse darkened with sweat, trading barbs with the cowboys like she was one of them. Which, as far as Sophie was concerned, she was.

By midmorning the heat had settled in for good and a couple of the boys had pulled their shirts off, which was nothing unusual and nobody thought twice about it. Connor was one of them. He was working bent over a bay's hind hoof at the far end of the shed, and whatever else the War had done to the man it had certainly changed his body. He was lean and hard, all whittled down, with a tattoo on his left shoulder, dark against the sun-browned skin, that Toby was fairly certain had not been there when Connor had left for the Army back in '41.

Parks was shirtless too, and the War had done its work on him same as it had Connor. But no tattoo, nothing that advertised where he'd been or what he'd done. That was the difference in the boy. It was all baked in. Somebody had taken the trouble to raise him right.

Sophie happened to be passing through just then with an armload of shoes, and her step slowed for a moment. Just a moment, and it probably didn't mean a thing, but her eyes found Connor and stayed there a moment too long before she caught herself and moved on.

Toby watched her go. She was a pretty girl, and Connor was a good-looking young man without his shirt on, and that was probably all it was. But Toby had been running crews a long time, and he knew how these things could start, quietly, without anybody meaning anything by it, without anybody even knowing it had begun.

Toby kept one eye on the work and one eye on the girl after that. He'd been watching Sophie Degarrin grow up on this ranch since she was barely tall enough to see over the corral rail. She wasn't a girl anymore, not really, though it would have taken a braver man than Toby to say so out loud. Her parents had their worries. He was beginning to have his own.

He checked on Mustard, Custard, Nip, and Tuck, the team of four big buckskin horses that would pull the chuck wagon on its long trek. They'd been given extra oats and gone over twice already, but Toby ran his hands down each leg and checked each shoe one more time. The team would cover two hundred miles before they trotted back into headquarters six weeks later. It would be a long, rough haul. Everything had to be right.

Ricky C de Baca turned up on the second morning, grinning and eager, newly assigned as this year's hoodlum. He was green as spring grass and appeared to be under the impression that his new position was some kind of promotion.

Toby walked him over to the hoodlum wagon. "This is yours for the next six weeks. You drive it camp to camp: drums of water, branding irons, rope corral, anything that won't fit in Ignacio's chuck wagon. Steady trot. You don't run this team. You take care of this rig, because if it breaks down out there, you're the one walking."

Ricky peered into the wagon bed with interest. "What's the rope corral for?"

"Holding the remuda when the wrangler brings them in. You string it up every time we make camp, and you do it right the first time. Two hundred horses pushing on a bad tie will go right through it, and then you'll spend the rest of your day chasing them across the flats instead of eating supper."

"Yes, sir."

"Now come on. You need to meet your boss."

Ignacio Mandragon was at the chuck wagon, standing on a crate and reaching into the depths of the wagon bed, rearranging things that did not, by any reasonable estimation, need rearranging. But Ignacio always rearranged things one last time. He had commenced on this journey many times before, and he had his ways.

"Ignacio, this is your hoodlum," Toby said.

Ignacio looked down from his crate and took the measure of his new helper with dark, unhurried eyes. Ricky straightened up.

"You cook?" Ignacio asked.

"Some," Ricky said.

"You chop firewood?"

"Yes, sir."

"Peel potatoes?"

"Yes, sir."

"Wash dishes without breaking them?"

Ricky hesitated just a fraction too long. "Yes, sir."

Ignacio looked at Toby. "He'll break my dishes."

"Probably," Toby agreed.

Ignacio sighed and turned back to the wagon. "Come here. I show you how my wagon is packed, and you do not move anything without asking me first." He pointed as he went. "Eggs are in the oat barrels. Break one and I send you home. Dutch ovens here, bean pot there. Flour sacks on top because flour and rain don't mix. The dried peaches are mine. I make the cobbler. Not you."

"Yes, sir."

"Good. Go chop firewood."

Sophie had been watching the exchange from across the way, leaning on a fence rail.

"Don't worry, Ricky," she called over. "Ignacio's cobbler makes up for everything."

"Is it that good?"

"It's a Conquistadora institution. You'll understand after the first one."

At last, after two days of hard work, everything was as ready as it was going to get. The aged chuck wagon and its harness had been given one last meticulous inspection. Alongside the tools and ingredients of its driver's trade, it bore tepees for the cowboys and was piled high with their fat and cumbersome bedrolls. Even so, plenty could go wrong in the coming weeks; it was quite likely that everyone, from cook to cowboys to hoodlum, would fill in as repairman and general handyman before the summer was through. Six weeks of it: the fresh pure air one day, the rolling red dust the next, and on some evening the scent of rain coming before you could see it. Toby knew every bit of it by heart. He wouldn't trade a single one.

Sophie, Kitten, and Christine had claimed their seats on the dark red fence that enclosed Casa Blanca's lawn. The day was already hot, although the sun had not been long in its morning climb. The air was dead still, without even a breath of breeze, though in a few weeks the summer storms would see to that, and the girls were more than willing to bask in the dense cottonwood shade while they waited. Behind them, a carpet of velvet-soft, vivid green-blue grass lay in a crescent, bordered by flower beds filled with roses and snapdragons. All her life, the quick crunch of gravel and the staccato click of boot heels on flagstone had heralded the approach of Sophie's father. This morning there were no such sounds, but the scene was set, awaiting only his arrival.

Across the way, Ignacio climbed up into the driver's seat. With the suppressed excitement he still felt, even after all these years, the cook solemnly gathered the reins in his able hands. He released the brake, clucked to his team, and nodded to Degarrin, who stood on the ground below. The wheels began to turn and the summer work commenced.

Ricky, a beat behind, scrambled up onto the seat of the hoodlum wagon. If this was old hat to Ignacio, it was brand new to Ricky. With a whoop he set his rig off after the chuck wagon at a good clipping pace.

"Ricky!" barked Degarrin. "Slow down! If you lame that team, you'll be pulling that wagon yourself."

"Yes, sir. Sorry, sir." At a sedate trot, but with a flourishing wave of his Stetson to the audience on the fence, the hoodlum and his wagon made their exit.

Amid laughs and waves, Kitten called, "We'll see you tomorrow, Ricky!"

"I'll live for the moment!" Ricky shouted back.

The dust rose and thinned behind the two wagons as they grew small against the flats. On the fence, the three girls were already talking about tomorrow, which horses they'd ride, which pastures they'd work. As far as they were concerned, nothing had changed.

Toby folded his string list into his shirt pocket. He had his doubts about that.

Chapter 3 — Dinner and a Trip to Town

DINNER AT LA CONQUISTADORA was one of her mother's favorite rituals, and ritual it was. The dinner hour had somehow become almost sacred, a tribute and nod of acquaintance to the past, a road map into the future. People dressed for dinner. Levi's were not seen past six o'clock of an evening. Tonight her mother surveyed the table with that look of deep contentment she wore when everything was exactly as it should be: a beautifully served meal, her husband, her daughter.

From through the swinging kitchen door there came an ear-splitting shriek and a clanging crash.

"Ay caramba! Madre de Dios!" came Rufina's cry as Degarrin, Sophie, and Louisa simultaneously sprang for the kitchen door and all the excitement.

Rufina came crashing through the screen door from outside and into the kitchen at the same moment all the Degarrins came pouring in from the dining room. Rufina was shaking and still babbling wildly when Louisa grabbed her by the shoulders.

"My God, Rufina! What happened? Are you all right?" she demanded.

Rufina gripped her boss's hand, squeezing the blood right out of it.

"Señora Louisa," she cried, still very agitated. "It was that goddamned snake! I went to the milk room to get a pitcher of nice cold milk, so Señor Degarrin could have a glass, just the way he likes it. That damned old snake was waiting for me! As soon as I came out the door with my nice old pitcher of milk, that damned red thing ran at me. I screamed and jumped. That pitcher of milk went flying up into the sky, and now, look at me. I'm covered in milk, dripping like a mop, and the devil only knows where the pitcher or the snake have gotten to."

Louisa comforted her cook. "Calm down, my dear. It was just that red racer again. He's chased me a few times, too. I don't like it either! I wish he would leave, but he doesn't seem to have any plans to. But for now at least, the snake has run off, you're fine, and look, here is Sophie with the pitcher. She has gone and found it, and see, it is fine, too."

Sophie brought a towel and began to wipe the still lingering milk drops from Rufina's hair and face. Louisa squeezed Rufina's damp shoulders and smiled encouragingly.

"There, everything and everybody is fine now."

Rufina was not so sure.

"That nasty red snake should not be allowed to live here with civilized people," she declared. "One day it was in the tree outside the kitchen door. It waited for me to come along and then it swung down, right into my face! It scared me nearly to death! Then it just wriggled away, laughing, I know! And now this. That snake should not be allowed to live here!"

"No, it should not," Louisa agreed.

"And Señor Degarrin, he should not be laughing at me either!"

"No, he should not!" Louisa again agreed, darting her husband a darkling look. "Sophie," she said, "please get your father out of here."

"Well, anyway, Mr. Señor Michael Degarrin," Rufina announced triumphantly, "there is now no cold milk for you to drink with your dinner."

"Just as well," Louisa assured her. "He doesn't deserve any anyway."

"No, he doesn't," Rufina agreed, but she had always been a sucker for Degarrin's charm and she was having to fight the twitch of a smile that was trying to break through her armor. When Degarrin winked at her she gave up and burst out laughing with him.

"Go on," she exclaimed, waving her arms at them. "Go on, and get out of my kitchen! How can I feed you helpless gringos when all you do is stand around and take up room in my kitchen?"

Having been shooed from the kitchen and back into her allotted place at the table, Sophie eyed her mother.

"Rufina and the snake might be just fine, Momma, but your silver pitcher is not so hot. It now has a nice dent in it."

"Oh, well," Louisa sighed. "At least this dent has a story to go with it. A lot of them don't, you know."

"So much for culture on the prairie," Louisa commented. "It's a constant battle, and sometimes losing is more fun than winning."

It was a battle that had been going on longer than any of them. The first investors in the great ranch, after it had passed from Spanish hands, had been British, men with money and backgrounds whose concept of rural life was rather elegant. The tone for life on La Conquistadora had been set by men reared on the great country estates of England, ratified by the manners and expectations of later investors from the mansions of Long Island. One of them had even built a lodge out by the lake with its own airstrip, so that movie stars and other luminaries could fly in to drink and gamble and carry on to their hearts' content. None of them had had any experience with the hardscrabble survival required on many homesteaded western ranches. They had walked into a complete kingdom, separate and firmly established by the Spanish dons, and they expected it to run accordingly. The rowdy West of some fact and lots of Hollywood fiction stopped at the fenced lawn of Casa Blanca and never even drifted near its front door. Then Louisa Madison Degarrin arrived from Virginia, added a twist of the Old South, and the matter was settled for good. People dressed for dinner. The red racer had not gotten that message.

None of the Degarrins had ever truly understood that La Conquistadora really was another world. They were not alone; the men and women who spent their lives living and working there never knew it either. But the cowboys who came and then went to work for other outfits just noticed that somehow nothing ever quite measured up to their memories of La Conquistadora.

As things returned to normal and food actually appeared before them, Louisa asked about the photographers. Degarrin had invited a pair of them out from Albuquerque, a fellow named David Harvey and his partner, Gary Sloan, to document life on the range. "The great

American cowboy, the 'last of the breed,' and all that," as Degarrin put it. Louisa had raised an eyebrow at that, but she liked having visitors and was curious to see what they made of the place.

"Oh, they're all over the place," Sophie assured her. "They've taken a million pictures of everything they see. All the cowboys constantly pose for them, every chance they get." Then, with a bat of her eyelashes, she confessed, "Of course Kitten, Christine, and I do, too."

"I would have been surprised if you didn't," her mother assured her. "What about you, Mike?" she asked. "Struck any good poses lately?"

"Of course not!" he answered instantly, but his blush betrayed him. "Well, not many anyway!"

Dinner progressed amidst more good-natured bantering, when Degarrin recalled something of a more serious nature.

"We are getting pretty low on vaccine at the wagon. Could you run into town in the morning and pick some up, Sophie? I phoned in the order to Doc Thompson and he'll have it all ready for you by about nine o'clock or so."

Sophie nodded. "Sure. I haven't been into town for a while. Can Kitten and Christine go with me?"

"I don't see why not," Degarrin responded.

"Is there anything you want from town, Momma?" Sophie asked. "Or would you like to come along?"

"I don't know," Louisa answered. "I haven't really thought about it. Now, let me see, is there anything pressing I have to do tomorrow morning?" She ran through a mental checklist. "I think everything is under control and this place can get along without me for a while," she concluded. "It's a date."

"Great," Sophie said. "Shall we still invite Kitten and Christine?"

"Whatever you want is fine by me."

"Then let's leave them at home this time."

Louisa was a little touched that her daughter wanted her to herself. "So be it," she said. "It will be just the two of us. Maybe we can even squeeze in time to shop a little."

"Little is about right," Sophie said. "What between Johnson's Dry Goods and Elyse's Dress Shop, I would imagine that a little shopping is all that's available."

"Well, we can look around, sometimes they surprise you. We found your beautiful cream cashmere skirt there. Remember? Maybe they'll have a few things suitable for school this fall."

"Maybe so, but I'm not overly optimistic."

Louisa looked at her a moment. "Sophie, are you absolutely sure that you don't want to go back to Randolph Macon for your sophomore year?"

"Momma, I'm sure."

"I just don't see why you didn't like it, dear. I loved it when I was there."

"I know you did, Momma. And it's not that I didn't like it; it was all right. But I just missed New Mexico too much. I missed the clear bright blue skies and the light and the feel of the air. Sorry, Momma, I guess I'm just a provincial at heart. The benefits of society and culture seem to be entirely wasted on me."

"Not at all, sugar," her father spoke up. "You are just a child of tierra encantada, the land of enchantment. It happens to everyone that stays around this state long enough. Look at your mother. You don't see her hotfooting it off to Virginia every chance she gets. In fact, you had to twist her arm just now to get her off this ranch for just a few hours tomorrow." "I know, it's true, it's true. The place has captured me. Actually, Sophie, I understand exactly what you mean. But I was hoping you would break free and see a little of the world, find out a little bit about other places and people."

"Well, Mom, you don't need to worry. You succeeded in shipping me out of here all last year. I saw lots of new places and met lots of new people. Besides, I've met people from all over the world right here at La Conquistadora, movie stars, senators, cattlemen from South America. And we've gone back to visit your family in Virginia every year, Momma. Even during the war Daddy finagled a way for you and me to go. So, calm down. I know there is a whole big world out there and I intend to see it all. I just intend to see it operating out of a home base right here in New Mexico, that's all."

"That's good enough for me, Punkin," Degarrin told his daughter. "Sounds like an excellent plan. Meanwhile, Miss Louisa, what has

Rufina whipped up for dessert? Any hope of chocolate cake and a little whipped cream?"

"How about cherry cobbler instead?" she answered.

"It'll do in a pinch."

Louisa picked up the silver bell beside her place at the table and gave it a practiced shake.

Rufina popped through the swinging door from the kitchen. "Do I hear Señor Degarrin's sweet tooth calling?" she asked.

Degarrin grinned. "That you do, Rufina."

"Just one little minute, then. Cherry cobbler coming right up. I've been warming it in the oven, just waiting for that little jingle bell." Rufina disappeared back through the door and the Degarrin clan sat back in anticipation.

Eight o'clock the following morning found Sophie and Louisa on their way to Clauson, a thriving metropolis of four thousand people, give or take a few. When people said they were going to town, they meant Clauson. Anything more exotic than grocery shopping, buying veterinary supplies, or browsing for an occasional new dress required a trip to Las Vegas ninety miles away, or considerably farther, to either Albuquerque or Amarillo. Fortunately, Clauson was also able to accommodate those who needed a broken leg or arm set.

Their primary quest was for vaccine to inoculate La Conquistadora's calf crop against blackleg and malignant edema. Secondly, they were willing to partake of whatever pleasures the little town had to offer on this bright summer morning.

Armed with the key to her mother's pink Oldsmobile, Sophie went to fetch the car. It was stabled in one of the ancient adobe outbuildings that made up the far-flung ranch headquarters, which ranged over several acres. To get there she went down the long portal, cut through the dining room and kitchen, where she paused to chat a moment with Rufina. Out the kitchen door, she walked across the back of the headquarters and down toward the creek. This back area was separated from the front driveway and main compound by a high wooden fence, a gate, and a cattle guard, all powerfully built, Sophie supposed, in case it ever became necessary to stop a speeding herd of buffalo. At any rate, fences at headquarters tended to be of wood, six feet high, topped by a flat board six inches wide, and painted a dull red that was guaranteed to rub off on the back sides of jeans and shirtsleeves. Sort of a red badge of courage. At one time or another in her childhood she had walked the top of every one of these fences. The flat tops themselves had been no trick at all, but to balance on the two-inch-wide gates, jiggling on their hinges, had been no small feat. Sophie had been quite proud of that accomplishment and she still was, although she had long ago given up the sport.

Continuing across the back compound, past the water tower and creaking windmill, past two repair shop buildings, the vegetable cellar, and the meat house, she finally arrived at two low adobe structures, built some eighty years before, that met at an angle to form the back boundary along the creek bank. Years before, these buildings had been stables or storerooms, but now instead of horses they housed cars and pickups, and a stack of decrepit and decaying tires that the rough ranch roads chewed through faster than anyone could haul them away.

The Olds's stall was in the heart of the angle, just a few feet from the encroaching creek bank. Presumably the creek had changed its course over time and the buildings had not intentionally been built so near the precipice. Another good flood or two and it would very likely be adios adobes, and maybe contents as well, if some future moving crew didn't move fast enough. However, on this clear June morning, none of this concerned Sophie in the least. She was here to retrieve her mother's car, which she did with a flourish. She wheeled the Olds out with practiced ease, spun the wheel, and since there was no one around to observe, hit the gas and sprayed gravel for twenty feet. Sophie and the Olds barreled across the back compound, flew over the cattle guard, spun past the maintenance shop and chuck wagon shed, to arrive in triumph at the north gate to the lawn of Casa Blanca, where her mother stood awaiting her chauffeur and chariot.

Louisa got into the car, shaking her head. "Sophie, I hope you haven't blown my engine just getting here from the garage."

"Oh, I doubt it, Mom. Oldsmobile makes a really good product."

"I hope so."

Sophie held her tongue. Her father insisted on a new Oldsmobile every couple of years as part of his arrangement with the owners (the one worldly and impractical thing about the man) and then rode the fences in them, every cattle trail from one boundary to the other, because that was what a good cattleman did. If they could survive her father, Sophie figured they could survive her.

The hands were at work around the saddle shed as they passed, finishing the last of the preparations before the crew moved out to join the wagons. Connor was among them. He looked up as the Olds went by, and their eyes caught for just a second before Sophie turned back to the road. In the rearview mirror, he was still standing there, still watching, long after the corrals had fallen behind them.

They were off, flying up the lane through the green arch of dipping, waving cottonwoods, then twisting and turning, cutting between the little mesas that would have barred their path. Before them was a steep hill with a tight turn at the bottom and another at the top. Hardly slowing and never hesitating, they charged up it, and were on top of the world. The mesa was miles across, and from this rolling, broken tabletop it seemed that one could see almost forever. The sky was clear to every horizon, not a line of weather anywhere.

This dramatic climb from creek-bottom lowlands to mesa top brought a smile to Louisa's face, as it always did, even after all these years.

"I love climbing up this hill with you, Momma. You always start smiling like the cat that just swallowed the canary."

"When I see this view, that is exactly how I feel. I just can't believe it. All this and heaven too."

"Oh, Momma, you are just too syrupy," Sophie complained.

"You feel exactly the same way too, Missy."

"Everybody does. You're just the only one who says it out loud."

"That, young lady, is because I am the only one capable of articulating my sentiments."

Sophie just smiled as she deftly slowed and swerved to avoid hitting one of her father's purebred Hereford yearlings. Such a collision would not have been an auspicious way to start the day.

The mesa was crossed before too many minutes passed. If the rapid ascent had been dramatic, equally impressive was arrival at the opposite side. With absolutely no warning the road bent around a fold in the terrain and there, swept out below them for miles, was a sea of grass across a red plain, finally broken in the distance by yet another rimrocked horizon. They sped down off the mesa and across that grassy expanse, their passage marked by a trail of high-floating red dust caught up infinitely in the breathless morning air.

Sophie's progress was halted at La Conquistadora's western boundary, where a locked gate stood across the road between adobe gateposts, stuccoed and painted white, that the red soil had long ago turned salmon. Brass plates were embedded in each post: one bore a three-pointed crown and the name La Conquistadora, the other read "Member, New Mexico Cattle Growers." Neither Sophie nor Louisa spared a moment or a thought for the gateway to their world. They used it as an exit, and once through that locked gate they joined the rest of the twentieth century.

In a mile or two they came to Peralta Lake, where the dam blocked the confluence of the Canadian and Red Rivers. The lake was rather enormous, particularly by southwestern standards, stretching its long reaching arms way up the rivers. Beneath its surface, made to look blue and beautiful by a trick of light and sky, stood deep canyons, hillocks, the skeletons of waterlogged and rotting trees, a cemetery, and the remnants of an abandoned village. In times of drought, the tops of the submerged hills sometimes appeared as islands through the lake's sinking surface. All that water, in a land of little rain, was a miracle in itself.

"Look how still the lake is today," Louisa commented. "It doesn't even have a ripple."

Sophie shifted her attention from the road to the lake. "There aren't any boats out, not a single one."

"No," her mother agreed. "No one seems to come out here much during the week. But I'll bet it is busy this weekend."

"No doubt."

The road ran smack on top of the dam and was narrow, with room for two lanes of traffic, barely. There was no room for error, and even Sophie paid close attention, sparing only an occasional glance for the water far below. Clustered at either end of the dam and ranging along the shoreline was a ramshackle settlement of weekend cabins, campsites, a couple of cafes, and a small hotel with a bar and dance floor grandly called the Lodge. Lots of local Saturday nights were whiled away downing beers and two-stepping at the Lodge.

Leaving this Mecca of civilization in their wake, they continued along the River Road, which wound along adhering to the course of the Canadian, the same path that Spain's explorers and slow-moving trade caravans had followed three hundred years earlier. The way was rough, even today. It had taken its toll on modern tires just as it had on the wooden and steel-rimmed wheels of long-forgotten carts and wagons.

"Here come the Narrows," Sophie said. She still felt that little thrill of excitement when approaching the Narrows.

"Remember how Daddy would always tell me, when I was little, about the Comancheros that were hiding there, waiting to attack unwary wanderers, and kidnap them and trade them to the Comanches?"

"Such lovely tales to be telling to a little girl," Louisa commented, as she usually did along here.

"True," Sophie agreed, "but I learned not to be unwary."

"Or to be a wanderer."

Sophie smiled and piloted them out of danger, leaving far behind the high-cliffed, rough-rocked Narrows, where many a clandestine action and evil deed had been carried out in the past, and would likely be again.

They rode on in silence, each lost in her thoughts of this and other journeys, both taken and still to come. The miles and the minutes passed in a comfortable and familiar quiet. After a while the ragged edges of the outskirts of Clauson gathered them in. They passed a scattering of fields and farms, then crossed over the railroad tracks on a bridge that had seemed so high to Sophie as a child but was really just an overpass, and drove into the streets of downtown Clauson.

"OK, Momma. What's first?"

"First, I think we'll stop by the Elk Drug Store and say hello to Myrtle and Clyde and make arrangements to pick up the vaccine on our way out of town. Then we'll drop in to see if Elyse has anything new in. We may as well start getting your school clothes together if we can."

They drove down the main street, which was mostly empty. People with somewhere to go were already there. The moms were still at home, feeding the kids or shooing them out of the house or even out of bed. The moms of Clauson would not be out on the town until later. By then, Louisa and Sophie would be on their way back home. For the moment, the town was theirs alone.

"Look," Sophie exclaimed, "there's Elyse unlocking her door even as we speak. Let's stop here first."

"Louisa! Come in, come in. I was just thinking of calling you. Sophie, I'm so glad to see you. I just got a new shipment in yesterday and there are a few things I think you'll like. Come and see."

Elyse led them into the back room, where an aged sofa sat behind a scuffed-up coffee table covered with piles of fashion magazines, some ancient, some brand new. A rocking chair with an afghan tossed over its back completed the haphazard but very inviting sitting area.

"Louisa, a cup of spiced tea? Sophie, I've got Cokes, too, if you would like that better."

But Sophie was already lost to them, engrossed in perusing a rack of new arrivals.

Louisa temporarily declined Elyse's hospitality. "I'd love a cup of tea in a minute, but first, I'm afraid I'm as bad as Sophie. I can't wait to see what you've gotten in."

"Be my guest." Elyse laughed and waved her toward the racks where Sophie was captured and enraptured by a mother lode of goodies.

The hunting among the racks was good this morning. Elyse brought forth, with a flourish, a little black dress with a white portrait collar. It was delightful and brought appreciative smiles to the faces of mother and daughter alike.

"Go ahead and try it, sweetie," Louisa urged.

While Sophie tried on the black dress, Elyse produced a blue skirt and sweater of the softest cashmere. "When I saw this at market I thought of Sophie. I believe it's just the color of her eyes."

"It's perfect," declared Louisa.

Numerous skirts, blouses, sweaters, scarves, and dresses later, Sophie's clothing thirst was slaked, as was Louisa's need to dress her daughter like a princess.

Only after this feeding frenzy was completed were the ladies able to retire to rocker and sofa, where they sat contentedly trading gossip and bits of news while sipping tea and nibbling shortbread cookies.

• • •

Although no one would have ever guessed it, Adam Connor was acutely aware of Sophie's absence from the wagon that day and hoped she would be back tomorrow.

Chapter 4 — Louisa

IT HAD RAINED DURING the night. Louisa Degarrin was an early riser. The first vague hint of light was her favorite part of the day. Not so her husband: Degarrin got up early because he had a lot to do and his ambitious nature wouldn't allow him to sleep in. Louisa rose before dawn because she loved to see the first streaks of light that heralded the birth of a new day. She liked to greet each day personally while its face was still fresh and clean from a night of rest, and no lines were yet written across its slate. It was even better after a night of rain. The dust would be laid and the air itself washed clean, its scent crystal clear and spring fresh.

Slipping from their shared bed, Louisa quickly donned her serviceable denim skirt and cardigan sweater set of red cashmere. It was always nippy out this early. Stepping onto the portal, she smiled with pure pleasure. It was perfect, better than she had imagined. No one else in the whole of headquarters was up but her. She had the place to herself. In the perfect silence and the murkiness of the coming day she was greeted by the sweet bouquet of mingled roses, honeysuckle, and trumpet blossoms.

Louisa crunched across the still-damp gravel of the walkway and through the gate onto the drive. On across the firm wet sand surface of the compound she strode, headed toward the creek behind the horse corrals. As she rounded the corner of the corral fence she could hear it before she saw it: the blessed sound of babbling water running in the often dry creek bed.

Through the trees she could see the ripples and swirls of red-brown water, tinted so by the red sand and soil of La Conquistadora.

Not too far away from where she stood was the sturdy little steel house and pens, painted the signature dull red of headquarters, where the pigs nominally lived. Louisa supposed the pigs had been at the ranch since well before the turn of the century, not these specific pigs, but pigs in general. Upon seeing Louisa, these specific pigs came snuffling and oinking over for a visit. This was a little unusual, as they were very seldom anywhere near their house. The pigs infinitely preferred ranging at will all over the far-flung compound, checking out the comings and goings of their fellow residents to staying at home. They were black pigs with a wide white stripe around their equally wide middles. Louisa had once suggested that they acquire some variety in the pig population and get some red ones, since red seemed to be La Conquistadora's color of preference. Her suggestion had been greeted with blank stares; La Conquistadora without black-and-white pigs would not be La Conquistadora. So the tradition continued and made itself felt in the form of six porkers waddling amiably toward Louisa, snuffling and grunting their greetings as they came.

"Good morning, Sigmund. And how are you, Alistair, and Blanche, and Myrtle, and Maud? Well, there you are, Grettle. My dear, I am very sorry to have to tell you, but I did hear you being discussed the other day. It seems the cook was commenting that Grettle was just about ready for the griddle."

Grettle didn't seem to be concerned, so Louisa decided not to worry about it either. Instead, she turned her attention once more to the wonder of La Cinta's flow as the pigs shuffled around keeping her company.

She wasn't the only one up this early. A little way downstream, a young cowboy was crouched at the water's edge, picking through the stones along the bank. As Louisa watched, he sent one skipping across La Cinta's current, three clean bounces before the water took it. He tried another and got four.

"You're getting good at that," Louisa called, and the young man straightened up, hat in hand before he'd even finished turning around. It was Danny Parks, the boy from Tennessee who had come on the previous winter, the kind of young man who took his hat off for a lady without thinking about it, because it had been taught early and never forgotten.

“Morning, Mrs. Degarrin. Didn’t expect to find anybody else out here this early.”

“I’m always out this early. Best part of the day.”

“Yes, ma’am, it is.” He looked out at the creek and shook his head, and there was something like wonder in his face. “I still can’t get over it, you know. Back home in Tennessee you just take a running creek for granted. Out here it feels like a present every time it rains. And the afternoon downpours, I never would have believed there’d be rain like that west of the Mississippi.”

“It surprised me too, once upon a time,” Louisa said. “I’m from Virginia. I thought I was coming to a desert.”

“Virginia.” Danny smiled. “That’s just a stone’s throw from Tennessee.”

“Practically neighbors,” Louisa agreed.

He nodded, glanced toward the bunkhouse, and put his hat back on. “I’d best get going, ma’am. Mr. Lloyd doesn’t take kindly to slow starters.”

“No, he doesn’t. Good morning, Danny.”

“Ma’am.” He tipped his hat and headed off toward the corrals, unhurried and easy in his stride.

She walked down the wet firm sand and stood by the shore for a moment, still accompanied by the more gregarious and curious of her flock. Along the bank, back a ways from the water, was a great tree trunk, the remains of a once-mighty cottonwood washed down long, long ago from somewhere upstream. It was now devoid of bark, worn and weathered smooth by time and the elements. Louisa settled herself upon its inviting expanse and sat for a few moments among the pigs, savoring the early morning face of La Conquistadora and wondering what other souls, recently or perhaps in ancient times, had paused here to do the same.

It still struck her sometimes, quietly and without warning, that she was here at all. She had been born and raised Louisa Madison of Charlotte, Virginia, and she had liked it very well. It had never occurred to her that she would leave that beautiful and civilized spot.

The ladies of her family stayed in Charlotte and had wonderful lives, or at least those surviving the Civil War and Reconstruction had, from all accounts. The thought of heading West had never crossed her mind. And never would have, had it not been for the fact that her father operated the still-large remnants of the family's ancestral plantation.

On this plantation, Major Madison had, over time and through dedicated effort, developed a prize-winning and much-renowned herd of registered Hereford cattle. An innovative young man named Michael Degarrin came calling one day in hopes of buying some of the much-heralded Madison Herefords. He wanted only the best, and that was why he had come to Charlotte and Major Madison's Fairfield Farms.

When he made the acquaintance of the family's youngest daughter, he had realized that prize Herefords were not, after all, the best that Fairfield Farms had to offer.

Her family had been appalled. She was too young; she had to finish school. New Mexico was too far away, too uncivilized; it was at the back of beyond. Louisa had not been raised and educated to waste away on some enormous, isolated, and godforsaken ranch in the middle of nowhere. Mr. Degarrin had best just take his cattle, or don't even bother with the cattle, just take himself back to New Mexico and forget all about Louisa and all this nonsense.

Michael Degarrin took his case to the fair Louisa and asked her what she wanted. She looked at the man before her, the dark blond hair, the lean, hard-muscled body, and knew he was the most handsome man she had ever laid eyes on. She also understood, instinctively, that he was one of the best men she would ever encounter. Louisa Madison gazed into his clear blue eyes and said, "I am going to love New Mexico and La Conquistadora."

On a fine May afternoon two years later, Louisa Madison graduated from Randolph Macon at two o'clock in the afternoon. At seven o'clock that evening she became the bride of Michael Degarrin, who proudly bore away the finest treasure ever produced at Fairfield Farms.

Louisa watched the red-brown water of La Cinta slide past and smiled. Twenty-some years, a daughter, a war, and a country of red dirt later, she had proven true to her word. Then, spying a smooth flat stone, she scooped it up and expertly sent it skimming across La Cinta's waters in four perfect skips.

"Not bad," she told her audience. "It's hard to get more than three." The pigs grunted their agreement.

That boy reminded her of home, not this home, the other one, the first one. Every cowboy on La Conquistadora took his hat off and said "ma'am"; that was just manners. But the soft drawl Danny put on the word, unhurried and easy, like he had all the time in the world, that was something different. That was the South talking. Tennessee wasn't Virginia, but it was close enough. Louisa knew the breed. She found herself entertaining the kind of idle thought that passes through a mother's mind from time to time and never quite leaves: if Sophie were ever to find a boy like Danny Parks, a Southern boy who could sit at her grandmother's table and hold his own, a steady young man who might just carry her daughter back to the kind of life where the ladies of the family stayed put and had wonderful lives, well. That would be a thought worth having.

It was a mother's daydream, nothing more. But it was a nice one.

Headquarters was beginning to come to life. The bunkhouse kitchen light was on. That meant Peggy Hampton had come down and was starting her biscuits. Soon she would have bacon popping in a vast cast-iron skillet, to be followed by eggs whipped lemon yellow for scrambling. Peggy filled in for Ignacio as bunkhouse cook while the wagon was out each year. These few weeks that Peggy cooked were the only time all year that a fluffy scrambled egg could be found at the bunkhouse.

Casa Blanca would be stirring as well. Michael Degarrin would be rising, if not shining just yet, impatiently waiting for her return. Her husband of over twenty years still retained some childhood traits, one of which was the eternal desire for the focused concern and attention of the lady of the house. As a boy he had wanted his mom to stay properly focused on him; as a man he wanted this of Louisa. He liked to get up and talk to her, plotting his coming day while he prepared to face it. For the most part Louisa found this a rather endearing trait and usually humored him in it. But sometimes she felt like an early morning reconnoiter on her own and left him to his own devices, knowing full well that he was perfectly capable of thriving without her. It was true, he was, though he was loath to admit he missed her presence on such occasions. But he did miss her always, and felt slightly abandoned and off center when he woke to find her gone from his bed and view. Well aware of this, Louisa bade the admiring pigs farewell and returned to Casa Blanca, where her spouse was gloomily in the process of putting his pants on, one leg at a time.

Her daughter was also preparing to take on the day, or more precisely, being taken on by it. Sophie emerged onto the portal looking as though the morning had already won. Her face was washed, her mascara was on. That was about it. She was still a long way from achieving brightness of eye and bushiness of tail. The race goes to those who endure, however, and Sophie had endurance. She had not succumbed to the blandishments of her bed, and Louisa supposed that counted for something.

"Good morning, Missy," Louisa greeted her woebegone sleepyhead.

"Morning, Momma," Sophie mumbled around a yawn.

Louisa slipped a steadying arm around her semi-asleep walking child and directed her into the little sitting room, where Sophie promptly collapsed into a deep comfortable wing chair, from which she regarded the world through glazed eyes.

Degarrin entered the room, radiating alertness. He paused to take in the same pitiful scene he viewed there most mornings.

"Louisa," he said, "this cannot be our child. Our child would be an early bird. Our child would already have an entire basket of worms by now. I believe she was switched at birth."

"Very likely," Louisa agreed. "However, it's probably for the best, as we apparently got the pretty one. Anyway, they tell me she is marvelous at midnight."

The dinner chime sounded, interrupting the little family's contemplation of each other. Smiling, Degarrin grabbed one of Sophie's arms while Louisa commandeered the other. Together they tugged her up and off toward the dining room.

"At least you got the pretty one. The other me is probably real ugly," was Sophie's only comment.

They had planned to leave for the wagon right after breakfast, Degarrin and Sophie to ride with the crew, Louisa because the pull of the camp was too strong to resist. She absolutely loved going out to the little wagon, an island of humanity in an ocean of grass that, blowing in the wind, made the waves and ripples of an inland sea. She liked getting there in time to have a cup of coffee and a sourdough biscuit left over from breakfast, in time to chat with Ignacio, the cook who could cook like no other. What he could do with hot coals and a dutch oven rivaled anything Louisa had ever sampled before. His peach cobbler was to die for, and, best of all, it was almost always available.

But breakfast was barely cleared when the telephone rang, a cattle broker in Tucumcari, wanting to discuss fall shipping arrangements. Degarrin disappeared into his office with a look that said this would not be brief. Sophie sat on the portal steps, restless, her boots tapping an impatient rhythm on the flagstone. She had come a long way from the glazed creature of an hour before.

Louisa left them to it. She had things to do while she waited. There were letters to be written, or else her family would know she had finally and irretrievably fallen off the edge of the world. There was laundry to sort.

Sorting through it, she came upon a list Degarrin had made the day before, entitled "Jobs for Pete." Across the wide drive, in the bunkhouse yard, ten pair of Levi's on stretchers danced on the clotheslines like legs with invisible torsos. Louisa smiled at the sight, then turned her attention to the matter at hand.

Pete was Rufina's brother. They were both the children of Miguel Mondragon, who had long been an institution at the ranch. It was Miguel who toiled endlessly around the sprawling headquarters, struggling to maintain fences and buildings in the face of sun and wind. The serene beauty of headquarters was Miguel's signature. Miguel's work ethic and love of a job done only to perfection did not seem to be genetic in nature. On one of her inspired days, Rufina could be awesome, but those days were few and far between. Pete, on the other hand, had never been afflicted with a single day of willing productivity or hindered by even a fleeting second of ambition. Pete's was a happily unexamined and uninspired life. The bone laziness that was the delight of Pete's life was the bane of his father's being. Louisa knew that without his list of jobs to do, Pete would be doing exactly nothing, which is what Louisa suspected Pete was doing at that very moment, with his sister's encouragement, in Louisa's own kitchen.

Louisa sighed at the thought. Just the evening before, Degarrin had confided to her that mutiny was brewing at the bunkhouse. Peggy and the few hands not out with the wagon were sick and tired of Pete appropriating the "so thick your spoon will stand up in it" cream that was solely for use in coffee. Pete would routinely confiscate the "coffee only" cream and enjoy it thoroughly on his morning cereal. By the time Pete got through tanking up on a little cereal with a lot of cream, there was never any left for anyone else.

First Ignacio, and now Peggy, had complained bitterly to Degarrin about this breach of protocol and disregard for common courtesy. Degarrin had never seen two such steady people so incensed.

"Peggy, for now, it's your kitchen and your dining room. Do what you have to do," he had told the outraged cook.

Louisa wondered where it would all end. Sighing again, she headed for the kitchen. Maybe she could persuade Rufina to try a new recipe, maybe something remotely American as Louisa knew it. All hope for something new and tasty was abandoned immediately upon entering the dining room. Clanging and banging of pots and pans that could only denote either pure rage or lunacy were emanating from behind the kitchen door.

"Oh, dear." Louisa quaked and almost balked. But reminding herself that she descended from heroes, or at least survivors, of Confederate and Revolutionary bouts, she peeked around the kitchen door.

"Rufina, is anything the matter?" she queried with what she hoped was cheerful oblivion.

"Miss Louisa," Rufina muttered, her words and tone drenched with bitter venom, "that Peggy a damned bad old woman. She did take off the cream to Pete."

"Oh" was about all Louisa could think of in response.

She was still contemplating the cream crisis when Degarrin

appeared in the hallway, hat in hand.

"Are we going, or aren't we?" He looked like a man who had been told his shipping costs were going up.

"We're going," Louisa said, and went to collect her hat.

• • •

The Comanche pasture was a good twenty-five miles from headquarters. Degarrin drove in silence, his mind still on the phone call, while Sophie sat between them watching the land unfold. The Comanche stretched from the rough rimrocks of the juniper-and-piñon-studded highlands down to the flats of the basin with its waving sea of grass. The soil was deep and rich, the finest grazing land in the world, Degarrin always said, and no one who had seen it had ever argued the point. That one pasture alone was larger than most ranches, and it was only one of many. Degarrin had done no settling, and the Comanche was as much his as it would ever be any man's.

They arrived just barely in time to catch mounts and join the drive. Sophie was out of the truck and striding toward the rope corral before Louisa had even found her footing, calling something over her shoulder about saving her a biscuit. Degarrin followed at a more measured pace, though Louisa could see his mood lifting with every step that brought him closer to horseback.

Louisa settled in at the wagon with Ignacio, a cup of his coffee, and one of his leftover sourdough biscuits, content to watch the morning take shape. This was what she loved: the quiet of the camp between drives, the shade of the fly, the smell of coffee and whatever Ignacio had simmering in the dutch oven, and the vast stillness of the country stretching away in every direction. From here she could watch for the telltale dust of the herd as it slowly approached across the flats and ravines. She could sit and be exactly where she wanted to be.

The drive came in before midmorning, four or five hundred head, from the look of it, the dust rising in a red-brown haze and the bawling audible long before the herd itself took shape. Louisa watched from the shade of the fly as the crew positioned themselves around the mass, holding it in a wide circle while the cattle milled and settled. Toby's crew was working so well and the work was going as smooth as satin. There was no better wagon boss than Toby Lloyd. He knew horses, cattle, and men right down to their souls, and he knew every inch of La Conquistadora. The empire and all its creatures, human and otherwise, were in good hands.

The cowboys rode in by ones and twos for a change of mounts, hot, dusty, grinning, the young ones showing off a little and the old ones not bothering. Sophie rode in flushed and dirty and looking entirely alive. She unsaddled Bogota and turned him loose, then carried her saddle toward the rope corral for a fresh horse.

Connor was there, changing mounts himself. He caught one of Sophie's string for her without being asked, just reached over and had the horse by the halter before Sophie was even at the rail. She thanked him with a word and a smile, and he said something back that Louisa couldn't hear, and they both laughed. It was nothing. It was the sort of thing that happened a dozen times a day among people who worked together.

But Louisa knew every one of her daughter's laughs: the loud one she used with the cowboys, the sweet one she saved for her father, the conspiratorial one for Kitten. This one was different. Lighter, less certain of itself. New.

Louisa watched Sophie saddle her fresh horse and ride back out to the herd, and she said nothing at all.

A little while later, Kitten and Christine came in to the wagon for water. They dropped into the thin shade beyond the fly, loose-limbed and easy, talking the way girls talk when they think no one is listening. Louisa was around the far side of the chuck wagon, refilling her cup from Ignacio's pot.

"...wouldn't mind finding out," Kitten was saying, and Christine laughed, a low, knowing laugh that was entirely too old for her years.

"You're terrible, Kit."

"I'm just saying what everybody's thinking."

They were looking toward the herd when they said it, and their eyes were not on the cattle. Louisa didn't need to follow their gaze. She pressed her lips together and poured her coffee. These were the girls her daughter spent six weeks with, sunrise to sunset, sleeping under the same canvas. Louisa had never much cared for it.

After lunch (Ignacio's peach cobbler having lived up to its considerable reputation) Degarrin and Toby talked over the next day's work while Louisa listened. They would move camp in the morning, work the rough country along the upper rimrocks.

"You all right with Sophie up in those canyons?" Degarrin asked, and Louisa knew the question was not for Toby.

She looked out to where her daughter was riding back toward the herd on a fresh horse, straight-backed, easy in the saddle, already calling something to one of the other riders.

"She'll be fine," Louisa said.

Degarrin nodded. Toby nodded. That settled it.

Degarrin tweaked his daughter's cheek and told her to mind Toby. Sophie rolled her eyes in a way that was pure nineteen. Then Louisa and Degarrin were in the truck, headed back the way they'd come, the wagon camp shrinking behind them until it was just a smudge of dust and canvas against the immensity of the Comanche.

They drove in the comfortable silence of a couple who had spent twenty years learning how not to fill every quiet with words. The flats stretched ahead of them, red and gold in the early-afternoon light, and Louisa watched the country pass: the grass running in the wind, the mesas standing blue on the horizon, the red dirt road unspooling endlessly before them. Not much was said. Husband and wife had spent countless hours following this same pursuit, driving the roads of La Conquistadora, checking on the condition of grass, roads, cattle, and fences, noting the ordinary and especially the out of the ordinary.

"Rufina tells me Peggy is a damned bad old woman because she took the cream away from Pete," Louisa reported.

"Well, did the two of them give notice?"

"Not yet. Maybe they won't."

Degarrin snorted. "I wouldn't mind if Pete decided he could live without us. But you need Rufina, and I don't suppose she'd stay if her darling baby brother were to leave."

"Oh, don't fret about that. I can get along without Rufina. When forced, I can cook and clean. Besides, she can always be replaced."

Degarrin knew it was hard to find a housekeeper and a cook who could cope with the splendid isolation of La Conquistadora. "I know you can, but I don't want you to have to. Let's just hope she stays and that Pete can get along without cream."

The road dipped into a creek bottom and climbed out the other side, the cottonwoods thick and green along the water.

"What was the call about this morning?" Louisa asked. "You looked fit to chew nails when you came out."

"Hendricks. Wants two dollars a head more for fall shipping. Says the trucks are all spoken for and we'll have to book early or take our chances." Degarrin was quiet for a moment. "Two more on top of ceiling prices that are already squeezing us half to death. Sometimes I wonder if this way of doing things has got a future, sugar." He shook his head. "It was easier when the Polly was running."

It was not like him to talk that way. Two dollars a head didn't sound like much until you multiplied it by fifteen hundred, and ceiling prices meant the cattle wouldn't fetch what they were worth even if they got to market on time. Louisa did the math and said nothing. The Stillmores had turned down his request for a new Oldsmobile this year, the first time she could remember. It was a small thing, and Michael hadn't said much about it, but Louisa had noticed. There were things about the arrangement with the Stillmores that kept her husband up at night, and she had learned when to ask and when to leave it alone.

The Polly. The little train that had once run from Clauson to Rogerton, right through the ranch. All the cattle had gone to market on the Polly in the old days, herded up to loading pens at Timber Canyon and put in cattle cars bound for Chicago and Kansas City. The Polly had served as ambulance and taxi too, when people needed to get to town for an emergency or just an important occasion. The Polly didn't run anymore. A victim of progress, its whistle was heard no more.

"That's not the only thing the Polly was good for," Degarrin said, and his grin had turned private, the one that meant he was reaching back for something.

Louisa knew that grin. She loved her husband's stories, and she could feel one coming. "Let's hear it," she said.

"Sugar, did I ever tell you about my adventure with a mad cow while the Polly crew looked on?"

"It doesn't sound familiar," Louisa said.

"Well, it must have been in the springtime of 1920 or '21, or thereabouts. It had been raining quite a bit and the creeks were running pretty regular. So somebody had to ride bog every day or so, you know, ride the creek looking for bogged-down cattle. Everybody else was tied up so it came down to me to do it. I took off on Tom Sawyer, a real good little horse, and one that was strong enough to pull a cow out of the creek bottom if she wasn't bogged down too bad, if it came to that. I was riding along from the 'Quistadora Farm to Fort McCamey, planning to ride back the next day. Well, of course before long I came across a cow bogged down pretty good, or pretty bad I guess you could say. She was stuck right near the railroad bridge. I hobbled Tom Sawyer and shucked off all my clothes, all except my hat, that is. She was stuck out in the water and there wasn't any sense in getting anything besides me wet."

"I bet you were quite a sight. I wish I'd been there to see it."

Degarrin grinned.

"Anyway," he continued, "there I was buck naked, all except for my hat, wrestling this cow out of the mud. Everything went fine for the most part until I got her free. Then she got mad. Now isn't that just like a female? After I had just risked my life to save hers, she turned around and tried to kill me."

"My goodness, was it really that bad?" Louisa asked, suddenly concerned for her husband's safety some twenty-five years before.

"Well, no, not really. But it plays a lot better that way, don't you think?"

"Most certainly," she agreed. "What happened next?"

"As soon as I got her out, she charged me. I grabbed for my horse but she wouldn't give me time to get him unhobbled, so I had to run around him with her getting closer every step. I could feel her breathing on my bare ass. Excuse my language. Naturally, while I am running and dodging for my life, the Polly came by. The crew of that little train sure cheered and applauded and even blew the whistle. They were a real appreciative audience, but I couldn't even take time to give 'em a bow. That cow was too darned close!"

Louisa laughed and laughed, caught up by the image of her husband, young and handsome, running naked from a fire-breathing cow before an audience of railroaders. She was still laughing when Degarrin slowed the truck and pulled off the road where a line of cottonwoods followed a creek bottom, the water still running from last night's rain, the shade deep and cool under the old trees.

He turned to her and she saw his expression change, the laughter gone from his face, replaced by something older and more certain. He caught her face in his two hands.

"Louisa, I'm not twenty-three anymore, and there's no cow and there's no Polly, but I would love to get naked right now with you."

"Right now?" Louisa was a little surprised but definitely interested.

"Right now," he affirmed.

"This seat isn't too roomy," Louisa commented doubtfully.

"My bedroll's in the back."

Years later, Louisa would proudly confide in her grandson that she had accomplished many things in her life, all without ever saying no to his grandfather. Sighing deliciously, she wrapped her arms around his neck and kissed him longingly, ending with a sharp little nip to his lip. "What are we waiting for?" was all she said.

Michael Degarrin was not a man hindered or hemmed in by conventionality, and neither, when it came down to it, was Louisa. A dusty, somewhat lumpy bedroll thrown down without ceremony on a patch of blue gramma grass in the shade of the cottonwoods was as fine a place as any she could think of.

Clothes shed, flesh to flesh, heart to heart, the afternoon was completely perfect. The sun filtered through the cottonwood leaves and dappled their skin, and the sound of the creek was the only sound in the world besides theirs. Louisa took him in, enfolding him and comforting him even as she drove him wild, and met him as she always had. Peak for peak, valley for valley, crest for crest. And in the final moments, his cry was matched by hers.

They had always been a randy couple, both ready at the drop of a hat (or any other item of apparel) for a quick tumble or a prolonged feast. Since they had the long hours of daylight left before them and no particular place to go, they settled down for a full-course banquet. Both were affected by the novelty of their locale, by the huge, high, blue bowl of sky above them, and the enormity of the land around them.

Louisa summed it up. “It’s as though we’re the only people on earth. Here we are for all the world to see, but no one exists to look or even care. I never felt so free in all my life.”

Degarrin propped himself up on one elbow and looked down into her upturned face, so open and so friendly, and Louisa saw in his expression the same thing she had seen the first time he ever looked at her, a man who could not quite believe his luck. Michael Degarrin was the only man Louisa had ever kissed. She just assumed this was how marriages were, and saw no reason to question it.

And so they whiled away a golden afternoon in nuzzling and kissing, whispering and talking, and making love because it was fun and felt good. And because they were blessed to love each other very much.

In distant years, when other memories had slipped away or just evaporated, this afternoon would shine clear in both their fading minds, as the best that life could offer.

Chapter 5 — Riding Bogota

TOBY SPLIT HIS CREW into two drives, one led by himself, the other by Juan Soliz, who, having practically been raised on La Conquistadora, knew every rimrock and wash as well as Toby did. Connor was assigned to Toby's drive, Sophie to Juan's. Toby kept the other two girls with him so that he could keep a close eye on their antics, if any. He was shortchanging all three girls' ability as riders and cowhands; every one of them was excellent in the saddle and quite skillful at handling cattle, even the wild range ones they would encounter today. Toby knew this quite well, but he always had trouble reconciling this knowledge with his equally accurate knowledge of their personalities and a predilection for high jinks. He always erred on the side of caution and split the ladies up whenever he could.

The two drives headed out, each leader periodically dropping riders off to work their portion of the ground. To find the recalcitrant cows and their calves was in itself no small feat; to drive them where they needed to be was yet another. To move several hundred cattle where they had no particular wish to go, and to do it quickly and with an economy of effort, was a finely choreographed dance played out over thousands of acres by a cast of artists.

Juan Soliz's drive dropped Sophie off along the base of Antelope Hills. The land here was open in some places and broken by ravines and benches in others, all generously dotted with juniper. It was a good place to be a cow. There was shelter, shade, lots to eat, and there were plenty of places to hide. It was a challenging place to be a cowboy.

While Sophie scanned for dots of red and white that would equal a Hereford, Bogota, who really was a major pest, was considering sowing the last of his oats. He decided to give it a go, and began to paw and prance. Sophie impatiently pulled him under control and continued her scout. Such high-handed treatment offended Bogota, who immediately worked himself into quite a state. In no time at all, he was up on his toes with ears twitching and rollers in his nose. Sophie ignored his tantrum and suddenly Bogota had had enough. He took the bit in his teeth and bolted, racing pell-mell through the juniper stands and leaping over little ravines and big yuccas with delighted abandon.

Sophie was simultaneously astonished and infuriated. Being doubly blessed with both a deep saddle and a paramount talent, she had no trouble keeping her seat, but she was getting more than a little fed up. She jerked him up and none too gently, which in turn made the horse even more ornery. Cold-jawing on Sophie, he paid not the slightest heed to the bit that was tearing his mouth, threatening to enlarge it by several inches. He also became very reckless, dodging and leaping and bestirring himself in ways that he would never have even considered in his right mind. Bogota even went so far as to buck, jumping into the air, kicking his back feet out, and turning and twisting in midair.

It occurred to Sophie that this could get dangerous, as her mount had obviously taken leave of what little sense with which the Lord had blessed him. It was time to call a halt, so she took up her left rein. She would just see how he liked running with his nose on the toe of her boot. Maybe she'd pound him between the eyes while she was at it.

Bogota wasn't buying. He was bow-necked and cold-jawed, and as determined to do exactly as he pleased as Sophie was determined he would do no such thing.

Sophie reassessed the situation. Bogota showed no signs of tiring and the best she had been able to do was get him turned a little to the left. Then she realized that that slight turn had been enough to send Bogota slightly uphill into the Antelopes. Sophie began to smile as she started working the headstrong runaway further around to the left. When he was turned enough that there was a pretty good incline laid out in front of him, Sophie was wearing a hell-born grin.

"All right, you sorry son of a bitch. Let's just see how you can run!" Kicking and spurring and screaming, Sophie sent a startled Bogota right straight up into the Antelope Hills. Like one possessed, she had lost all sense of caution and didn't particularly care if both she and horse came to a crashing end.

Bogota discovered a suddenly reborn sense of self-preservation, not to mention exhaustion, and slowed down dramatically. Sophie would have none of it. She kept right on kicking and spurring and screaming. Bogota was too tired to go on long before she was. Finally horse and rider stood still, both aquiver, well up the steep side of a rough foothill. There was no doubt as to whom the victor's laurel would go.

Gathering both her wits and her reins about her, Sophie said, still panting, "Let's work some cattle."

Bogota made no protest.

Having called a truce, Bogota and Sophie picked their way down the hillside they had just torn up. This trip, however, both were mindful for the first time of rocks, cactus, and uneven ground. Their descent was considerably more decorous than their ascent had been. Once down on more habitable terrain, horse and rider commenced their cattle quest. At some point they merged into the team they should have been from the start. Bogota's constantly flicking ears showed that he was as diligent in his search as Sophie was in hers. When he bothered to apply himself, he was a pretty good cow pony; otherwise he would not still be enjoying life on La Conquistadora. Only the good remained.

Once a cow was spotted, Sophie directed her mount toward it and Bogota knew what to do. Heading for the cow, he would get behind it and drive it and its calf, along with any other cattle that happened to be found near it, down toward the roundup ground. Bogota was watching for cattle too, and would head toward them without Sophie's cue if he saw them first. Sometimes it was hard to tell who was directing this project, but that's what being a good cowpoke and pony was all about. Now and then a cow or two, or more, would try to cut back and make a dash for cover, preferring not to be rounded up that year. But Sophie and Bogota were always right there, racing in pursuit, whirling, and always turning them back, then chousing them well down toward the flats where the drive would pick them up. After one particularly challenging duel with three stubborn cows and their confused calves, Sophie hugged Bogota's wet, sweaty neck to tell him all was forgiven and that he was a "good'un."

As the morning wore on, they reached the end of Sophie's allotted territory, the land behind them successfully scoured of cows and calves.

"Well, hoss, I think we've done a real good job in spite of the bad start we got off to. Even ol' Toby won't be able to complain about us."

Satisfied with their achievements and adventures, the pair trotted down from the foothills. In the distance, the main drive was evidenced by the rising dust and endless bawling of several hundred head of herded cattle a couple of miles away. Sophie's little gather had had enough antics for one morning and was content to be headed along toward the drive. Relaxing in the saddle for the first time that morning, Sophie tilted her face up to the sun. The sky was a flawless blue, not a cloud from here to the horizon, but the heat was thick and pressing, the air dead still. She calculated that she and her charges should intercept the herd in a half hour or so.

However, a cursory glance soon gave lie to Sophie's optimism of just a few moments before. The little herd moseying along in front of her, claimed at such effort, now seemed meager indeed. Its number, she decided, was not likely to impress Toby, who would probably decide that her wages were scarcely justified, even though she worked for free.

"I swear, Bogota, I think I work harder than any hand on this place. And I don't even get paid for it. I must be crazy. But what we have got to do, right now, is find some more cattle, muy pronto."

To remedy this problem, Sophie concentrated her sight on the terrain around her, sweeping her trained and practiced gaze across the land, searching not for movement so much as for a variation in color and an unnatural uniformity of shape. Sophie's eyes knew what they were looking for, and in just a few moments they had ferreted out shadowed shapes and patches of red that would materialize into a score or so of calves and cows on closer inspection.

Yelling and chousing, Sophie and Bogota got their wards into a run and well started toward the drive. The momentum of flight would unite them for a little while, and by the time her little herd lost its brief cohesion and started to break apart, to be swallowed up once more by the hills and brush and by the washes and ravines, Sophie would be back to put a stop to their disappearing act. Meanwhile, Sophie and Bogota, all differences forgotten, worked in perfect unity, loping gracefully from one little bunch of cattle to the next. If a calf tried to bolt or a cow to balk, Bogota was blocking its path or hurrying it along with a nip on the rump before such bovine thoughts were even completed.

"Good boy, Bogota!" Sophie praised him with a pat on the neck when, a few minutes later, they were pushing their regrouped herd, along with their new acquisitions, toward the thickening dust and rising crescendo of the drive.

Sophie's contribution pushed the drive's tally up toward four hundred or maybe more. It had been a good morning's work for all La Conquistadora's crew, but the day was young and there was still a lot to be done. First the growing drive had to be maneuvered to camp, which in itself was no small feat. The drive was an independent creature, a flowing carpet of red and white with a life all its own. Some of its members were rowdy and raucous, with much snorting and pawing and butting of heads. Others were quiet and stoic, calmly plodding along, moving with and yielding to the ebb and flow of the currents within it.

"Hey, Sophie," Tommy Ryan called out from the dusty depths of the drag, "come on back here."

Sophie just laughed and waved. "Not in this lifetime," she yelled back. Riding drag was not her ambition for that day, or for any other.

"Better come on back, Sophie. This is where all the fun is," Frankie Evans joined in his crony's invitation as he effortlessly laid a loop around the hoof of a surprised, and then irritated, calf.

"Not much fun if you get caught," Sophie called back.

Frankie just smiled and tossed another perfect loop. His smile was that of a man who was young, and who spent his mornings on horseback under a high blue sky. He had neither thought nor worry to waste on a boss's wrath.

As the drive progressed toward the wagon, Sophie relaxed a little. She would never have admitted it to a single soul, but if her dad or Toby were anywhere near the wagon or the drive, she was always a bit nervous, worried that she might not acquit herself quite well enough. She knew that she was as good a hand as any of the cowboys, but still, she always had that tease of tension and butterfly flutter to keep her company.

Almost all the scattered riders were in now, their gathers swelling the main drive larger and larger. She could see Danny Parks loping in from the east with a good-sized bunch of his own. Sophie watched Adam merge his finds into the flowing herd and knew a moment's delight as he casually dawdled in his efforts until she was carried alongside him by the movement of the drive.

"Well, Sophie, how did you and old dog food there get along?" he asked.

"Pretty well. But he did try to run away with me," Sophie confessed.

"Did you get him stopped?"

"No."

"Dog food! Shame on you. Now you stop running away with this girl, right now," Adam commanded the pooped Bogota, who, with complete indifference, totally ignored his heckler.

"I ran him straight up the Antelope Hills and pretty soon he got tired of being a runaway."

Adam laughed.

"I reckon he won't try that again."

"I reckon he won't," Sophie agreed. "Unless of course he wants another go at high-speed mountain climbing."

They rode together for a while after that, not saying much, just moving with the drive. It was easy, being beside him. Sophie didn't think about it, which was the thing. With the other cowboys she was always performing a little, always aware of herself. With Adam she just rode.

The wagon was in sight now. Ignacio was there somewhere, invisible in the shade of the fly, preparing lunch and making sure there were biscuits and leftover bacon and steak for a quick sandwich, with plenty of hot coffee to wash it down. It had been quite a while and many hot miles of riding since breakfast.

Up ahead, Toby was scattering riders to get the herd halted and held in a wide circle. The herd would be "worked" now, two or three men riding in to search out bulls and dry cows, cutting them free. It was a skilled job, requiring a top hand on a top cutting horse. Degarrin almost always cut the herd, as did Toby, and sometimes Sophie, who was very good at it. She had two or three mounts in her string that she considered to be fine cutting horses, and she always changed to one of these for working the herd, just in case her services were requested.

At camp, the remuda had been wrangled once again and was standing penned in the rope corral. In ones and twos the cowboys rode in for a quick stop at the wagon for a much-needed drink, a quick sampling of Ignacio's offerings should their stomachs think their throats had been cut, and a change of mounts.

Chapter 6 — Working the Herd

SOPHIE RODE IN FOR a change of mounts, but stopped by the wagon before heading for the rope corral. Leaving Bogota hobbled for the moment, she stepped under the fly and immediately appreciated its shade. The morning coolness was long since gone and sweat had been sliding down her back and between her breasts for some time now. The temperature drop in the shade of the fly was most welcome, as was Ignacio, who could be counted on to baby her a little. A glance around told her that her mother had not arrived yet. That meant there wouldn't be any ice for her to filch. All the ice her mother would bring with her from headquarters was to be used for everyone's enjoyment at lunch, and not before. Sophie was the only one Ignacio let cheat, slipping her a cube or two early, on the sly, if no one was looking.

Ignacio watched her come up to the wagon, hot and looking a little tired.

"Missy Sophie! You been working too hard. Let these worthless cowboys go out into the sun and work like dogs! You should be sitting here in the cool talking to me while I make the best cobbler and sourdough biscuits in probably the whole world, most certainly in New Mexico. Come over here and get yourself a biscuit and a drink, then you'll feel better."

"You know, Ignacio, I think you may be right, about your cooking and about the worthless cowboys, too." Ignacio handed her a biscuit and a tin cup, which she filled with a dipper brimming over from the galvanized water bucket. The shade had done what it could to preserve the water's nighttime cool, but the sip Sophie took was still close to room temperature. But it was wet, and wet was what Sophie wanted at the moment. The water tasted good and so did the biscuit. Completely revived, Sophie was ready once more to have at it.

"Sophie, do you figure you've loafed around here in the shade long enough, or are you planning on taking up residence?" Tommy Ryan inquired as he walked over from where he had just hobbled his horse. Tommy was a good-looking kid of twenty or so, with waving blond hair and green eyes, both of which were mostly hidden by his wide-brimmed straw hat. Sophie was not moved by Tommy's looks. She had known him too long to even notice them. She and Tommy had been encountering one another around the place for years. His father had been an on-again, off-again hand at La Conquistadora since before Tommy had been born. Now Tommy worked there full time and thus far had evidenced a far steadier character than that of his father. But then Tommy was still young; there was plenty of time ahead for him to go to the dogs.

"No, I've been waiting for you. I figured you couldn't find your way back to the herd by yourself," Sophie told him.

"Now, children, behave," Kitten said as she joined the group. Sophie could see that Tommy's looks were not lost on Kitten in the least. While Kitten watered and fed herself, she eyed her target speculatively.

"I saw you were riding Rebel today, Tommy. He sure is a beautiful horse," Kitten purred.

"Yeah, he looks all right. He's a wild one, too. That's why I like him."

"Maybe you'll let me ride him sometime. I like 'em wild, too."

"Oh, yeah?"

"Yeah."

Tommy and Kitten eyed each other in a whole new light. Tommy grinned. "Maybe I will let you try him. Think you can ride him?"

"I know I can," Kitten answered, looking him right in the eye. There was nothing sheepish about Kitten.

Oh, brother, Sophie thought. Here we go.

Not having much interest in the budding range romance she was witnessing, Sophie abandoned the fly's shade and went to collect Bogota. On her way, she encountered David Harvey with his ever-present camera.

"Hi, David. How are you doing?" she asked.

"Just fine, Sophie, just fine. How about you?"

"I couldn't be better. Are you having any luck with your picture taking?"

"Oh, yes. We sure are! Gary and I are taking some photographs that I think will become classics. We've gotten some great branding pen scenes, and the remuda is always good for a roll of film. The horses are always so cooperative, the way they all crowd up against the rope corral and pose for the camera. A couple of days ago we heard from a major hat company. They are interested in putting some of our shots on their hat boxes. Just think, Sophie, you might go into a store fifty years from now, and a thousand miles away from here, to buy a cowboy hat and see this summer on the box."

"What a nice thought!" Sophie exclaimed, much taken with that image of the future. "I hope so! I'm so glad everything is going well for you."

"Everything is going great, Sophie. And besides that, Gary and I are having the time of our lives. We will always remember this summer."

"Me, too," Sophie said, turning to go.

Turning photographer again, David snapped off yet another series of shots, capturing Sophie's grace as she retrieved her mount and rode off to the rope corral for a change of horses, where Bogota was glad to be unsaddled and turned loose.

Sophie decided to ride Mary Lou for the afternoon work. Why Mary Lou was called Mary Lou was one of life's great imponderables. For some reason the young cowboy that had first ridden him as a bronc had so dubbed him, and so he was called, then and forever after. Whatever his name, Mary Lou was a natural-born cutting horse. He and Sophie loped back to the herd with anticipation; they might just get to do some cutting today. It soon became apparent to both horse and rider that this was not going to be their day to do much of anything. Toby, Degarrin, and Adam were already inside the herd, cutting out everything that was not a cow and calf pair. This left Sophie and Mary Lou with no option but to take up a mundane holding position on the edge of the herd. With nothing to look forward to, Mary Lou promptly went to sleep.

Horses were sleeping all around the sea of cattle. Their riders weren't too excited, either.

Frankie Evans, having gotten in his prohibited roping practice earlier in the day while riding drag, now sat slouched in his saddle with his right leg crossed carelessly over his horse's neck, a comfortable but precarious position that didn't appear to concern him in the least.

Time passed as it always did, with the sun climbing toward its zenith and the heat settling in heavy and still. Not a breath of wind. Far to the west, white clouds were stacking up over the mountains, tall and flat-bottomed, but they were somebody else's weather for now. Thoughts turned to food and a break from the sun, perhaps even a chance to grab forty winks for those who could go to sleep at the drop of a hat and wake up raring to go.

Inside the herd, Degarrin, Toby, and Adam were swiftly and surely maneuvering the bulls out. Bulls had to come out first; left in the roundup, they were nothing but trouble and a pure nuisance. Degarrin was moving a group of three or four bulls through the roundup toward its edge when the bulls decided to fight. Bulls pawing and butting heads was a common enough occurrence, often done out of boredom or for no reason at all. It rarely amounted to much. These bulls were no different and started a typical ruckus, but then for no reason, either apparent or obscure, two of them decided to get serious and attack in earnest. Charging and hooking at each other amidst flying dust and enraged snorting, the two wreaked havoc throughout the herd with an irritated Degarrin following along behind.

There wasn't anything much you could do about two idiot bulls that had decided to do battle, except stay out of the way. Degarrin tried to steer them toward the edge of the herd as best he could, and Adam and Toby converged on the scene with the same idea. The bulls did not want to be steered and were undeterred by the riders' efforts. They were, however, irritated by them. Arriving near the edge of the milling, uneasy roundup through their own efforts, they each whirled and simultaneously spotted new targets for their wrath.

Sophie's spurs and heavy hand on the reins brought Mary Lou back from the land of nod with a jolt. Being both a natural athlete and possessed of a healthy self-preservation instinct, Mary Lou woke up at a gallop, being guided by Sophie around the herd and past riders who were already moving to cut off the four thousand pounds of destruction that were on their tail.

About the same time that Sophie and Mary Lou took off like a rocket, Frankie got a chance to test his theory that he could stay with any horse under any circumstances. His mount was Dandy, and Dandy's eyes stood out on stalks when he realized that a very large, and very angry animal, with horns, was about to mow him down. In one move he whirled and took off for safer climes. Whether or not Frankie went with him was not one of his concerns. Dandy almost spun out from under Frankie, but his theory held true and he just managed to save himself from the wrath of el toro by grabbing the saddle horn with one hand and a handful of mane with the other, while untangling his leg and reaching frantically for his stirrup. It was a close call for Frankie, but not for Dandy. The bull never had a prayer of catching that fleet-footed runaway. In fact, it took a little effort on Frankie's part to get him stopped, and then only after the bull had been turned back.

It took the combined efforts of Degarrin, Toby, and Adam, along with Danny Parks and three other cowboys, to turn the bulls and get them headed toward the rest of the day herd that had just been cut out from the main herd. As quickly as it had started, it ended. The bulls tossed their heads, slinging slobber and snot all around, and then, suddenly bored again, dropped their heads almost in unison and began to graze.

Adrenaline rushes began to recede in both horses and riders as pulse rates slowed toward normal. Sophie let her breath out without ever realizing she'd held it, and Frankie thanked his lucky stars. Degarrin rode past, saw that she was fine, and his only comment was, "I'm glad your mother wasn't here."

"Me, too," Sophie said, a little faintly.

Adam came riding close behind his boss. As he rode past, he gave Sophie a wink that left her smiling.

That little commotion over with, things went a lot more smoothly. Degarrin and Toby worked the herd for shippers and dry cows, cutting out everything that wasn't going to earn its keep on grass. When they were satisfied, the herd was penned and Tommy Ryan put the last calf through and closed the gate. It was time for lunch.

Chapter 7 — A Day at the Wagon

LOUISA CAME TO THE wagon because she liked it and because she was expected, expected to show up with the ice and maybe some cookies as well. As a Dutch oven and an open flame were Ignacio's primary tools, cookies were not on his menu unless she brought them. And she usually did. She could be counted on. She was the reason La Conquistadora's crew was spoiled and accustomed to having iced tea for lunch. Ignacio loved being spoiled; so did everyone else. Louisa was a great favorite. She would have been liked anyway, but probably not so well without the treats she brought. But Louisa Madison Degarrin was Virginia bred; as a good Southern girl, she would not have dreamed of going calling empty-handed, even to her own husband's roundup.

That morning, Rufina had started the brownies right after breakfast. By the time Louisa came down to the kitchen to discuss the supper menu and start breaking out the ice, they were cooled enough to slice. One pan for the wagon, one left in the pantry, for Rufina and Pete, though neither had asked and Louisa hadn't offered. It wasn't necessary. While the wagon was out, the freezer at Casa Blanca was jammed full of ice cube trays and little else: fifteen trays, now broken out and their contents sacked up in double paper bags and packed in a heavy canvas duffel bag that was supposed to help keep the ice frozen as long as possible. Nothing had been said about buffing the dining room floor. Louisa intended to let that thought sit a little while longer.

Finally the ice, the brownies, and Louisa herself were loaded into the car and gone. She stopped by the Hamptons' house to pick up Peggy and her niece and nephew, who were visiting from Fort Sumner, a little town a hundred miles away. The kids were Patsy, who was six, and her eight-year-old brother, Billy. Both were looking forward to visiting the wagon. Both were excited. Billy was bubbling over and Patsy's shy little eyes and face were glowing with anticipation. She was proudly wearing her brand-new bright red denim pants and a red-and-white-dotted shirt. On her feet were Billy's outgrown and cast-off cowboy boots, but her momma had polished them up all bright and shiny. Patsy thought they looked brand-new.

Billy didn't worry about his appearance. He knew he was a cowboy, all right, and he just couldn't wait to get out there with the rest of them. With each passing minute and every mile the children's excitement grew, and when neither one could stand another second, they were finally there.

Before their eager eyes lay the camp: the chuck wagon under its great white canvas fly, the cook fire with its Dutch ovens and ever-present coffeepot, and Ricky filling a water bucket beside the hoodlum wagon. It was a whole little civilization out here on the prairie, and at the moment it was missing only one thing.

Billy scanned the camp with growing dismay and was not shy about sharing his opinion. "What kind of outfit is this, anyway?" he demanded of no one in particular. "No horses, no saddles, and no cowboys, either. Just a bunch of women and my sister! I've been robbed!" He turned to Louisa. "Where are the horses? Where are the cowboys?"

"Don't worry, sweetie," Louisa told him. "All the horses and cattle and cowboys you could ever want are over there where you see the dust in the air. They're working the herd and will be along after a bit. Just be patient."

Billy was a little appeased, but not too much. He figured he'd waited long enough to be around some real cowboys and here he was, waiting again. As soon as Louisa stopped the car, he was gone, racing toward the wagon and hardly hearing, much less heeding, her instructions to slow down and be careful.

Patsy was of a shyer and more cautious nature. Upon climbing out of the back seat, she cast a hesitant glance from the unfamiliar scene before her to her aunt and slid her hand into Peggy's.

"Come on, baby doll, we are going to have so much fun!" Peggy assured her. With eager steps, the three ladies headed for the wagon.

Her gifts presented and appreciated, Louisa settled onto a bedroll with Ignacio and Peggy. Billy was already off exploring, and Patsy sat shyly on a bedroll near her aunt, her feet not quite touching the ground.

"I left brownies in the pantry for Rufina and Pete," Louisa mentioned. "Pete was probably through the kitchen door before we cleared the gate."

Ignacio smiled.

"Right about now they're sitting at that table spooning heavy cream into their coffee and agreeing with each other that the bunkhouse boys are crazy for not using it on their cereal." She shook her head with a fondness she didn't bother to hide. "I've tried to tell Rufina: the heavy cream is for coffee, the light cream is for cereal. She nods, she smiles, and then she uses the heavy cream on everything. Pete's just as bad. It's the one battle I will never win. And if that floor goes unbuffed one more day, the cream will be the least of Rufina's worries."

"Some battles are not worth winning," Ignacio offered.

"And it's all on company time," Louisa added.

Ruben Munoz sat on the ground nearby, his back propped up against yet another bedroll. Ruben was the ranch's windmill man and blacksmith. He also ran the branding iron each afternoon. Ruben was a near genius and could repair anything, even a shy little girl's first visit to the wagon. Louisa watched him smile up at Patsy and hold out his hand.

"My name is Ruben, and what is yours?"

"Patsy," she answered very softly.

"Then, Patsy, let us shake hands and be friends."

"All right." The voice was still a little soft and a little shy, but the smile was from the heart and her eyes were starting to shine as Patsy held out her hand.

Joining her on the bedroll, Ruben admired her red pants. "You know," he said, "I was just sitting here wishing I had someone new to talk to. Someone besides Ignacio, because I've known Ignacio forever and I don't have anything new to say to him."

"I know what you mean," Patsy assured him earnestly. "That's just how I feel about Billy. I get real sick of him."

"That's Billy?" Ruben asked, motioning toward Billy, who was busy poking around the harness draped across the tongue of the hoodlum wagon. Ruben hid his smile as he saw her nod, without much enthusiasm.

"He's my brother," she informed her new friend.

"Is he a bad brother?" Ruben inquired.

"Usually he's okay. But he's a real pain right now, because he thinks he's a cowboy and all."

"Oh. Well, some cowboys are like that, you know."

"You're not. You're nice."

"But I'm not a cowboy."

"You're not?" Patsy asked.

"No, I'm a windmill man and blacksmith. I make sure the animals have water to drink and the horses have shoes."

"Oh." Patsy was totally confused but wanted to be nice to her new friend, so she said, "I have real shoes at my aunt's house, but today I'm wearing my boots." She stuck her legs out so Ruben could fully appreciate her footwear.

"Those are much nicer than the horses' shoes," Ruben said. "Which reminds me of what I was telling you. I was here lonely, wishing for someone new to talk to, when I saw you coming. I saw you when you were far, far away because of your bright red pants."

"Did you really?" Patsy asked, astonished.

"I did. Yes, I spotted you miles away, at the top of the hill near headquarters. The reason I could see you was because your pants were so bright and so red."

Patsy wasn't sure that was such a good thing. "Do you like them?" she asked worriedly. "Billy says they're dude pants. Maybe I shouldn't have worn them."

Regretting his teasing, Ruben hastily redeemed himself. "No, no. Your red pants are beautiful. They are the perfect thing for a beautiful little girl to wear to the wagon. All the cowboys will adore you."

"You're being silly." Patsy giggled.

"Come along." Ruben stood up and held out his hand. "I'll show you around the camp and make sure we can keep your brother from being bit by a rattlesnake."

Smiling up at him, Patsy placed her hand in his, and Ruben had a fan for life.

Louisa watched them go. She settled back and let the morning wash over her: the quiet camp, the distant hum of the herd being worked, the smell of Ignacio's cook fire and whatever he was conjuring in those Dutch ovens. There were worse places to spend a morning.

The sky had turned white along the edges with the heat, though overhead it was still that hard, deep blue. The air had a weight to it that hadn't been there a week ago. Louisa fanned herself with her hat and watched the heat shimmer above the flats.

A couple of riders came loping in ahead of the main crew to change mounts, Danny Parks and Adam Connor among them. Danny stopped by the fly long enough to fill a dipper and tip his hat.

"Morning, Mrs. Degarrin. Somebody told me there might be brownies."

"After lunch," Louisa told him. "Not before."

Danny grinned, the kind of grin that conceded defeat gracefully, and headed for the rope corral with Connor. On his way past, Danny stooped to tell Patsy her red pants were the finest he'd seen in New Mexico, and the girl lit up like a little lantern. Louisa watched him go and felt the quiet thought stir, the one she couldn't quite let go of.

Louisa was still smiling when she heard the commotion, a horse's squeal, sharp and high, and then a child's cry that froze her where she sat. Over by the rope corral, one of the horses the early riders had brought in was lunging against its hobbles, ears flat, teeth bared. Billy was on the ground not three feet from the animal's hooves, too scared to move.

Connor got there first. He scooped the boy up with one arm and had him clear before the horse could lunge again, then handed him off to Ruben, who had come running with Patsy in tow. It was over in seconds. The horse settled. Billy did not.

"I just wanted to pet him," Billy said in a small voice. His chin was trembling but he wasn't crying, not quite.

"That one doesn't take to petting," Connor told him, not unkindly. "Some horses are like some people. They'd rather be left alone." He glanced at Ruben, who looked stricken. "He's all right. No harm done."

Louisa reached them and gathered Billy to her, feeling his heart hammering against her ribs like a trapped bird. She looked up at Connor, and what she felt was so simple it should have been easy: gratitude, pure and plain. He had been right there. He had not hesitated.

"Thank you," she said.

Connor just nodded and walked back to the corral. Louisa held the trembling boy and watched him go. She was grateful, of course she was grateful. And something else, in some small back corner of her mind that had no name yet. Connor was becoming a presence in her family's life, and Louisa did not yet know what kind.

Ruben had brought the children back to the shade of the fly, Billy subdued for the moment and keeping close, Patsy clinging to Ruben's hand as if she'd never let go. About that time, Frankie Evans closed the gate on the cows and calves in the branding corral, and excitement struck all over again. Up from the corral came galloping a whole posse of cowboys, enough to make Billy forget his recent humiliation entirely. Patsy was thrilled to note that there were even three cowgirls.

Everybody looked hot and a little bushed. Mike was among them, but Louisa knew that look; something was chewing on him. He'd tell her when he was ready, and not before. It had been a big gather, maybe even a little bigger than he would have liked. Louisa knew her husband's views: two hundred to two hundred and fifty calves were enough to brand in one day, and today they would be pushing that outside limit, if not breaking it a bit. It couldn't be helped now, and besides, it just showed that La Conquistadora had a hardworking, top-notch crew. Still, big brandings were hard on the cattle; the calves had trouble finding their mothers in the crowded confusion.

Sweaty and tired, the crew clustered around the water can,

dumping dippers of water over their heads, the cool water running down their backs, welcome after a long morning in the dust. Sophie pulled a red bandanna from her pocket and dipped it in the water. When it was thoroughly soaked, she placed it around her neck under her long, thick, heavy hair.

"It's at times like this that I'm always so tempted to cut this mess off," she commented to Christine, whose brown locks were cut short and chic.

"You'd be sorry if you did. It takes a certain air to wear short hair," Christine assured her.

Kitten had joined them in time to hear this smug comment. With a wink at Sophie's haughtily raised eyebrows, she sniffed disdainfully and said, "Christine, you're right. You most definitely have a distinct air about you."

Christine stuck her tongue out at both her friends and headed for the shade of the fly. There was little for Sophie or Kitten to do in response but follow along in her wake. Sophie was still too hot, so she strolled along with both arms raised over her head, holding the thick long mane up high off her neck.

Watching her daughter approach, Louisa was struck by how provocative her child looked at that moment, all the more so because her pose was so totally unconscious. Oh, brother, she thought. I hope no one else is paying any attention to her. But she caught Adam Connor's eyes following Sophie from where he had settled onto a bedroll in the shade, and she looked away before she could read what was in them.

Even though the drive was a big one, it had been gathered pretty quickly. It would be a little while before Ignacio called that lunch was ready. There would be time for a little peace and quiet, and even forty winks for some. Old Toby was in the forty winks camp.

About the time Toby got settled good, little Billy got bored. After such a promising start, galloping pell-mell up to the wagon, the cowboys had let him down. These cowboys didn't act the way Billy figured cowboys were supposed to act at all. All they did was sit or lie around and sleep, or drink iced tea or lemonade. But if Billy had been a Boy Scout, he'd have been a good one. He was prepared for just such a lull in the festivities and took it upon himself to liven things up a little. Pulling a comb and a piece of tissue paper from his pocket, he proceeded to play his idea of a tune. Old Toby was not pleased with this course of events. Whether it was his selection of song, or his rendition thereof, that Toby found objectionable was anybody's guess. Toby was a very large man who got up very quickly and without even one word of warning picked Billy up and then rolled him up in the bedroll that he had just vacated. Only head and feet were left sticking out. There would be no more before-dinner music from maestro Billy.

Tommy Ryan watched Old Toby deal with little Billy and then came over and sympathetically squatted down beside him. "You probably think things are looking pretty grim and couldn't possibly be any worse," he said. "But let me tell you, they could be a whole lot worse. When I was a kid, I messed around and got on the wrong side of Old Toby, and you know what he did?"

"What?" mumbled a much-abashed Billy, who was thinking seriously about crying.

"He stuck my head between the spokes of a wheel on the chuck wagon, and I got trapped there. He didn't let me go until everybody had finished eating and saddled up and left."

Billy didn't say a word, just looked at Tommy with wide eyes and decided to be very good.

Tommy just nodded and walked away.

Joining Tommy beside the iced tea urn, Kitten said, "You know, you didn't stay stuck in that wheel with your head between the spokes until everyone had eaten and left. The way I remember it, you yelled and screamed so loud my dad had to pull you out right away so you'd shut up."

Tommy ducked his head. "You have way too good of a memory, Kitten. I like my version a lot better."

"Launchee! Launchee!" Finally, Ignacio called the words they'd all been waiting to hear, and La Conquistadora's crew and visitors lined up to eat, with Louisa gallantly shown to the head of the line.

Chapter 8 — Distant Thunder

THE WAGON HAD NOW been out on the open range for close to three weeks, and they had been long weeks of hard work without so much as even a day off. Everybody was tired and everybody was ready for a break. Today La Conquistadora's cowboys would work until noon, and then they would have two days off. Rodeo weekend had arrived in Clauson, as it did each summer at this time, and calling a halt on La Conquistadora to enjoy the festivities was a time-honored tradition. Secretly, Degarrin and Toby begrudged their crew the time off. They were from the old school and believed in pressing on at all costs. They thought a good time for a day off was when the work was all done next fall. As they were the only moss-backs on the place, no one else shared their view, and a Christmas-like anticipation and suppressed excitement filled the early morning air.

Adam was up before most of them, but that was habit, not enthusiasm. He liked the mornings best, before the day got loud.

Alejandro Romero, called Ally Oop by the gringo boys who couldn't say his name, was a methodical man who maintained high personal standards, even when camped miles from anywhere in a sea of grass. Every morning he shaved with a straight-edged razor and a bowl of hot water poured from the kettle that was always hot and full above the coals of the cook fire. Gary Clancy, a cowboy still young and pretty green, watched him in fascination, as he did every morning.

"I still don't see how you do that, Ally Oop. How can you shave with that damn thing and not cut your throat? And how the hell can you do it and not even use a mirror?"

Clancy asked this question every morning and every morning he got the same answer.

Alejandro stretched his neck and expertly ran the razor up his throat to his chin, leaving a swath of clean, smooth skin in its wake. With another flick of his wrist the blade was rinsed and ready to cut another path. Before continuing, he gave his admirer a smile and an offhanded answer.

"I don't need a mirror. I know where my face is."

Clancy shook his head. "You're amazing, Ally Oop. There's nobody else like you."

Every morning, the same exchange, word for word. He supposed if Alejandro ever changed his answer, Clancy would fall right off the bedroll.

No one felt very enthused about working that morning. The roundup was quick and sketchy at best, and the branding that followed didn't take long. All the cowboys knew that they would have to make up for their laxness and work double hard for a day or two after their break, but it was worth it to start their holiday a little early.

Adam's horse told him something was wrong before he could see it. The bay had been moving a little short on the left front since yesterday, but this morning it was worse, a hitch in the stride that wasn't going to work itself out. Adam pulled up and swung down. He ran his hand down the leg, lifted the hoof, and found what he expected: heat in the fetlock, a little swelling. Nothing terrible, but the horse was done for the day and probably the next few.

Toby rode over and looked at the leg without getting down. He didn't need to.

"Take that horse in to headquarters. We'll be along by noon." He paused, considering. "Might as well stay put. Don't be late Monday morning."

"Yes, sir."

Toby was already turning away. Adam gathered the bay's reins and started walking.

• • •

It was a long walk to headquarters, and Adam didn't mind a bit. He led the bay at a slow walk across the flats, keeping the pace easy on the bad leg, and for the first time in three weeks he was alone. No herd, no dust, no voices. Just the land and the sky and the sound of his own boots on the ground.

The sky was high and clean above him, though to the west a line of clouds was building, white and flat-bottomed, with the kind of height that hinted at weather still a few days off. The air had that weighted feel to it, heavier than it had been at the start of the summer, as if the season was holding its breath. Adam had learned to read a New Mexico sky the way some men read a newspaper, and what he read now said the monsoons were coming. Not today. But soon.

Sophie Degarrin had asked him about the clouds the other morning, whether they meant rain. He'd told her not yet. He'd thought about her question longer than it probably deserved.

He'd missed this. All of it: the enormous silence, the way the land opened up and kept opening until the distance swallowed every edge, the smell of juniper and dust and sun-heated grass. Four and a half years he'd been gone, and he had missed every day of it. There had been times in Belgium, in the snow and the noise and the dying, when he'd closed his eyes and tried to put himself back on a horse on these flats, tried to feel the sun on his shoulders and hear absolutely nothing. Sometimes it worked and sometimes it didn't. The times it didn't were the worst.

She'd been a kid of fourteen when he left for the war, running around the corrals in bare feet. She wasn't fourteen anymore. That was the kind of thing a man noticed whether he meant to or not.

He didn't think about the war much. It was behind him, and he was not the kind of man who looked over his shoulder. But the war had left its marks: the tattoo on his shoulder, which was a young man's foolishness and couldn't be helped, and his feet, which were something else entirely. They ached this morning, as they ached most mornings, a dull grinding soreness that had been with him since the Bulge and that he had learned to ignore. It was worse in the cold, which was a problem for a man who lived outdoors, but on a morning like this, warm and still, it was bearable. He had never mentioned it to anyone on the ranch. Cowboys didn't complain about their feet. Cowboys barely acknowledged having feet.

The bay walked well enough at the slow pace, and so did he. Two sore creatures making their way home across the flats, one hobbled by a fence he'd blundered into, the other by a war he'd been sent to. Neither one had had much say in the matter. But the morning was warm and the pace was easy, and they were both still walking, which in Adam's experience was about all you could ask.

He wondered what she was doing right now, and the picture that came was one he couldn't seem to shake: Sophie at the water can a few days back, soaking a red bandanna and wrapping it around her neck, then walking off with both arms over her head, holding all that heavy hair up off her neck. She had no idea how she looked. Adam did.

He let his mind wander where it wanted. Mostly it wanted to stay right where he was, on this land, under this sky, heading for a place he'd chosen to come back to when the choosing was the only thing that kept him sane. La Conquistadora was not his ranch. He was a hired hand, drawing wages, and he knew the difference. But a man didn't have to own a thing to belong to it, and Adam Connor belonged to this country the way a cottonwood belonged to its creek, not because someone had planted it there, but because the roots went down and the water was good and there was no earthly reason to be anywhere else.

And there she was again, in his head, uninvited and in no hurry to leave.

The red roofs and waving green trees of headquarters came into view as he dropped off the rimrock and into the little valley. He hadn't expected to be glad to see the place this early, but he was. The buildings sat in their cottonwood shade as they always had, white walls gone golden-pink from years of wind-borne sand, the green shingled roofs bright against the sky. La Cinta ran along behind the old adobe horse barn, its banks thick with cottonwoods whose leaves caught every breath of air and turned it into a sound like water running over gravel. After three weeks on the open range, headquarters meant a return to the twentieth century: electricity, a hot shower, and a bed to sleep in for at least a couple of nights. Adam was ready for all three.

He put the bay in the small corral behind the barn, pulled the saddle, and checked the leg again. The swelling hadn't gotten worse. He ran cold water from the trough over the fetlock, holding it there until the horse got bored and tried to pull away, then turned him loose with hay and a bucket of oats. The bay would be fine with a few days' rest. Horses were tougher than people gave them credit for, and more honest about their pain.

The headquarters compound was quiet and empty, everybody still out at the wagon, the bunkhouse dark, Casa Blanca sitting white and still behind its wall of cottonwoods. Adam stood in the shade of the horse barn and listened to absolutely nothing. A mockingbird was working through its repertoire somewhere in the trees along the creek. That was it. The whole place was his, and for a few minutes he just stood there and let it be.

Then he headed for the bunkhouse, because a hot shower was waiting and he wasn't going to waste the head start.

• • •

He heard them before he saw them: the crew coming off the rimrock in a loose bunch, horses picking their way down the switchback trail, the rattle of spurs and bit chains carrying across the still air. Toby was in front and the rest were strung out behind him in no particular order, every man already calculating his shower time and what he was going to put on for the social.

Adam was sitting on the bunkhouse porch by then, clean and shaved, wearing a clean white shirt he'd dug out of his war bag, his good boots crossed at the ankle on the railing. He watched them come in and felt the comfortable satisfaction of a man who'd gotten there first.

While his hands were happily piling into the bunkhouse, Toby headed straight for his own house just up the lane. Adam didn't blame him; the man wanted Annie's cooking, his own bathtub, and a little peace.

Down at the bunkhouse, the hands lost no time in getting to the table. Peggy knew the boys would be starving when they got in from the wagon and she had dinner ready when they got there. She had cooked a huge standing rib roast, set off by a mountain of mashed potatoes, yellow with butter; a big bowl of fresh green beans with bacon and lots of dark drippings, coleslaw, a big tossed salad, and dinner rolls. Peggy knew greens were as rare as hen's teeth at the wagon and a yeast roll even scarcer. She noted with a cook's pride that Ignacio was digging in right along with the best of them.

Looking up, Ignacio's eyes met hers and crinkled in pleasure. "A very fine meal, señora," he said. "You can come and cook at the wagon anytime."

A rowdy chorus of agreement came from Ignacio's disloyal following seated around the table.

Blushing, but pleased nonetheless, Peggy declined. "I'll leave that to you, Ignacio. Those boys would drive me crazy."

"'Nacio's pretty crazy himself, Miz Hampton," Tommy Ryan assured her. "You know what he did to me?"

"I have no idea, Tommy. What did he do?"

"Well, the other day I got this boil..."

"Don't tell me where you got it, Tom," she hastily interrupted him.

"No, ma'am," he agreed. "Anyway, I asked 'Nacio there if he had any medicine that would help a boil, and he said he sure did. Then he dug around in a box for a while and finally came up with this dusty old bottle. 'Here,' he says, 'put this medicine on it and it'll draw your boil, it'll draw the poison that's causin' it right out.' So I said okay. Well, let me tell you, that stuff burned like fire. I thought I was gonna die. The next morning, old 'Nacio says to me, 'How'd that medicine work on your boil? Did it draw all right?'"

Tommy paused for effect. Adam took a drink of his iced tea and waited.

"I looked at him and said, 'It darned sure drawed all right, 'Nacio. It drawed tears.' And he fell down laughing, thought that was the funniest thing he'd ever heard."

Tommy's indignation was lost in the laughter of his concerned companions, and it was some time before Peggy could wipe her eyes and offer him her sympathy.

Toby arrived not long after, having found Annie's note on the kitchen table and no Annie in the house. He was not pleased, but he was hungry, and a full plate improved his mood in direct proportion to his decreasing hunger. By the time he'd cleaned his plate a couple of times, he was once more willing to rejoin the human race.

After lunch, the bunkhouse emptied out, some men headed for the showers, some for naps, some straight for the ironing board and their good shirts. Miss Louisa's ice cream social was at half past two, and nobody intended to be late. Adam was already clean and shaved. He sat on the porch and watched the afternoon settle over headquarters, the light going long and golden across the compound, the cottonwoods throwing their shadows east. His feet ached less than they had this morning. The bay was resting in the corral. The sky was building to the west, white clouds stacking into something that might mean business in a day or two.

It was a good day to be exactly where he was.

Chapter 9 — Ice Cream Social

COWBOYS WERE A COURTEOUS lot, and punctually at half past two, they started their trek in twos and threes across the driveway from the bunkhouse to the front gates of Casa Blanca. Adam fell in with Danny Parks and Juan Soliz. Danny had shaved and put on a clean shirt and looked about ten years old. Juan was telling them both about a map rock he'd found up at the Indian Rock mesa, and Danny was full of questions, for he had a hunger for the old things on this ranch that Adam recognized because he shared it.

The herd instinct prevailing in the younger crew, Jeff Hendricks, Frankie Evans, Gary Clancy, and Tommy Ryan came in one good-looking mass. Opening the gate, they stepped out of the rough-and-tumble, sometimes violent cowboy world into an imposed and enforced island of civilized peace with touches of elegance. The girls they were used to riding and working with in sweltering heat and dust were nowhere to be seen. Instead, they saw before them a new Christine and Kitten, dressed not in the familiar Levi's of yesterday, but in sundresses showing backs and freckled shoulders.

Kitten stood cool and pretty in pastel pink in the shade of the huge old cottonwoods. Tommy stopped dead. Adam watched the kid's face go through about four expressions in the space of a second and settle on something that looked a lot like surrender.

"Hi, Kitten. You look really nice," Tommy greeted her, surprising even himself with his gallantry.

Kitten, who had never before seen Tommy shined up like a new penny and on his Sunday best behavior, was equally impressed. "Why, thank you, Tommy. You look mighty handsome yourself."

They each actually blushed and stood at a loss for words. Then Kitten remembered that she was just Kitten and this was just Tommy, albeit a new and improved version. Laughing, she grabbed his hand. "Come on, Tommy, you've got to say hello to Miss Louisa, and be sure and tell her what a lovely time you're having." And with a saucy glance she hauled him across the lawn toward their hostess.

"It's just started and I'm already having a hell of a time," Tommy assured her with an appreciative grin.

"It can only get better."

The bluegrass lawn was as soft as velvet under the heels of cowboy boots and the seats of their pants. Louisa wore a crisp white blouse with a ruff at the neck, tucked into a full circle skirt with a border print of enormous full-blown roses. Adam had to admit she was quite a sight, the kind of woman who could stand on a lawn full of cowboys and make every last one of them mind his manners.

Sophie was at one of the refreshment tables. He'd been looking at her for three weeks in dust and sweat and work clothes, and that had been fine, better than fine, but this was different. Cleaned up and smiling in the shade of the cottonwoods, she looked like her mother. He could see it now, in the way she carried herself and the way she smiled at people, and he felt a tightening in his stomach and in his Levi's that he sincerely hoped wasn't as obvious as it felt. She poured him a glass of lemonade and handed it to him with a smile.

"Having a good time, cowboy?"

"Getting better," he said, and meant the lemonade. She laughed, and he felt his face go warm. She moved on to pour for someone else. Adam took his lemonade and found a place on the grass.

Danny was already settled nearby, his long legs stretched out, his hat beside him. He had a voice you could listen to all day, a deep Tennessee drawl that sounded like it came from another century. Adam liked him. Everybody liked Danny.

There was a great trestle table that Ruben Munoz had built for the occasion, sturdy enough to support an entire roasted ox should the occasion ever arise. At the moment, it was graced with five-gallon tubs of chocolate, strawberry, and vanilla ice cream. For the true connoisseur, Annie and Ruben had combined their considerable talents and efforts to produce several hand-cranked freezers full of homemade peach to complement the Clauson Creamery's offerings. The peach was a big hit and was going fast. Adam made sure to get a bowl before it was gone.

Sophie came by with a fresh pitcher of lemonade, and Danny was on his feet before she could pour, taking the pitcher and filling cups while Sophie stood talking with the boys for a minute. Danny said something that made her laugh, and she swatted his arm and moved on to the next group.

The afternoon passed slowly and without effort, the way good afternoons do on La Conquistadora. Adam liked the stories that came out at a time like this, stories about arrowhead finds and Indian campgrounds and old-timers who had ridden for the ranch fifty years ago. Layer upon layer of people, all the way back to whoever had first seen this country and decided to stay. It was all the same place, and it remembered them all.

Danny had gotten quickly to his feet when Winston Mallory came walking up, and gone to bring a chair for the venerable old man, which was accepted with a gracious smile. That was Danny. You didn't have to tell him what to do. He saw what needed doing and did it, and it never seemed to cost him anything.

It was getting on toward the end of the afternoon when Adam noticed Danny hanging back, waiting for the crowd to thin. He had something in his hand, wrapped in a red bandanna. Adam didn't think much of it. He finished his lemonade and set the paper cup in the grass. Across the lawn he could see Sophie helping her mother fold a tablecloth, the two of them laughing about something. It had been a good afternoon, in good company, and he was in no hurry for it to end.

• • •

The kitchen of Casa Blanca was in the oldest part of the house, its wing a hundred or so years old, maybe more, no one knew for sure. Its walls were old adobe and no corner was square, a condition that would have driven a German hausfrau to distraction but that worried

Rufina not at all and Louisa very little. There was a short step up into the dining room and a good step down into the pantry. The early Spanish builders had not been blessed, or cursed, with the possession of a level. Those that followed, followed suit. The house had over thirty rooms and halls and nooks and crannies. It also had seventeen steps up or down that added either to its charm or its disgrace, depending on one's point of view. Louisa loved it and considered it charming. Sophie figured that was the way the house was supposed to be. Despite their widely differing origins, it was the kind of home they had both grown up in.

Rufina came up the step from the pantry carrying the large chocolate cake she had made that morning.

"Oh, Rufina, let me have a piece. It looks way too good to wait for," Sophie begged.

"Ask your momma. I'm not the boss."

"I thought you were," Louisa commented, and then added, "All right, I guess we can cut one end off and then just cover it up with icing." Louisa had as big a sweet tooth as anybody and could usually find a way to sneak a few goodies.

"Wait!" Degarrin objected. "We don't want to eat it plain, do we? We want it iced first."

As this idea met with universal acceptance, the cake was promptly cut, slathered with icing, and gobbled down by all in a most egalitarian manner. Degarrin had been perched on the kitchen counter for the better part of an hour, being in the way and offering unsought opinions and advice that no one heeded but remaining unbanished because a man in the kitchen was such a rare and wondrous thing. Toby had wandered in not long after and was promptly welcomed into the feminine realm for the very same reason and was soon offering his ignored opinions as freely as was his boss.

Sated by the feeding frenzy and realizing there was very little more fun to be had in the kitchen, Degarrin and Toby strolled out to the horseshoe pit by the vegetable garden, where they commenced a leisurely game in the company of zucchini, crookneck squash, and green chili. The women got down to some serious preparations.

Sophie didn't mind the work. She liked the preparation almost as much as the party itself, when the house smelled of cake and everything was clean and set out and ready. Through the kitchen window she could see the lawn and the tables and the cottonwoods, all of it waiting. This was her mother's favorite party of the year, her own tradition, something brand new that she had introduced to La Conquistadora. Occasionally there was something new under the sun. Every summer, on the first day of the Clauson rodeo and dance, at half past two in the afternoon, Louisa held her ice cream social. The guest list included every La Conquistadora employee and a few people Louisa considered special who had known the ranch in the past. It surprised and delighted her that upon receipt of one of her invitations, people seemed willing to drive across the country to honor it.

There were moments when Sophie was struck with startling clarity of just how truly beautiful her mother was. Watching her now across the lush lawn, surrounded by cowboys in freshly pressed snap-button shirts and Levi's with knife-sharp creases, Sophie was confronted, for at least the thousandth time, with the full power and potential of her mother. It was awesome and wonderful, also a little scary.

Sophie was at the refreshment table pouring lemonade when Adam Connor came through the line. She handed him a glass with a smile.

"Having a good time, cowboy?"

"Getting better," he said. There was something in his face that made her laugh, though she couldn't have said what it was. He took his lemonade and moved on, and Sophie turned to pour for the next in line without giving it another thought.

Danny Parks came through not long after, polite as always, thanking her for the lemonade and asking if she'd saved him any of the homemade peach ice cream. She hadn't, but she pointed him toward the trestle table and told him to hurry. He tipped his hat and went.

Drifting across the lawn a little later, she caught the end of an exchange between her mother and Jeff Hendricks that made her smile.

"Did you ride him?" her mother was asking, with the same

attentive look and smile that had encouraged every man she'd ever known to pour his heart out.

"Well, of course, ma'am," Jeff answered, surprised she'd even asked.

Laughing, and loving his genuine astonishment, Louisa assured him, "I just knew you had, Jeff. I would have been surprised if you hadn't. I don't even know why I asked!"

Jeff laughed too, a little embarrassed. "I can't ride 'um all, Miss Louisa, but I can sure ride old Midget."

From Jeff's scornful tone, Sophie concluded that Midget's bucking left a lot to be desired.

She could see Danny Parks across the lawn, settled on the grass with the other cowboys around her mother's yellow chair. He had that easy way about him that Sophie liked. Some men had to work at being comfortable with themselves and with everybody else, but Danny just was. He was telling a story, and from the way the boys were leaning in, it was a good one. Danny always had a good one. Sophie smiled and went back to the table. There was more lemonade to pour.

• • •

Louisa was quite a favorite with the hands, and the cause of more than a few crushes. Jeff Hendricks was just one of the boys who was more than a little smitten. Without ever even realizing it, he would instinctively measure women by her standard, and usually find them lacking and somehow disappointing. Louisa didn't know this, but she knew Jeff, and she knew how to draw a young man out.

"Are you having a good time this summer, Jeff? Have you had to ride any wild ones?" she asked with the same attentive look and smile that had encouraged every man she'd ever known to pour his heart out.

"Oh, yes, ma'am! Why, just this morning when we saddled up, Midget started bucking with me, and when I got a chance to look around, there were two other horses bucking, too. There was more of a rodeo at camp this morning than there will be in Clauson tonight. Old Toby said he'd never seen anything like it, with so many bucking at once. I guess they just got each other going."

"Oh, I would have loved to have seen that! What a sight." There were lots of times when Louisa understood and secretly shared her daughter's love and yearning for the cowboy's life on the range. As an afterthought she asked, "Did you ride him?"

"Well, of course, ma'am," Jeff answered, surprised she'd even asked.

Laughing, and loving his genuine astonishment, Louisa assured him, "I just knew you had, Jeff. I would have been surprised if you hadn't. I don't even know why I asked!"

Jeff laughed too, a little embarrassed. "I can't ride 'um all, Miss Louisa, but I can sure ride old Midget."

Louisa was forced to conclude from Jeff's scornful tone that Midget's bucking left a lot to be desired.

Across the lawn she spotted Degarrin talking with Fred Hampton. From their expressions she could tell it was business. Fred was no doubt bringing the boss up to date on fence conditions and projects around the ranch. La Conquistadora had hundreds of miles of fence; just maintaining them was a full-time job for several people. Fred was the foremost among that group. He had started out on the fencing crew years ago as a teenager and had been there ever since. Degarrin was convinced he was the finest fence builder there was anywhere, and the proof was in the pudding. La Conquistadora was renowned for its fences.

Not far from her father, Louisa could also see Sophie at one of the refreshment tables. She was pouring a glass of lemonade for Adam Connor and laughing at something he had just said. Louisa found herself smiling too, for it was hard to see Connor and not smile. But she watched him take his lemonade and head for the grass with his face pinker than the lemonade in his glass, while Sophie, still laughing, turned to pour for the next in line without so much as a backward glance. Louisa had been a young and pretty girl herself, once. She recognized that look.

He was so very good-looking, with waves of sandy hair that would probably go brown eventually to match his eyes, and a dimple in his left cheek that appeared when he smiled and probably got him out of more trouble than he deserved. Then he would be dark and handsome instead of fair and handsome, but he would never be tall and handsome, for it was too late for that. He carried himself well, though, which made him seem taller than he was.

That described her husband, at least. She didn't know about Adam Connor.

Louisa's wool-gathering was interrupted by Annie Lloyd at her elbow.

"Come on, Louisa, it's time for us cooks to have some of the feast we've been toiling over for the last couple of days. Just about everybody else has been served and is already enjoying the fruits of our labor."

Louisa saw that she was right, and together they headed for the great trestle table that Ruben Munoz had built for the occasion. Ruben believed in doing things on a grand scale, and the table bespoke his beliefs. Louisa was sure it could support an entire roasted ox should the occasion ever arise. At the moment, it was graced with five-gallon tubs of chocolate, strawberry, and vanilla ice cream. For the true connoisseur, Annie and Ruben had combined their considerable talents and efforts to produce several hand-cranked freezers full of homemade peach to complement the Clauson Creamery's offerings. The peach was a big hit and was going fast.

Among those who had helped empty the freezer of homemade peach was Danny Parks, a young man from Tennessee. Danny had the most beautiful speaking voice that Louisa, or just about anyone else, had ever heard. It was low and deep, with the rich drawl that Louisa missed from the Southern days of her youth, the accent pure and untainted by any of the Texas twang that she often heard from New Mexican lips. Danny called out to her now.

"Miss Louisa, won't you come and join us? We've saved a place just for you."

They had indeed. An old-style lawn chair, heavy and made of wood, bright yellow in color with a steeply slanted seat, sat vacant and waiting for her in a little sea of smiling cowboys. Returning smile for smile into their upturned faces, Louisa accepted. "Who could resist such an invitation?" she asked, taking her place in their midst.

After a few moments of greetings and a little ice breaking, Louisa's eager court got down to the business of bringing her up to date on their latest finds and adventures. She was always an appreciative audience for the cowboys' tales and wanted to know all about their doings.

Juan Soliz started them off.

"Miss Louisa, I've been meaning to tell you about this but I just haven't had the chance to until now. Back in the spring, I was prowling around over at the Indian Rock mesa, you know, where the antelope drawings are?"

Louisa nodded. She knew exactly where he was talking about. It was one of her favorite places on the ranch, a point off the Antelope Hills whose base was littered with great boulders that in some ancient, long-past day had broken off the sandstone rimrock that circled the top of the point. The great red boulders and the outcroppings of stone around the base of the point had provided the same refuge to passersby as they had in ancient times. The most casual survey informed even the most negligent of observers that many a tribe had passed their days and enjoyed protection there. Scarcely a surface was without a drawing carved or pecked out by some long-gone artist. The rocks abounded with deer and antelope and almost anything at all that had been deemed worthy of note. Thus this special place came by its name, for it was truly the Indian Rock. Louisa thought of it as a kind of Metropolitan Museum of Ancient Indian Art. No one else thought of the Indian Rock in such high-toned terms, but everybody who had ever laid eyes on the place was fascinated and intrigued by it.

"I went on past the drawings we all know and have looked at lots of times, but then I went on and started climbing up on some of the boulders higher up the cliff side," Juan continued. "Anyway, I started climbing and I came across some drawings I didn't know were there, and that I'd never heard anyone else ever mention."

Now he had everybody's attention.

"You found some new drawings at the Indian Rock?" Louisa asked. This was the kind of thing she really loved. Back in her student days at Randolph Macon, her major had been history, her minor archaeology. One reason she loved La Conquistadora so much was because to her it was one vast field trip.

"I pulled myself up on a really big rock. It had a flat, fairly smooth surface and was lying almost level. The rock was covered with drawings like I'd never seen before. There were a few animals like you'd expect to see, but not many. There were peaks pecked out that looked to be hills, and then some lines down the surface and across it too, like trails. I think the rock is a map."

"A map?" Louisa asked. "Juan, I really want to see this map rock! Can you tell me how to find it, or do you need to show me?"

"I think I can tell where is good enough that you can find it. If you can't, I'll show you some afternoon after the branding."

Louisa and the other cowboys sitting on the grass around Juan listened carefully to his instructions. Louisa wasn't the only one planning a trip to the newly found map rock. This led to reminiscences of great arrowhead finds and favorite Indian campgrounds around the ranch. Louisa told the boys about taking Sophie to the grinding holes in the Buffalo Flats pasture when Sophie was just a little girl, with a box of Grape-Nuts cereal and a metate. They had had a grand time being Indians and grinding up Grape-Nuts in one of the deep, well-worn holes. When they left, they had put a flat rock over the hole, with the Grape-Nuts still in it. Sophie had thought they should leave the cereal for any Indian spirits that might come back to visit their old home and be hungry. Louisa had thought that a wonderful idea. She guessed the Grape-Nuts were still there, unless a hungry spirit had happened by. That was years ago, but she had never gotten back by to check.

Cake and ice cream almost gone, only the dregs of lemonade remaining, the boys' talk turned from the past to the future. The rodeo and dance that evening were the next big events on their horizon.

"Are you goin' to the dance, Miss Louisa?" Frankie asked. He fancied himself a pretty good two-stepper, and a twirl or two around the dance floor with the boss's wife would have suited him just fine.

"No, we're leaving that to the younger generation this year. But, Frankie," Louisa smiled, the belle never far below the surface, "dance a dance for me."

"Yes, ma'am, I sure will," Frankie said.

Winston Mallory, one of Louisa's and Degarrin's most honored and favorite guests, had walked up in time to hear this last exchange. Although a very old man now, Winston was something of a legend. He had been up the trail with the great cattle drives and had cowboyed on La Conquistadora before the turn of the century and for a few years after. Louisa considered him her greatest find, and he was on every guest list she had ever compiled. Sometimes he came just to stay and visit for a while and to remember and share with them his younger days on this special place. In Louisa's opinion, Winston Mallory was the West. He was also a true gentleman, and very well spoken. When he talked of the past, those long-gone days were as real to Louisa as if she had been there with him.

Upon Winston's approach, Danny had quickly gotten to his feet and gone to bring a chair for the venerable old man, which was accepted with a gracious smile. Louisa watched Danny settle the chair and step back, and thought, not for the first time, what a fine young man this was. He had the instincts that couldn't be taught and the manners that could only come from good raising. A good Southern boy.

Seating himself, Winston commented that in his day La Conquistadora had had the dancingest man he had ever seen.

"That would have been a long time ago, maybe thirty, forty years. Two brothers worked for the ranch then, Jim Greene and his brother Fred. They were both real good hands. Jim was one of the finest riders I have ever known. But let me tell you boys, and Miss Louisa, that feller could play the fiddle even better than he rode. He could fiddle the birds down outa the trees. Jim Greene was a mighty popular man on a Saturday night. But not as popular as Fred. Fred could dance the night away, moved just as smooth as silk, like a river flowing. There wasn't a lady alive that didn't love to dance with Fred, for he made 'em all look like they were as good as he was. Boys, if you want to be as popular as can be with the girls, a real lady killer, just learn to dance like a dream."

Winston settled deeper into his chair, his eyes bright with the memory.

"Anyway, on Saturday afternoon these two would come ridin' in to headquarters to get cleaned up and dressed up. Now, because Fred was a real dancer, he took it right serious. When he headed out to a dance, he always had his bowler hat and shiny, polished-up dancing shoes in a flour sack, tied on behind the saddle. He was the only cowboy I ever ran across that carried his dancing shoes and hat around with him. And there they'd go, Fred with his flour sack and Jim with his fiddle case tied on with the saddle strings, resting nice and snug along his horse's side. Of course, they always rode their prettiest, fanciest mounts. When Jim and Fred rode out on a Saturday afternoon, they were always just miles from Saturday night."

Frankie was delighted with Winston's story. "Hey, the Greene boys and me would have got along fine, they were my kind of guys!"

"You would have," Winston agreed. "They were fine men, and fine cowboys."

"Mr. Mallory, it must have been wonderful on La Conquistadora then, when the ranch still had buffalo and hardly any fences," Danny said with longing in his voice. Danny was just a little too romantic for his own good, in Louisa's opinion. He very likely wished he hadn't missed the Civil War, either, she thought. Silly boy.

Winston looked at Danny, eager and longing a little for the age that he had missed, and smiled. "With those buffalo around, you had even fewer fences. Those old woolly rascals would go through a fence like a hot knife through butter. The fence crew just went around behind them. But the good old days were pretty good," he said. "I had a helluva lot of fun, and so did most everybody I knew. Things were really popping around the old La Conquistadora ranch. But those days were hardly different from the way the ranch is now. The land is still the same, and the cattle and horses are bred up to be even better than they were then. You don't have line camps, but you have electricity and automobiles, so it doesn't take two or three days to try to get across the place. It looks to me like the ranch hasn't changed all that much, and that things are still hoppin' around the old La Conquistadora."

Winston's summation met with general approval, and Danny was satisfied.

Most of the guests had drifted over and joined the crowd around Louisa and Winston. Realizing this, Louisa took advantage of the situation to thank her guests.

"Thank you all for coming to our little party this afternoon. Of course, you are all welcome to stay as long as you like and for as long as the cake and ice cream hold out, but I know you have a big evening to get ready for, and I don't want to hold any of you up."

Toby spoke from the back of the little crowd. "Miss Louisa, on behalf of everybody here today, we all want to thank you for having this party for us today. Everything was real nice, and we all enjoyed ourselves."

"It was truly my pleasure," Louisa responded to Toby's little speech and the voices of agreement that followed it.

Danny had been waiting for a moment to speak to Louisa without an audience, and as some of the guests began to drift away, he approached her.

"Miss Louisa?"

"Yes, Danny."

"I have something I want to show you. The other day when we were working the Creek Pasture, I was riding along across those little sandy flats with the tepee rings. You know the place?"

"Of course I do, Danny. The old Indian campground, with the stones just waiting to hold down the sides of the next tepee. I've always liked that place, but I've never found anything really good there, although I always expect to. Did you find something fabulous?"

"I'll let you decide," he answered. Reaching down to his boot, he pulled out something wrapped in a red bandanna handkerchief. Danny grinned.

"It was too big to go in my pocket," he explained, "at least not if I was going to be doing any sitting around socializing."

"I see," said Louisa, dying to do just that.

"Well, here it is." Danny unwrapped the red bandanna, and there in his hand Louisa saw an absolutely perfect eight-inch spear point, the extraordinary creation of an artisan and craftsman of a long-gone civilization.

"Danny, that is exquisite. It is the most beautiful and perfect thing I have ever seen found on this ranch, and you know how many arrowheads and scrapers and pottery shards and things this place has yielded up. But this is the best. It always seemed to me that that campground had to have some treasures, and here one finally is. Congratulations, Danny, but how did you come across it?"

"Remember when it rained and the wind blew so hard about ten days ago? We worked that part of the Creek Pasture the next morning, and I happened to get assigned to the sand flats part. I'm like you, Miss Louisa. It always seemed to me that the campground should have been a great place for hunting arrowheads, but I'd never had a lot of luck there, either. I think the sand just keeps shifting and reshifting over whatever is there. When I came along, the conditions were perfect. The wind and rain had cleared it off, and with the sand still being wet, it hadn't had time to shift back over. I was just riding along and glanced down and there it was, just as perfect as can be."

"It is just as perfect as can be." Louisa had been examining the spear point while Danny spoke. "There is not a single flaw anywhere on this point. Whoever made it knew exactly what he was doing. The owner must have been very unhappy when it got lost."

"I imagine so," Danny agreed.

"Isn't it remarkable that something so fine and exquisite could have lasted such a long time without being broken or damaged in any way?"

"Miss Louisa, I want you to have this. It's everything you say it is, and I knew you would appreciate it more than anyone I know. Eventually, you might have found it anyway."

"Are you absolutely sure, Danny? It's your find. Are you certain you want to give it away?"

"I wouldn't give it to anyone but you, Miss Louisa. But it's a part of La Conquistadora, and there's no telling where all it may have been in the past, but it should stay here at home now."

Louisa was touched. What a fine young man this was.

"Danny, if you are absolutely certain, I will accept it. Not for me, but for the ranch. There is quite a little collection of special things found here on the ranch on the fireplace mantle in the dining room. I don't know how it got started. The collection was there when I came, and Degarrin says the same thing. There are some interesting things on that mantle, among them a cannon ball and a long-roweled Spanish spur. Your spear point will go beautifully there, and will always have a place of honor."

"Thank you for taking it, Miss Louisa. I'll always like thinking of it here where it belongs. I'd better get going now. I've got things to do before leaving for town."

"Oh, Danny, before you go," Louisa stopped him, "I wanted to ask you something. I heard you got into a little scrape a day or two ago. Are you all right now?"

Danny looked puzzled for a moment, then laughed when he recalled the incident she was referring to. "Oh, that! That was nothing, Miss Louisa. I'd already forgotten all about it. I was heeling a calf on Roosevelt and messed around and managed to catch the calf and my own horse's front legs, too. I don't know who was more surprised, me, the calf, or Rosie."

"But, Danny, that could have been so dangerous," Louisa voiced the concern she'd had since the incident had come to her ears.

Danny waved it off. "It's only tricky, Miss Louisa, if you stay caught."

With these comforting, lighthearted words, Danny tipped his hat and was gone.

Watching him stride away toward the bunkhouse and his big night on the town, Louisa could only shake her head in the exasperation of age, tinged with just a touch of envy, toward the careless confidence of youth.

Degarrin came across the lawn to her, a golden brownie in his hand.

"I love these things," he told her.

"I know. I do, too. They're pure brown sugar and butter. Deadly, but delicious," Louisa agreed.

"I'd say your soiree was quite a success, everybody's got a full belly and a smile on their face. It will make all the columns tomorrow."

Louisa laughed and put an arm around her mate. "I was thinking the very same thing. They'll likely be reading about it in Charlotte."

"Then why so glum?" he asked her.

"Oh, I was just listening to Danny make light of his near disaster. How can he be so foolish?"

Now it was her husband's turn to laugh. "He's twenty-two. That's what being twenty-two is all about. Besides, nonsense like that happens around here all the time, but you usually don't hear about it, that's all."

Noticing the spear point in his wife's hand, Degarrin changed the subject. "Where did you get that lethal weapon?" he asked.

Louisa explained the acquisition of her latest artifact, and the two started toward the dining room to arrange its new home. Seated in the cool and shady depths of the portal, they found Winston. He was sipping a bourbon and water, enjoying life and the vivid green and bright orange of the blooming trumpet vines that screened his perch.

"You know, Winston, there is something I've always meant to ask you but never seem to remember to," Louisa said.

"Ask away, my dear."

"Do you by any chance know anything about the history of the walnut, marble-topped sideboard in the dining room?"

"I should say so! I recall clearly the day that dreadful thing arrived. It was not alone, you know. There were several other matching pieces as I remember. The freighter lugged it all down here from Las Vegas in a horse-drawn wagon, and the trip took the better part of a week, I believe. Upon arrival, it took that large and brawny man and three cowboys to get it all unloaded. I was one of those cowboys and, probably as a result, have never been overly fond of that marble-topped Victorian stuff."

"Winston! I rather like that piece. All the rest of the furniture you helped unload that day is still here, in various bedrooms. In fact," Louisa paused, suddenly struck by her thought, "the dresser in your bedroom is one of those very pieces!"

"Yes. I rather thought it might be," Winston commented dryly, to Louisa's delight and Degarrin's amusement.

"We are on our way to the dining room. Come along and point out to us all the shortcomings of my beloved sideboard," Louisa invited.

"It will be my pleasure."

In the dining room, while Winston held forth, beguiling Degarrin and Rufina, who had come out of the kitchen, with tales of another time, Louisa, smiling as she listened, made a place for Danny's spear point on the mantle over the little corner fireplace.

Chapter 10 — After the Social

SOPHIE WAS FEELING MORE than a little stuffed, having sampled liberally of cake and ice cream as well as a few of her father's favorite golden brownies. She decided a little stroll was in order, especially since the cleaning up was nearly done and Rufina had just run her out of the kitchen, a fate she had not protested in the least.

Sophie stepped through the kitchen's deep doorway, set as it was in nearly three feet of adobe, and paused to look around her domain. No sign of life was to be seen. The cowboys were either sprucing up, napping, or were long since on their way to town and beer. The back side of the headquarters compound was silent and deserted, just the way she liked it. To the west, the clouds had been building all afternoon, tall and white on top, flat and dark underneath. The air had that heavy, waiting feel it always got before the monsoons.

She could appreciate at her leisure the pink and red tones mixed with the yellows that blended to color the whole place. All the buildings had started out a bright white, but years and years of being blasted by the wind-borne red sandy soil had long since turned them all a golden, rosy hue, a shade that went quite nicely with the green shingled roofs and the red slate atop the old adobe horse barn along the creek. The barn was thought to be the oldest structure on the place. Standing and contrasting with it all were the bright green dancing leaves of the cottonwoods that were found everywhere and clogged the banks of the creek for miles.

A large swing, of the type found on many a veranda, hung, as it always had, from a thick bough just beyond the kitchen door. The swing had been Sophie's companion since childhood and called to her now, as ever. But today Sophie turned a deaf ear and headed instead for the horse corral behind the barns. Yesterday, Fred had brought in a yearling colt, one of the ones that had been halter-broken last winter. The little fellow had had a bad accident and gotten cut up in a barbwire fence. Something must have badly scared him, because he had bolted right through it. Fred found the hole in the fence and then the injured horse, which he brought back to headquarters to be doctored. The colt's name was Domino because he was black with a white star and four white stockings. He was a pretty fellow but would probably always have a scar where he had gashed open his chest on the fence.

Sophie had helped Fred clean the wound yesterday, and she and her father had held Domino steady while Fred stitched him up.

Examining his handiwork, Fred had commented, "It ain't very pretty, but this little guy didn't leave me a lot to work with. It will most likely leave a scar, but at least the wound will heal now and won't get infected." Fred had not been happy about that assessment. He loved horses and hated to think of one being hurt.

"He'll be fine, Fred. It's lucky you found him when you did," Degarrin had reassured him.

Now that her mother's ice cream social was over and Sophie had some spare time on her hands, she thought she had better go and check on the little colt and make sure that he stayed on the mend.

Domino was a bit on the shy side, still not too sure people were to be trusted, but even so, he was not averse to a little company. But when Sophie got to the corral behind the barns, Domino already had a visitor.

Adam had haltered the colt and was talking to him and rubbing him as he inspected the stitched-up gash above his front legs. The late afternoon sun was turning his hair almost gold, and his hands on the colt were slow and sure. Sophie stopped walking and just watched him for a moment before he knew she was there.

"What's the diagnosis, doc? Will he ever play the violin again?" Sophie asked.

"Like a virtuoso. He may have a little more trouble winning the Kentucky Derby, though," Adam said, looking up from his examination. "So you got worried about him, too? So did I. But it seems we're Johnny-come-latelies. Fred has already come and gone, and this guy is in as good a shape as he can be."

"I should have known Fred wouldn't neglect him," Sophie commented, stroking the colt's neck. "Did you have fun at Mom's party?" she asked, for something to say.

"You bet! That's a really nice thing for you all to do, having all of us over for a get-together like that. There are a lot of places where that just wouldn't happen. Most folks like Miss Louisa and your dad wouldn't cross the line and mingle with the hired help like that."

"We're not snobs! Of course we mingle with the people who work for us."

"I know." Adam grinned. "That's what I just said."

But even as she smiled back, Sophie knew they were snobs. Mingling was all right on occasion and under certain circumstances. She looked forward to her mother's ice cream social as much as anyone and had just as good a time. But in the back of her mind the thought always lurked that her mother enjoyed playing Lady Bountiful, and that the whole thing smacked a little too much of noblesse oblige. She knew very well about the line, and that if you crossed it too far there would be certain trouble. The line was the reason her mother did not approve of her helping with the cow work when the wagon was out and why she didn't automatically get to ride out with the cowboys the rest of the year. The line was the reason she wasn't allowed to wear shorts around the headquarters, although she could wear them in downtown Albuquerque. It was the reason they dressed for dinner every night and she was expected to practice the piano every day.

Sophie didn't even want to think about it. She would rather think about Adam, who was so handsome and so nice.

"Do you like it here, Adam? You had the whole world to choose from, and had seen a lot of it in the war. Why did you come back here?"

"What I saw of the world during the war made me want to come back to this ranch all the more. The world is a very brutal place, and it's all because people make it that way. Here at La Conquistadora there's lots of beautiful land and very few people to mess it up. There is order and no chaos. This ranch follows a pattern, year after year. After being in that mess in Europe, I started appreciating continuity and peace and quiet. I sometimes feel this place is timeless, like it's caught somehow in a wrinkle in time. When the old-timers talk about the eighties and nineties, they could be talking about yesterday."

"That really is true," Sophie agreed. "When I look at old pictures, the only reason I know they weren't just taken is because the saddle backs are too high and the cattle aren't pure Herefords."

Adam nodded. "That's exactly what I mean. The reasons Winston Mallory loved working here are the same reasons I love it, too."

Suddenly deeply curious, because his reasons might be hers too, Sophie asked, "Why, Connor, why do you suppose it means so much to you?"

"I can tell you exactly why. It's because of the people here. They keep their word and respect your privacy. And it's because the cattle and the horses are the best on earth. But most of all, it's because the land is so vast and empty, and the sky is so high and such a blue, and it's because the light is so soft and golden it brings out every color it touches. When it plays across the flats and lights the canyons, well, Rembrandt should have been here. Maybe some great artist will find this place someday and capture the way it really is."

Sophie listened to his words and was strongly moved.

"My God, Adam. You are a poet. You just expressed exactly what I feel but have never quite figured out how to say."

"Maybe a poet will find this place sometime, too. I've had a lot of time to think about it, and I've seen a lot to compare it to. La Conquistadora is as close to heaven as I will ever come, Sophie."

The two stood and regarded each other in silence. Soul mates, not just with each other, but with everyone that had ever been touched by La Conquistadora, which was just about everybody that had ever touched it.

While talking to Sophie, Adam had taken the halter off Domino and now held it in his hand. He looked down, surprised to see it there.

"Speaking of old and wondrous things around here," Sophie said, "I guess you know the story of the weighing scales over there?"

Adam looked at the scales a few feet away. He shook his head. "What about them?" he asked.

"Well, they used to be over at Fort McCamey. You know the wagon camp there now, down on the river, with the brick corrals?"

Adam nodded. Old Fort McCamey was, of course, known to everyone. He had spent many an afternoon sweltering in the heat of those hot, closed-in brick corrals.

Sophie continued. "Back forty or fifty years ago, they sent a crew over there to dig up the scales and see if they were still usable. They were buried three or four feet deep by then, because the fort had been abandoned for a long, long time. But they dug around and finally found the scales. The installation book was even bound under one of the beams. The scales were brought back here and the instructions in the book were followed. And there they are, working as good as new."

"Is that right?" Adam asked curiously. "I've helped weigh bulls on those scales lots of times. One time I weighed a cowboy named Tubby Burke because I couldn't believe a horse could carry something around that weighed three hundred pounds."

"I remember him. Did he really weigh three hundred pounds?"

"Pretty darned close. I've heard Toby say those scales are accurate to a quarter of a pound. Tubby weighed in at two ninety-eight and a half, if I recall right. He would have made about three of you, I guess."

"Not quite three," Sophie said.

"Hop on and let's see." Adam headed for the scales.

Sophie knew she weighed a hundred and twenty-three pounds and wondered if the fabled old scales were as good as everybody bragged.

"Okay," she agreed, and stepped through the gate Adam held open for her. Sophie was now penned in a corral with six-foot fences of railroad ties, built to hold three-thousand-pound bulls. While Sophie considered the novelty of her situation, Adam went to the weighing booth and took her measure.

"One twenty-two and three-quarters," he announced with a questioning look.

"I guess Toby was right when he always brags they're within a quarter pound accurate," Sophie acknowledged.

Adam came back to let her out but paused, regarding her through the steel gate, his hands resting on the rungs.

"Is your dance card all filled up for tonight?" he asked her.

Sophie put her hands on the gate rungs, not far from his, and gave him a long and searching look. Her mind swiftly considered possibilities and calculated consequences. This would be a real good time to be cordial but discouraging.

"My dance card still has a space or two left," she said.

For a long moment, through steel bars painted a dull red, brown eyes and blue eyes met, each searching the other, taking stock.

"Then I'll see you tonight," Adam said, and opened the heavy gate for her.

Chapter 11 — Heat Lightning

KITTEN AND CHRISTINE WORE Levi's and snap-button shirts. Sophie wore a black skirt and a red sleeveless blouse. Christine and Kitten fit right into the denim-clad crowd of girls and women, cowboys and men. Sophie stood out. She always stood out when she dressed like herself instead of dressing for the range, and tonight she had dressed like herself. Her two friends exchanged a glance that Sophie had been getting since she was fifteen and had long since learned to ignore. Their goals were different, after all. Sophie had always proclaimed her intention of marrying the governor's son or some such thing. Christine and Kitten just wanted a good-looking cowboy.

The VFW Hall in Clauson was not much to look at (cinder block and a concrete floor and enough cigarette smoke to cure a ham) but the band was loud and willing, the beer was cold, and every cowboy within fifty miles had showed up in his best shirt and his cleanest hat.

Sophie spotted Adam almost at once. He was near the bar with a beer in his hand and a half circle of girls around him who had found the best-looking cowboy in the building before the band finished its first song. One of them, a tall brunette Sophie had never seen before, had her hand on his arm and was laughing up at him as though he had just said the funniest thing in the history of the English language. Adam was smiling and talking to all of them, easy and unhurried, and he didn't seem to mind the brunette standing close enough to read his watch. Sophie watched for a moment and felt something shift in her chest that she did not care for at all. She had spent the afternoon at a horse corral looking into those brown eyes through the bars of a bull pen, and here he was, surrounded by every unattached girl in the county. Maybe what she had felt that afternoon was nothing special. Maybe it happened to him every Saturday night.

Danny Parks found her before she could dwell on it. He came over with his hat in his hand and his Tennessee manners on full display and asked if she would care to dance. Sophie said she would love to. Danny was a good dancer, easy to follow, and he talked the whole time in that deep drawl of his, telling her about a big old mule deer buck he had nearly ridden over that morning at the wagon. Sophie enjoyed herself. Danny was good company, the best company, and she told him so when the song ended.

"Why, thank you, Miss Sophie. I enjoyed it too," he said, and tipped his hat. He glanced at her, followed her eyes to where Adam still stood with his admirers, and grinned. "That Connor sure is easy on the eyes. I'm going to have to work a whole lot harder to get noticed with him in the room."

Sophie looked at Danny and thought what she always thought when she looked at Danny Parks. He was a very handsome man, with those dark eyes and that deep voice and manners that would have made his grandmother proud. He had never had trouble with girls and he knew it. The modesty was pure Danny; he had seen something on her face and was making light of it. He just wasn't for her. She had no idea why not, and she didn't feel like working it out tonight.

"Danny Parks, if I had a sister I would point her straight at you and tell her not to let go."

He laughed and went to get himself a beer. Sophie watched him go and thought he was just about the nicest young man she had ever met. He was like a brother, or a cousin, someone you were always glad to see and never once had to think twice about.

She was still thinking that when she looked across the floor and saw Adam Connor looking back at her. He said something to the brunette, set his beer on the bar, and came strolling toward them without a backward glance.

He was in clean Levi's and a pressed white shirt, and the smile he gave them could have lit up the room. Christine held her breath, hoping she was the one. Kitten confidently struck her picture pose. Sophie looked at Adam Connor and stopped thinking about Danny

Parks altogether.

"Sophie, would you like to dance?"

"I'd love to," she said, for the second time that evening. The words were the same. Nothing else was.

Christine's hopes and Kitten's confidence were both disappointed, but Sophie was already gone, two-stepping across the floor with Adam before either of them could say a word.

Sophie was a good dancer. She glided like a swan on water, responding almost intuitively to her partner's leads, and she could carry on a conversation while doing it, which was more than most girls managed. She knew all of this about herself. But she had never danced with Adam Connor, and the moment he took her hand and led her onto the floor, she understood that everything she knew about dancing was only half the picture. Adam moved as though the music's beat and rhythm went directly to his muscles, bypassing all mental processes entirely. He was graceful and effortless, without any conscious effort whatsoever, and Sophie, who had danced with a hundred partners, felt for the first time in her life what dancing was actually supposed to feel like. He made her better than she actually was, he made it look easy, and he had absolutely no idea he was doing any of it. With his looks and his moves, Adam Connor would have been a gift to Hollywood. If the thought had ever crossed his mind, he just would have laughed and gone back to La Conquistadora without a second thought.

"You're a lot of fun to dance with, Sophie," he told her.

She almost laughed. "Thank you, Adam. You're a great dancer, did you know that?"

"Oh, well, I wouldn't say that. There's not much to dancing, you know. Anybody can do it."

"Adam, I've danced with a million guys and you are without doubt the best partner I have ever had. Not just everyone can dance, and no one I have ever encountered moves like you do."

He shrugged off her praise as though she were complimenting his bootlaces. He genuinely did not know. Sophie found that so charming it almost hurt.

For a moment he looked as though he wanted to say something

else, but he just smiled and led her into the next song, a waltz.

The waltz changed things. It brought them closer than the two-steps had, close enough that Sophie's hand found the hard curve of his shoulder through his shirt and stayed there. His hand settled at the small of her back, warm and sure, and his other hand held hers as lightly as if she might want it back, but she didn't. He smelled like soap and something warm underneath that was just him. During a slow turn his jaw brushed the top of her hair and he didn't pull away and she didn't want him to.

Then more two-steps, and a polka or two.

Between dances, Sophie went back to her friends for a drink of water. Christine gave her a look.

"I don't think Miss Louisa would approve," Christine said.

"Of dancing?" Sophie asked innocently.

"Of the way you two are dancing," Kitten said, grinning. "You know, Sophie, you always get what you want."

"I don't always get what I want."

"Name one time you didn't."

Sophie couldn't, offhand, and she wasn't about to stand there and try. She turned back toward the floor, and as she did she heard Christine say, quietly but not quietly enough, "Sophie is the only one with a shot at Adam Connor, and it's one she better not take."

Sophie took it.

Caution thrown to the wind, Sophie and Adam danced the night away. They never noticed when Kitten and Tommy disappeared for an hour or more and came back glowing and a little rumpled. But not as glowing as Adam and Sophie, who never left the dance floor at all. Song after song, two-steps and waltzes and a jitterbug that left them both breathless and laughing. Sophie lost track of the room, the crowd, the smoke, the band. There was nothing but the music and the way Adam's hand felt at the small of her back and the way he looked at her when he thought she wasn't paying attention. She was always paying attention. She knew the weight of his hand at her back by now, and the way his thumb traced her spine during the slow songs without his knowing he was doing it. His shirt had come untucked on one side and his hair had fallen across his forehead and he looked better for it. She caught him looking at her bare shoulder once, just for a second, before his eyes came back to hers. She hadn't fixed her own hair in an hour. She didn't care.

But even with the perfect partner you can't dance nonstop all night. After one particularly energetic jitterbug, Sophie declared she needed air and liquids. Adam, who had broken into a sweat himself, agreed. He bought two bottles of beer at the bar and headed outside with Sophie. The dance hall, which was also the VFW Hall, had a porch and railing that ran across the front and down the sides. It was a good place to cool down, or to get heated up, judging from some of the couples dimly visible in the shadows.

The sky had changed since they'd gone inside. The clouds that had been building all afternoon were stacked high and dark now, and along the western horizon, heat lightning flickered silently across the flats. The air was heavy and still and waiting.

"I hope beer is okay?" Adam asked, handing Sophie a bottle.

"Beer is great," she assured him, taking a sip.

There was a tiny breeze brewing that felt good after the heat and hustle of the hall. An infinitesimal gust blew a strand of Sophie's long blond hair across her cheek. Adam began brushing it away, an excuse to touch her face, and they both knew it. But the strand remained untouched, finally moved by the breeze itself. Instead, Adam's hand lingered, close but not quite touching, and Sophie did not pull away.

For the second time that day, brown eyes and blue eyes met for a long moment. The same eyes that had searched each other through the red-painted steel bars of the corral that afternoon, but closer now, and without any bars between them.

"I've never known anyone like you, Sophie. You're from a whole different world."

"I thought I'd known lots of cowboys just like you, Adam. But you're not the same."

Their voices were low, almost whispers. Their heads so close together that when their lips touched it could almost have been by accident. But the depth and the length of the kiss was no accident. The touch of encircling arms, hesitant and uncertain at first, but soon powerful and possessive, was no accident either. Sophie had been kissed before. She had never been kissed like this.

Her mother's voice was in her head for just a second (the line, the rules, the reasons she had rattled off to herself not six hours ago) and then it wasn't.

Finally Adam broke away.

"This is getting out of hand, Sophie. We'd better go back."

So they went back, and danced until the last song ended. Before leaving the dance floor, alone in the milling crowd, Sophie caught Adam's shirt sleeve.

"Adam," she said urgently. "I know these things just happen sometimes. I don't know what I'm really feeling. You probably don't either. There are a lot of complications, but let's agree that if it seems like a good idea, we'll meet tomorrow. No pressure on you or on me to show up. And no hard feelings either way, life just goes back to normal."

The relief on his face was so plain she almost smiled. He hadn't known what to do, and she had just solved the problem for him. Sophie didn't mind. She was good at solving problems, and she understood perfectly well that what they had just done could not be undone by standing on a dance floor pretending it hadn't happened.

"It's a deal," he agreed. "What time? What place?"

"The horse corral to check on Domino, after supper at six thirty. Adam, whatever happens, I had a wonderful evening. I'll never forget it."

"Me too, Sophie."

Outside, the first low rumble of thunder rolled across the flats from the west.

Chapter 12 — Sunday

ADAM WOKE EARLY. THE bunkhouse was dark and full of the sounds of men sleeping off the dance, and he lay there for a while, staring at the ceiling and thinking about what he had done.

He'd kissed the boss's daughter. Or she'd kissed him. It didn't much matter who had started it. What mattered was that it had happened, and that he'd liked it, and that she had asked him to meet her tonight at six thirty, and that he had said yes.

He'd have to be crazy to get mixed up with the boss's daughter, and he'd have to be double crazy to even think about getting involved with Miss Louisa's only child, a child that lady had definitely not produced and raised to settle for one of the hired hands.

But crazy or not, lying there in the dark thinking about Sophie Degarrin and the way she had felt against him and the taste of her mouth, he was hard before he finished the thought. Adam pulled on his jeans quick and quiet before anyone in the bunkhouse could wake up and see him, and went outside.

The headquarters compound was quiet. The big cottonwood by the saddle shed stood enormous and still, its bark furrowed deep as a man's thumb, and a magpie worked its way through the lower branches without any hurry at all. The Degarrins were off inspecting the kingdom in Miss Louisa's pink Oldsmobile and wouldn't be back until lunch. Rufina had the day off and had gone to Santa Cruz with Pete. The hands who weren't still sleeping were drifting around the compound with the aimless look of men who had nowhere to be and nothing to do and weren't sorry about either one.

Tommy Ryan was sitting on the bunkhouse porch with his boots up on the railing. He spotted Adam and grinned like a man who had been waiting all morning.

"Well, well. If it ain't Fred Astaire. How's Miss Sophie this fine morning, Connor?"

"I wouldn't know," Adam said.

"You sure seemed to know last night. What was it, every song? I lost count after about the fifteenth."

Clancy looked up from the magazine he was reading. "It was more than fifteen."

"Thank you, Gary," Adam said.

"You're welcome," Clancy said, and went back to his magazine.

Tommy wasn't finished. "I'm just saying, partner, you two looked awful comfortable out there. Like you'd been dancing together your whole lives. And then you disappeared for a while, and when you came back you looked even more comfortable."

"We went outside for some air."

"I bet you did."

Adam could feel his ears getting hot and he didn't like it. He looked at Tommy and Tommy looked back at him, still grinning, and there wasn't a thing Adam could say that would make it better.

Tommy leaned back in his chair and laced his hands behind his head. "You know what they say, Connor. There's three ways to get a ranch. You can buy one, you can inherit one, or you can marry one."

Something went very still inside Adam's chest. Tommy was grinning the same grin he'd been grinning all morning, but the words hung in the air between them like smoke.

Danny Parks came around the corner of the bunkhouse with a cup of coffee. He took in the scene without breaking stride, looked at Tommy, and the easy good humor left his face.

"That's enough, Tom," Danny said, and there was nothing easy or quiet about it.

Tommy looked at Danny and the grin faded. He hadn't meant it the way it landed. Adam could see that. Tommy Ryan was a lot of things, but he wasn't cruel, and the look on his face said he'd heard his own words a beat too late.

"I was just kidding, Connor."

"I know you were," Adam said, and walked on down toward the corral, because it was either walk away or stand there and let everybody see what Tommy's joke had done to him.

The trouble was, Tommy wasn't wrong. They had looked comfortable. They had danced every song and stood too close and gone outside together and come back looking like two people who had just done exactly what they had just done. Adam had been so wrapped up in Sophie that he hadn't thought about who was watching. Everybody had been watching. And if the crew knew, then Toby knew, and if Toby knew, then Degarrin would know by Monday. There was no putting the toothpaste back in the tube.

He walked down to the small corral to check on the bay. The leg was better, the swelling almost gone. He ran his hand down the fetlock and the horse stood for it without pulling away. Adam wished he could say the same for his own feet, which had been aching since he woke up and would be aching all day. Dancing all night on a concrete floor was not something the army had improved them for. He turned the horse out with a pat on the neck and leaned on the fence for a while, looking at nothing in particular. To the west, the clouds were building again, stacking up white and flat-bottomed the way they had every afternoon for a week now. The thunder last night had come to nothing, but the sky was making promises it meant to keep sooner or later.

Sophie was probably still asleep. She'd danced until the last song ended and then stood there in the milling crowd and laid out a plan like she'd had it in her pocket the whole time. Meet tomorrow, no pressure, no hard feelings, life goes back to normal. She was like that, quick and sure about things that left him standing flat-footed. She had solved the problem because he hadn't known how to, and he wasn't sure what that said about the two of them, but it was nothing he wanted to think about too hard.

He thought about it anyway.

She was Degarrin's daughter. She was going off to Randolph Macon in the fall, her mother's school, a place where the daughters of people like the Degarrins went to learn whatever it was they learned there. She would meet young men from good families with prospects and futures and the kind of money that didn't come in a pay envelope once a month. She would marry one of them, and she would look back on this summer the way people look back on any summer, from a long way off and probably not too often. Adam would be a name she half-remembered, if she remembered him at all.

And he was a hired hand. He drew wages and slept in a bunkhouse and owned nothing in the world but his saddle and his war bag and a bay horse with a sore leg. La Conquistadora was not his ranch. He had come back to it because it was the only place that made sense to him, the only place that had kept him sane when nothing else could, and he had put all of that at risk because Sophie Degarrin had kissed him on a porch and he hadn't had the sense to stop.

Then Adam thought about how Sophie wouldn't show up anyway, and how most likely she had just been entertaining herself last night. These thoughts made him feel a little bit relieved, but a whole lot more disappointed than anything else. Then he would recall long blond hair, an oval face with blue, blue eyes, the prettiest girl he'd ever seen, and he'd start feeling a little bit in love.

"I'd have to be crazy," Adam told himself, again.

She was probably awake by now. Probably stretched out on that screened-in porch of hers in the west wing, the one covered in so much ivy it was like a green cave, reading a magazine and not giving him a second thought. She'd be turning the whole thing over in her mind and coming to her senses, if she hadn't already. She'd think about her mother and her father and the line everybody knew about, and she'd think about Randolph Macon and the governor's son or whoever it was she was supposed to end up with, and by six thirty she would have talked herself right out of it. That was what girls like Sophie did. They didn't end up with hired hands. They came to their senses.

Adam spent the rest of the day going around and around that tempting but forbidding maze of thoughts.

The hours crawled. He checked the bay again, though the bay didn't need checking. He cleaned tack that was already clean. He sat on the bunkhouse porch and watched the light crawl across the compound, slow as paint drying, and tried to read a magazine somebody had left on the railing and couldn't get past the first page. The sun was in no hurry and neither was the afternoon. Adam ate supper at the long table with the rest of the hands and couldn't have told you what was on his plate.

A little after six, Adam walked down to the horse corral behind the barns, because Domino needed looking at. That was why he was going. The colt needed checking and he had said he would check on him. That was all this was.

He haltered Domino and talked to him and ran his hands over the stitched-up gash above the colt's front legs. The wound was healing well. Fred's work was holding. Adam took his time about it, because there was no reason to hurry. He was just a man checking on a horse.

He heard the gate open behind him and turned.

Sophie was standing there, and everything Adam had spent the day telling himself fell apart in the time it took her to smile. Her hair was down and the evening sun was in it, and she was looking at him the way she had looked at him through the steel bars of this same corral two days ago, except that now she was inside the gate and there was nothing between them at all.

"Adam," Sophie said, lingering on the name, "long time, no see."

"Too long," he agreed, stepping to meet her.

So it was that, pressed heart to heart, in Domino's condoning presence, Adam kissed Sophie in the evening light without a drop of beer or a clap of thunder or the slightest excuse that it might have been an accident.

Chapter 13 — Back on the Range

GETTING BACK IN THE swing of things was harder than Sophie had imagined it would be. Adam Connor seemed to invade her every waking thought. How she was going to carry on, business as usual, she could not imagine. But carry on she must, and so she pulled herself out of bed in the predawn darkness, climbed into her Levi's and boots, and got on with the day. Outside, the sky had a heaviness to it that hadn't been there a week ago.

"Get in, get in, get in," Sophie ordered her troops as she started up the Chevy pickup that had been on the brink of worn out before the war and was now well past that condition.

"We're in, we're in, we're in," Christine grouchily informed their chauffeur. She and Kitten settled in for another careening, bone-jarring dash to the wagon, courtesy of Sophie's driving skills.

"I didn't see much of you yesterday, Sophie." Kitten kept a watchful eye on her friend as she made this comment. She was fishing and didn't want to miss any clues.

"I didn't see any of you yesterday, Kitten. I just figured you and Tommy Ryan were holed up in a hay rack somewhere."

Fishing expeditions were never very productive where Sophie was concerned.

"That's an idea worth considering. So tell us, since we're dying to know, what's the deal with Adam Connor?"

"Well, don't die. I'd have to stop and throw your carcasses out, and that would make me late to the wagon. Here's the deal. He is a divine dancer, as I'm sure you noted. We are madly in love, will be marrying at Christmas and plan to have at least three children. None of whom,

I might add, will have you as a godmother. Any more questions?"

With this answer, Sophie turned her blue eyes on her passengers and smiled charmingly. At this inattention the old Chevy, in a spurt of its last remaining vigor, made a break to escape the rutted road and head for open pasture.

"For heaven's sake, Sophie, keep your eye on the road, or we'll all be wearing wings shortly," Christine exclaimed.

"You might. I'm not so sure about Kitten, though."

Sophie's reply was nonchalant, but she redirected her attention to the road. She had been as startled as Christine at their near detour.

"What about you?" Kitten teased. "Shall we order a pair of wings for you? Or maybe a little pitchfork?"

"I," Sophie assured them, with her nose in the air, "shall be leading the choir. My wings will very likely be gilded with gold and will no doubt be quite perfect. Whereas yours, Kitten, will be smoking and singed from your near escape."

Christine, satisfied that Sophie wasn't going to wreck them (just yet, at least) and who really did want to know the true scoop, joined in.

"Sophie, what did you really think of Adam? I had no idea he was such a fabulous dancer! We were all so jealous watching you two dance. You were perfect together."

Sophie glanced over at Christine, who really was a sweet girl and as good a friend as you could ever want. She frowned slightly and answered her truthfully.

"I never had more fun in my life than I did Saturday night, Chris. I will remember it always. It was perfect."

"Do you think he'll ask you out on a date?" Christine voiced the question of the hour.

Here was danger. She and Adam had agreed that secrecy and discretion were their best hope. So looking her dear friend right in the face, Sophie lied through her teeth.

"What would be the point of that? I would be sent off to Randolph Macon quicker than you could blink your eye. You know the unspoken rule as well as I do. He's one of the cowboys, a hired hand, with no prospects and no future. He's not someone I'd even be allowed to consider. I would have a better chance of dating an elephant than Adam Connor."

All that Sophie said was true. She watched Christine and Kitten settle back in their seats, the worry leaving their faces, and she knew the lie had done its work. A romance between Sophie and Adam would have caused a lot of problems. Degarrin and Miss Louisa were nice people, up to a point, but they weren't people you wanted to cross, and Christine and Kitten knew that as well as anyone.

Sophie kept her eyes on the road and did not let herself think about how it felt to lie to her two best friends in the world.

• • •

The mood at the wagon that morning was upbeat. The cowboys were glad to have had a break (life on the range, a million miles from town, could get a little monotonous) but now they were just as glad to be back at work. If these men had wanted to cope with civilization and modern society, they would not have sought out La Conquistadora as their place to live and work. Every one of them was at least a little bit of a maverick. They were all happy to be back on the emptiness of the endless rolling prairie, under the high blue sky.

Dawn had just broken over the little encampment on the plains when the girls, in their exhausted Chevy, arrived. The cook fire was already going, smoke drifting flat across the grass in the still air, and bedrolls lay thrown back under the fly where men had left them in the dark.

Ignacio was delighted to see them, as were the rest. Only he didn't mind saying so.

"Hijas, welcome! It has been days since you have been here! We are so glad to see you!"

Christine laughed. "Iggy, it's been all of forty hours, maybe, since we've been here!"

Ignacio paid her no heed at all. He was far too busy welcoming his favorite girl.

"Miss Sophie! You are beautiful this morning. Far too good to be in the company of this worthless crew! You had better stay in camp with me this morning," he promptly informed her.

Sophie beamed at him. They really were pals. "Ignacio, best friend of my childhood, you know I'd love to stay in camp with you. But you know these guys goof off if I'm not around to keep them in line! Without me they'd probably bring in only three cows and no calves this morning. Isn't that right, fellows?"

She turned and viewed her audience, the picture of innocent inquiry. Ignacio immediately agreed with her while the crew hooted. Christine and Kitten got themselves cups of coffee and a biscuit and settled in to watch Sophie work the crowd, as they had been watching her work crowds since they were old enough to notice.

"In my next life I want to be Sophie," Kitten said. "I've watched her do that all my life, and I have never figured out how she does it."

"As best I can figure, it's a gift," Christine said. "It has to be. She puts absolutely no effort into it, and it comes as naturally to her as breathing. But, after years of observation, I have decided that part of it is that she doesn't really give a damn whether they like her, or what they think of her. And because she doesn't care, they want her all the more."

"You might be right," Kitten said thoughtfully. "But I'll tell you what, if I took that high-handed approach, there wouldn't be anybody speaking to me. Nobody would put up with me. They'd just figure I was a real bitch and avoid me like the plague."

"That's because you don't have the gift. Sophie's got it in spades, so does her mom. It must be genetic."

"That's why I want to be Sophie in my next life," Kitten repeated, smiling as she watched the show.

Sophie came back to the fire for a cup of coffee and didn't argue with Christine's theory. She had never figured it out herself.

Sophie caught Adam's eye across the fire and looked away.

Toby took one last sip of coffee. Rising, he emptied the rest onto the cook fire, which hissed and steamed in response. Tossing the tin cup into its waiting bucket, he headed for the rope corral. On this signal, without a word, the command to start the day's work was given. Everyone scrambled to follow suit, leaving Ignacio and Ricky to tend the camp in their absence.

At the rope corral, Joe Allen, with great elan and a single circle of his arm and a flick of the wrist, was tossing effortlessly perfect hoolihans around the necks of surprised horses. He repeated this act as fast as each cowboy could call a name and get his bridled mount out of the corral. Sophie called Muffin, Kitten called Junebug, and then Christine called Rebel.

Joe Allen never missed a beat. He just roped Rebel and handed him over. Toby, however, and everyone else, sat up and took notice. Rebel was not a horse in Christine's string. One of the reasons he wasn't was because he was very hotheaded and on occasion just barely rideable. Rebel was in Tommy Ryan's string and one of his favorite mounts, because of course Tommy didn't like a horse unless it was about to blow up under him at all times. It had taken considerable wheedling on Christine's part to persuade Tommy to turn Rebel over to her for the day.

Toby gave his daughter a searching and not-best-pleased look. Sophie knew what that face meant. Christine was a fabulous rider, better than Tommy Ryan in fact, but Toby was a father first and he would have preferred not to have her on that horse.

Saddling up near her dad, Christine grinned at him. "Relax, Daddy. You know how Tommy is. He gets these horses stirred up himself, just so he'll have more fun. Rebel won't give me any trouble, or at least none that I can't handle. He'll enjoy a break from Tommy."

Danny Parks passed by just then, leading his ride for the day. He paused for a second to smile at Christine and pass a quick glance over Rebel.

"Well," he said, "he's looking a little twitchy, but nowhere near as bad as Tommy usually has him by now." "You two will do fine today," Danny told them.

Christine passed the same infectious grin on to her father. "See, Daddy, it'll be okay. If Danny says it'll be fine, then it will be. Nobody can read a horse like Danny."

Toby just shook his head, but Sophie could see he was satisfied. Nobody argued with Danny Parks when it came to horses.

Danny was, by common agreement, the best rider on the ranch and possibly the best rider any of them had ever seen. Sophie had heard the story of his tryout ride from just about everybody on the place, and it had grown some in the telling, but everyone agreed on the parts that mattered.

Danny had come to the ranch with the last of winter, just back from the war. He had said he was from Tennessee, that he was a good hand and that he could ride anything. Toby had never heard of such a thing, a kid from Tennessee that could ride a bucking cow pony? If Danny had said he was from Texas, Toby wouldn't have doubted him so much, but doubt he did, and so did Degarrin.

Toby had sized the young stranger up and told him, "Well, sir, we've got a rough string or two that need to be ridden, but we'll have to try you out first before we take you on. In the morning, we'll have a test ride right after breakfast. Go on over to the bunkhouse for tonight."

"Yes, sir. Thank you, sir." Danny was a very courteous young man. His momma had raised him right.

The next morning, right after breakfast, the remuda was brought pounding and whinnying into headquarters. Degarrin had Joe Allen rope Whirlwind for the tryout ride. Whirlwind was just about the worst horse for pitching on the place. Toby or Degarrin usually rode him, but only because there wasn't any young bronc buster to dump him on.

"If Whirlwind doesn't unload this kid, he's got a job for life," her father had said to Toby as they watched Danny unconcernedly toss his saddle up onto the twitching sorrel's back, apparently oblivious to the flat, laid-back ears and rolling eyes.

Suffice to say that Danny rode Whirlwind that morning, rode him to a standstill, and laughed while he did it. Toby and Degarrin had never seen a prettier ride. Whirlwind did all his best tricks, tried everything he knew, with a few new touches as well. Danny stuck with him every pitch and twist of the way and never even thought about coming off. He was grinning when he finally stepped off the exhausted horse.

Her father had walked up to him and put his hand out. "That was the finest ride I have ever seen, son. Welcome to La Conquistadora. It's your home for as long as you care to stay."

Since that winter morning some six months ago, Danny had come to like his new home just fine. At the moment, though, he was a few yards away about to climb aboard an ornery and unpredictable little horse aptly called Little Bit, as that was about all he was worth. Degarrin was always meaning to send the nag off to market but somehow never got around to it. Some days Little Bit was angelically well behaved and could have been a kid horse. Other days, for no apparent reason whatsoever, he was just as likely to break in two and buck until he was pooped. There was just no telling with Little Bit. He was not a big horse and he wasn't very good at bucking either, but he had a lot of heart and he always gave it everything he had. Danny thought he was a real hoot and just loved to ride him.

Danny stepped up and wasted no time getting his seat, in case Little Bit got rowdy. Little Bit had decided this was his day and he immediately broke in two. He leapt as high as he could and, throwing his back feet out behind, came down as hard as he could. He did this over and over. The more Little Bit bucked, the more Danny laughed. Everyone had stopped to watch. Cowboys were laughing and shouting advice. Not everybody on that crew could have stayed with Little Bit, but Danny made it look so easy that, from the safety of the ground, they all thought they could.

"Fan him, Danny, fan him!" Frankie Evans shouted.

"Don't let him get his head down!" cried Jeff Hendricks. "He'll unload you if he gets his head down!"

In all the excitement, Sophie had found her way over to Adam's side without quite planning it. He was grinning at the show, and when he turned to her, the grin was the same one he wore for everyone, easy and unconcerned. But something in his eyes was not easy at all, and it was meant for her alone.

"That little pony couldn't unload Danny, even if Danny went to sleep up there," Adam said.

Sophie nodded, but mostly she was caught by Danny's gaiety and nonchalance. As his mount went pitching off with him, she could see Danny looking back over his shoulder at all of them, laughing and showing his white teeth in a delighted grin, as if sharing a good joke with his friends.

"He's an incredible rider, isn't he?" Sophie asked, rather rhetorically.

Adam nodded, his eyes on the horse and rider. Danny might have been a centaur, so much a part of Little Bit did he seem, anticipating his every move and flowing with him as though they were one.

"He's the best I've ever seen," Adam answered without shifting his gaze from the prairie ballet before him.

Little Bit was not ready to quit. He bucked in close to the wagon, and then pitched straight through Ignacio's cook site, tap-dancing through the fire trench, kicking the coffee pot, and sending Dutch ovens flying.

An equally incensed Ignacio added his voice to the hubbub. "Hey! Señor Danny, keep him away from here! He does not belong here, bucking through my kitchen!"

"Sorry, Ignacio!" Danny called as he and Little Bit rounded the chuck wagon.

"I've never seen a horse buck through a campfire before," Degarrin commented to Toby.

"No, that's a first for me, too," Toby agreed, shaking his head.

Apparently that was also Little Bit's last best effort. All his energy gone and Danny still very much on his back, he just gave up. Standing with his front legs straddled far apart, Little Bit put his head down to the ground and bawled. His mournful lament was so startling that everyone just stared at him for a moment before bursting into laughter.

"That is another first, Degarrin. In all my years, I've never seen such a thing! I've never even heard of such a thing," Toby informed his boss in complete amazement.

Degarrin couldn't even answer, he was laughing so hard.

Danny slid off and put his arm around his squalling horse. "Poor Little Bit. Poor, poor Little Bit." He consoled the little pony in true sympathy. "No one can ever say you didn't give it your best shot."

Sophie watched Danny with his arm around that ridiculous horse and thought he was just about the best man on the ranch.

Little Bit and Danny's dance had provided some unexpected and mightily enjoyed entertainment, but it was growing late. Buffalo Flats was the name of the pasture they would finish working today, and it was time to get started. La Conquistadora's riders followed Toby out onto the plain and into the day's work.

Buffalo Flats was not a hard gather, being only of moderate size when compared to most of La Conquistadora's pastures, and the terrain was not rough. In fact, most of the rugged country was behind them now, already worked. Toby didn't have to spread his riders so thin since there was less ground to cover today. He decided to send the girls off together, so they could keep an eye on each other, and if Christine had any trouble with Rebel, she wouldn't be far from help.

Sophie had been looking forward to today's work, not just because it was great to be back on the range doing what she loved best, but because Buffalo Flats was one of the prettiest pastures on the ranch. La Cueva Creek ran through it, cutting a meandering path that ambled and rambled on for miles, not just through Buffalo Flats, but through the entire ranch on its way to its final appointment with the river. The creek was fed by springs all along its winding length and was never dry, making it one of La Conquistadora's true treasures. As a result, there was a double-sided ribbon of green that ran along its banks, composed for the most part of cottonwoods and tamaracks. La Cueva lent a lovely contrast to the sea of often less-than-green grass through which it cut its course.

The pasture had taken its name from the remnants of one of the last great buffalo herds to have called northeastern New Mexico home. They had chosen this place as their favorite range. By the early years of the century the herd numbered only about twenty, led by a tough and aged bull. For a long time La Conquistadora operated around the buffalo as best it could. But finally the powers that be had gotten tired of replacing fences wherever the independent-minded bull had decided to lead his followers. So it came to pass, in a most unusual trail drive, that the buffalo were herded, as well as buffalo could be herded, to what would become the Philmont Scout Ranch. There they reigned supreme, and fences were the least of their worries.

As Sophie, Christine, and Kitten rode along the shaded creek bank, the buffalo had long been gone, but their range would ever bear their name. Christine had her hands full with Rebel, who had come by his name quite honestly, for he simply hated to be controlled in any way, shape, or form. A summer of Tommy Ryan's high-handed riding style had only made him worse. Despite her glib assurances to her father, and Danny's faith in her ability, Christine was riding at the edge of her considerable skill, and Sophie could see she was loving every minute of it.

"I don't know why you think that horse is so wonderful," Kitten commented as she watched him snort and paw his way along. "He is a complete pain in the ass."

"I like to ride him because he's a challenge," Christine said.

"Well, you can have him. I wouldn't want to mess with him. He looks hopeless to me."

"That's just as well for you, then, because Tommy wouldn't let you ride Rebel anyway."

"Tommy only handed him over to you this morning for the very simple reason that he wants to get more from you than just a two-step the next time there's a dance. Or maybe before."

Sophie, long accustomed to Christine and Kitten's sniping, having heard it all their collective lives, had not been paying much attention to them. Instead she had been thinking about the buffalo and whether their descendants liked it at Philmont. Sophie was of a sentimental nature and wished there were more of them around than just the ancient stuffed one in the ranch's office, mounted above the equally ancient walk-in vault. That buffalo had seen better days.

However, always interested in intrigue, she perked up and forgot about the past plight of buffalo, being much more interested in the present plight of Christine.

"And so, Chris," Sophie joined the conversation, "what are young Mr. Ryan's prospects? Do you predict a bright future based on his past achievements?"

Christine raised an eyebrow, a trick she had practiced diligently until perfected, and quizzed right back, "And so, Miss Degarrin, what are the not-so-young Mr. Connor's prospects?"

Sophie laughed. She merely assured her friends that Mr. Ryan's prospects were far sunnier than Mr. Connor's.

"Be that as it may," Kitten changed the subject, "if we don't split up and find a whole bunch of cattle to drive in, I can promise you one thing for sure: we will all be fired off this crew!"

"Knowing our dear papas as we all do, that could definitely be true," Christine commented.

Faced with this prospect, the girls parted company and set about their task with eyes peeled, riding hard to make up for lost time. Under the influence of Christine's spurs and new no-nonsense attitude, Rebel soon lost any urge to rebel.

Chapter 14 — Degarrin Disappears

THE NEXT MORNING FOUND Degarrin, along with the rest of the cowboys, prowling his domain on horseback. Sometimes he rode with the crew, sometimes he elected to ride in his pickup over the ranch's miles of roads. The ranch was so vast that it took constant travel to watch over it properly, and lack of vigilance meant trouble, anything from general decay to cattle rustlers and old-time squatters. So Degarrin maintained an eagle eye, and today it was from the back of Sandy, one of his favorite mounts.

Sandy was a young horse and still had a lot to learn, but he was a quick study and a beautiful goer. He had a splendid jog trot that would comfortably eat up the miles and a lovely running walk that would do the same. But in Degarrin's opinion, his nicest gait was a slow, easy lope that would have been the envy of any show ring when the judge called, "canter." Sandy wasn't likely to ever encounter a show ring and no judge would ever lay eyes on his beauty, but Degarrin's praise and affection surely equaled any blue ribbon.

Today they trotted up the well-beaten cow trail onto the Talosa Mesa, where they loped along, Degarrin with a grin and Sandy with happily flicking ears. From the mesa top Degarrin could see thirty miles in every direction, nothing but grass and sky and the pale line of another mesa on the horizon. The sky to the west was thicker than it had been, a haze along the rim that said the season was turning whether anyone was ready or not. Far below, a handful of pronghorn drifted across the flats, and way up above them the buzzards were making their slow circles the way they always did. Everything was a wonderful experience for Sandy. He had true joie de vivre. When they had gathered all the cattle they could find, Sandy and Company, with a flourish, pushed them together into a tidy herd and took them down the same trail. Horse and rider were quite proud of themselves.

After all these years, Degarrin had never become even slightly inured to this life. He never took miles of spectacular country, a clear endless day, and a great horse for granted. Each was a gift, as was this life he led, a life he ran for people who had never seen it from the back of a horse and never would. If they ever decided they were done with it, there wasn't a thing he could do but pack his saddle and go. But that was a worry for another day. Sometimes he still couldn't believe he got paid to do this. It was like breaking into a bank and being commended for a job well done. He simply loved it.

Down off the mesa, Degarrin and Sandy soon encountered another of La Conquistadora's finest. Adam Connor was off across a great sacaton flat, pushing the fruits of his morning's labor through the big bushy clumps of sacaton grass in the general direction of the roundup ground. Still feeling expansive, Degarrin raised a hand in greeting, which was promptly returned. The two little herds were not far apart, and they moved to join them into a single gather that they would drive in together.

Degarrin and Sandy guided their charges out onto the sacaton flat. It was slow going because sacaton, somewhat akin to the pampas grass found in lawns, is a big plant that grows in large clumps, and Sandy and the cows and calves had to pick their way carefully through several acres of it. Some of the clumps stood chest-high on the horse, and the pale seed heads rattled against Sandy's sides as they pushed through. Degarrin could see Adam on the far side, holding his bunch and waiting.

One moment they were ambling along enjoying themselves, and the next moment they weren't.

A calf jumped right out from under Sandy and spooked him. Sandy shied and backpedaled, as was his standard response to life's more startling surprises. Degarrin was exasperated but not surprised. Not surprised, that is, until tierra firma evaporated from under Sandy's hooves and the two of them found themselves dropping into a well of darkness.

The hole they fell into was ten or twelve feet deep, the sky just a disk of blue above their heads. Holes like this were sometimes washed out under a heavy turf of sacaton by the summer rains, invisible from above until some unlucky soul found one the hard way. It was just their luck. The hole was about five feet across at the top, and although considerably wider at the bottom, it still wasn't much room for a startled Degarrin and a very scared Sandy. Sandy, in typical young-horse fashion, panicked and began to whirl and kick, frantically looking for a way out. Degarrin's wiser counsel and attempts to calm him down were completely ignored, and the situation rapidly escalated to one of real danger.

Degarrin managed to get free of his mount and scramble back under a little overhang. From here he had a close-up view of thrashing hooves, flying stirrups, and whirling horse belly. After having gone so beautifully all morning, his day was rapidly going downhill. He was not optimistic.

Then he heard Adam's voice from somewhere above, and the relief that washed through him was almost physical.

"Degarrin, Degarrin! Can you hear me? Are you all right?"

He couldn't see much past Sandy's whirling, but he could hear the worry in Adam's voice and he was not about to question how fast the man had gotten there.

"Degarrin, where the hell are you?"

"Adam! Adam! I'm over here, under the overhang."

"Are you hurt?"

"No, I'm fine so far, but Sandy's doing his best to change that."

"So I see." Degarrin could tell from the steadiness in Adam's voice that the man already had a plan. "I'll get a rope on him and get him out of the way."

From below, Degarrin heard Adam shake out his lariat, and a moment later the loop dropped expertly around Sandy's neck. Sandy yielded to its authority at once, glad to have a human back in charge, as his own efforts hadn't helped him at all. Adam held Sandy back out of the way while Degarrin crawled out from under his overhang and carefully approached his still skittish horse.

Holding Sandy's bridle right at the bit and being careful to stay close by his shoulder, Degarrin assessed his predicament. "Adam, I believe the best thing to do would be for me to put the rope around me, unsaddle Sandy, and then you pull the line taut and be ready to pull me up real quick. Just before you pull me and my saddle up, I'll take the bridle off of him. I hate to leave him down here in this hole, bridled. He could go nuts again and get hurt."

Adam nodded. "That'll do it, Mr. Degarrin. We'll have you out in no time at all."

True to his words, the earth gave Degarrin back almost as quickly as it had taken him. A few minutes saw Adam and his boss bidding adieu to a very unhappy but considerably calmer Sandy. Toby would send a couple of boys back later with shovels to dig the bank of the hole down enough for Sandy to scramble out. He would be safe enough down there now that the saddle and bridle were off, but Sandy was far from happy to be abandoned, and as Degarrin settled behind Adam's saddle with his own saddle and bridle in hand, Sandy could be heard whinnying for help. It sounded like the cry of a ghost horse calling from the depths of the empty range.

The going was slow and cumbersome, but neither Adam nor Degarrin had any intention of sacrificing the morning's efforts. Picking their way along and taking their time, they brought their combined gathers in to the roundup. Sandy was the only one that had been left behind.

Chapter 15 — First Storm

THE LATE AFTERNOON SUN was still high above the horizon, although it was nearly six o'clock, and it set the western sky aflame as it went. In all his travels Adam had never seen sunsets to rival those found in New Mexico, where the color washed the sky more than halfway up its arch and lingered on and on until finally twilight came and rang the curtain down.

Back at the wagon, talk turned, as it inevitably did, to the topic of women. Favorite tales of true love and tragic betrayal were trotted out and put through their paces. Reminiscences were shared of conquests, both actual and imagined, and of the ones that somehow got away. Over final cups of coffee the cowboys shared their hearts and their laments, and Adam sat with his and listened.

Danny Parks had the last word, as he often did. His rich, deep Tennessee drawl was a commentary on all their lives when he said, "It's funny, when we're at the ranch, all we talk about is women, and when we're with women, all we talk about is the ranch."

Nobody argued the point. Bedrolls were laid out under the fly, and those with tepees crawled into them. The time for talk was done and now it was time to dream.

• • •

Morning found a La Conquistadora of a different complexion. Clouds had rolled in during the night and the sky was low and leaden with more than a hint of rain in the offing. Business went on as usual. Rain was not a cause for distress; it was a blessing on the range, the bread and butter of the entire enterprise. A storm in the making was something for Toby to bear in mind, and he planned the day's work while keeping a weather eye.

Toby opted for a short drive, with everybody back in by eight thirty or nine if it looked like the bottom was going to drop out. That plan decided upon, the wagon boss dispatched his crew about their business and likewise set about his.

As the morning progressed, the cloud cover grew thicker and darker. A wind came up, and it was clear to everyone that it was just a matter of time before a torrent let loose.

Lightning began to flash, followed closely by the rumble of nearby thunder, and the ranges of La Conquistadora were transformed into a hostile world of danger. Of an accord, every cowboy, wherever he was, turned both his horse and his gather toward the wagon and headed for home.

The gathers were all in and the abbreviated drive was not large and would easily fit into the branding corral. The crew, working in perfect precision, got the herd penned in record time. The last pair was scarcely through the gate when the downpour commenced with a crash of thunder and a blaze of lightning.

With the drive corralled and their work done, the cowboys took off in a run for the wagon about a quarter of a mile away. Adam had gotten off Laramie, one of his least favorite rides, to shut the corral gate. Laramie was an awfully pretty little horse, a sorrel with a white star and just a patch of white on his nose that gave his face a nice balance. But with Laramie, beauty was just skin deep. He wasn't much of a cowhorse and he was extremely housey. Right now his primary object in life was to get back to the wagon with the other horses, and the quicker the better. In his view, giving Adam time to mount up would just be a needless waste of time.

After a little scuffle, Adam was up in the saddle, dripping wet and far from pleased. Cold rain pouring off his hat brim and down his back, combined with Laramie's shenanigans, put him in a mood as foul as the weather, and he jumped the horse off in a gallop.

A run for home was exactly to Laramie's liking, so he headed for camp with abandon, never even breaking stride when he jumped a mesquite bush that got in his way. On the other side of the bush there was a hole that caught both horse and rider by surprise. Laramie hit it straight on and was thrown for a loop. The horse, with Adam on his back, turned a complete flip in the air and landed in a wet and frightened, breathless heap. In the best of circumstances, Laramie would never have been classified as calm. In this circumstance, near hysteria might best have described him, but as bad as things were for Laramie, they were worse for Adam.

Adam had stayed with his horse over the mesquite bush and through the airborne acrobatics, and he was still with him when Laramie scrambled up and started his maddened race for the wagon. He had actually lost his seat and come off the horse, but his left foot was caught fast in the stirrup and there was no way for him to escape. In a few moments he would surely be dragged and kicked to death.

All this flashed through Adam's brain with the speed of light. When all was said and done, it was hopeless. But Adam had not survived the brutal war in Europe for nothing. He had walked away from the Battle of the Bulge, and he didn't believe in hopeless. Faster than he could even realize, he sized up the situation and grabbed Laramie's tail, the only part of the hell-bent runaway that he could reach. With a death grip on that tail, Adam was able to hold himself up high enough off the ground to keep from being dragged or kicked, for the moment at least.

So far, so good. But what next?

Things were beginning to look a little bad. Actually, things were past looking very bad, and it occurred to Adam that there might not ever be a "next." Laramie had gone even crazier when his tail was grabbed, kicking and twisting in a frantic attempt to free himself of whatever it was that had him. He was about to succeed.

Adam conceded this fact and realized that his luck had finally run out.

It had been a mesquite bush that contributed to the problem, and it was also a mesquite bush that delivered a tiny ray of hope when one of the reins snagged on a limb and was dragged alongside him. Adam did not wait for opportunity to knock twice. He seized the stray rein and wasted no time winding it around his left hand until he had

Laramie's head pulled around so tightly that all the little horse could do was whirl and not run and kick. Adam was now the vortex of a whirling maelstrom of pelting rain, terrified horse, and wet leather. His left foot still trapped in the stirrup, his right hand grasping Laramie's tail, his left wound as tightly as possible in bridle rein, Adam, stretched a little thin, was spinning almost nose to nose with his horse.

Things had taken a definite turn for the good in the last few heartbeats.

Adam decided his tail grasp would have to be traded for a grab at a saddle string. Until it was actually the moment to attempt the switch, he had not realized how attached he had become to Laramie's tail. He hated to let go. It might not work and he still might be kicked and dragged to kingdom come. He let go of the tail and made a desperate grab for a saddle string. His efforts were rewarded, and with that handful of saddle string and the motivation that only impending death can give, Adam was able to pull himself out of disaster's way and up into the saddle. If he hadn't still had a slippery situation to contend with and a crazy horse to control, he would have felt weak with relief. But there was no time for relief. It was still raining, Laramie was still nuts, and Adam had had better days. Later he could only assume that habit and reflex had piloted horse and rider back to the wagon. He really couldn't remember much about it.

Up ahead was camp. Dry, with a fire and coffee. The other cowboys were already there, either still hobbling horses or making a dash for the comfort of the fly. A few were already under its shelter, grinning and laughing about the weather. The whole thing had taken maybe a minute, if that, although to Adam it had felt like a lifetime. No one had even noticed.

Adam sank down on a bedroll under the fly. He wasn't sure his legs would hold him if he tried standing. Coffee cup in hand, he took a little teasing for being the last one back to camp.

"On old Laramie, I figured you'd beat us all back. You must have really made him behave. I bet he wasn't very happy," Frankie said.

"Yeah," Adam admitted. "We had a little tussle. There wasn't anybody very happy."

Somehow, the time never seemed right to tell of his whirlwind experience. It was pretty far-fetched, anyway. Maybe some distant evening he would reminisce about it around the campfire over a final cup of coffee before turning in for the night.

The next morning Adam's back let him know that it, at least, knew all about his wild ride. It had been violently jerked around and was now registering a complaint. Being a good GI, Adam decided the best course was to ignore it. The pain proved stronger than his resolve, and by evening he gave up. A trip to Las Vegas and the chiropractor was the only solution.

After supper he saddled a horse and rode over to the old Clauson road that lay a couple of miles from the wagon camp. The road ran along the river, and there was a phone booth there, the only connection with the outside world for quite a ways. In the old days, before the paved highway was put in miles to the west, the little booth and the telephone lines that marched across the pristine isolation of the prairie had been a welcome means of communication for many a passerby. Over the years that phone on the empty, open prairie had become nearly sacred to cowhands and passersby alike. To Adam that evening, it was as welcome a sight as it had ever been to anyone.

He dialed headquarters and reached Degarrin. Someone would be at the river crossing the next morning to take him to Las Vegas. Good enough. Adam and his back suffered through the night and were glad to see the break of day.

Chapter 16 — The Trip to Las Vegas

WHEN THE PHONE RANG at headquarters that evening, Sophie was closer to it than anyone else and picked it up. It was Adam, calling from the phone booth on the old Clauson road, asking for someone to drive him to Las Vegas in the morning because his back was hurt, though he didn't say how.

Sophie told him someone would be at the river crossing first thing in the morning and hung up the phone.

Her father was in the office going over tallies with Toby. Sophie stood in the hall for a moment, catching her breath, and then walked in and told them Adam had called and needed a ride to the chiropractor.

"I'll run him in," she said, as casually as she could manage. "I need to pick up a few things in town anyway."

Degarrin glanced at Toby. Toby shrugged. Neither of them thought anything of it. Sophie ran errands in Las Vegas all the time, and someone had to take the boy.

"Take your mother's car," Degarrin said. "And drive careful on that switchback."

Sophie promised she would and went to her room before her face could give her away.

She barely slept that night. She lay in bed and stared at the dark ceiling and thought about Adam Connor and what she was doing and what she was about to do, and every time she tried to talk herself out of it she remembered the way he had looked at her across the campfire, and the look in his eyes that had nothing to do with words, and she stopped trying.

• • •

Sophie was up before dawn. She took her mother's pink Oldsmobile and drove the empty road with the windows down and the morning air cool on her face and her heart behaving in a manner that was quite improper for six in the morning. The headlights picked up the pale trunks of cottonwoods along the creek and the shapes of mesas standing black against the barely lightening sky. Twice she slowed for arroyo crossings where the road dropped into cuts deep enough to swallow the car, the Oldsmobile bottoming out on the far side where the ruts were deepest.

She saw him before he saw her, a rider coming down to the river from the far side, sitting his horse a little stiffly but otherwise looking like any other cowboy heading out for the day's work, except that this one was heading in the wrong direction entirely and riding straight toward her.

Sophie pulled the car off the road and got out and waved.

Adam's surprise was visible even from across the river. He had not given much thought to who would be taking him to Las Vegas, but it had never even dimly occurred to him that it might be the boss's daughter. Sophie could see it in the way he pulled up short and stared for a moment before putting his spurs to his horse and crossing the river toward her.

The river was calm enough today, and he crossed without trouble. All things considered, it was a good crossing.

Sophie had the trunk open when he got there, and Adam's saddle, blanket, and bridle were soon stowed. Released from service, his horse promptly plunged back into the river and went right home to the wagon and his friends in the remuda. That taken care of, Adam directed his attention to Sophie.

A smile lit up his eyes and his whole face. Sophie beamed back.

"I should call a cab more often," he told her.

"I've been thinking of going into the business," she assured him.

Sophie felt a little nervous, and suddenly very shy. Out of nowhere, it seemed that she hardly knew Adam at all. There was no music and dancing to break the ice, no mutual concern for an injured colt to bridge the distance. She was standing on a dirt road in the early morning light with a man she could not stop thinking about, and she had no idea what to say next.

Adam took charge. Turning to her with a wide, happy smile that made her heart turn, he told her, "I can't tell you how glad I am I hurt my back. If it means I get you all to myself for a whole day, I'll never take myself off the injured list. Pain is a small price to pay."

Sophie began to relax and then to smile. This Adam was familiar and not a stranger at all. It would just be a little strange to be alone with him in a car for the first time.

She said, "Here, maybe you better drive," and handed him the keys. She slid into the passenger seat and leaned over to open the car door for Adam.

Her smile changed to a look of anxious concern as she watched him crawl in behind the wheel and wince in pain.

"Are you all right?" she asked.

Putting the car in gear, Adam thought about acting tough, but his back really hurt. He gave her a halfhearted, sheepish grin.

"I've been better," he confessed.

"Do you want me to drive?"

"No, it's gonna hurt whoever drives. Might as well be me. It'll make it that much easier if I decide to abduct you."

Sophie perked up. "Are you planning to? Abduct me, I mean."

"I don't know, I'm still thinking on it."

"Well, if you decide to, please let me know. I wouldn't want to miss my own abduction."

"Yes, ma'am," he said. "I'll keep you informed."

"But, Adam, I'm a little concerned. Do you think you can handle an abduction with your hurt back?"

He shook his head and looked at her with a twinkle in his eyes. "I don't know. That's why I'm still thinking on it. I might be able to, if you were to cooperate."

"What would I have to do?" Sophie asked.

"Drive."

"I'd have to drive myself for my own abduction?" Sophie demanded. "Wouldn't I be abducting you, then?"

"Maybe, but I very likely wouldn't complain."

Sophie considered that scenario for a moment. "I don't think that would actually qualify as an abduction," she said. "That sounds more like an elopement."

"We could do that, too," Adam assured her.

Sophie blushed a little and glanced away. "I'm very sorry you got hurt, but I'm awfully glad you're here with me right now," she told him.

"You can't have one without the other," Adam said.

Sophie laughed and said, "How did you hurt your back anyway? I haven't heard a word about it. Or is this all just a clever ruse?"

Adam sat up. "You are not going to believe this, Sophie. It happened to me and I can't believe it!"

"I haven't told a soul. You'd be the first. If I tell you, will you keep it a secret?"

"I don't know. This sounds like too deep a mystery for me."

"No mystery, just too bizarre to be believed."

"Well, tell me and then I'll tell you if it's believable."

When Adam had recounted his and Laramie's adventures, Sophie just shook her head. "You're right, that is just too wild. It sounds like something out of a Saturday matinee. But it's too crazy not to be true. But, Adam, you could have been hurt, you could have been killed!"

"I was hurt! I am near death at this very moment. That's why we're going to the doctor. I may not live to see another sunrise. In fact, I probably won't live 'til sundown. These could be my last hours. You'd better give me a final kiss."

Sophie was startled into laughter and turned in surprise to look at him. But his delight was infectious, and suddenly a kiss seemed the very thing that was needed. It proved to be quick and light but full of gaiety and promise.

"Has the abduction begun?" Sophie asked, still laughing.

"Maybe," Adam answered.

Sophie looked around and realized they were starting up the long switchbacked hill that would take them up out of the river country and onto the high plateau that led to Las Vegas and the high mountains beyond.

"This road has always scared me a little," Sophie confessed, peering out the window and over the ledge of the roadbed and down the steep drop-off to the panorama spread out below them. "But what a fabulous view it is."

Adam took his eyes from the climbing road and looked down and out across the miles of open, empty land. He had to agree. "I read an old-timer's account of this land once," he said. "He said that when he was a young man and would ride out on these highlands and look out over all this huge country and know there wasn't a fence between him and Mexico and maybe even far beyond."

Sophie nodded and continued gazing out over the vast scene spread out below them and to the horizon. "I love this land," she said quietly. "I love everything about it, but most of all I love the space. I missed it so much when I was in school in Virginia last year. All the endless openness, how it makes you feel so small and yet so great, all at the same time."

Adam nodded. "Let's stop at the top and take a little break," he said. "Just walk out along the edge a little and enjoy it all for a while. I've missed it too, these last few years."

At the top, Adam parked her mother's car off the empty road, and the two walked hand in hand along the edge of the great plateau. After a time they paused and sat down side by side on one of the outcroppings of rimrock that marked the mesa's edge. Together Adam and Sophie gazed out across their land in shared silence and content.

Adam slipped his arm around her and hugged her tightly, his cheek pressed close against her hair. He closed his eyes, and Sophie closed hers.

She put her arm around his waist as well and wished the moment would never end.

"I wish I could spend my whole life with you right here, just like this," she said softly. It was a childish wish, not possible at all. But Adam didn't laugh or ridicule it at all.

"I wish you could too," he murmured. "Sophie," he said softly, after a moment.

Sophie waited for him to continue. When he did not, she pulled away a little and looked up at him. "What, Adam?" she asked.

"Sophie," he continued, "do you think there is such a thing as love at first sight?"

"I think there is," she answered.

"So do I."

When their lips met it was as though each had found a missing puzzle part, so good was the feel, so perfect the fit. Lying back on that high mesa top with the world spread out around them and beneath them, and with the sky draped over them in a vast canopy of blue and white, Adam and Sophie felt they were at the very center of the universe. If the moments before had been perfect, they were now totally surpassed.

The glow of perfect joy lasted throughout the day, even through the chiropractor wrenching Adam's back into place.

Sophie and Adam returned to La Conquistadora with a perfect understanding that evening. When Sophie delivered Adam back to the river crossing where Danny, with an extra horse, was waiting to meet him, she delivered half of a couple.

Chapter 17 — Moving Camp

IT WAS ANOTHER MOVING day for the chuck wagon and cowboys of La Conquistadora. They had been working out of the Juniper Breaks campsite for two days now. The rough and rugged, steeply canyoned country had been worked clean, scoured of cattle that had then been culled for shipping and all the calves stamped with La Conquistadora's renowned three-pointed crown. Or so Toby hoped. Anything missed would have to wait for the fall work, or maybe even next spring's. At any rate, it was time to move on. The days allotted to the Juniper Breaks were spent. The next stop was Las Vegas del Oro, a pretty camp in a pretty pasture, named for the acres of sunflowers that dotted it, some of their blooms as big as a man's head. Sophie's mother had always wished there was a line camp on one of Las Vegas del Oro's rises, where she could just sit on the porch, her eyes and spirit soaking in the great splashes of gold out across the flats, the multitude of blossoms turning in unison to track the sun. Sophie understood the wish. It was that kind of place.

There was a lot to be done before the wagon could move on, and by the time Sophie, Christine, and Kitten drove into camp, the crew had it nearly finished: the rope corral taken down, the wagons loaded, the remuda ready to go. Their timing was perfect. Not only was the work all done by the time they were saddled up, but the morning's best show was just about to begin.

As the last bedroll found its place atop a large can of dried pinto beans, Juan Soliz, Adam Connor, Frankie Evans, and Danny Parks prepared to "jerk the fly." The fly, freed from the anchoring guy ropes that had held it taut to supply shade and shelter to cook and crew, was now just twenty by thirty feet of heavy canvas, draped limply across the wagon bows. But not for long. Never averse to putting on a show for the audience, especially an audience of three pretty girls, the four cowboys performed to perfection that day. In unison they leaned into the tug that started the canvas sliding up and over the bows, then a quick little run to stretch it straight and flat on the ground. Guy ropes tossed into the center, Danny and Juan gave the fly a fold this way, Adam and Frankie a fold that way, then a lap from each end, and the fly was folded. In one fluid motion, four hard bodies bent and, lifting the heavy canvas on high, dashed for the wagon. Danny and Juan stopped with their end of the folded fly against the side of the wagon. Frankie and Adam, in a single motion, flipped their end up and over, to be perfectly caught by Gary Clancy and Tommy Ryan, who were waiting on top of the wagon to receive it and tie it down.

The feat was performed well, and Sophie, Kitten, and Christine expressed their appreciation with an enthusiastic round of applause. Six cowboys, all of whom loved a grand gesture, turned and again in perfect unison bowed to the ladies.

Meanwhile, Custard, Mustard, Nip, and Tuck had been harnessed and hitched to the chuck wagon by four other members of the crew. The prettiest four-horse team on the range was ready to pull that chuck wagon over any road that came their way, and pull it at a clipping trot all day long if need be. But if they were the prettiest, they were also the feistiest. Only working every two or three days and being pampered with extra rations of oats each morning, the team had energy to spare, and then some. When they were harnessed and hitched up to the wagon, the horses knew it was time to go, and the quicker the better. A cowboy had to stand at each eager horse's head with a very firm grip on the rein to prevent the chuck wagon from being hauled out of camp without its driver. The team, the chuck wagon, and the cook had to be taken care of, for without them, there would be no home on the range for La Conquistadora.

Sophie had maneuvered and arranged things so that she would be the one tagging along, leading Adam's horse, so that he could rejoin the drive after that adventuresome first half mile. In Sophie's biased opinion, things were going very well today.

Ignacio knew his team and their antics well, and he could certainly drive them, and he did it routinely. But those four big horses were always full of fire early of a morning when the air was cool and their bellies were full of oats. They ran away every single time they were hitched up, and sometimes it was a wild trip. A cowboy was always assigned to ride with Ignacio for that first jolting half mile or so, to help him handle his unruly charges. Most of the cowboys hated this task. It was one thing to be in the saddle up on the back of a hot-blooded horse, even a pitching horse, where you were in charge, but it was quite another to be bounced around on the seat of a not-too-well-sprung wagon being dragged along behind the surging rumps of four big, strong runaways. There was only one cowboy who loved it. Adam Connor would take any man's place, anytime, who didn't want to start the day with a shot of adrenaline. Sophie could see it in his grin and shining eyes whenever he climbed up on that wagon seat. He did love the rush.

When Ignacio was settled on the wagon seat, Adam turned for a split second and winked at Sophie before springing up beside the cook. Sophie suppressed a smile, her shining eyes rivaling the sun's brilliance, had anyone taken note. But no one had noticed, not even Ignacio, who normally didn't miss a trick where his favorite girl was concerned. At the moment, the only thing on Ignacio's mind was the upcoming wagon ride. Sophie knew the only thing he didn't like was the first half mile, and even though he considered Adam to be completely crazy, he was glad to have him along.

"Okay, Ignacio, you take the wheelers and hold them up pretty tight. I'll take the leaders."

"You sure you know how to handle the leaders, Señor Adam?" Ignacio asked nervously.

"Of course I know how to handle the leaders. I'm going to handle the leaders the way I do every time we move camp. I'm going to steer them as straight as an arrow. And I'm going to hold them up, but not so much that your wheelers get caught up in the stretchers, go down, cause a wreck, and send us all to meet our maker. Okay?"

"Okay, Señor Adam. I have faith in you."

"You ought to. We haven't been killed yet."

"Today could be the day."

Adam just grinned.

"Are you ready, Ignacio?"

"I am ready."

"All right, boys. Let her rip," Adam shouted to the men holding the team.

The four cowboys jumped back and the four horses leaped away. Each horse lunged for his bit and grabbed it. Wagon and all were gone in a swirl of dust and horsehide, punctuated by enough wild Spanish to make Sophie wish she were completely fluent.

Sophie stayed well to the rear and maintained a sedate trot, leading Adam's horse alongside her. The last thing she wanted to do was encourage the runaways any more than they already were. From behind, the spectacle was something to see: the wagon lurching and bouncing over the rough ground, the four big horses pounding along with great abandon, snorting and tossing their heads. Four heads bobbed in unison, their manes waving like flags. Sixteen powerful legs churned up the earth, topped by heaving flanks and broad, deep chests now wet with sweat. Mighty muscles bunched and released over and over again with each leap forward. Ignacio's hat was just visible above the dust, and Adam was up there beside him, leaning forward into the run with the easy balance of a man who was having the time of his life.

After a while the team began to slow, the wild charge settling into a trot, and then Ignacio pulled the chuck wagon to a halt. The team did not protest.

Sophie came up at a lope, leading Adam's horse.

"God is good and generous, we live another day," Ignacio told Adam as he took the leaders' reins from him.

"You're right, Ignacio, God is indeed good and generous," Adam agreed as he climbed down from the wagon seat.

With a wave to Sophie and a nod to Adam, Ignacio and his four transformed charges trotted off to the next campground.

Adam walked over to where Sophie sat her horse, reached for his own horse's reins, and looked up at her.

"Hi, Baby," was all he could say.

It was enough. Without a word, Sophie leaned down from the saddle and kissed him full on the lips. When he returned the kiss, as deeply as he had received it, Sophie felt something give way inside her that she knew would never go back to the way it was before. They were an inseparable island, alone in the vast sea of waving grass, a small stronghold in that rippling ocean of green.

The two reluctantly parted. After all, they were not truly alone in the universe, and there were still cattle waiting to be worked. Adam mounted Cougar, the horse Sophie had led out for him, and together he and Sophie jumped their steeds off in a lope across the grassy flats. Both felt a great joy and contentment to be riding together that day, through the waves of grass under the great arching blue sky with fluffs of cloud tossed across it. The day and the company were perfect. Even the horses seemed to feel the glory of it all. They seemed to have no bottom, loping freely and easily, as though they could go on forever.

A rifle cracked somewhere off to the north, some cowboy a mile away taking a shot at a coyote. Sophie barely registered it. Adam did. He went rigid in the saddle for a beat, his hands locking on the reins, and Cougar felt it and broke stride. It was over in a second. Adam's hands eased and the horse settled back into his lope, but Sophie had seen something cross his face that she could not name, something far away and not good, and then it was gone and he was smiling at her again as though nothing had happened. She did not ask. She had no idea where it had come from or what it meant, but it was from somewhere she had never been and she knew better than to go poking around in it.

The moment, however, ended rather abruptly when Cougar gave a nervous whinny that brought forth an immediate answer in kind from Sophie's horse, Jake. One quick glance around and they knew the reason for their mounts' excitement. The ground over which they so happily loped was thick with rattlesnakes. An expanse of land was simply crawling with them, and the riders were suddenly as edgy as their horses. Sophie was terrified of snakes. To fall here, she was sure, would mean certain death. To Sophie it was a scene from hell itself.

"Sophie, are you all right?" Adam asked her sharply.

"I don't like this at all," was her answer.

All Sophie's intelligence told her to look ahead and not down, to ride for the horizon and not to even think about the snakes that were everywhere. But all she could do was stare at the snaky, rattling ground in horrified fascination, and all she could think about was poor Jake, trying to find a safe place to put four hooves among all those snakes.

The sun had been at work for some time now, and the snakes were rapidly losing their nocturnal languor. Some had long since lost it altogether and just wanted to get out of there. As a result, there were masses of rattlers crawling and writhing about in confusion, just trying to escape from the sheer numbers of their fellows. Add to this chaos two very nervous galloping horses, and the result was a lot of confused and angry rattlesnakes.

Before her eyes Sophie watched the carpet of scaly backs heave and sway beneath her passage. Some wriggled frantically to crawl away. Others coiled and struck at anything, or at nothing, their tails raised and buzzing with the rattle Sophie had been taught from childhood to listen for and be so very wary of. The sound cried danger to her ears and always had. Everywhere she looked it seemed she saw either a buzzing tail or gaping jaws with venom-filled fangs out and ready to strike in less than a heartbeat. Her head felt light as she stared, mesmerized, at the seemingly endless ripples of scaly black and tan below her. Her breath came in short, fast gulps, and she knew that the lovely land of golden flowers was far away, that now she was lost here, marooned in this awful tempest of danger and certain death.

"Look, Baby, all we have to do is keep moving and lope on through them. See, we're almost to clear ground now."

Adam's voice seemed to come from a long way off, but Sophie heard it. She was surprised and glad that, like the sun, it burned away the fog she had been lost in for a moment. She looked where Adam pointed, and sure enough, just ahead, the mass of undulating snakes was beginning to thin out and finally be replaced by open grassland. Once out of the snakes, Sophie's relief was enormous.

"Adam, in all my life I have never seen or even heard of anything like this, have you? There must have been hundreds of them at the very least, maybe even more."

"No, this is a first for me, too. There must be a den nearby or something. Anyway, Baby, I suggest we just keep on riding and never look back. That's a whole lot more snakes than I feel like taking on. How about you?"

Sophie felt better with the ocean of snakes behind them, so she was able to smile a little, although her face was still on the pale side.

"You see me riding, but you don't see me looking back, do you?"

Adam laughed. Sophie could tell the snakes had shaken him more than he wanted to let on. He was quiet for a moment, and when he spoke again his voice had a catch in it that Sophie hadn't heard before.

"Sophie," he said.

She looked at him.

"I know we've got a lot of work to get done this morning, but meet me somewhere for a few minutes, all right?"

"Of course I'd love to meet you," Sophie answered. "Just say where. But are you okay? You're awfully pale all of a sudden. Those snakes must have scared you more than you thought."

"Yeah, they did," Adam agreed. "Listen, we are both supposed to be working the Indian Rock Mesa side of this pasture. Meet me there, near the drawings, in an hour and a half. That will give us time to get a respectable number of cattle gathered and shoved down to the roundup ground."

"You've got a date, cowboy," Sophie told him. With a wave of her quirt she was gone, galloping off toward a stand of giant sunflowers, her earlier concerns forgotten.

Chapter 18 — Sophie and Connor Share an Apple

SOPHIE PULLED JAKE TO a walk as she came up through the broken ground of Indian Rock Mesa. She could see Adam ahead, standing in the shade of a piñon with Cougar's reins looped over his arm. He had his pocketknife out and was cutting slices from an apple, sharing them with his horse. Neither of them knew she was there.

She sat her horse for a moment, watching. The terrain was rough and scattered with piñon and sandstone boulders, many of which were covered with the drawings of long-departed Indians. Sophie's mother had always said that a visit to Indian Rock was a visit to an ancient art museum, and Sophie had always agreed with her. Adam loved this spot, which was why he had chosen it. Sophie could see it in the easy way he leaned against Cougar's shoulder, his eyes moving across the kingdom spread around him and above him and out across the flats. The shadows cast by high white clouds created great shifting swaths of darkness across the land below.

"Any for me?"

Cougar's head flew up. Adam spun around, and Sophie had herself a captive audience.

"I was afraid I wasn't going to be able to sneak up on you, but both of you were so caught up in your apple eating no one noticed Jake and me."

"Sweets for the sweet." Adam held an apple slice up to her.

Smiling down at him, she reached for the apple. Sophie felt a peace and contentment so profound that she knew, just for a moment, that she was caught up in a rare and perfect day. In taking the apple slice, her fingers touched Adam's, and Sophie felt a jolt that went clear to the pit of her stomach. She had never experienced such a thing before. Startled and confused, she glanced at Adam, and her blue eyes were helplessly captured in the lock of his searing brown gaze. Sophie briefly wondered if she could ever escape and doubted she would ever want to.

In one fluid move Adam pocketed his knife and stepped up against Jake's shoulder, his chest grazing Sophie's booted leg. Without conscious thought, he raised her small hand, apple and all, and pressed a deep kiss into her palm. No word was spoken, but Sophie, heeding his primitive call, slid weakly to the ground. Her knees felt unsteady, as did her stomach and her head and her heart. Sophie wondered if she were dying and stared, mesmerized, at the hand that had just received Adam's kiss, and at the red-and-white flesh of the apple that still lay there.

She had never felt this way in all her nineteen years. She had never been swept off her feet by Cupid's cyclone. Acting again on instinct and without conscious thought, Adam took the apple slice from Sophie's limp fingers and held it up to her lips. Forever and always Sophie would remember eating that apple slice from Adam Connor's strong, firm fingers as the most intimate moment of her life.

When the apple was finished, Adam cupped Sophie's cheek with first one hand and then the other. Then slowly, for there was all the time in the world, he lowered his lips to Sophie's, to savor and linger over their kiss and the sweet faint taste of apples.

Sophie's hands slid up Adam's broad chest, and she could feel his hard, tensed muscles bunched under her light touch. She marveled for a split second that he, such an experienced and mighty man, a warrior, was here in the arms of little nineteen-year-old Sophie Degarrin. But then his tongue slipped between her parted lips, and his touch and his kiss thundered through her blood, setting her aquiver. It felt as though every cell in her body was separately but simultaneously vibrating, releasing awesome and overpowering sensations that swept through Sophie in waves. Responding in kind, kissing as she was kissed, returning touch for touch, caress for caress,

Sophie lost all track of time and place. She was completely lost in a world of desire, and love, and lust.

After a while she surfaced enough to notice her arms were tight around Adam's neck, one hand lost in the tangled waves of his thick hair. She was also vaguely aware of his surging anatomy pressed tightly against her middle. That scared her a little, but then she succumbed once more to the feelings that flowed all through her. Sophie surrendered to that hot exploring tongue and to the hands that roved sensuously over her, touching her hair here, her neck there, stroking and caressing her arched back, then trailing lower to cup and knead the firm behind tucked safely away inside her Levi's.

Sophie had always considered herself a young sophisticate, if not actually a woman of the world, but this was too much. She was getting scared of the sensations she had never remotely experienced before and yearnings and desires she didn't know if she could, or even should, control. She pulled her face away to catch her breath and try to regain her bearings.

Adam slowed his assault until his kisses became nothing more than a slow, soft pulling on the tender curve at the base of Sophie's neck. It seemed to Sophie that just that light tugging alone caused all her insides to surge through her from side to side in response to each sweet pull of Adam's lips. Sophie was powerless and stood waiting, grateful for the support of Adam's arms, until he had had enough.

The two rested, entwined, drawing strength from one another and then sharing it between them. Leaning back a little so they could face each other, blue eyes encountered brown in mutual searching and probing. Neither was sure of where they had been or where they were going. Sophie smiled first. Lips curved, eyes alight, her whole body beamed.

"Wow," she said.

Then Adam responded in kind. He couldn't help himself. His eyes began to sparkle, and a foolish grin he could not suppress came over his face. "Damn, Sophie. You are one hell of a woman. I was afraid I might die."

"Me, too. We could have died and gone straight to heaven together."

"Might not have been heaven."

"No, it would have been heaven."

Adam laughed and gave her a light kiss on the lips, then stepped back and glanced at his watch. "Hell, Sophie, we've been at this for half an hour. We've got to get going."

"Oh, dear! You're right. Here, don't step on your hat." Sophie grabbed Adam's straw hat from the ground where it had thus far escaped from being trampled.

Adam put the hat on and looked around. The horses had wandered off a hundred yards or so.

"Sophie, the next time we have a romantic rendezvous, let's try to remember to hobble the horses."

"Will they come if you whistle?"

"Not unless we've somehow gotten into a movie. Sophie, you angle across down below them and that'll keep them from heading down the hill. I'll try walking up to Cougar. He'll most likely let me catch him."

"Good luck. Jake's a real pain in the rump to catch."

Sure enough, Cougar proved cooperative and Jake didn't. But once mounted, Adam had no problem with Jake. Not wanting to waste time or pussyfoot around, he simply took down his rope and quickly slapped a loop around a surprised Jake's neck.

"Hey, he can kiss, and rope. What more could a girl ask for?" Sophie said.

"Child, you ain't seen nothing yet."

When Sophie was mounted on Jake, Adam turned serious. "Okay, little one. Do you know where you're supposed to be?"

"I think I should ride like hell for that break over there. I figure that's where I'd be if I hadn't taken this little reprieve."

"That's right. And, Sophie, try to pick up some cattle so it'll look like you've been busy today."

"I have been busy, Adam. I was thinking of putting in for overtime."

"I'd give you overtime and a bonus, too."

"I'll see you at camp," Sophie said. Still glowing, she turned and galloped away across the sunflower flats.

Chapter 19 — Danny's Day

THE SKY WAS FLAWLESS, blue from one rim of the world to the other, and the smoke from Ignacio's cook fire went straight up and stayed there, not a breath of wind to bend it. The wagon had reached its destination by midmorning and without incident. As always, the team had worked all the silliness out in the first dashing half mile and thereafter performed like the old hands they were. Through the concerted efforts of Ricky and Ignacio, the encampment on the prairie looked as if it had been there forever, or at least longer than a few minutes. Lunch preparations were well underway, and delicious aromas were fast becoming unmistakable when Louisa Degarrin arrived.

She sniffed the air appreciatively and smiled at Ignacio.

"Seems I've gotten here just in time, Ignacio."

"Any time is the perfect time for you to arrive at our humble camp, Miss Louisa," Ignacio gallantly assured her.

Seating herself on a bedroll, Louisa waved a greeting to Ricky, who was off near the woodpile collecting an armload of fuel. She looked around in satisfaction. She liked the wagon when it was a quiet, peaceful island with Ignacio calmly going about his tasks, before the hurly-burly of the cowboys' arrival. Knowing this, Ignacio left her to her thoughts. There was no need to entertain this lady. When she wanted conversation, she would start one. Meantime, both would enjoy a quiet while, all to themselves. Ricky, too, was used to this routine and did whatever chores he had without comment or commotion.

Ignacio stood at the shelf that folded down from the back of the chuck wagon to make his worktable and methodically picked through a mound of dried pinto beans. Good plump pintos met with his approval and were swept into his pot. Shriveled ones and pieces of gravel and dirt were disdainfully shoved to the side to fall discarded to the ground.

Louisa watched Ignacio's concentration as he sorted his beans and smiled again. The selected beans were destined to simmer until noon tomorrow, when she knew they would be delicious. As would be the steaks or the roast or whatever else he chose to prepare. Eating at the wagon was always a tasty experience. Louisa loved it, and she especially loved it when the wagon was camped here at Las Vegas del Oro, where the acres of sunflowers made a glorious splash of color across the land.

"Ignacio, this is my favorite campsite on the whole ranch, I do believe."

"Yes, I know. It is one of mine, too, Miss Louisa. But you need to be enjoying it with a cup of coffee and some of my peach cobbler that I saved just in case you paid us a visit."

Louisa had little choice, had she wanted one, which she didn't. She knew full well that Ignacio's cobbler bordered on the divine and peach was her favorite. The first bite was heaven, and the second even better. She was contentedly munching and sipping strong black coffee when the first trails of dust became visible in the sky off to the east.

"Here they come." Ricky heralded the first appearance of the herd.

It was some time later that the first riders came in to change horses. Then, with fresh mounts and hardly a pause, it was back to the roundup ground where the herd was restlessly stirring. The air was filled with the lowing of cows and calves calling to each other in the crowded, dusty confusion and with the occasional trumpeting of a bull.

Louisa watched with pride as her husband and her daughter rode into camp together. Both were as at home on the back of a horse and as one with their mount as any rider in the finest Virginia hunt club. They were a sight that any eyes could appreciate. Louisa walked out to meet them at the rope corral.

Hopping down from Jake, Sophie took off her straw hat and mopped her brow with the back of her hand. Freed from the restraint of the hat, her blond hair fell down her back and floated a little in the breeze.

"Hi, Momma," she said.

"Hi, yourself, Missy. You look mighty content today."

"I am mighty content. I have had a fabulous day thus far and expect it to only get better. The sky is high, the sun is bright, and sunflowers are pure gold. You should ride out and see them off the road, Mom. How could the day be any better?"

Degarrin interrupted to suggest that the three of them take a little ride after the branding to show the sunflowers off to Louisa.

"You haven't been on a horse in a while, Louisa. You need to take a ride every now and then or you'll lose your touch."

As Louisa was a champion rider, this sally brought forth a laugh.

"You know, Mike, I've been worried about that very thing. Do you think you have a horse I could handle?" Louisa asked.

"Don't worry, Momma. If Daddy doesn't have something rideable for you, I'll wake up one of my tired nags for you to ride," Sophie assured her mother.

"Thank you, honey. I'll consider it a date and just hope I can keep up with the two of you."

"We'll wait if we have to," her husband said with the smile he saved for Louisa alone.

It would be fun to ride out with her family that afternoon. When Sophie was a child, the three had ridden quite often together, and it had been such fun. As Louisa watched them ride back to the herd a few minutes later, she was once again filled with pride, but also with a little added sense of anticipation.

Later, in the shady refuge of the wagon fly, the crew took a breather while waiting for Iggy to call "lunchee". Louisa, seated a little apart, observed the whole and made special note of her child's glowing beauty. It seemed to her that Sophie looked a little more radiant today than usual. Unable to pinpoint the source of this subtle change, Louisa shrugged it off as just the healthy effects of a little extra sunshine and exertion.

Her meditations were interrupted by Ignacio's call to lunch, and she gladly rose to take her place in line. She found Adam Connor behind her in line for chuck. He chatted casually about the weather, the condition of the sunflowers, and the prospects for further rain. All were safe topics, and Louisa found him pleasant company.

Danny Parks, on the other hand, found Miss Louisa's company far too delightful to be passed up, and promptly settled down beside her for a cozy visit. Across the group, Louisa caught her husband's eye and saw the poker face cracking into a smile.

Danny touched the brim of his hat. "Good morning, Miss Louisa. How are you today?"

"I'm fine, Danny, and you?"

"Oh, I'm as right as rain. Have you made it over to the map rock yet? Juan took me over there a few days ago. It was something else."

"I haven't gotten there so far, but I'm thinking I'll get a free minute later this week and that's at the top of my list of things to do. It sounds fascinating. I know I'll love it."

"I think you'll like it. If you have any trouble finding it, just let Juan or me know."

"I will. Oh, by the way, I gave your spear point a place of honor on the mantle in the dining room. It looks great there and gets lots of attention. We had a visitor for lunch a few days ago from the Museum of New Mexico. He really coveted your find."

"Did you give it to him?" Danny asked.

"Certainly not! It's a La Conquistadora treasure and here it will safely stay forever, or at least as long as I'm around to guard it."

"Good. I'm sure it wants to stay here at home and not go traveling. Oh, I almost forgot." Reaching into the pocket of his Levi's, Danny pulled out an almost perfect arrowhead. "I found this a couple of days ago riding across the sandy area over near the point of San Hilario Mesa. I think that must have been an Indian campground. There are still a lot of stones there that I figure had to have been tepee rings."

"I think you must be right. I've found some pot shards there myself. But tell me, Danny, how on earth do you find such great things? Your spear point is absolutely perfect and this arrowhead only has a little chip or it would be perfect, too."

Danny laughed. "I don't know," he said. "I just sort of see them sometimes, riding along."

Louisa shook her head and smiled at him. "I don't see how. I walk along, staring at the ground, searching and searching. Sometimes I finally find something, but usually not."

Danny just grinned at her, then took a sip of iced tea and chewed on his sourdough biscuit. He seemed a little lost in thought, so Louisa turned her attention back to Ignacio's excellent offerings.

Danny interrupted her contemplation, saying, "I'll tell you how I find arrowheads and things if you won't die laughing and tell me I'm completely crazy."

Louisa perked up. She loved a secret as well as anyone. "I'm not laughing," she answered him. "As for crazy, I'll need a little more proof."

"This might prove it," he told her.

"Try me and see."

"Okay." Danny paused for a moment, taking time to chew and think. "When I first came to work here, I loved the thought of Indians living here, riding the same land I was riding, maybe walking just exactly where I was putting my feet. It's hard to explain."

"I think I know what you mean. I think that feeling is a big part of La Conquistadora's appeal. Lots of times I've had a kind of eerie feeling that only a second of time separates me from those people. Their feel is still here, and so is their place. The only thing different is a blink in time."

Danny looked at her with smiling eyes. "That's exactly what I mean, only you said it better than I ever could. Well, anyway, I spent a lot of time thinking about Indians as I rode along. I was always looking for arrowheads, but I never saw any, never came close to finding anything at all, even though I wanted to more than anything. Then one night I had a dream. This old, old Indian man was in my dream. He said he was going to help me. Then he showed me every kind of arrowhead there was, and all the spear points, and knives and scrapers and a whole lot of other things, too. Ever since that dream, it seems like my eyes are trained to know what to look for and where. I can just see things now. I probably still miss a lot, but it sure seems like, if there's anything near me at all, my eyes just seem to be drawn to it as plain as day. That spear point I gave you practically jumped up and down, and then into my pocket," he said.

Louisa had been mesmerized by Danny's words.

"That's a wonderful story, Danny. Do you think you were an Indian in a former life?"

"Maybe." Danny was still grinning at her. Because Miss Louisa hadn't laughed and didn't seem to think he was any crazier than maybe he was, Danny told her something else. "Maybe I was an apprentice, trying to learn how to make the different kinds of points, and the old Indian was my teacher. Maybe I couldn't make them right until I could really see them, so the old Indian showed me all the possibilities."

Louisa nodded her head, and the two sat in companionable silence. Louisa, seated on a dusty bedroll, sipped her tea and gazed out across the great sweep of grass.

"Danny."

"Yes, Miss Louisa?"

"Maybe you were the old Indian."

Danny's eyes met Louisa's with an arrested expression.

"I never thought of that," he said, a little wonder in his voice. "That would be nice, wouldn't it?"

Louisa just nodded.

"Well, boys," Toby told his crew, "I'd love for us all to spend the afternoon here, chatting in the shade, but we've got cattle to work."

With these words, lunch was ended and the crew mobilized. There were horses to catch and calves to be branded.

Louisa drove her car down and parked it right outside the gate to the branding pen. She always did this when she was at the wagon. Louisa enjoyed sitting in her pink Oldsmobile and watching the branding from its comfortable interior. She much preferred this to perching on a fence in the broiling sun.

The daily afternoon scenario was playing out before her. The large corral was filled with cows and calves and cowboys. Also present were Christine, Kitten, and Sophie. The branding pen was hardly the place Louisa liked to see her daughter, but she had resigned herself to the fact that Sophie was not about to be left out. So there she was, expertly wielding a vaccinating needle and striding about the corral as if to the dust and dirt born. Watching Sophie, Louisa couldn't help but smile. She would never admit it, but in a way it was gratifying to watch her daughter perform so ably in the rough-and-tumble cowboy world. Louisa was secretly proud that her child, who could be such a lady, could also more than hold her own in that dusty melee before her.

As the branding wore on, the air became thicker and thicker with the fine dust kicked up by cows and calves, horses and boots. The afternoon sun shining through the suspension of dust cast a golden haze across the scene. Through it Louisa watched her husband and Danny Parks expertly heel calf after calf and then drag the startled calf out of the herd to be grabbed by the flankers. It was late in the season now and each pair of flankers had long since become a perfect team. With a minimum of effort and no confusion whatsoever, each calf was thrown to the ground and stretched out by the flankers, ready to be branded, castrated, earmarked, and vaccinated. The La Conquistadora crew could brand two calves a minute when things were going well.

In the corral, things were going very well indeed. Degarrin was roping perfectly, making catch after catch. He was a great roper, but Danny, who was matching him catch for catch, was just as good. Both men were grinning. It was fun to be horseback on such a day and roping with an equal. It was an honor to be asked by Toby to rope, and it was an honor that only the wagon boss could bestow. Even Degarrin had to wait for Toby's nod. All La Conquistadora's cowboys thought they were fine calf ropers, and some were, but Danny and Degarrin were the best.

Louisa could see her husband shaking his head and smiling the wider as he watched Danny's fluid grace in the saddle. She knew what that look meant. In just a while, Danny would be better than he was. It was only age and a million more tosses that let her husband hold his own against the young man now.

Watching from her car, Louisa smiled, too. She loved to watch her husband, but watching Danny was just as good.

Danny's loop settled so easily against the calf's leg, and the calf so cooperatively stepped right into it. Danny smiled his thanks and turned Chaco, his favorite mount, toward the branding fire. The rope, tied on to Danny's saddle horn, was stretched tight as Chaco dragged the bawling calf behind him.

The young heifer went a little crazy when her first calf was pulled squalling away from her. Such a thing had never happened before and she ran after her baby. In her confusion and concern, she crashed into the taut rope and knocked Chaco off balance. Danny automatically tried to steady his horse, but things went from bad to worse. The calf scrambled up when the line went slack and began to run with its confused mother.

When the still-heeled calf hit the end of the rope, cow, calf, and Chaco went down. The suddenness of it all took Danny and everyone else in the pen by surprise. Chaco twisted a little at the last second and Danny hit on the saddle horn. The wind was knocked out of him and he was dazed for just a heartbeat. But Chaco wasn't dazed and he wanted up and out of that mess right then. His thrashing hooves were searching for footing when one found Danny's ribs instead. Determined and frightened, Chaco gathered himself and with one mighty effort scrambled to his feet. Danny, still in the saddle, rose with his mount, but Louisa could see he was hurt. It had all happened so fast that no one had had time to react with anything more than a frozen stare of fear.

The rope had gone slack again, and in all the confusion, Chaco and Danny had wound up between the panic-stricken calf and its still-crazy mother. The heifer bawled and bawled, calling to the calf that was now lost from her view. The calf responded with an ill-planned dash to the safety of its mother's side. The path it chose led right under Chaco, who, with heaving sides and rolling eyes, saw it coming. The horse decided he had had enough, and he jumped and kicked, just wanting to be rid of the pesky bovine nuisance.

Chaco's whirling and kicking had accomplished what the calf alone probably could not have. Danny was now locked down in the saddle, his right leg clamped in place by the rope that now stretched tightly from his saddle horn, across his leg and under Chaco's belly, to the squalling, jerking calf.

Chaco continued in his headlong struggle to get free, whirling and kicking and trying to jump away. Danny, superb rider that he was, tried to calm and control the frantic horse. But it was a futile effort. Chaco was beside himself with confused rage, and Danny was gasping in pain and breathlessness.

There was a scream from Louisa as she jumped from her car and a curse from Degarrin as he leaped from his horse. Now the scene resembled a rodeo bull ride gone bad with the clown unable to reach the rider in trouble. Although it only lasted seconds, it seemed like forever that the rampaging Chaco kept Danny tied in the saddle and kept help out of reach.

Acting instinctively, Sophie threw down her vaccinating needle and ran for Chaco. Frankie and Adam had acted on the same impulse, but Adam was a little closer and a little quicker. "Get back, Sophie!" he ordered as he seized her arm and threw her behind him and out of harm's way. Then he grabbed for the reins and in a second had the headstall firmly in hand as well.

"Steady boy, steady boy," Adam murmured, moving with Chaco, staying right by his bobbing head. Chaco was glad to have a human with him that acted in charge and was calming down a little.

Toby and Degarrin were on the scene as well, trying to get to the rope that was causing all the trouble. The calf, making one last charge, hit the end of the rope and snapped it tight around Chaco's front legs. As Chaco once again crashed down on the dirt floor of the branding corral, Toby finally made it to the tight and jerking rope that now held the calf, Chaco, and Danny all prisoners. Toby brought the razor-sharp castrating knife slashing down, cutting Danny and Chaco free at last.

Freed from the calf, Chaco was still held by the rope twisted around his front legs. Further infuriated and terrified by this new restraint, Chaco lashed out, trying desperately to get to his feet. Adam had jumped away from the falling horse but was now down on the ground once more at Chaco's head, doing all he could to calm the horse and keep him still. It was hopeless. Chaco was anything but calm. His slashing hooves cut up the dirt of the corral, adding to the golden haze of dust that hung in the dead-still air.

Danny's head grazed the ground when Chaco fell, and the blow packed some punch. Louisa, frozen at the gate, saw it happen and remembered what Danny had told her at the ice cream social, that when you stayed caught was the only time that it was tricky. And Danny was staying caught, and there was nothing she could do.

Chaco heaved and jerked about, his churning hooves still searching for solid footing and escape. One of those hard, steel-shod hooves found Danny's beautiful dark head instead. From that collision, Danny felt no pain and thought no more.

Adam crouched on Chaco's neck, holding his head down and trying to force him to be still. Chaco finally did lie still, but it was because he just gave up, not because of Adam's strength and determination. The rescuers' efforts rewarded, they set to work cutting Danny free and pulling him to safety. Chaco, too, was cut loose and climbed shakily to his feet, Adam still at his head. But Adam's eyes, and everyone else's, were on Danny.

"Is he all right?" Adam asked for everyone.

Degarrin, kneeling beside Danny's still form, lifted his hand from the pulseless neck and his eyes from the spreading stain of red through Danny's thick, dark hair. He raised stunned eyes to all who breathlessly watched and shook his head.

"We were too late for Danny." His voice was hardly a whisper and filled with despair.

In that corral on the prairie, bathed in a golden haze of dust, there was the stunned silence of disbelief. Then, as stubborn disbelief reluctantly gave way, the dust and dirt on every face was washed away in a pour of tears.

Chapter 20 — Moving On

THERE WERE MORE HARD-STARCHED and creased Levi's and snap-button shirts at Danny's funeral than there were town clothes. When cowboys gather their gear to go on wagon work, they don't pack their suits, even if they own one. But that was all right. The still-stricken mourners were dressed the same as the guest of honor. Danny, in his simple casket, wore the same uniform of the range as did they.

The gathering was small. The only family Danny had present were those who had adopted him into their hearts, and he they, at La Conquistadora. Danny would go home that afternoon to Tennessee and to his blood kin there. The trip would be by train at La Conquistadora's expense. Louisa had wanted to keep Danny at the ranch, resting in the tiny little burial ground in the fruit orchard at headquarters. But his mother wanted Danny returned to her in Tennessee, and Louisa had had to give way.

"He would have wanted to stay here," Louisa had told Degarrin. She was sure of it. Danny would not have wanted to leave this open land where you could see forever and where the Indians had walked and the buffalo run.

But Degarrin doubted it. "Your childhood home is where you think back to in times of trouble. Danny was not so far from those days when home and mother meant happiness and comfort. I think he'll be better off ending in the same place he started."

Louisa said no more, but she knew in her heart of hearts that Degarrin was wrong. Danny had been just like her and would never willingly have left La Conquistadora, never to return. There were other things she had imagined for Danny, quiet hopes she had never shared with anyone. Those, too, were gone now.

The service was held at the First Baptist Church in Clauson, because there wasn't any other, and Danny's family was Baptist. Louisa suspected Danny had not confined himself to any one organized denomination, or even one religion. Certainly this little church, pretty though it was, seemed inadequate to hold his spirit.

"Momma." Sophie squeezed her mother's hand to get her attention. She wasn't coping too well and needed her mother, although she was loath to admit it.

"Momma, you seem lost in space. Like you're only here in body, and just barely that."

Louisa heard her child's anxiety and all the unspoken cries. She gave Sophie's hand a reassuring squeeze.

"I'm right here, baby, and I'm just fine. How about you? How are you holding up?"

Sophie could only shake her head. She couldn't talk at all as her face crumpled up into a fresh wash of tears. In present memory, at least, no one had ever died at La Conquistadora. It was Sophie's first personal encounter with death, and she did not like the stranger at all. She would have been far happier not to have made its acquaintance for a long, long time, and to have its calling card be the loss of Danny was more than she could bear. Louisa put her arm around her daughter as Degarrin did the same. Holding Sophie between them, the little family sat huddled together, one tight unit, and listened as the music Louisa had chosen rolled over them.

Filling the church with rare beauty, the choir sang "Above the Hills of Time," because it was lovely and set to the melody of "Danny Boy," and then concluded with "Amazing Grace," because the title summed Danny up so well.

The service was followed by a luncheon in the church hall. The ladies of the congregation provided casseroles and deviled eggs, which were gratefully, if automatically, consumed by the still-stunned mourners. It was still unbelievable that Danny would not be joining them any minute, that he would never join them all again. The cowboys were uncomfortable having to confront and be bombarded by so much raw emotion. Emotional terrain was their most dreaded territory, the place where their footing was least sure and a stumble and fall the most likely to occur. The meal was eaten in haste and the hall soon emptied. The ladies of the Clauson First Baptist Church were not surprised. They had known it wouldn't take long. It never did to feed a crew of working men, whether at home or at church.

Louisa and Degarrin paused just outside the church door to speak with the pastor and to thank the ladies for lunch. In the parking lot, the cowboys were gathering among the pickups, wondering what to do next. There was to be a memorial service and the placing of a marker in the orchard cemetery back at the ranch, but that wasn't until sundown.

"What do we do now?" Frankie asked no one in particular. "What are we supposed to do with a day off, between funerals?"

"It's either back to the ranch or go to a bar," Tommy Ryan said.

From the church door Louisa could see Sophie and Adam standing together in the parking lot. Sophie, drawn and pale, was still balanced just barely this side of constant tears. Adam was equally pale and maintaining a very tight control, so tight a control that it fairly crackled. Sophie said something Louisa couldn't hear, and then her face crumpled and she began to cry again. Adam just put his arms around her and held her close to his heart.

Louisa watched this scene from a distance and filed it away. She vaguely realized that she had lately been filing away quite a few bothersome bits and pieces to be looked at when time allowed. But not today, no, not today. This was Danny's day.

The sun set that night on the cemetery's new marker. It was placed in a simple ceremony, with no preacher and no great fanfare, but with deep love and sadness. Throughout the coming years, Danny's marker was often visited by both those who had known and loved him and by those who only knew and revered his legend. But as the myth of Danny developed, it was the story of a great cowboy, a gifted horseman with dancing eyes and a flashing smile in a handsome face. It never related his kindred spirit and devotion to those who walked and rode this same land before him. Louisa Degarrin never told that side of Danny. Instead, she stored it away and treasured it in her heart.

The wagon work went on. There were only a few days left, but still a lot of cattle to be worked. Spirits were low, and that worried Degarrin, who liked a contented crew. He did not want a crew that was beginning to see disaster and early demise in every ride and tricky situation. A cowboy's life was made up of rides and tricky situations. That's what made it a cowboy's life, and that's also what made it fun. In Degarrin's view, those who didn't like adventure and a little risk should have stayed in town.

Things needed to be lightened up a little.

Degarrin discussed his worries with Louisa. When Sophie arrived home from the wagon that evening, Louisa talked to her about it, too.

"Sophie," she said, "do you think we need to do something to lighten the boys' mood a little?"

"Yes, but I don't know what. This summer has been so wonderful, until now, that is. It was bad enough to lose Danny, but now nothing is fun at all. I don't think it's what Danny would have wanted. He loved everything about La Conquistadora, and I don't think he would have wasted a single day here moping around like everybody is doing now. I think he would be having fun no matter what."

"I think you're right, Sweety. I think Danny would be mighty disappointed in us all. So what shall we do?"

The two ladies sat in silence thinking for a moment. Then Sophie perked up a little.

"You know, Mom, it's been so hot lately. Just this afternoon, Kitten was saying it would be so nice to go swimming just to cool off. The wagon is camped just a few miles from Price Canyon. Maybe everybody could go over for a swim tomorrow afternoon after branding. What do you think?"

Louisa thought about it. Price Canyon was an arm of the lake that stretched up into La Conquistadora. It was easily accessible, and a swimming party in the high heat of summer might be just the thing to revive flagging spirits.

"Maybe so," Louisa said tentatively.

"We could make it a picnic," Sophie said, liking the idea the more she thought about it. "We could have sandwiches and maybe potato salad and cookies for dessert. It might be a nice change."

Louisa was warming to the idea. She could easily organize the food and festivities for a swim party on the lake.

"But, Sophie, there is one little problem. What will the boys use as swimsuits?"

"What's wrong with their birthday suits?" Sophie asked her mother very innocently.

"Not a thing!" Louisa agreed enthusiastically. "It will be so much easier to organize a smaller party, too. Because of course the guest list will have to be cut. But you and Kitten and Christine won't mind staying home, will you? I'll tell you all about it when I get home."

"And exactly why would you be attending a nudist colony swim meet while I stay at home?" Sophie asked, eyes a-twinkle and smiling.

"Because I, unlike you, am a married woman. A passel of birthday suits on cowboys won't bother me a bit."

"Well, I think it might bother Daddy. I imagine somewhere on this place there are enough of something that will pass for bathing suits so that a totally nude orgy need only be a last resort."

"Well, only if you insist. Although I was quite looking forward to it."

"I'm sure you were, Mom."

The next afternoon found the cowboys of La Conquistadora, with Christine and Kitten, packed into pickups bouncing along the dirt road that led to Price Canyon. Sophie was already on her way there with her mother, who, as hostess of the outing, had requisitioned her presence and help. Peggy Hampton and Annie Lloyd were also there to help out. Enough swimwear had been turned up to accommodate those who were not too picky and critical, and there were enough refreshments to satisfy even a hot and hungry crew of cowboys.

Price Canyon was rather spectacular. It was not your typical bucolic bathing scene. The canyon was just that, a deep, rugged canyon that had filled up with water when the dam was built. The bluffs of the canyon wall towered above the water in all but one small place where you could walk down a slope from the road to a small beachhead. Here the water was fairly clear and the bottom sloped off for quite a ways before it fell away and the lake got really deep. It was a good place to swim and play.

Everybody piled out of the pickups and looked around for the best place to trade boots and Levi's for swimsuits. It was decided that the girls would stay behind the pickups while the men headed for a cluster of sizable boulders strewn nearby. The girls were ready first and sat on a tailgate, waiting to whistle their admiration or hoot their disgust.

Frankie Evans led the way, tenderly picking his way barefooted across the prairie toward the water. His body from the neck down was ridiculously white. From the vee of his neck up he was as brown as a berry. Frankie was not alone. All his fellow Anglos shared the albino-bodied, chocolate-faced look, although some also had chocolate lower arms. Only the Mexican boys showed to advantage. The sudden appearance of a barefooted pack of fish-belly-white cowboys, with more than a few knobby knees and faces that didn't match, picking their way down to the water was almost too much for the girls. But what tipped them all over the edge and into helpless laughter was the big cowboy hat that was perched atop every head in the pack. When met with such a reception, the pack froze where it was, bewildered. Then each one looked at his neighbor and then at himself. Light began to dawn. They really did look pretty silly. Tentative, sheepish smiles turned into grins that quickly dissolved into laughter as well. Price Canyon resounded with the noise. The situation was only compounded when, at water's edge, the cowboys took off their hats to reveal albino foreheads that matched the rest of their bodies. The proud cowboys of La Conquistadora resembled nothing so much as they did a herd of badly striped zebras. The only ones to escape the zebra look were the Mexicans, who showed their monochrome coloring to advantage.

Louisa watched in pleasure as the cowboys and the three girls entered the water and began to enjoy its cold contrast to the hot day. It wasn't but a few minutes before there was squealing and splashing to match a beach scene anywhere. The dour mood was broken and the melancholy atmosphere that had descended on La Conquistadora began to lift. Louisa, Peggy Hampton, and Annie Lloyd had set up beach chairs in the shade of the pickups and Louisa's car. From there they sipped iced lemonade and nibbled on oatmeal cookies while watching the antics in the lake. Of course Tommy Ryan had promptly singled Kitten out for his teasing and, in Louisa Degarrin's opinion, forward behavior. Louisa noted that Kitten and Tommy's behavior did not seem to meet with any objection from the girl's mother. Louisa concluded, correctly, that Tommy was precisely the type of boy the Lloyds expected their daughter to marry and spend a lifetime scrimping by with.

While Louisa dwelt rather smugly on the inferior outlook and prospects of the Lloyds, the Ryans, and their like, she blindly watched the watery scene before her, lost in her thoughts. Slowly her mind began to take in the scene, and what she saw began to register. What she saw shattered her air of complacent superiority and slammed her right up against the hard, cold wall of reality. Her beautiful, golden, the-sky's-the-limit daughter was riding on Adam Connor's shoulders, engaging in a free-for-all water fight with Kitten, who was similarly mounted on Tommy Ryan's shoulders. All four were laughing and happy, their eyes aglow. They were having the time of their lives. Through the splashing droplets of Price Canyon and under the hot, glaring sunlight of La Conquistadora, the four may as well have been mirror images. Louisa could see absolutely no difference between her daughter and Kitten Lloyd. They each wore the same expression of utter happiness, with flushed cheeks and shining eyes.

Seated on a wooden lawn chair, in the shade of a pickup truck, out in the middle of the vast New Mexico prairie, Louisa knew the truth as clearly as if Sophie had shouted it to her face. Her daughter, her only child, the one who had always assured her she was going to marry at least a governor's son, was in love with Adam Connor. Adam Connor, who was a drifting saddle tramp, just another Tommy Ryan, a nothing.

Louisa was filled with absolute rage.

"Over my dead body," she screamed to herself. "No, over her dead body! No, over his dead body!"

Louisa was beside herself with fury. Smiling, she continued to play hostess, making sure everyone had plenty to eat and drink and was having a wonderful time. No one had a clue as to her inner battle, certainly not Sophie or Adam.

Through it all Louisa kept repeating to herself, "Act natural, be a good hostess, smile. Don't let Sophie suspect a thing. I have got to get out of here. I have got to get home. I have got to talk to Degarrin."

It was only in times of real trouble that her husband became Degarrin instead of Mike. All afternoon Louisa never thought of him as anything other than Degarrin.

After supper that evening, Louisa and Degarrin went for a little drive. This was a typical way for them to end the day. Degarrin kept a tight watch over the expanse that was La Conquistadora, and one last look around was the way he liked to bid farewell to the sun each day. But this evening, Degarrin was concentrating on his wife's words rather than on the condition of roads and fences, cattle and windmills.

"Louisa, you have to be exaggerating. It can't be as bad as you seem to think. Sophie is a very bright girl. She is our daughter, for goodness' sake. She knows what's what, and she knows what is acceptable and what isn't. I can't believe she would be so foolish as to let herself fall for some cowboy."

"She is only nineteen, Mike, and Adam Connor is extremely handsome and likable. I can easily imagine that she let her head be turned by him. But I don't care how handsome and likable he is, or anything else. This just won't do."

"No, of course it won't," Degarrin agreed. "It's not even to be considered for one second. But maybe it's not as bad as you think," he repeated hopefully. "We raised Sophie right, and she has a lot of sense. Let's see what she has to say before we get too excited."

"When?" Louisa asked. "When shall we talk to her?"

Degarrin considered for a moment before replying. "If there is a problem, which there may be if you're right, we don't want it to go all over the place. The wagon work will be completed in two more days, and all the extra hands will be paid off and gone. It's too bad Adam is one of our full-time cowboys. Otherwise he would be on his way in three days."

"Could you lay him off with the others?" Louisa asked hopefully.

"No, there is not a reason in the world to justify it. He is probably our number one hand and a fine man. He'd be just about perfect if he had never noticed Sophie."

"Well, he did," Louisa stated flatly.

Degarrin was still considering the best way to handle the situation. "We had better wait a few days. When the chuck wagon is back under its shed and the extra crew is gone, things will be back to normal. Then we can talk to Sophie and get to the bottom of this without making a stir."

And so their plan was made. A lot could happen in a few days. Maybe Sophie would suddenly get excited about going off to Albuquerque and the University of New Mexico, or maybe Adam would just go away. Or maybe not.

In mid-July, just a day or two over six weeks from the afternoon Ignacio and Ricky had trotted the chuck wagon and hoodlum wagon out of headquarters to start the summer work, they smartly trotted them back in, and the work was done. The remuda was turned into the summer horse pasture. The chuck wagon was unpacked and parked under the wagon shed, the hoodlum wagon back in the barn. Ignacio returned to the bunkhouse kitchen, and Peggy Hampton returned to her home chores, tending to the needs of husband and daughter rather than the motley bunkhouse crew. Sometimes she missed it, that motley crew being easier to satisfy and more appreciative than the other two.

For many of the cowboys, it was one last night at the bunkhouse, one last luscious breakfast cooked up by Ignacio. Louisa walked down that last morning to say her goodbyes.

"I'm gonna miss these sourdough biscuits, Iggie," Tommy Ryan said.

"You'll be back next year, Tommy. The biscuits will not have changed. They will wait for you," Ignacio assured him.

"Yeah, I might be back," Tommy said.

"You had a good time, Señor Tommy?"

Tommy nodded. "I had a good time, Señor Ignacio."

Ignacio nodded. Then he continued to eat his breakfast with the rest of La Conquistadora's crew. Louisa knew he would remember them and miss them. But there would be next summer and other days, thousands of other days. Some would come back, some would never be seen again, but other young men would come in their places, and the days and the summers would go on and on.

Frankie Evans, Tommy, and Gary Clancy stood outside the bunkhouse in the still early-morning light of their last day at La Conquistadora. The birds were singing in the cottonwoods. An occasional little puff of cotton floated through the air. The sky was the same high, clear blue dome it almost always was, dotted here and there with clouds that might build into an afternoon shower, or might not. Down by the creek the pigs could be seen snuffling along, scouting for something to eat. It was just another La Conquistadora morning.

But to the boys it was the end of an idyll, the end of an adventure. They would not forget it. No one ever forgot a summer wagon work at La Conquistadora. There was just something about it.

Frankie breathed deeply and looked around. "I'm going to miss this old place. I had the time of my life."

That about said it all, so after one more look around, they headed toward the office to pick up their pay.

Chapter 21 — The Monsoon

SOPHIE WALKED IN A golden haze. She had always been happy. La Conquistadora was that kind of place, and she was that kind of girl. But she had never been happy like this.

Sophie was completely consumed by thoughts of him, with the way he walked, the width of his shoulders, the depth of his voice, the beauty of his eyes, and with memories. Her body as well as her mind remembered the touch of those arms, the strength and the power they held, and the feel of his body against hers, lean and hard. Sophie watched for him constantly, and the sight of Adam always brought her pleasure, but sometimes the rare and stolen glimpse was almost overwhelming. Such was always the case if she happened to see him striding about the headquarters. Adam always strode, he never walked or sauntered. He moved with purpose and conviction. But the view that always caught Sophie in the solar plexus and left her breathless, if not helpless, was Adam on horseback. Because Adam on horseback was perfect, there was simply nothing better. He was a total man, so confident, so in command.

It was almost time for breakfast. Sophie stood in the morning cool of her adobe room and gazed out the window across the drive to the bunkhouse. They should be coming soon. Sure enough, she could hear the rumble and the drumming of hundreds of hooves. Adam was bringing the remuda in, and Sophie held her breath. There was no better way to start each day. The dash of two hundred horses galloping past her window in flashes of sorrel and bay with the occasional splashes of white or black was awesome. But the best was yet to come. The best came last.

Suddenly the best whirled past. Adam, so relaxed and so in tune with his mount that they were merely extensions of one another, passed before her window with the flash of a secret smile and an infinitesimal nod.

Sophie sank against her wall and slid down it to the floor, where she sat for a moment consumed with passion and wonder. She had made a decision in the night, or perhaps it had been made for her by all those days and stolen hours. The next time she and Adam were alone, she would hold nothing back. She would give herself to him completely and become his.

"How did I ever end up with such a man?" she wondered.

It was hard to think about breakfast just then, but Rufina was imperiously ringing the dinner gong, so Sophie pulled herself together and headed down the long portal to the dining room. The sky to the south was heavy and dark along the mesa rim, the clouds stacking in shades of purple and gray. The monsoon had been building for weeks. It looked like it might finally mean business.

When Sophie ducked into the dining room, her mother was in the process of seating herself, her father standing behind his chair, waiting politely for Sophie to sit down before doing so himself. With a quick smile, Sophie slid into place. It was a familiar ritual, the kind that develops character and binds a family with tradition.

"You look mighty happy this morning, pussycat," her mother said with a smile. "To what do we attribute this ravishing glow?"

"Lots of sleep and proper nutrition," Sophie promptly assured her mother.

Everybody smiled at everybody. Sophie was so caught up in her private world that she failed to take note of the chill in the room. It was an uncomfortable coolness that she had only encountered a few times with her parents, but on those rare occasions it had never been followed by anything good. Today was no exception.

When breakfast was over and the family was leaving to set about the day, Louisa said casually to her child, "Sophie, stop by the little sitting room for a minute before you take off. Your dad and I want to talk to you about something."

"Sure," Sophie said, and tagged along behind her parents from nineteen years of habit. She noticed the vivid orange of the trumpet vines and saw a hummingbird drinking from one, its wings beating in an invisible whir.

"Look, Momma! See the hummingbird!"

Normally it would have been a shared joy. Today Louisa's only response was a perfunctory smile and a polite nod.

Inside the cozy little sitting room where Sophie had had some of the happiest times of her life, Louisa took a seat at the antique desk along one wall while Sophie plopped down in a worn and familiar wing chair. Degarrin remained standing.

Sophie looked at her parents expectantly, her eyes still shining.

"Sophie," said Louisa, "I have noticed lately that you seem to be paying quite a lot of attention to Adam Connor. Is this my imagination or is there something going on there?"

"Adam is a terrific guy! And just exactly what do you mean, is something going on?" Sophie was caught completely off guard by her mother's questions. Before she could recover, Louisa bulldozed on.

"Your father and I are not pleased. Any relationship at all with him will not be tolerated in any way whatsoever."

"Mother, just exactly what are you talking about? Oh, and you too, Daddy, I suppose you're in on this too?" Finally Sophie's emotional antennae were picking up the alarm signals she should have detected far earlier. Days earlier, in fact. Not that it would have made any difference.

"Sweety, your mom's just worried about you, and so am I. She didn't mean to jump down your throat or get your hackles up. Just tell us what is going on, if anything, between you and Adam."

Sophie was on red alert now.

"What do you mean?" she asked again. "And why are you asking me all this anyway? It's a free country, and what business is it of yours who I like, anyway?"

"Well, Sophie," her father continued inexorably, "you are our only child and we had figured on something a little better for you than a cowboy drifter that any floozie in a cheap bar could have picked up."

"Daddy, that is the rudest, most hateful thing I have ever heard you say! Adam Connor is not just some cowboy drifter. He is a fine man.

He has honor and integrity. He is a war hero, for God's sake! Adam Connor fought and was wounded. He nearly died for this country!"

"I wish he had!" Louisa spat out, unable to stay out of the fray.

"Momma, I won't ever forget that, and I won't forgive it either." Sophie's voice was ice cold, and there was something in her eyes when she looked at her mother that gave Louisa pause.

"All right, all right. Let's just calm down and think about this sanely for a moment, if we can." Louisa decided she had badly overplayed her hand. It was time everybody cooled off a little.

Degarrin wasn't ready to cool off just yet. Turning on his daughter, he asked her in a voice dripping in sarcasm, "What kind of a future do you envision, exactly, for this paragon of yours? This hero?"

"Well, I haven't really thought a lot about it, Daddy, but I'm perfectly sure we can come up with something quite wonderful. And a damned long way from here."

"What is that supposed to mean?" Louisa demanded, suddenly tuning into the first faint alarm bells going off in her own head.

Sophie didn't speak at all for a few minutes. Instead she sat lost in thought. She knew this was make or break time.

"Look," she finally said, "I know you had other plans for me. Plans that didn't allow for me falling in love with someone like Adam. But if you'll just step back and look at it, it isn't bad at all."

"Not bad, not bad at all!" Degarrin snorted.

Sophie ignored his interruption and continued.

"I'm sorry, sugar, but you are going to have to give him up," her father said gently. "It just won't do. He just isn't right for someone from your station in life. You can't go out and hitch your star to a man who slaughters the English language. Someday soon, when you get back to school, you'll meet someone who is right for you and you'll be able to forget all about Adam Connor."

"He doesn't slaughter the English language," Sophie said, so softly it went scarcely heard.

Sophie sat with her head bowed, tears sliding unheeded down her cheeks. She was thinking of the happy life she had had, a lot of it right here in this room, with these two people. All through the years these two had assured her over and over that they loved her. This was the first and only time that love had ever been tested. And it had come up short.

"Adam has his G.I. Bill benefits," Sophie said at last. "He's talked about going to school. He could go to UNM with me. Once he has his education and a good job, he will be just like anyone else you would have wanted for me. Only he'll understand our ranching life, our whole culture. He will fit right in. He won't be a stranger that you have to explain every little thing to."

Sophie's words were reasonable and she had a point. But it was not a point either her mother or her father found palatable.

"Adam Connor will never understand our culture, and it is an insult to us and to yourself to even think such a thing. I cannot imagine that you could even dream of lowering yourself to such a depth. That young man will never be acceptable, and he will never be anywhere near what we wanted for you." Louisa finished speaking and sat straight-backed and rigid, two spots of bright color in her cheeks.

Sophie knew it was hopeless. They would never compromise on this. To them she was eternally a child whose life belonged to them, and not at all to her.

"I can't do it," Sophie said. "I can't let him go."

No more was said. Sophie went to her room to wash her face and try to gain some composure. She would talk to Adam when she was more in control. They had plans to make.

Sophie was thinking out the course of action that she and Adam would have to take. She just assumed that her mother and father would go on about their lives as though they had no daughter and had never had a daughter. She was planning a future when the knock came at her door, and her father's voice, quiet and flat, told her that Adam was waiting in the office and wanted to see her.

Sophie crossed the sand and gravel drive with a heavy heart and reluctant steps. When she learned that her father had confronted Adam face to face, she knew her plans had suffered a major setback. When Degarrin willingly sent her, unchaperoned, to Adam's side, she recognized that the blow may well have been fatal.

Entering the office, Sophie took one look at Adam and knew that the very worst had happened. In his arms she felt the hot tears rise up as well and fought them back.

"Tell me what happened," she whispered, afraid to know but knowing already.

Adam told her.

"I'll go with you," she said fiercely. "I don't need this place or them. I need you. If you leave me now, I know I will never get over you. It will be like a piece of me is gone forever. You'll leave with my heart, and I know I'll never get it back."

"No," he whispered back. "You say that now, but you will get over it. Quicker than you think. You're so young and so beautiful. You can do so much better."

"No I can't."

"You can't give your parents up, Sophie. You can't say goodbye forever to La Conquistadora. I know you say you can, but you can't. Sophie, I can't be the cause of you losing it all. You would hate me, and I couldn't bear it. I just couldn't. It's what you are, Sophie. All this is what makes you, you."

"No it isn't, Adam. I'm what makes me, me. I always will be."

"I have to go now, Sophie," Adam still whispered, afraid to say the hateful words aloud, for once spoken and released upon the wind, they could never be recalled. But for such purpose, a whisper served as well as a shout. The destructive force was just as great.

"No!" Sophie's cry of anguish ripped the silent office, but could not drown out the whisper that still vibrated there.

"No!" she cried again. "Please don't leave me," she begged. "Please, please. You don't understand. Please, please don't go." Her pleading was pitiful, as though her very life depended on it.

"I have to, Sophie. I love you too much not to go."

The door closed softly, gently, behind him when he went. Sophie sat huddled and defeated, her head down on the desk, and cried.

She cried for Adam and for herself, but somewhere beneath the grief a harder knowledge was taking shape. All her life, Sophie had gotten what she wanted, and it had never cost anyone anything. Now it had. What she wanted had cost a good man his livelihood and the only home he had found since the war. What she wanted had cost her parents their only child.

Much later, when all of her tears were spent and the reservoir was finally dry, she raised her head and stared at the familiar wall. A lot of her life had been spent in this room, too. Above the vault was the ever-watchful buffalo that had observed her grow throughout the years. Her father had lifted her a thousand times to pat its black, dry nose and rub its shaggy coat. On one wall hung the map of La Conquistadora that her parents had drafted one long summer when Degarrin had decided to take up surveying. That was before their daughter's time, and the two had tramped the ranch together, mapping out the land and their future. That future had held many hopes and dreams and several children. But only Sophie had heard the call and come. Now Sophie was about to go.

Sophie pulled her chair over to the vault's closed door. She climbed up on its seat and patted the buffalo's dry, black nose, and rubbed his thick, rough coat.

Before leaving the office, Sophie made two telephone calls. One was to Christine, who immediately said that there was nothing she would rather do than drive Sophie into town that afternoon.

The next was to her Aunt Tessa in Albuquerque. Tessa Morgan was Degarrin's sister, and her visits to the ranch had always been bright spots in Sophie's life. She was fun, loved her brother in an irreverent way, was very fond of Louisa, and flatly adored Sophie.

"Aunt Tessa?"

"Yes, Sophie. How are you, dear?" her aunt said immediately, as though she was right next door and they spoke on the phone at least three times a day.

"Aunt Tessa, could I come stay with you for a few days? Just until school starts."

"Of course," her aunt responded promptly, as Sophie had prayed, but known all along she would.

"I mean right now, today."

"That's what I thought you meant. And the answer, of course, is of course. Are you all right, Sophie?"

"No. I'm really not, Aunt Tessa." Sophie's voice had developed a decided tremor.

"Are you going to be all right, sweetheart?"

"Yes, ma'am. I'm going to be just fine if you'll only meet me at the bus station at five o'clock this afternoon."

"I'll be there with bells on, Sophie."

"Thank you, Aunt Tessa."

The tremor was gaining ground, making it almost impossible for Sophie to speak. But she had said all she needed to. Chris would help her, and Tessa would be there.

Sophie didn't show her parents any anger. She didn't seem hurt, and she didn't make a scene. She seemed as cold as ice and was someone they didn't even know.

"I'm going to Albuquerque to Aunt Tessa's until school starts. Christine is taking me to the bus. Her father doesn't know anything about it. You've made enough trouble for one day. I hope you won't make any more over this for Chris and her family, or for Aunt Tessa. Oh, and if you don't want to pay for my college anymore, I don't care at all. If I decide I still want to go, I'll do it on my own."

"Of course we'll pay for your college," her father snapped, not liking the situation at all.

"Suit yourself," said Sophie and left the room.

When Christine came for her, Kitten was with her, determined to show her friendship and support to the very end if need be. And so the three who had grown up with each other, whispering and giggling, and even riding the range, rode off together one last time.

The trip to Clauson was a quiet one. There didn't seem to be too much to say, and Sophie didn't feel like talking anyway. She felt like looking at the land and the sky that were La Conquistadora. Riding down the long red road, Sophie gazed out across the flats to the distant mesas and soaked in the essence and the beauty of this lovely place where she had been a child and had grown up.

Christine and Kitten were careful with her, and Sophie was grateful for their silence. By tomorrow the whole ranch would know. The girl who had always gotten everything she wanted had reached too far, and a good man had walked away because of it. Sophie had always been the one her friends envied: the ranch, the parents, the charmed and golden life. Nobody would envy her now.

• • •

Adam walked into the tempest with no knowledge or anticipation of the coming attack. But even had he been forewarned, he would not have acted differently. He could not have abandoned Sophie, and he would have faced Degarrin under any circumstances. He just would have known it was coming, as he had known when a big allied assault was looming or a big Nazi push was shaping up. Maybe it was just as well he was taken by surprise. At least he hadn't spent time and energy worrying about it.

Every cowboy who ever lived and worked on a big outfit knew better than to fall for the boss's daughter. Danny Parks had known better. Danny had been sweet on Sophie in his quiet way, but Danny understood the line and never crossed it. It's only tricky if you stay caught, Danny had told him once, easy and unhurried, the way Danny said everything. Danny hadn't stayed caught. And Danny was dead now, killed in a branding pen, and none of it had kept him alive.

Adam had known from the beginning that he was holding a losing hand. A drifting cowboy with nothing but a saddle and a war record against one of the most prominent ranching families in New Mexico. He had known it the night of the dance and he had known it every morning since. But knowing and stopping are different things. After the war, after watching good men die who had done everything right, a man stopped expecting that keeping his head down would save him.

Degarrin didn't waste any time or energy on formalities or niceties. He just started right in.

"Adam, I want to talk to you about my daughter."

It didn't sound to Adam like Degarrin was talking about living, breathing, beautiful Sophie. It sounded like he was referring to one of his favorite belongings, a horse, or maybe a nice piece of real estate.

"Her mother and I are very concerned about the relationship between you two. I brought you in here to tell you that it has to stop. No, to tell you that it already has stopped. It's over and you're out of her life. Permanently."

Adam didn't say a word. He just stood looking at Degarrin, sizing him up. He would be easy to take. Pompous, overconfident, accustomed to being the unchallenged king of the roost all his life. It would feel good to beat the hell out of Michael Degarrin.

Although Adam could maintain a stoic and unreadable face, his eyes were another story. When he was seriously crossed, or when danger and the enemy encroached, they turned a chilling cold, fury etched in ice.

While Adam believed he showed Degarrin only an inscrutable poker face, he had actually turned on him the look of murderous rage that comrades and enemies alike had witnessed across the battlefields of Europe.

Adam's assessment of Degarrin was basically accurate. He had worn the mantle of authority for so long and with such success that it had never crossed his mind that there were people who would not bow to his wishes immediately upon his expressing them. But he had never encountered a decorated warrior before. Degarrin decided to change his tactics.

"Son, I have absolutely nothing against you, personally. You're one of the best cowboys we've ever had here. Maybe the very best, and that's saying a lot. It's just that you and Sophie are from different worlds. Neither one of you belongs in the other's."

"You're saying I'm not good enough for your daughter," Adam said, cutting through the rhetoric.

There was a long pause. Finally Degarrin broke the silence.

"That's what I'm saying. You two are from different classes. She was not raised to throw herself away on a hired hand, drifting from job to job. Living by the strength of his back and the health of his body, broken down at forty and with nothing saved and no hope. Never able to provide her with a home or any security, but giving her kids he can't afford. My wife and I did not cherish and provide for our only child to watch her sink down into an underclass of poverty and hopelessness."

"That's a pretty strong case against a man you hardly know," Adam commented. "What does Sophie say?"

"Sophie says you're wonderful and that the two of you will light the world on fire."

Adam smiled the faintest smile, glad to know Sophie had stood bluff and hadn't let them cow her.

"And that is the primary reason I'm here talking to you now," Degarrin said, banishing the smile. "I know Sophie very well, better than you ever will. She is very headstrong and stubborn when she doesn't get her way. In this situation it is a given that she will do something very foolish which we will all regret. If she is not stopped, she will no doubt run off with you and break her mother's heart, and mine, and ruin her life completely."

That didn't sound like such a bad scenario to Adam. If he could just get Sophie away from here for a while, everything could still turn out all right. Once he showed these Degarrins that he had plans and had no intention of spending his life as a saddle tramp, it could all work out. Once he had a chance to show them that, if given just a little time, he could provide very well for Sophie and give her all the best of everything, all would be well. They might even someday be glad he got their precious daughter, and even find him to be the perfect son-in-law.

"I'm not going to stop her." Degarrin once more interrupted Adam's thoughts. "You are."

"How do you figure that?" Adam thought Degarrin had surely taken leave of his senses. There was no way Adam was going to let Sophie get away if she wanted to go with him.

"You are going to leave her for the same reason I'm here talking to you right now. Because you love her. You know how much her mother and I mean to her. You know how much she loves this ranch. La Conquistadora is her anchor, it's her identity. This is her kingdom, she is a princess here, it is what sets her apart from every other girl, and always will. You don't want her to lose any of that, the ranch, or her mother, or me. These are the things that make Sophie who Sophie is. Without them she isn't Sophie anymore, she's just another girl, a ship without an anchor. If you ever see her again after today, that's all she'll be."

"What do you mean?"

"I mean if Sophie leaves with you, she can never come back to this ranch. Neither you nor she will ever be welcome here again. She can never bring her children here, and it may be a very long time, if ever, before her mother or I will want to see her, and we will never want to see you."

Adam was stunned by the cold callousness of Degarrin's words.

"You are talking about your daughter. The only child you have. One of the most wonderful people in the world, certainly the best person I have ever met. How can you treat her like that? How can you love her so little?"

"We would do it because she would have disgraced us all. But we are not going to have to, are we? Because you are going to leave her today, aren't you? Because you love her too much to be the cause of her being stripped of everything she holds dear."

Adam sank down into a hard, straight-backed wooden chair and sat still and silent, his head in his hands.

"I guess you win, Degarrin. I'm just sorry for Sophie. You and her mother are all she has now. Her worst enemies in the world are all she has to count on now."

Degarrin was infuriated by the words, but Adam took no notice. Standing up, taller than Degarrin, Adam put his hat on, a blatant and deliberate display of bad manners and no respect.

Adam looked Degarrin up and down, the murderous look back in his eyes. "I'll be going in a few minutes. But I want to see Sophie first."

Degarrin's first impulse was to refuse. Then he thought about the message in those eyes.

"I'll send her over." Degarrin reached into the desk and held out an envelope. Adam took it without looking at it and slid it into his shirt pocket.

Adam stood alone in the office, waiting.

Sophie came in, and one look told him she already knew. He held her and felt her tears against his chest and fought back his own.

"Tell me what happened," she whispered, and he told her.

"I'll go with you," she said, and the fierce certainty in her voice nearly broke him. She meant it with everything she had. If he said yes, she would walk out that door with him and never look back.

But he couldn't say yes.

"You can't give your parents up, Sophie. You can't say goodbye forever to La Conquistadora. I know you say you can, but you can't.

Sophie, I can't be the cause of you losing it all. You would hate me, and I couldn't bear it."

"No it isn't, Adam. I'm what makes me, me. I always will be."

But Adam wasn't listening. He knew he was right. As hard as it was, it was better to leave her now while she still loved him than to watch that love wither into misery and despair, and maybe into something worse.

"I have to go now, Sophie," he still whispered, afraid to say the hateful words aloud, for once spoken and released upon the wind, they could never be recalled. But for such purpose, a whisper served as well as a shout. The destructive force was just as great.

"No!" Her cry ripped the silent office. "Please don't leave me. Please, please. You don't understand. Please, please don't go."

"I have to, Sophie. I love you too much not to go."

The door closed softly, gently, behind him when he went. Adam Connor walked across the drive. At the bunkhouse, one of the hands waited by a ranch truck, engine idling. The man had his orders: drive Connor as far from La Conquistadora as a tank of gas would carry them.

He took one look at Adam and didn't ask what had happened.

"You played a hell of a hand, Connor. It was an honor sitting at the table."

Adam nodded. He collected his gear from the bunkhouse and threw it in the bed of the truck. Before climbing in, he looked across the drive at the house. Through the front window, he saw Louisa watching him go. She had let Degarrin do the talking, but she was the one who had set it in motion, and they both knew it. Adam touched the brim of his hat to her. It was not a gesture of respect.

He climbed in and they drove out past the corrals where he had worked the horses every morning of his time here, and out of La Conquistadora. He was leaving more than Sophie. He was leaving the ranch that had become his home, the first place since before the war where the work made sense and the land felt right and a man could sleep through the night. The sky to the south was black, the clouds boiling over the mesas.

Adam did not look back. He had learned long ago, in the rubble of a dozen shattered towns across Europe, that looking back was something you could not afford.

• • •

Degarrin's heart sank when Sophie ducked into the dining room that morning, her face aglow. This was going to be bad, and his poor Sophie didn't even see it coming.

Degarrin had not built what he had built to watch it end this way. Thirty years of work (the ranch, the presidency of the Cattle Growers' Association, the standing invitation from the Secretary of Agriculture's office, the reputation that carried weight from Santa Fe to Washington) none of it had come without cost, and none of it would survive his only daughter marrying a hired hand.

He stood behind his chair, waiting politely for her to sit down before doing so himself, and studied his daughter's face across the breakfast table. It suddenly struck him, for the thousandth time, how very beautiful this child of his was. He watched Louisa examine her and saw the set of his wife's jaw and knew the conversation they'd been putting off could not be put off any longer.

"You look mighty happy this morning, pussycat," Louisa said. "To what do we attribute this ravishing glow?"

"Lots of sleep and proper nutrition," Sophie assured them, and everybody smiled at everybody. But Degarrin's smile was hollow. He knew what was coming and he knew his daughter did not.

When breakfast was over, he heard Louisa deliver the line they'd rehearsed, casually, lightly, as though it were nothing at all. "Sophie, stop by the little sitting room for a minute before you take off. Your dad and I want to talk to you about something."

"Sure," Sophie said, and tagged along behind them, and Degarrin watched her notice the trumpet vines and the hummingbird, watched her face light up with the pure, uncomplicated joy of a girl who still believed the world was kind.

"Look, Momma! See the hummingbird!"

Louisa gave a perfunctory smile and a polite nod. It was the cruelest thing Degarrin had ever seen his wife do, and he knew worse was coming.

Inside the sitting room, he remained standing. He knew he had to be there, but he wished he weren't. Sophie looked up at them both with shining eyes, and Louisa began.

"Sophie, I have noticed lately that you seem to be paying quite a lot of attention to Adam Connor. Is this my imagination or is there something going on there?"

Degarrin watched his daughter's face change. He watched the shock register, watched her try to recover, watched Louisa bulldoze on before Sophie could find her footing. He heard himself say things he had rehearsed but hated ("Sweety, your mom's just worried about you, and so am I") and watched those words do nothing at all to soften the blow.

When Sophie fought back, he felt a surge of pride he could not show. When she invoked Adam's war record, his honor, his integrity, Degarrin knew she was right about all of it. And then Louisa said the unforgivable thing.

"I wish he had!"

Degarrin saw the look in Sophie's eyes when she turned on her mother, and he knew something had just broken that would never be repaired.

"Momma, I won't ever forget that, and I won't forgive it either."

He heard himself turn sarcastic ("This paragon of yours? This hero?") and watched Sophie fire back without flinching. "A damned long way from here," she said, and meant it.

Degarrin tried to be gentle. "I'm sorry, sugar, but you are going to have to give him up. It just won't do. He just isn't right for someone from your station in life." He heard himself say "cowboy drifter that any floozie in a cheap bar could have picked up" and winced inwardly at his own cruelty, but he said it because it needed saying and because Louisa needed to hear him say it.

Sophie's words about the G.I. Bill, about UNM, about Adam fitting in, they were reasonable and she had a point. But it was not a point either he or Louisa found palatable. Louisa delivered the final verdict, straight-backed and rigid, two spots of bright color in her cheeks. Degarrin said nothing.

"I can't do it," Sophie said. "I can't let him go."

Degarrin felt a stab of pain he never forgot, one that left as its memento a vague and nagging twinge that faded in and out but lingered on and on.

She went to her room, and Degarrin went to the office and called Adam Connor in.

He knew what this was going to cost him with the crew. Every hand on the place had worked alongside Adam Connor, and most of them liked and respected him. When word got out (and on a ranch, word always got out) they would not forgive Michael Degarrin for running off the best cowboy La Conquistadora had ever had. But the hands had seen this coming. Every last one of them had watched Adam Connor play with fire, and every last one of them knew how that ended.

The young man walked in with no idea what was coming. Degarrin didn't waste any time on formalities or niceties. He just started right in.

"Adam, I want to talk to you about my daughter."

He said the words he had prepared, that it had to stop, that it was over, that Adam was out of her life permanently. He expected the young man to argue, to protest, perhaps to plead. What he got instead was silence, and a pair of eyes that made him take a step backward in his own office.

While Adam believed he showed Degarrin only an inscrutable poker face, what Degarrin actually saw was the look of murderous rage that had been forged across the battlefields of Europe. Degarrin had never encountered a decorated warrior before. He decided to change his tactics.

"Son, I have absolutely nothing against you, personally. You're one of the best cowboys we've ever had here. Maybe the very best, and that's saying a lot."

It was the truth, and Degarrin meant it. But truth and kindness were not the same thing today, and kindness was a luxury he could not afford. He laid out his case: different worlds, different classes, broken down at forty, kids he couldn't afford, poverty and hopelessness. He said it all and meant none of it personally, and knew that didn't matter.

"That's a pretty strong case against a man you hardly know," Adam said, and Degarrin had to concede the point, silently, to himself.

"What does Sophie say?"

"Sophie says you're wonderful and that the two of you will light the world on fire."

Adam smiled, and Degarrin felt something shift inside him that he would spend years trying to name. That smile. This man loved his daughter, and his daughter loved this man, and Degarrin was in the process of destroying them both.

He pressed on. He told Adam about Sophie's stubbornness, about the foolish thing she would do, about breaking hearts and ruining lives. And then he played his final card.

"You are going to leave her for the same reason I'm here talking to you right now. Because you love her." He laid it all out: the ranch, the identity, the princess, the anchor, the things that made Sophie who Sophie was. He told Adam what would happen if Sophie left. No return, no welcome, no children at La Conquistadora, no mother, no father.

"How can you treat her like that?" Adam asked him. "How can you love her so little?"

In later years Degarrin would often recall Adam's words and ask himself the same thing. But at the moment no such second thoughts distracted him.

"Because you are going to leave her today, aren't you? Because you love her too much to be the cause of her being stripped of everything she holds dear."

Adam sank down into the hard, straight-backed wooden chair and sat still and silent, his head in his hands.

"I guess you win, Degarrin. I'm just sorry for Sophie. You and her mother are all she has now. Her worst enemies in the world are all she has to count on now."

Degarrin was infuriated by the words. But when Adam stood up, taller than him, and put his hat on (a blatant and deliberate display of bad manners and no respect) Degarrin said nothing. The murderous look was back in those eyes.

"I'll be going in a few minutes. But I want to see Sophie first."

Degarrin's first impulse was to refuse. Then he thought about the message in those eyes.

"I'll send her over." He reached into the desk and held out the envelope he had prepared that morning. He had put more in it than what was owed, enough to carry the young man a long way from La Conquistadora and make sure he had no reason to come back. Adam took it without counting it and put it in his shirt pocket.

He quit the office, wondering why he felt so much the loser when he had won, hands down. He was losing a good man. The best cowboy the ranch had ever had, but that was the smallest part of it. Adam Connor was an honorable man, a man of real courage and integrity, the kind of man Degarrin might have been proud to call a son under different circumstances. But honor without standing was not enough. Degarrin told himself that, and almost believed it.

He found Louisa at the front window. She was not watching her favorite view. She was watching Adam Connor walk away under a black sky, and there was no apology in her face. Louisa had always wanted Sophie with Danny Parks, safe, appropriate, a match that belonged to their world. Adam Connor had been the danger all along, and Louisa had been slow to see it. But once she did, she had moved without hesitation.

The monsoon was coming. Degarrin could feel the pressure dropping. Every hand on the place would be needed when it hit: stock to move, gates to check, arroyos that would run in minutes. And he had just sent away the best one.

Toby came to the office door that evening. He didn't come in, didn't sit down, didn't take his hat off.

"You put a man in a truck and drove him out past the gate with his gear in the bed." Toby's voice was level and quiet, which was worse than shouting. "That's not letting a man go, Mike. That's leaving him for dead."

He turned and walked back to the bunkhouse. Degarrin had no answer for him, because there wasn't one.

When Sophie left La Conquistadora that afternoon, Degarrin and Louisa were stunned. They had gotten exactly what they had wanted, but things had not gone exactly as they had planned. Adam Connor was gone, but so was their daughter.

They had waited nervously for her to return from her meeting with Adam. They hoped she wouldn't be too angry or too hurt. They hoped she wouldn't make a scene. They hoped things would be back to normal as soon as possible.

Sophie didn't show them any anger. She didn't seem hurt, and she didn't make a scene. She seemed as cold as ice and was someone they didn't even know.

"I'm going to Albuquerque to Aunt Tessa's until school starts. Christine is taking me to the bus. Her father doesn't know anything about it. You've made enough trouble for one day. I hope you won't make any more over this for Chris and her family, or for Aunt Tessa. Oh, and if you don't want to pay for my college anymore, I don't care at all. If I decide I still want to go, I'll do it on my own."

"Of course we'll pay for your college," Degarrin snapped, not liking the situation at all.

"Suit yourself," said Sophie and left the room.

Degarrin stood at the window and watched Christine's car come up the drive, watched Kitten climb out of the back seat to hold the door for Sophie, watched his daughter walk across the gravel with a suitcase in her hand and her back straight and her chin up. She did not look at the house. She did not look back.

Adam Connor was gone. And so was their daughter.

The sky opened. The monsoon broke over La Conquistadora with a fury that rattled the thick adobe walls and drove the hands from the corrals to the shelter of the bunkhouse porch. Rain hammered the drive until there wasn't a boot track or a tire track left in the gravel. By morning the arroyos would run and the dust would be laid and the land would look as clean and new as it always did after a storm. Those who were left would collect the scattered pieces and move on, because there was stock to tend and work to do.

Chapter 22 — Clearing

AUTUMN CAME AS EVER to La Conquistadora, with touches of October's crispness and hints of November's cold lurking just around the corner. It was only October, and the month Louisa had always claimed as her favorite, yet she felt the chill of winter despite the warmth of the sun and the gold of its light. The days were spectacular, as they always were that time of year, the last hurrah, the swan song of summer. The monsoon was a memory now, the arroyos quiet, the land washed clean and settling into the dry clarity of fall. The sky had put away its summer storms for the high, pale blue of October, so vast and still it seemed like it might never cloud again. But the chill Louisa felt was not brought on by shortened days or falling temperatures. Hers was the chill that sprang from an autumn of the heart.

Sophie had been gone close to three months now. Tessa relayed the news that she seemed fine, if a little thinner. That was what Tessa said, carefully and cheerfully, and Louisa had learned to hear what lived between those careful, cheerful words. Tessa missed the niece that bubbled and giggled. But she was gone, and in her place was a girl who was seldom available and always distant. The rest Louisa pieced together from what she could observe herself: the phone calls Sophie cut short or didn't answer, the letters that didn't come, the silence that had settled over her daughter like a door quietly closed. Sophie had not talked, not to Tessa and not to Louisa or Degarrin. The familiar Sophie had gone away. Louisa, Degarrin, Tessa, and even Sophie, herself, could do little more than hope that she would come back soon.

It irritated Louisa to have Degarrin and herself on the outside of whatever Sophie had built around herself. She just wanted to grab her daughter by the shoulder and give her a good shake, shouting at her to "stop it, just stop it!" But underneath the irritation and the anger there was the relentless crawl of fear that grew a little every day. Louisa knew her daughter very well. She knew from a lifetime of experience that if something really angered Sophie, she never forgot. There was no doubt about it. Louisa and her husband had made Sophie not just angry, but furious. They had hurt her, too. Had messed up her plans and had tampered with her life.

These not too pleasant thoughts were going through Louisa's mind as she drove across the cattle guard. Sitting around the house did no good. Degarrin was somewhere on the ranch, busy with the fall shipping, which at least gave him something to do. Maybe she would feel better if she took a little drive.

Having no particular destination in mind, Louisa drove up the steep winding road east of headquarters out of habit more than anything else. Up on the plateau, she just kept driving. Finally, up ahead of her, she could see the rimrocks of the Indian Rock Mesa. Looking at the red stone bluffs, Louisa was suddenly reminded of Danny. Another very special person she had lost. Beset by a most unusual bleakness, it occurred to Louisa that the summer had yielded a bitter harvest indeed. But memories of Danny could not be darkened, even by such a heavy hand as death itself. He had been such an embodiment of laughter and life that at thoughts of him, Louisa began to smile, and suddenly she knew her destination. Although she had always meant to, Louisa had never gone in search of Juan's and Danny's map rock.

"Well, Danny, I could certainly use a little guidance today. Maybe your map will do the trick, now if only I had a map to find it."

But Juan had told her well. The map rock was where the last Indian guided by it, and Juan and Danny, and maybe a long-forgotten cowboy or two, had left it, waiting for Louisa's coming.

It was a great sandstone boulder, resting at only the lightest of angles, but well up the mesa side. Its face was flat and very smooth, ideal for the lines and drawings that long-gone navigators had pecked out and chiseled. Standing at its apex, Louisa looked down on the rock's decorated surface. She was mystified and tantalized.

"What did it mean?" she wondered. "Was that winding dotted line a trail? And this one perhaps the river? Were these mountains and hills? Or none of the above?"

Scattered here and there across the map rock were the outlines of animals: deer and antelope, a snake, and even a man. It certainly seemed to be a map, but of what? Louisa felt the depiction before her was the key to something, but to what, she did not know.

"Am I looking at the ranges of La Conquistadora? Or of some distant hunting ground? Or is this perhaps just the result of boredom, or artistic expression, or both?"

Louisa had voiced her questions to the sky and land around her, but no answer was given in response. Sighing, she sank down to sit upon the rock. The morning sun had warmed its surface and the mild heat felt good against her skin. For some time Louisa sat enjoying the silence and the sunlight, studying the map rock and its mystery. But she could not read the past and would never know its meaning. She thought of Danny again, and what he had told her once about the old Indian who came to him in a dream and showed him how to see what was hidden in plain sight: every kind of arrowhead and spear point and scraper, all the things left behind by people who had walked this same ground. After that dream Danny's eyes knew what to look for, and he could find what others walked right past. Louisa wished she had that gift today.

Sighing yet again, she turned her thoughts from the past to the present and to the future. This turn of view brought no more clarity and certainty than had her perusal of the past.

"I wonder if I was wrong about Adam?" She voiced the thought that had been nagging her. "I wonder if I should have listened to Sophie instead of to all my prejudices? I didn't want him in our family because I thought he wouldn't fit and wasn't good enough. I thought he would destroy our family and all it stood for, but it seems like our family is destroyed anyway. He might have fit just fine, and he might have been quite good enough. Sophie said he was." There was a long pause of silence and then that sigh again. "At any rate, putting up with Adam, be he perfect or deplorable, would have been a lot better than not having Sophie anymore. I hope Sophie comes back. Please, God, don't let her stay gone forever."

Hot tears slid down Louisa's cheeks to be dried by the warmth of the sun's timeless rays.

When Louisa returned home later that day, she had regained her composure. Only the Indian Rock Mesa and its map rock were privy to her doubts and fears, only they witnessed her buried remorse.

The next morning Louisa wandered into the kitchen, drawn by the warm smell of cinnamon and the low sound of voices. Pete had dropped by to see his sister. Rufina greeted him with delight.

"Pete! Mi hijo, I am so glad to see you! Come in, come in and sit down. You look so tired, I know you have been working too hard."

Sinking into a chair at the kitchen table, Pete was forced to agree.

"Yes, it's true. I have been working very hard. But I decided this morning that I must go and see my sister, I must make sure that she is well. So here I am."

"Yes, here we are and I am fine as always, Pete. But I worry about you. You look thinner. I just baked cinnamon rolls, your favorites, I know. You must have one, or several. Miss Louisa won't mind."

Pete nodded agreeably and waited patiently while Rufina scurried to fetch a warm, fragrant cinnamon roll and a cup of rich coffee for him.

"Sister," Pete commented while he waited, "Miss Louisa seems troubled and Señor Degarrin is most unpleasant lately."

"Yes, all the world knows that. It's Miss Sophie. I don't think she has called or written since the day she left."

"It's a pity," said Pete.

Rufina's razor-sharp knife sliced out Pete's cinnamon roll. "Humpf." She snorted. "Señor Degarrin and Miss Louisa bring all their troubles on themselves. I do miss Miss Sophie, though. I like that girl."

Rufina placed a cup of coffee and the cinnamon roll in front of her little brother. "Here you go, Pete, I hope you like the roll. There are more where it came from."

"You have cream for the coffee?" Pete asked his sister.

"Of course I have cream! So thick and good you can stand a spoon in it!"

Pete and Rufina smiled at each other. Louisa stood in the doorway with her coffee and watched them, and thought that in La Conquistadora's kitchen at least, the world was perfect.

Chapter 23 — Said and Done

AS AUTUMN SLIPPED AWAY toward winter, Sophie settled into life as a student at the University of New Mexico. She realized that she was fading away from life in the peaceful harbor of her Aunt Tessa's adobe home on Las Lomas Street near the university. She and her aunt discussed her depression and deep sadness. They decided she needed to be with people her own age who were busily engaged in living their lives and forming plans and dreams.

"Sophie, I know every day is hard for you. If I could make the hurt go away I would. But I can't, and I love you too much to let you just fade out and stop existing. When I was in college I was in a sorority, and it was great fun. I think some fun is what you need."

Sophie just looked at her and shook her head. "Aunt Tessa, I can't."

"Yes, you can," her aunt responded with determination.

Sophie pledged a sorority and took up residence at the Alpha Delta Pi house. The place was brimming with girls who were very excited about everything, but mostly about the abundance of G.I.s back from the war. The sorority house was abuzz with the ecstasies and lamentations of loves gone either right or awry. Even though she knew she needed human contact, stories of love, either good or bad, were not something Sophie could tolerate at present. She spent her time studying hard, to block out thoughts of Adam, or else wandering around the campus and its surrounding tree-lined streets, thinking endlessly of him. The studying bore the best results, and Sophie easily made the dean's list. The endless walking kept her legs in shape and her mind in turmoil. Adam, or the lack of Adam, dominated and obsessed her. She dreamed of the day he would come for her, and she watched constantly for his arrival. Sophie imagined that magic moment over and over again. Sometimes it would be in the student union, sometimes at the sorority house, other times as she was walking across the campus. She never doubted that he would come. The only thing that ever changed in her scenario was the location of their meeting.

Christmas came and went, but Adam did not. Sophie could not stand the thought of a La Conquistadora Yuletide. For the first time in her life, she spent Christmas away from home. As far away as she could get, in fact. Accepting a sorority sister's invitation, Sophie found herself in the mountains of Vermont and there she enjoyed a New England holiday with all its snow and traditions. Nothing could have been further from luminarias and La Posada. Sophie had known she wanted distance and change, but in Vermont she discovered how she missed the old and the familiar. But no one ever knew Sophie wasn't having a wonderful time. She laughed, she toasted the season, she skied and skated, and even dashed through the snow in a one-horse sleigh. Sophie threw her heart into everything, and was appalled at how little she felt. It was as though all her heart and half her mind were missing. She knew it wouldn't do, but there seemed to be little, if anything, she could do about it.

The spring semester came and went. Every letter from La Conquistadora said, "Sophie, come home..."

Occasionally she would even reply, but she didn't go home. Instead she spent the summer working on a dude ranch in Wyoming instead of the real thing in New Mexico. She could see the worry in Tessa, and the letters from La Conquistadora carried the same quiet concern. In truth, Sophie began to worry too. She knew it wasn't right to still feel so little, as though she were observing the world through a windowpane, and to still have Adam roaming somewhere in her mind every single waking moment and often in her dreams as well.

As time went by, the seasons and semesters came and went, but the presence and the memories of Adam never left, never even faded. The days continued to flow past, like a river of time, but Adam never came.

"I must put all this behind me. Today will be different," Sophie assured herself each morning when she rose. She continued to throw herself into any and everything, frantic to make a connection, to feel something other than abandonment and despair. As a result, Sophie became an honor student, and by her senior year, the chairman of almost every committee, and the life of every party. Life became a frenetic whirl, going faster and faster, but providing less and less.

In the end it was Joe Carpenter who slowed it down.

Sophie had noticed him around. It was hard not to, because wherever she was likely to be, Joe was certain to be there. He was tall and solid and persistent without being pushy. By sheer determination and tenacity he dented the armor that she wore unawares, and got her attention. Joe took on an identity and became a real man to her and not just a dance partner and beer bust buddy.

Joe asked Sophie to dances and to the movies, and to anything else that came along. Sometimes she accepted, sometimes she didn't. Joe never got upset or even discouraged when she turned him down. He just kept on asking.

What Sophie learned about Joe Carpenter over time came in pieces. His family was from Midland, West Texas, the heart of oil country. He had served in the Army, first in Africa and then in Europe, and had come to UNM to complete his final year in college. His European sojourn had taught him to love mountains, and when he came home he found that Texas was just too flat. He was a law student now, contracts and property, which he planned to combine with his geology training to wheel and deal in the oil business. He planned to be the richest member of his family, maybe the richest man in Midland.

Sophie could not have cared less about his future plans and showed almost no interest in hearing about them. She knew this about herself and was not proud of it, but she could not seem to help it. Joe, for his part, never seemed to mind. He kept coming back, undaunted, and Sophie found herself grateful for it. She could see that he saw something in her, and that he had decided she was worth the trouble.

Spring was in the air, its promise floating lightly on the evening breeze, caressing Sophie's cheeks and ruffling her still long, honey-colored hair. She was sitting on the balcony of the sorority house, facing east, watching the western sunset color the Sandia Mountains watermelon pink. It was a spectacular show, and one that was staged nightly. Sophie never grew tired of it and seldom missed an evening's performance.

"I thought I'd find you here," said Betsy Loftus, stepping through the door and onto the balcony.

"Here I am," Sophie said.

"Still looking blue," Betsy commented after an examining glance.

"Do I?" Sophie asked, a little concerned. It was not supposed to show, ever.

"Only to the discerning eyes of your bosom pals," Betsy assured her.

Both girls sat in silence and watched the vivid pink fade out to ordinary twilight.

"Do you think you will ever get over him, Sophie? It's been such a long time now."

"Apparently not, Betsy, and certainly not for a lack of trying."

"I'll vouch for that. You have definitely not spent your time languishing and wearing the willow."

"No," Sophie agreed. "I haven't, but I might as well have. I don't seem any better today than the day he left."

"I guess it just takes time," Betsy advised for the thousandth time.

"It's been time," Sophie responded, also for the thousandth time. "I don't have any more time. School's out in a couple of months. I don't know what I'll do then."

"You could go to graduate school."

Sophie looked bored.

"You could go to Europe."

Sophie looked skeptical.

"You could do what I'm planning on doing."

"Which is?"

"Get married."

"What?" Sophie looked absolutely astonished.

"Sophie, don't look so astonished. You know I'm getting married. At least I hope you do. You are supposed to be one of my bridesmaids, you know. Unless of course it slipped your mind!"

"I know you're getting married, silly. But I'm not!"

"Well, I've been thinking, and I think you should."

Sophie scrutinized her friend, searching for signs of derangement. Finally she said, very calmly, "Betsy, you have lost your mind."

Betsy grabbed her friend's wrists imperatively and looked her square in the eye. "I don't think so, Sophie. Listen to me for a minute."

On seeing her friend's determination, Sophie resigned herself to her fate and waited patiently for Betsy to voice her plan. Sophie had long since learned that there was no stopping Betsy when she got going.

"I'm listening," she prompted.

"Well, it's been three years, and he's not going to come back. That's obvious, by now."

Sophie made no comment. She couldn't. In her heart of hearts, she still imagined the day that Adam would come back into her life. She just couldn't seem to let go of that belief, that silent hope.

"You've got to forget him. Or at least make his memory manageable. I'm thinking if you were married, you'd have a new direction, a new trail to blaze, so to speak. I think you have to get something really major between Adam and you. Otherwise he's always going to be available, just a call away. You could end up wasting your whole life waiting for that call, and I don't think it's ever going to come. If you're going to have to spend your life without him, and you are, at least don't do it alone. Don't let him beat you that way! You offered him the best, and he turned it down. Don't let yourself dry up and wither away in bitterness because he let you down and is never coming back! Lots of times the one you want is not the one you get. I really think you should take the very best guy available, get married, have a family, and live your life to the very fullest. Otherwise, Adam Connor and your mother and father will have beaten you lock, stock, and barrel."

Betsy's impassioned soliloquy stayed with Sophie far longer than she let on, and made a deeper impression than she wanted to admit. In a curious way, Betsy's words sort of made sense to her and took on the ring, almost, of wisdom.

As a result, Sophie began to view her court with a more assessing eye, sizing up who might and might not do. There was really no contest, of course, Joe Carpenter being the only possible choice. He stood so far above the others. Sophie was not sure what to feel about that, but she knew it was true.

When Joe proposed to Sophie in early May of 1949, she was very honest with him.

"You are handsome and smart and awfully funny. I like you very much, but I don't love you like I should. Not like I should anyway, if I'm going to marry you."

"I love you enough to make up for it. Fifty percent of your love is better than a hundred percent of anyone else's. Sophie, I want to marry you because I love you totally. I want to take care of you, and get whatever the burden is that you're carrying off of you. You need a rest and some tranquility. I've watched you be a whirlwind for three years, and I think you're just about to fly apart. Marry me, baby, and I'll take care of you, and we'll have a lot of fun, too."

There Joe stood, smiling down at her, strong and solid. Sophie realized that this was someone who would care for her and stand by her, and who would very likely love her far more than she deserved. She was beginning to like the idea of being Joe Carpenter's wife.

"Where would we live?" Sophie asked tentatively.

"Anywhere you like," Joe said.

"Not around here," she said. Sophie didn't want to be anywhere near La Conquistadora. She needed to close that chapter and seal it with some distance.

"Not around here," Joe agreed. "Actually," he said, "I was thinking of Carrolton, down in the southeastern part of the state. It's nice there and far enough away from your folks to give you some peace, and close enough to Midland to let me do some business there, but far enough away to give us both some peace from my family."

Sophie was warming rapidly to the plan Betsy had laid out for her. Life with Joe Carpenter might prove very nice, she thought, certainly better than Betsy's alternative offering of withered and wasted bitterness. So it came to pass that Sophie went to bed an engaged woman that night.

Lying in bed, Sophie considered the new turn her life had taken.

She was very hopeful that she had made a wise choice. It was past time for her to get on with her life. In the darkness Sophie listened to her radio, turned down low and playing just for her that night. Vaughn Monroe was singing about ghost riders in the sky. "A ghost rider, that's what Adam is," Sophie thought. "Only he's riding through my heart and through my mind. Just like he rode with me through the tall grasses of La Conquistadora under the high blue skies of summer." Sophie could see them all, Adam and Danny, Frankie, Tommy, Kitten, and Christine, and herself riding forth on a summer's day. She could feel the warm breeze of summer on her cheeks and fell asleep, never knowing the warmth was that of tears, and not a breeze at all.

BOOK TWO

Prologue — Summer of 1969

KYLE LEANED ON THE hood of his Camaro and hardly felt the sear of the sun-baked metal through his Levi's. The car had been sitting in the Carrolton Senior High School parking lot all day long, and even in May, the southeastern New Mexico sun could be relentless. Jason watched his best friend with concern. Kyle knew Jase could tell he was getting singed, he had to be. Jason had already hopped off the hood for that very reason, but seeing Kyle's face, he knew that Kyle was scarcely aware of the pain.

Kyle's dark blond hair had been blown across his forehead by the skittish breeze that had been rising and then fading away all afternoon. His left hand was carelessly thrust into his pants pocket; only the slight tapping of the fingers of his right hand against his denim-clad thigh betrayed his inner agitation. Other than that, he looked calm and in control. Kyle suddenly glanced at his worried friend and flashed a smile that never touched his eyes.

Kyle could feel the rage welling up inside him, and he knew Jason could feel it, too. They had been friends long enough that neither had much trouble reading the other. Once in the car, Jason ordered him, barely in time: "Don't pop the clutch! Just act normal, like nothing's wrong."

Kyle's eyes snapped to meet his friend's. He hadn't said a word to Jason about Amy, but as usual, Jase had correctly summed up the situation without any need for words. Jase was right, he thought. Why give her the satisfaction? Better to show he didn't care. So, just as normal as could be, he swung the Camaro out of its space, comforted by the deep, familiar purr. Cruising toward the exit, he even paused to call a greeting across the fast-emptying lot to Bobby McFarland.

"Hey, Bobby, you going to Hunter's tonight?"

"Hell yes! You'll be there, won't you?"

"Yeah, see you there." So Kyle had kept his cool. No one but Jase would ever know what he was feeling as he watched the rearview mirror and saw Amy lean up against Joel Cannon, just the way she used to lean up against him. He knew exactly how it felt, and a red wash of anger and hate and jealousy poured through him. Kyle suddenly wanted to kill someone; the only problem was who.

Before he could decide, Jase spoke up again. "Don't look. Just drive. Just drive and drive and drive and forget all this shit."

The silver-gray Camaro bore its silent passengers away from the campus, through the quiet streets of Carrolton, some of them green tunnels of cottonwood trees. Out on the empty highway, Kyle opened it up and let the speed and the wind do whatever it could for him. Carrolton fell away behind them, and way off to the west the mountains were just a distant purple, giving a shape to the horizon. To the east, the ground rolled down to the river, a series of hills and breaks laced with little canyons and steep gullies.

After a while, the wind and the speed began to comfort Kyle, and he let the speedometer drift down and down until old Hal, the state trooper that patrolled that stretch of road when he wasn't drinking coffee at the Ramada Inn, would have done no more than wave at them in passing.

"When we broke up, I knew it was going to be bad. I just didn't know it would be this bad," Kyle commented quietly.

Jason was busy digging through a pile of cassettes on the floor between his feet. A whiny, heartbreaker country-western song was playing on the radio. Jason was listening to it with a grin, it sounded just like him, and they both knew it. Jason found what he was looking for and, instead of hazarding a response, popped a cassette of Steppenwolf into the tape player to change the mood. The sounds of freedom and rebellion immediately rocked through the car, and Jason grinned at Kyle, who did not grin back.

Kyle knew Jason well enough to know that part of his friend was just as glad the big Kyle and Amy romance was off, at least for the moment. He could see it in the way Jason relaxed when the subject came up, the way he breathed a little easier. But he could also see that Jason felt a little bad about feeling good; after all, Kyle was his best friend, and he didn't like to see him suffer. Still, with Amy out of the picture, maybe things would go back to normal. Forever and ever, it seemed, the two of them had liked Amy in just the same way: as just a girl they had grown up with and had always known. Then, a year or two ago, Kyle had started to see her in a different way, and things had gotten way out of hand. Women just complicated things, especially when they managed to really get to a guy. Kyle was living proof of how messed up a girl could get you.

"I guess you could get her back. It was your idea to break up. She never wanted to. She'll come back if you ask her to. Listen, she was pretty gone on you. All you'd have to do is call her up, and she'd drop shitface Cannon fast enough." Kyle could hear the reluctance in Jason's voice even as he said it. But it was true, and they both knew it. Amy loved Kyle. The real problem was that Kyle loved her, too.

"I know. But if I go back to her, I'll have to promise to marry her. I know that's what would happen. It's what she wants, and I know I'd wind up doing it sooner or later."

"You were already sleeping with her. Why would you have to get marriage into it? Why screw up a good deal?"

"'Cause it's what she wants. I don't want to use her or hurt her. She wants to get promised, and then she wants to get engaged, and then she wants to get married when we graduate next year."

"So get promised and engaged and married. Shit," Jason said seriously.

"Bullshit. I'm not ready to even think about getting married. Neither is she, but at least I'm smart enough to know it."

"Well, I'm glad that's settled. Let's go over to Romero and get some beers. Juan'll let us have some. Ever since we got elected co-captains of the football team, he's forgotten what an I.D. is."

Juan Soliz ran a hole-in-the-wall cafe and bar grandly styled La Cantina del Sol. The name never caught on, and it was generally called The Canteen by the gringos or La Cantina by the Spanish speakers.

Romero was a little Mexican village, just a wide spot in the road, really, up the river from Carrolton. Whatever local color Romero managed to possess was supplied by La Cantina del Sol. It was the heartbeat of the tiny town, the place where all news was created, based without preference on either fact or fallacy. Its cool adobe walls and dim duskiness had watched romances both flourish and flounder. Here, gloom and despair had been known to deepen, keeping perfect pace with the dropping level in a tequila bottle. Here, as well, Carrolton girls sometimes got the giggles on wine-filled Saturday night dates. You were not supposed to be able to get liquor in New Mexico if you were under twenty-one, but old Juan could turn a blind eye to the youth of the ones he liked. He had always liked Kyle and Jason, and had often allowed Kyle's señorita, Amy, to be one of the Saturday night gigglers. The boys thought he sometimes let them drink a little because they were big tough football stars. But he let them drink because they were boys, and he wanted them to grow up to be men. La Cantina del Sol was a good place for them to try on manhood, try the taste of beer and maybe something harder, a good place for them to bring their girls and inch toward growing up. It was a good place for them, here under Juan's slow old eyes that never missed a thing. Jason and Kyle would have been chagrined and irritated to learn that their parents felt them to be as safe with old Juan as they would have been at home on the sofa with them. Had they known, they might never have gone back, which is why the mothers and fathers, and Juan Soliz, never let on.

The highway had bypassed Romero years ago, and there were only two ways to get there: either you wanted to, or you were lost. Over the years, old Juan had relieved many a young man's thirst and hunger and a few of their distresses. Right now, on a sizzling afternoon, Kyle and Jason were among the few who wanted to get to Romero. So, where the highway and the old road split, they took the narrow, faded ribbon that dipped in a wide rolling arc down to the river. The bridge was an old one and narrow, built for the cars of decades past. It sat high and narrow, not low-slung and wide like the Camaro that hurtled across it now. Once safely across the river, the road meandered along the bank until it wandered into Romero, as if by accident.

Romero had probably never had any dreams of grandeur, but if it had, they had long since dried up and sailed away on the wild west wind. The town sort of sprawled around a central plaza, typical of many Mexican communities. The plaza was grass and dirt in about equal parts. At its center was a weather-beaten bandstand, badly in need of paint, its lumber warped and grayed in places from years of neglect by all but the weather. Why Romero had a bandstand, nobody seemed to know. The town had never had a band, and what musicians it could muster up found playing a guitar in the comfort of their own homes preferable to a mosquito-thick visit to the bandstand. But the bandstand was nice; it gave dignity to the plaza, and the children loved to scramble in and over it. It was a part of Romero, and so, whenever it reached a certain state of decay, someone would always go and nail a new board or two in place. Sometimes there was even talk of everyone getting together for a fiesta and painting the bandstand.

The river wasn't far away, and the long roots of the cottonwoods were able to tap into its moisture. So the plainness and the brownness of Romero were relieved each year by a canopy of green leaves shifting restlessly in the slightest breeze. Those same teasing puffs of air floated tiny tufts of cotton from the trees across the plaza and all through the town, decorating it here and there with bits of summer snow. So, between adobe walls and the leafy shade of summer, there was shelter in Romero from the sun's white heat.

Not much was happening in Romero when Kyle and Jason wheeled into town. A couple of old-timers sat across the way on the post office steps and disinterestedly watched a group of kids play a squealing, sweaty game of tag on the plaza. The arrival of the Camaro caused a brief stir of interest, ebbing as soon as the boys were recognized. They were regulars, their novelty long since worn off, if it had ever existed in the first place, which was questionable. Kyle had been coming to Romero since before he was a toddler. His mother, known to the people of Romero as Miss Sophie, had always loved to come to Romero. She would sit in La Cantina and visit with Juan over a cold drink and a squeeze of lime. Miss Sophie had been coming to Romero since before Kyle had been thought of. Just as the town had watched

Kyle grow up and in some fundamental way considered him one of their own, Old Juan had watched Miss Sophie grow, and his concern for her was equally deep.

The Soliz family was from Encantada, up in the northern part of the state, not far from the vast expanse of La Conquistadora Ranch. For four or five generations, Soliz men had ridden that range, and Old Juan had been a part of their ranks. Back in the twenties, Mr. Michael Degarrin had come to La Conquistadora, to run it for the Stillmores, the very wealthy eastern family that owned all those miles of fence and the sea of grass that was La Conquistadora. But the Stillmores seldom ventured out from their Massachusetts kingdom of sand, salt air, and Atlantic blue. They never came to really know their second kingdom, that which was officially known as El Rancho de La Conquistadora.

But that was all right, just as well, really, because Michael Degarrin had taken to the place as though it were his own. He could not have loved it more if it had been his birthright. His family (his wife, who came to be known to all on the ranch as Miss Louisa, and his daughter, Sophie) both came to share his devotion to La Conquistadora. While the rest of the country was roaring through jazz and Prohibition, La Conquistadora took no notice. While the rest of the nation was struggling and starving through the Great Depression, La Conquistadora was like a world apart: there was no hunger there at all. Its pastures were filled with cattle, its gardens rich with vegetables and flowers. Fruit came from the orchard, and the little dairy herd of Jersey cows and one proud old bull paraded past Casa Blanca each morning, either to or from the milking room. When Degarrin first set eyes on La Conquistadora, he took one look around and called it home.

"This is where I will stay forever and sink our roots," he said. "This is where I will someday bring a wife, and where we will grow old." That was how it all unfolded.

Juan Soliz was only fourteen years old but was already one of the hands when Degarrin arrived, and he continued on through the years, as other Soliz men had done before him and would continue long after him, as well. Juan had been one of the many who had caught Miss Sophie's horses for her, tossed her up on their backs, and watched her bounce away. And when she bounced a bit too much and ended up in the dirt, he was just as likely to be the one who picked her up, brushed the tears away when necessary, dusted her off, and tossed her back up again. If Kyle was Romero's, Miss Sophie was Old Juan's.

After the war and college and all her troubles, Miss Sophie had left La Conquistadora and come to Carrolton, the bride of Joe Carpenter, a young up-and-coming lawyer. Carpenter had come up and come far; he had in fact grown rich. Joe Carpenter had never known the land, and he had never been a cowboy. Maybe that was why she married him. It had not been a big event, and while a far cry from a grand celebration, Degarrin and Miss Louisa had seemed pleased, and hopeful.

About that time, Old Juan's joints were getting stiff and he was tired of having his spine beaten down from the constant jarring of a life on horseback. He looked around and found Romero, where the winters were a little warmer and he had some cousins to make him feel welcome and a little bit at home. It was really just a coincidence that the village was so close to Carrolton, Miss Sophie's new home. But it was a happy coincidence all the same.

Thus, very early in the fifties, Romero got a new citizen and a new establishment. La Cantina del Sol was born. Sophie Louisa Degarrin Carpenter came often; it reminded her of home.

At the moment, though, it was her son who briefly blocked the doorway, pausing for a moment while his eyes adjusted down from the bright afternoon glare.

"Hola, hombres, entren, entren." Juan waved them into the room. He was of the old school and always came to shake the hands of his special guests.

Slouched on bar stools covered in creaking rawhide, the boys rested their elbows on the hard, cool surface of the shiny red tiles of Old Juan's bar and relaxed, drawn into the serenity of La Cantina. La Cantina seemed somehow to exist outside of time, in a way that most places did not, with its once-bright hanging serapes, a little faded now, and its dark, deep leather booths where it seemed eternity itself would never intrude.

Old Juan gave them both a bottle of golden Mexican beer to keep them occupied while he fried up some tortilla tostadas for them. He watched with the pleased satisfaction of a true aficionado as the boys worked through the first bites.

"God damn, Juan!" exclaimed Jason, wiping his eyes. "What did you put in this stuff? It's hotter than hell!"

"Whew, that's the truth," Kyle agreed, wiping both lips and eyes.

Juan watched as the boys settled back and sighed in contentment, with cold beers in hand and satisfied looks on their faces.

"School is out?" It was a rhetorical question. Juan knew as well as anyone that school was out. He'd had his grandkids underfoot yammering about it for ages past. But it was a question that took him where he wanted to go.

"Yeah," Kyle answered, "school's out all right."

Jason, deeply absorbed in his beer, was slow to catch the question. When it did finally penetrate his cortex, he started a little and scurried to respond. "Yes, sir, school is definitely out." He, like Kyle and most of the other Mason County kids, had had good manners pounded into him by very determined parents, particularly courtesy to his elders. Jason was a little worried that Old Juan might take offense at the tardy reply.

It was rare indeed that Juan took offense at either of these two, but he respected courtesy, so he smiled at Jason and nodded the tiniest of acknowledgments, dismissing the incident.

"And so, por la mañana, it is off to La Conquistadora with the two of you?" Again Juan's question was purely rhetorical, as Miss Sophie had that very day graced the patio of Old Juan's cafe. She had dined on enchiladas verdes, Juan's specialty (and perhaps made a little more specially for her) and toasted Old Juan and the world and La Conquistadora with Dos Equis beer and had spoken of her son.

Kyle's response was not enthusiastic. "Yeah, looks like I'm off to the big roundup, but not alone, old Jase here is going with me."

"You do not want to go?" Old Juan only partially feigned surprise. Kyle could see it in the old man's eyes; in spite of his conversation with Kyle's mother, he was still amazed that any young man would hesitate to summer at La Conquistadora. He knew no better place on earth.

"Well, you know," Kyle said, just a little defensively, "I thought there would be some things here in town I'd be doing this summer, instead. But that kind of fell through."

Jason spoke up before the silence could settle. "Not being able to take care of little Miss Amy this summer freed you right up to go be a cowboy." He thumped Kyle on the shoulder a few times for emphasis and grinned at him. "We're going to have a blast, and I can't wait."

"Okay, okay, don't knock me off the damned bar stool!" Kyle began to laugh in spite of himself.

Kyle raised his near-empty Corona. "To La Conquistadora and, in the immortal words of Ray Price, 'to the good times.'"

"To the good times." Jason happily raised his beer on high.

Old Juan's glass, filled with a little tequila and a lot of lime, was lifted ever so slightly as he joined in the toast, but his eyes glowed and he spoke from the heart. "To the best of times."

He held the glass a moment longer than the boys did. Then he set it down carefully, as though it were something fragile, and said, almost to himself, almost not at all, "You go to her while she is still what she is."

Kyle didn't know what to make of that. Jason didn't seem to hear it. Old Juan smiled at them both and wiped the bar with his cloth, and the moment passed.

• • •

His old and weary eyes, for a moment, were not so old and weary. In his mind's eye, Juan saw himself, a younger, stronger man, at La Conquistadora, in a horse corral one early, distant morning long ago.

It was still an early hour and not yet full light. Juan stood back out of the way, under the slanted tile roof of the long saddle shed that stood between the rock wall of the back horse pens and the dull red-painted wooden front corral. The shed floor was deep in soft dirt, kicked up and milled down again by the comings and goings of booted cowboys and the hooves of horses across the span of many years. Before Juan was a seething sea of horseflesh, mostly sorrel, highlighted by an occasional gilding of white, or bay, or dun, or black. This sea of horses was lit by the golden light of early morning, the same clear light that always had, and always would, entice artists to this New Mexico world. The shining light, mixed with the dust raised by over two hundred sets of hooves, blended to create a soft golden haze. Juan Soliz looked across the horses and through the haze to the main house, with its sand-stained adobe walls topped off with dark green shingles. These shades were accented by the bright and different greens of giant cottonwoods, all spread out before a backdrop of climbing sandstone, rimrocked hills, and the early morning sky of flawless blue.

Juan purred almost reverently at the scene before him. “This world, and heaven too.”

The living, moving scene before him shifted with the appearance of the ranch foreman, Toby Lloyd, his daughter Kitten, Christine Hampton, and Sophie Degarrin.

Seeing the approaching girls, Juan’s beautiful smile was a flash of white in the cool dimness of the shed. He turned to his fellow cowboys. “Care to place a bet as to whether the ladies will be joining us on this year’s roundup?” he asked.

Watching as the girls grew closer, the rest of the crew smiled with him. They all knew Toby’s views on range-riding girls, especially his daughter, who thought they were cowboys.

“No takers, Juan,” cowboy Junior Allen answered for them all. “Toby and Degarrin can’t hold out against that bunch. I’m already planning on spending my day shoeing their mounts.”

“I’ll shoe horses all day long if it means Miss Sophie will be riding with us,” Juan stated.

There was a general murmur of agreement from the Conquistadora crew.

• • •

In the familiar comfort of La Cantina del Sol, Old Juan remembered that day well past twenty years ago as if it had only been yesterday.

Next day found Kyle and Jason fast asleep well past the hour Kyle's grandfather, Degarrin, would have considered a good departure time. About the time Degarrin started to watch for their arrival, the boys finally got their act together enough to pack up the Camaro and head for La Conquistadora, some two hundred and fifty miles away.

Sophie walked Kyle to the car, her arm around the waist of her beloved only child. Kyle's arm was tight around her shoulder, as well. There were those who found Sophie Carpenter a little, or a lot, impatient, overbearing, and even overwhelming. Her son was not of that number, and neither was her husband. These two, who knew her best, also loved her best, for her flaws as well as her virtues. Kyle had loved her all his life and could not even imagine a mother he would have rather had.

Joe Carpenter stood on the porch and watched them go. It was there in his father's face: the quiet, steady devotion, the way he tracked Sophie's every movement as though she were something rare that might slip away. After over twenty years of marriage, Joe Carpenter still marveled that he had actually persuaded her to stay as his wife. Kyle knew that about his father. He had always known it. Sophie had a restless heart and there was a wild wind to her spirit that even Kyle could feel at times, like the sun upon his skin.

Up at La Conquistadora, where the boys were expected by afternoon, Louisa was already fretting. "She will have a million things on her mind besides horses and wagon work," she told her husband. "By now I would have thought she would have outgrown it, anyway."

As to that, Degarrin hazarded no comment, and Louisa set about her day's activities with an easier mind.

Chapter 1 — More of Summer, 1969

EVENING FOUND KYLE AND Jason ensconced at Louisa Degarrin's dining table, one on either side of their hostess. At the head of the table sat Kyle's grandfather, Michael Degarrin. Degarrin had gotten over his ill humor that the boys had not arrived at what he considered a reasonable hour. He had expected them in time for lunch and had not coped well with their five o'clock appearance. Kyle had told Jason on the drive up that his grandfather made flying trips to the edge of the mesa to watch for arriving dust trails, and that his mother had not called ahead as she'd promised. From the way Degarrin was holding his jaw, Kyle figured the old man had spent most of the day looking for a plume of dust that never came.

Kyle's grandmother, on the other hand, seemed simply glad to have them there. She had told Kyle on the phone that she wasn't sure he'd come this summer, and her delight that he had, and that he had brought his friend, was plain on her face.

Kyle took the formality of dining with his grandparents as a given, as constant and unfailing as the sunrise. The dining room smelled of roasted meat and fresh bread and the faint sweetness of the roses Louisa always kept on the sideboard. He noticed things, though. He always had. The way his grandfather's hands went flat on the tablecloth when he was displeased, the way they relaxed when the first course came. It was at this very table that he'd had his table manners drilled into him. For Jason it was clearly another matter entirely. His momma had raised him right and he could handle himself anywhere, but Kyle doubted his friend had ever dreamed that people dined like this routinely. If you needed more tea, Kyle's grandmother rang a little silver bell and the cook came in, took your glass away, and returned it in seconds, full of ice and tea with a wedge of lemon and a sprig of mint. If you wanted another dinner roll, the same lady appeared with a woven basket, pulled back a linen napkin for you to make your selection, and then disappeared back into the kitchen to wait for the next summons from Mrs. Degarrin's silver bell. Everybody acted like this was business as usual: the cook, the Degarrins, Kyle. From the look on Jason's face, he was beginning to guess it was.

Degarrin wasted no time laying out the ground rules so there wouldn't be any confusion the next day.

"We start early tomorrow morning, boys. Breakfast is at six thirty, right after that we'll get you started shoeing your string."

"Yes, sir," Kyle answered.

"Yes, sir," Jason quickly echoed, though Kyle could tell from his face that he had no idea what the man was talking about. Looking up, Jason caught Louisa's eye. She gave him a wink so quick he would have doubted it happened if it hadn't been for her merry smile.

After dinner Kyle took Jason for a tour around the headquarters.

"Kyle, you always told me your grandparents lived on a ranch. This is not just a ranch. This place is huge. This headquarters is like out of a movie, it's a whole village! It even has its own post office and zip code! This place is not a ranch. It's a goddamned kingdom!"

"That's how Granddaddy sees it. But any way you look at it, La Conquistadora is an impressive place."

They passed the tack room door on the way, old wood silvered to the color of ash, with horseshoes nailed above the frame and big hand-forged strap hinges that looked like they had been there since the place was built.

They walked the rest of the compound in the last of the light: the saddle shed, the corrals, the old cook shack with the hand-painted sign. Kyle noticed things he hadn't noticed before, or hadn't thought to notice. A section of coyote fence leaning inward where the posts had rotted at the base. A gate that had been wired shut rather than rehung. The paint on the cook shack door, which had once been barn-red, had faded to the color of dried blood and was peeling in long curls. None of it mattered, really. Ranches were always like this; things wore out and got fixed or didn't. But something about the accumulation of small neglects made the place feel different than he remembered, as though it had gotten old when he wasn't looking.

They passed the orchard on their way back. Through the iron gate Kyle could see Danny Parks's memorial under his grandmother's roses, and beside it a second marker, the stone still pale. Jimmy Lucero. He'd been on the crew two summers back. Quiet kid, good with horses. His draft notice came that fall.

He didn't mention it to Jason. Jason was in love with everything he saw.

Breakfast was as fancy as dinner had been. Jason thought it was a trip. Everybody else thought it was normal. Afterward, Louisa joined the boys on the porch to watch the remuda come in. The morning was still, the sky high and clean above the mesas, the same sky it had always been. The horses came pounding up the road in the early golden light, their hooves raising a fine cloud of dust that hung in the still air and caught the sun like something suspended between earth and heaven. Kyle had seen the remuda come in every summer of his life and it still stopped him cold. When the horses had galloped past and into the corral, Jason turned to Louisa with shining eyes.

"This place is wonderful, Mrs. Degarrin."

"I think so."

"I'm going to love it here."

"I do, too."

Degarrin materialized beside them. "All right, Kyle, Jason. Let's get going. We've got a lot of work to get done today."

"Yes, sir." The boys' answer bounced off Degarrin's back. His boots were already tapping down the portal and toward the gate. His two newest hands hurried to catch up. Louisa strolled along behind at her own pace. She wouldn't want to miss a thing, but she had seen it all before.

Toby Lloyd had made the final string assignments the night before. He was under the saddle shed shoeing horses and seeing to it that his short-order farriers were doing the same thing. Quite a few cowboys were busy under the saddle shed, shoeing their rides. Some of the boys knew what they were doing; some didn't and took a little more supervision. The great remuda of La Conquistadora had to be shod. With Toby in charge it would be, and in fact almost was, already. George Price, Larry McIntire, and Sam Cook were all pretty good cowboys, but best of all, they could put shoes on a horse in a hurry. And that's what Toby had them doing.

Sam Cook took Jason in hand and went to work on Tinamite. Sam was tall and quiet, with big square hands that looked like they could shoe a horse or deliver a calf with equal ease, and a slow smile that put people at their ease before he said a word. Belying his name, Tinamite was huge. He stood over sixteen hands and looked like a lot better horse than he was. He routinely was given out to the greenest hand each year.

Sam put his hand out to Jason in greeting. "I'm Sam Cook. Come on and I'll help you get shoes on this old nag." While they worked, Sam told Jason about his family. His great-great-grandfather had left the family plantation, or what was left of it, after the Civil War, departing the South and all it had been, to go to Texas. Once there, he had abandoned his landed-gentry past and started over, running a stable and blacksmith shop beside a river crossing on the cattle trail to Kansas. By all accounts he was successful in his new home and he never looked back. If he sometimes missed the old home place and his life before, no one ever knew it. When asked, he told people he had left Alabama to get away from the hopelessness. Maybe he had. Anyway, he had been a hell of a blacksmith. His great-great-grandson figured the ability was genetic. He was getting on to being a pretty fair smith and farrier himself.

Jason watched Sam deftly handle Tinamite's feet, rasping a little off a hoof here and there until he was satisfied with the fit of a shoe, then pounding horseshoe nails down through the hoof and out the shoe, to be swiftly and surely twisted off and tossed away with a powerful flick of the wrist. The ring of hammer on iron carried across the shed, and the acrid smell of hot steel on hoof drifted through the morning air. Bars of sunlight came through the shed's open sides and laid bright stripes across the packed-earth floor, catching the dust that every hammer blow sent up.

Jason was obviously impressed; Kyle could see it from across the shed. He'd been watching Sam's hands himself, the sure, unhurried reach for each tool, the way he never fought the horse's weight. This was a world his friend knew absolutely nothing about, and Sam seemed to be an expert in all of it. Basking in the attention, Sam was moved to generosity toward his fan.

"You done much riding?" he asked Jason.

"Some," Jason hedged.

"Well, it don't really matter much whether you have or not. There ain't nothing much to riding a horse. And from the looks of your string, they didn't give you any wild ones. You won't have no trouble handling these ponies. And you'll be doing so much riding it won't be no time at all before you'll be an old pro at it."

With these encouraging words Sam finished shoeing Tinamite. Turning to Jason, he grinned. "You ready to shoe the next one?" he asked.

"Sure." Between them that day, for better or for worse, that string got shod and a friendship was born.

Across the shed, the shoeing of Kyle's string was going less smoothly. One of Kyle's horses was a rangy roan named Diamond Jim, who may have been a diamond, but perhaps not of the first water. Diamond Jim was just plain ornery, that was about all you could say of him. Today he was being his usual bratty self. After rearing up a few times, kicking a few times, and jerking his hoof away from Larry McIntire's hands innumerable times, Larry, a wiry, red-faced young man who ran hot in all weather and hotter when provoked, finally got tired of Diamond Jim's silliness and George Price's free advice on what to do and how to shoe. George was Larry's opposite in every way, long and loose-limbed, with a lean face permanently arranged in an expression of mild amusement, as though the whole world existed for his commentary. Kyle kept his mouth shut and tried to be helpful and stay out of the way, all at the same time. Larry ran out of patience long before George showed any sign of winding down. Even without being advised to do so, Larry got his lariat around Diamond Jim's feet and threw him to the ground, much to everyone's surprise. Observing Larry hogtying the astonished roan, George sized up the situation.

"That's good, Larry. That's good, all right. You can throw a horse to shoe him," George assured his compatriot.

"Yes, goddamn it, George. I know you can throw a horse to shoe him. I just got through doing it!"

George thought Larry's touchiness a great joke. He wholeheartedly continued to critique Larry's efforts and technique, and watched him pound the last two shoes on Diamond Jim, who had lost all interest in playing this game. Consequently, the horse was lying limply on its side looking more dead than alive, when Toby came over to check their progress.

"What are you trying to do? Kill that horse? It looks like you succeeded! Hurry up and get him up on his feet, I hate to see a horse mistreated."

"This damned nag has been mistreating me this last hour! What about that?" Larry wanted to know.

"Well, what about what?" Toby answered. "That horse is just a poor dumb animal. What's your excuse?"

Larry was incensed, which made George laugh all the harder and brought a twinkle to Toby's eye. Toby just shook his head and looked mournful. "Do you boys think, between you, that you could show Kyle how to shoe a horse, plain and simple? Like Sam's over there teaching Jason?"

"Well, my great-great-granddaddy was a Don Juan instead of a damn blacksmith. That's why I'm such a great lover instead of a great horse shoer."

"Larry, I don't believe that's a word," was Toby's only comment as he returned to the far end of the saddle shed where he and Degarrin were finishing up their shoeing work, far from the cowboys' antics.

There was only one horse left to be shod in Degarrin's string of mounts, and that was Teddy Blue, Degarrin's favorite horse of all time. Jason looked up from his own shoeing project to see the fanciest horse he had ever seen. Although his experience with horseflesh was not great, it did not have to be to appreciate the animal before him. Jason directed newly appraising eyes at Larado, the horse he was helping Sam shoe.

"How come this horse looks like bargain-basement dog food and that horse looks like filet mignon?" he asked.

Everybody grinned and George chortled. "Because Larado is dog food and Teddy Blue is filet mignon. That's why you get to ride Larado and Mr. Degarrin has Blue."

There wasn't anything blue about Blue. He was a sorrel with a perfect white blaze, four white stocking feet, and a blond mane and tail. His coloring was perfect and his conformation was better. Teddy Blue was also smart as a whip, fast as lightning, and could turn on a dime and give you change. He was also a better cowboy than most men. When Blue was working cattle, he somehow transmitted a message to the herd that he meant business, that all bovines had better do what he wanted and then get out of his way. If they didn't, Blue bared his teeth and bit. Drawing blood was one of Blue's talents. Except for calves, he never bit a calf. With calves, he was extremely careful, nudging them along with his head, or maybe nibbling them with his lips, but never his teeth. Teeth could wait until next year when the babies were older and should know better.

"The horse is red. So, why do they call him Blue?" Jason asked.

Kyle shrugged his shoulders. "He's named for one of Granddaddy's heroes, I think. Some old guy named Teddy Blue."

"Really? I didn't know that," Larry commented. "I figured he was named Teddy Blue just because he was named Teddy Blue."

"Oh, yeah, that's a real good reason," George said. "So, who was this Teddy Blue cat, anyway?" he asked Kyle.

"I don't know. Some old cowboy, I guess. If he was Granddaddy's hero, he's probably dead by now, too."

Suddenly aware of Toby's watchful eye, the boys forgot about Teddy Blue and fell back to work.

"Come on, Blue, old boy. Let's get these shoes on you and then I'll give you some oats and turn you out to run with your friends." Degarrin talked to his old pal as he straightened his mane and rubbed his neck.

Blue had no objection and the shoeing went fast and without a hitch until the last foot. Degarrin was busy working on Blue's left forefoot, trimming and rasping away, when Blue got a little bored. He began to lean on his master, just a little at first. Then a little more.

Degarrin ignored this. After all, he was nearly finished and Blue had been very cooperative, up to now. Blue didn't like being ignored. So he leaned a little more. When Degarrin was just about supporting the whole horse, he finally yelled at his old buddy. Quite a few times, in fact. Blue decided to try something else. When Degarrin least expected it, the horse yanked his foot away and placed it on the ground. Degarrin picked it up again without comment and continued rasping. Teddy Blue was feeling mischievous today. He decided to try his luck again and see what happened. He yanked his foot out of Degarrin's grasp and stamped it firmly down on the ground, his eye rolled back to catch Degarrin's reaction. Blue felt his master's reaction before he saw it.

In one fluid movement Degarrin belted Blue in the belly with the rasp and Blue picked up his foot and put it back in Degarrin's hand. Degarrin grinned and without any further incident finished shoeing his favorite horse in the whole world.

The wagon had a two-day head start, and when the crew finally rode over the last rise and the camp came into view below, Jason pulled up beside Kyle and stared. The chuck wagon sat at the center under its great white canvas fly, the cook fire already sending up a thin line of smoke, Dutch ovens lined up along the edge of the coals and the coffeepot blackened and steady over the flame. To the side stood the hoodlum wagon, the supply rig that hauled everything the chuck wagon couldn't: water drums, branding irons, rope corral, extra firewood. Big thick rolls of heavy canvas, belted with leather straps, lay end to end along the inside of the fly, forming a kind of sofa wall that marked out the camp's living room from the miles of prairie beyond. Downwind, a loop of heavy rope strung between posts held the remuda, or would, once the horses were brought in.

"It's a whole little town," Jason said.

Ignacio Mandragon met them at the chuck wagon with the unhurried authority of a man who had been running La Conquistadora's kitchens since before either of them was born. He looked Jason up and down with dark, appraising eyes.

"You touch my wagon, you ask first. Eggs are in the oat barrels; break one and I send you home. Dutch ovens are mine. The dried peaches are mine. I make the cobbler."

"Yes, sir," Jason said.

"He means it about the cobbler," Kyle told him afterward. "It's a Conquistadora institution."

Life on the range agreed with the boys. Kyle and Jason were given their own tepee, which they pitched with the help of Sam Cook and the advice of George Price. In the few days that the wagon had been out, Kyle and Jason had come to love their new lives as cowboys. The first few days had been a little rough, especially on their bottoms. Even Kyle had been more sore than he thought he would be. After all, he had grown up riding horses, but he had never before ridden the long hard miles of a roundup and cattle drive. However, youth and endless seasons of football, basketball, and track stood the boys in good stead. Sore muscles soon stopped aching and the life of a cowboy riding the open range began to work its spell.

"You know, Kyle, I think old Juan was right. This just may be the best of times."

"Yeah," Kyle acknowledged. "You have to give it to old Juan, I guess he knew what he was talking about. This really is a lot of fun."

"Yeah, and we're getting so good at it."

As to that, Kyle didn't comment. He had spent a lifetime hearing the exploits of dudes critiqued and ridiculed and wasn't about to take on airs or assume any premature claim to credit or skill. In the company they were keeping, that would only be riding for a fall. It was better to go slow, listen up, work hard, and keep your ego in its place.

Jason had never encountered the ranching culture before and, unlike Kyle, was not tuned in to its pitfalls. From the way he carried himself, he had little doubt that he was developing into a fine hand at breakneck speed. Kyle had to admit, Jason did have the makings of a fine hand; the problem was that his idea of his progress was just a little bit accelerated. But he was so likable and so willing that no one seemed to mind, and Jason, from the look of him, took the crew's patience for agreement.

Jason's first assignment to riding drag came on the third day, and he learned two things from it. The first was that drag was the worst job on the roundup: nothing but dust and stragglers and the south end of northbound cattle. The second was that it was also, if Toby wasn't watching, the best place on the drive to practice your roping. The slow-moving dregs of the drag were perfect targets, and every young cowboy on the crew used the dust for cover while they laid loops on anything with legs. Degarrin and Toby did not want La Conquistadora's range cattle harassed and made skittish by the roping antics of junior cowboys. Therefore, roping the drags was strictly forbidden. Therefore, it constantly occurred.

• • •

The prank presented itself during those first days at the wagon, when Jason was still fresh enough to take everything at face value and the crew was still entertained enough by his eagerness to leave him that way.

George Price was the architect. George had a lean face that seemed permanently arranged in an expression of mild amusement at the world and everything in it, and he possessed a seemingly bottomless supply of advice on all subjects, most of it unsolicited and some of it even useful. In Jason, George had found the most willing audience of his career.

It came up naturally enough on a morning when the riders had scattered out to work a sweep of pasture south of camp. George and Larry McIntire were riding with Jason when the young man pulled up and started to swing his leg over the saddle.

"Where are you going?" George asked.

"I need to take a leak."

George looked at him with the patient disbelief of a man watching someone do things the hard way. "Off the horse? You're going to get all the way down and all the way back up again just for that?"

Jason hesitated, one boot still in the stirrup. "Well, yeah."

"Nobody out here does that, Jason," George informed him. "You just stand up in your stirrups, get yourself squared away, and take care of your business. The horse doesn't care. He's been around cowboys his whole life."

Jason looked to Larry, who was sitting his horse a few yards off with a face that gave away nothing.

"That right, Larry?"

"I have never once gotten off a horse to take a leak," Larry said, which was close enough to the truth to survive without a tremor.

Jason climbed back into his saddle and filed the information away with the same good faith he brought to everything else. The instruction had arrived in exactly the same tone and manner as every other piece of cowboy wisdom that had come his way, casually, as if it were so obvious that it barely needed mentioning. Like loosening your cinch before you swim a creek.

The opportunity presented itself later that same morning, when Jason had been working a draw by himself and the call of nature had grown more than he cared to bear. He looked around. Nobody in sight. He recalled George's instructions. Stand in the stirrups. Get squared away. Simple enough.

Jason stood up in his stirrups.

Robin Hood had been plodding along in a state of comfortable half-sleep, paying no particular attention to anything, when his rider's weight shifted suddenly upward and forward in a way that no rider's weight had ever shifted before. The horse's ears went up. He took a couple of quick, uncertain steps to the side.

Jason, standing tall in his stirrups with both hands engaged and his balance already gone, was not in any position to correct anything. Robin Hood, sensing something was wrong but not sure what, took another couple of steps. The angle changed. Physics, which has no sense of humor and takes no one's side, followed its natural course.

What had started as a forward trajectory became something else entirely. The stream ran down the inside of Jason's jeans, along the saddle fender, and onto Robin Hood's side.

Robin Hood had been a patient and cooperative horse through any number of adventures already that summer. He had tolerated his rider's enthusiastic overmanagement, endured some fairly questionable rein handling, and accepted a number of indignities without serious complaint. He drew the line here. He jumped sideways with a conviction that very nearly deposited Jason on the ground, then broke into a stiff-legged, offended trot that bounced his wet and mortified rider in the saddle until Jason could gather him up and bring him to a halt.

Jason found George and Larry at the noon water break. His jeans were still damp and his expression was the kind that warns sensible people to keep their distance.

"Something go wrong out there?" George inquired, with the mild interest of a man receiving news from far away.

"You son of a bitch," Jason said.

"Now, what happened?" George asked, all innocence.

"You know exactly what happened. I tried your cowboy method and I pissed all down my leg and all over the horse."

George considered this for a moment. He appeared to give it genuine thought, which was generous of him, and then he nodded slowly.

"Well, Jason," he said, "I told you how to piss on the horse, and that's exactly what you did."

He let that settle for just a moment. "Good thing I didn't tell you how to piss off a horse."

The water break came apart. Larry, who had been holding together since Jason rode up, was finished, doubled over, gasping for air. Sam Cook, who had heard the whole story secondhand that morning and had been waiting patiently for the payoff, finally let go of whatever composure he had left. Kyle, riding in just in time to catch the last exchange, didn't even know what had happened yet and was laughing anyway, because everybody else was laughing and because the look on Jason's face was a thing to behold.

Jason stood his ground for about five seconds. Then the corners of his mouth gave way, and the battle was lost. He started laughing, too, because he was Jason, and because it was, if he was honest about it, exactly what George had told him to do.

He was still a little damp at lunch. Toby, who missed nothing where his crew was concerned, offered no comment beyond a brief and unreadable glance in George Price's direction. George received it with spotless innocence.

• • •

While Kyle was accepted because he belonged and always had, and because he rode well and easily, putting in a good day's work without fail; and Jason because he was so eager and willing; there was one member of the crew who proved that nothing is ever perfect. The blight on the otherwise perfect La Conquistadora landscape took the form of Rick Howard, a Texas blowhard from the panhandle. He claimed to have done some cowboying for a big-name outfit or two there, and had of course been their best hand. Everything he had ever done before and every other ranch he had worked on was far and away superior to the meager offerings of La Conquistadora. Nothing suited him and everything needed to be changed and improved: the food was bad, the crew was bad, the horses were worthless, and the cattle were culls, even the ranch itself wasn't much. He had expected better from the fabled La Conquistadora.

The crew, in cowboy fashion, held its peace to see how this blight would be dealt with. But their anticipation was not that of amused indulgence, as with Jason. It was based in simmering dislike that was steadily building.

One of the summer work's most tedious tasks each year was rounding up the cattle on La Reyna Mesa and bringing them down onto the flats at La Reyna camp for branding and culling. The grazing on the mesa was excellent, with thick grass and quite a bit of juniper for cover. For years the prime grazing had gone to waste until Degarrin had had the bright idea to try for a water well up there. Everyone thought he was crazy, and he was beginning to wonder himself, when finally, after several dry holes, the driller hit water. Then everyone said he was a genius. Degarrin claimed that he had never doubted it. Now, with the windmill pumping away year after year, the cattle and deer and antelope had a great home with a wonderful view.

The downside to La Reyna Mesa was that there was only one way up or down. This was by way of a beaten-out, two-rut rocky road that was little more than a trail, slipping through the only break in La Reyna's thick rimrock and then winding down the mesa side to the prairie below. As a result, the cattle who ranged there had a tendency to grow wild and woolly, especially those who had managed to avoid being rounded up for a year or two, or even more. Making the La Reyna gather could be quite an adventure.

The day had come and the boys were ready. George and Larry and Sam had told Kyle and Jason all about what might be found up there. Jason knew in his heart of hearts that today would be his day. Today he would really shine.

Toby was unusually terse that morning, and Jason noticed the older hands were quieter than usual. The combination of a marginal trail and spooky cattle could be a problem. It was still early in the work, and this was not the day for cowboys who didn't know what they were doing.

"Who are you riding today, Sam?" Kyle asked his new friend.

"Copperhead. He's got a lot of go and that's what you need to work La Reyna. There's a lot of land to cover up there, you need a strong horse that won't quit on you."

"That sounds like good advice. I guess I'd better ride Jim Bridger, he's my best goer," Kyle said. "How about you, Jason? Who are you riding today?"

"I better ride Blue Bird if energy is what we're looking for," Jason answered.

That morning Toby just mounted up and galloped off toward La Reyna Mesa. He would scatter his riders when they reached the top. The cowboys fanned out behind him, riding at a brisk gallop, working any potential silliness out of their mounts before they reached the mesa. Kyle and Jason joined in the gallop, riding side by side with delighted abandon. There was nothing in their experience to equal racing across an endless land, borne on pounding hooves, with the wind on their faces and the sun in the air. They were riding forth on a summer morning under a high blue canopy to do the work of men, in the company of men. It was a fine sensation, but one so rare that once experienced it was remembered forever.

Everyone galloping on the prairie that morning felt the same abandon and the same exhilaration. Surrounded by the thunder of hooves and the blowing of horses amid the calls of their fellow cowboys, Jason and Kyle began to smile. Catching each other's eye, the smiles grew into grins of pure delight. Swept away by a common thrill of that same delight, the cowboys of La Conquistadora began to whoop and holler. At first just a few were heard, but then the mood was caught by all, and even Toby joined the chorus.

All too soon, it seemed, La Reyna's climb was reached. Jason and Kyle pulled their horses up, still laughing and beaming at each other. Jason sat his horse for a moment, looking out across the flats they had just ridden, the land falling away below them in every direction, and Kyle saw something cross his friend's face, something quieter than excitement, and deeper.

"This life is the best! It is incredible! I can't believe we get paid to do this every day!" Jason exclaimed.

"I can't either," Kyle agreed. "It really is pretty fantastic, isn't it?"

"That run just now, with all the other guys, was out of sight. It had to have been better than sex!" Jason continued.

Kyle, who had actually had sex, and liked it very well, wasn't sure he could agree with that.

"Well, I don't know if I'd go quite that far, Jase. But it was damn close."

The boys started up the trail to the top of La Reyna Mesa.

Just as expected, working the mesa proved difficult. The cattle were more wild than not, preferring to run where they pleased rather than where a mounted rider tried to herd them. But La Conquistadora's cowboys were top drawer, and their cowboying skills exceeded the cattle's abilities to run and hide. After a few hours of sweating, hard riding, and more than a little cussing, the roundup was made. Now the hard part began.

Degarrin, on Teddy Blue, conferred with Toby under the blazing sun. The herd of recalcitrant bovines now had to be negotiated down off the high mesa top and collected up at the bottom before being steered to corrals for branding. It had already been a long, hard day and it still had a long way to go.

Bob Turner was sent to pilot the leaders down and hold the first of the herd at the bottom. He was an old man, over sixty, but he had spent many years working cattle and riding the ranges of many far-flung ranches. La Conquistadora was the ranch he had returned to the most over the years. He knew its expanses, and its folds and ridges as well as any man. Before long there was a winding ribbon of bawling, skittish Herefords stretching down the mesa side. Things were going pretty well.

Jason had been galloping back and forth, working the hell out of the herd that was still on the mesa top, waiting to start down. He kept the edges of the herd neat and trim, without so much as a hint of a straggler. It was clearly pissing him off that he was having to do all this cowboying by himself. The rest of the cowboys just sat their horses, watching both the cattle and Jason work themselves into a sweat.

"Oh well," Jason muttered to himself, "somebody's got to do this job! I guess if no one will help me, I'll just have to do it myself."

To show he was more than equal to the task at hand, Jason redoubled his efforts. Kicking and spinning and turning, he shouted and herded that herd. Jason was a cowboy with a mission, like a cowboy in a movie. He would get the job done, even if he had to do it himself.

Kyle watched his childhood friend's transformation into top hand with a growing grin.

"Why are you sitting there on your ass while I do all the work?" Jason demanded of Kyle as he rode past. "Why don't you kick that old nag of yours and help me a little?"

"Well, Jase, my old horse is kind of tired. And besides, it looks to me like you're doing quite a job by yourself."

Totally disgusted, Jason rode away.

Toby had been monitoring Jason's efforts with an ever more jaundiced eye. He rode over to where Jason was working so hard, and being such a hand.

"Son, I want you to do something for me," Toby said to Jason.

"Yes, sir."

"You see that little rise over there with the juniper bush?"

"Yes, sir."

"Well, I want you to ride over there, and get off your horse, and sit down in the shade of that juniper, and watch these cows go down this hill."

"Yes, sir."

Toby Lloyd, Degarrin on Teddy Blue, and the crew of La Conquistadora herded a lot of cattle down off the mesa and onto the flats below that summer morning.

That same morning on La Reyna Mesa, Jason learned an awful lot about working cattle and being and becoming a cowboy.

• • •

Toward the end of that first week at the wagon, when the days had settled into a rhythm that Kyle's body was only just beginning to accept, George Price announced after supper one evening that it was time to go skiing.

Jason looked up from his plate. "Skiing?"

"Sand skiing," George said, as though this explained everything.

Sam Cook went to the chuck wagon and rummaged through one of Ignacio's crannies, those mysterious compartments that seemed to exist outside the normal geometry of the wagon and held things no one knew were in there until they were needed. Into this same findable-only-by-Ignacio category fell barber shears that looked suspiciously like the shears used on horses' manes and tails, straight-edge razors that only old Alejandro Romero had ever been able to use safely, and a tin of liniment that Ignacio swore by and everyone else swore at. Sam rummaged past all of these and produced a rolled-up cowhide, stiff and cracked from years of rolling and unrolling. What set it apart from any other old hide were two holes cut into the front end and a loop of lariat rope threaded through two more slits a couple of feet back.

"What do we do with that thing?" Jason asked, not entirely convinced.

"You stand on it," George said. "Somebody ties the other end to a saddle horn, and you hold on and try to stay upright."

They rode the quarter mile down to the creek, every man saddled, because nobody on a ranch walks anywhere when a hundred and fifty horses are standing within earshot. Kyle had grown up knowing this, but Jason still looked a little amazed every time the whole crew mounted up to go a distance a man could cover on foot in five minutes. The creek bed was bone dry, a wide pale ribbon of packed sand and fine gravel that curved away between low cutbanks fringed with salt cedar and the dusty green of young cottonwoods. The late sun had dropped behind the mesa and the sand had cooled just enough to hold a bootprint without burning through the sole.

Sam dallied a lariat through the holes in the hide and handed the coil up to Larry McIntire, who was already mounted on a big bay and looking pleased with himself. Larry was not a man who needed an excuse to run a horse, and his red face was already lit up at the prospect. George spread the hide flat on the sand.

"Let her rip," George said.

Larry put his spurs to the bay, who dug into the sand and took off at a gallop. George leaned back and let the rope do the work, shifting his weight with automatic ease as the hide skimmed across the packed sand in a spray of grit that caught the last of the light. He made it look easy, the turn at the far end, the second pass back, and he was grinning when Larry eased up and trotted the horse back to the starting point.

"Your turn, Jason," George said, stepping off the hide and dusting himself.

Jason needed no encouragement. He stepped onto the hide, took the rope handle in both hands, and nodded at Larry with the confidence of a man who had never been dragged across anything at speed.

Larry kicked. The horse jumped. Jason lasted about forty yards before the hide caught a ripple of harder ground and bucked sideways, and he went rolling through the sand and came up spitting grit. Larry swung around and rode back with the same mild concern he might have shown a dropped glove.

"That was good," George observed. "You almost made it look like you meant to do that."

"Let me go again," Jason said.

He went again, and stayed up longer, and went again after that. Every man on the crew tried his hand at it with varied success. Kyle rode the hide twice and managed to stay upright both times, though the second run ended at a sand drift that deposited him in a manner that was not entirely graceful. Sam, being Sam, rode it quietly and well and did not feel the need to say much about it afterward. Larry, who turned out to be a surprisingly good skier when he wasn't busy running the tow horse, argued that he was clearly the best. George disagreed, on principle, and cited specific deficiencies in Larry's form that only an expert eye could detect.

By the time the sun had made its farewell, the western sky going from gold to deep rose to something close to violet, the color washing halfway up the arch and holding there as if it had no place else to be, they were all played out and ready to call it a day. They rode back to camp in the thickening dusk, the horses walking loose-reined and unhurried, their hooves quiet on the grass. The mesa stood dark against the last of the light and the first stars were coming through above it. Kyle sat easy in the saddle and watched the sky and felt something settle in his chest that he hadn't known was unsettled. The land was enormous and still and it did not care that he was there, but he was glad to be in it all the same.

Chapter 2 — Adam Arrives

KYLE FLANKED CALVES THAT afternoon teamed up with Larry McIntire. Jason was paired with George Price and, after his lesson under the juniper tree, had decided to take advantage of any coaching that might come his way. He listened sharply whenever George happened to pass along a clue or two on the fine points of calf flanking. They were both learning quickly, and it would not be very long before their days of calf wrestling were over, replaced by smooth, efficient flanking that would be noted and valued. Not so happily progressing were Sam Cook and his partner, Rick Howard. Not surprisingly, calves were flanked differently and better on some other ranch, in some other place, according to Rick. Sam was a mild-mannered and patient young man, but even he was growing more than a little tired of Rick Howard. It showed in the set of Sam's jaw and the way he'd stopped answering back.

Every afternoon in the branding corral, it was normally Degarrin who ran the Conquistadora brand, stamping each calf with the renowned three-pointed crown. But today Degarrin had elected to rope, so it was Toby who wielded the hot iron while Degarrin heeled calves and dragged them out of the herd. The iron hissed each time it met hide, and the smoke drifted up sharp with the smell of singed hair, a smell that lived in their clothes and followed them to their bedrolls at night. Joe Crooks took Toby's usual job castrating, while Ben Brumment wielded the vaccinating needle. Tom Slaten would be sharing the roping honors with the boss that afternoon, as La Conquistadora always had two heelers to keep up a steady supply for the flankers.

Even though it was still early in the season, the cowboys were coming together to work in unison as a team. Things were going well, and It showed in the way his grandfather and Toby moved through the corral without needing to say much to each other.

Kyle noticed his grandfather keeping one eye on the road. When a pickup pulled up beside the corral and a man stood talking to Louisa at the gate, Degarrin wasted no time.

"Let's take a little break, Toby," he said, riding toward the gate.

"Whew, I'm ready for a break, all right," Kyle told Larry as they headed toward the water barrel that sat on the tailgate of a pickup parked in the corner of the corral. Gathered around the water barrel, the cowboys drank dippers of cold water and poured others over their heads and down their backs. The water was so cold it made Kyle's teeth ache, and when he poured a dipper down the back of his neck, the shock of it against his sun-heated skin was the finest thing he'd felt all day.

Sam went up to Jason and slapped him on the back.

"You're doing real good, Jase. It looks like you just about got calf flanking nailed down. Next we'll have to work on roping. You're already about three-quarters cowboy, I figure by this time next week, you'll be all the way there."

"Thanks, Sam. After this morning, I guess I still have a long way to go."

"Working cattle's like anything else, I guess, Jason. You just have to take a little while and get the hang of it, then it's like falling off a log. It's not a real big trick to outsmart a cow."

Jason grinned back at Sam.

"Speaking of roping, Sam, did you see who showed up just now?" Larry asked.

"Yeah, I saw. I'm glad I'm not the one roping with Degarrin, 'cause you know he's going to give him his horse."

"You know it. Hey Tom, did you see who you're going to be roping with?" Larry asked a little gleefully.

"I sure did. But that's all right. I don't mind looking the fool, but I'd rather it was you."

"Yeah, you wish," Larry answered.

"What are you guys talking about?" Kyle asked.

"See that guy your granddaddy's handing his horse to?" Sam answered for them all.

"Yes."

"That is the world champion calf roper. That's Adam Connor."

Kyle just watched. Hero worship is contagious. Kyle and Jason came down with a full-blown case that afternoon, joining the epidemic that already held sway at La Conquistadora. They had been impressed with Degarrin's and Tom Slaten's roping skills. Jason couldn't imagine anyone better than Degarrin. Kyle could, because he had seen his grandfather rope when he was a younger man with a surer eye and a stronger arm. But both men's efforts lost their shine when held up to the bright light of Adam's perfect loops, each tossed so lazily and landing so surely. Adam rode and roped with the grace and élan of a natural and a champion. He was the stuff heroes were made of.

The last calf had been roped, the branding irons put away, and the cows and calves sprayed for ticks and lice. The branding-iron smoke still hung in the corral, a thin blue haze that smelled of singed hair and tasted like copper at the back of the throat. Above the pens, a pair of buzzards rode the thermals in slow circles, patient and unhurried, the way they did all day every day on La Conquistadora. The day's labors were drawing to a close when the cattle were turned out of the corral and held in a loose herd while the mothers found their babies and paired up. Before finally calling it a day, the cowboys mounted up one more time and drove their charges out a ways into the pasture, away from camp and back where they belonged, on the wide ranges, grazing.

Adam joined in the little drive. Kyle watched him as they rode. The man seemed at home on this land in a way that went deeper than a summer's visit, as though the ranch were as much a part of him as the roping. Kyle knew parts of the story, more than his grandparents realized, probably. They had told it in pieces over the years, the way families do with things that are not quite comfortable to speak of directly, and Kyle had been listening longer and more carefully than they gave him credit for. Adam Connor had worked on La Conquistadora a long time ago, the summer Kyle's mother was nineteen. Something had happened, and Adam had left. Years later, after he had made quite a name for himself on the rodeo circuit, he and Degarrin had run into each other at the state fair in Albuquerque. Degarrin had held forth his hand in something close to friendship, and Adam had accepted. From that time forward, Degarrin and Louisa had made Adam welcome at La Conquistadora. Louisa had never invited him to stay overnight in their home; some barriers, it seemed, could not be crossed. But he had dined there on numerous evenings, and many times had stayed once more in La Conquistadora's bunkhouse and ridden forth of an early morning with its crew.

What the nature of that old connection was, exactly, Kyle had never been told. His mother's name came up around Adam Connor the way a bruise comes up around a bump, slowly, and tender to the touch. Kyle knew better than to press.

But watching Adam now, the way the man's eyes moved across the land as if he were memorizing it, the way his hand rested on the saddle horn with the quiet possession of someone who had once lost this place and knew it could be lost again, Kyle thought of something his grandmother had said on the phone last spring. She hadn't been talking to Kyle. She'd been talking to his mother, and Kyle had picked up the extension to make a call and heard Louisa's voice, tight and careful: Your father is tired, Sophie. He's more tired than he lets on. Kyle had hung up softly. It wasn't the words that stayed with him. It was the way his grandmother said "tired," as if she meant something larger than sleep could fix.

Riding beside the herd, Adam seemed distant for a time, as though his mind were somewhere else entirely. Then he smiled, and whatever shadow had been on him passed, and he looked friendly and approachable again. Kyle rode closer and decided to try his luck.

"Mr. Connor, I'm Kyle Carpenter," Kyle said, holding out his hand. "I wanted to tell you how much I admired your roping this afternoon. I don't guess there was ever anybody better than you when it comes to riding and roping."

Adam grasped the offered hand and shook it firmly.

"I'm glad to meet you, Kyle, and thanks for the compliment. There are probably more, but I know for sure there was one fellow that could outdo me at roping and riding and at just about everything else, any day of the week."

"Who?" Kyle asked, not at all convinced.

"A boy named Danny. He was a cowboy right here on this ranch."

"Danny Parks," Kyle said matter-of-factly. "I've heard my grandparents talk about him, and my mother, too. He must have been something really special. Momma and Grandmother always get tears in their eyes when they talk about Danny."

"So do I," Adam said softly. Then, studying Kyle's face, he smiled with a warmth that seemed to come from somewhere very deep. "So, you are Sophie's son. I've heard a lot about you. I am very glad to finally meet you. I knew your mother a long, long time ago."

Kyle smiled back. Adam seemed like a genuinely good person, and the way he said Kyle's mother's name carried something in it that Kyle couldn't quite place but recognized all the same.

Kyle was already up the next morning, coffee in hand, when Jason settled onto the bedroll beside him to watch the sky lighten in the east. Dawn was just a few minutes away and its overture lit the morning air and gave chase to the shadows and darkness of the night. Few had been the occasions in Jason's life that he had been both awake and alert to greet the day. But at this moment, he could see why Kyle's grandmother said that morning was the very best of the day: a clean start, bright with promise. A meadowlark was singing from a fencepost somewhere behind the wagon, and the coffeepot sat by the fire's last coals, ticking as it cooled.

"What are you sittin' there smilin' like a jackass for?" Rick Howard demanded to know as he sat down beside Jason on the bedroll that was now way too crowded for Jason's taste.

Jason's bright start had just taken on a serious cloud.

Rick sat there, scowling across the endless prairies, past the mesas near and distant, toward the new day.

"I hate this place," he said. "I should have stayed in Texas."

Jason had been looking at the ground, the way he sometimes did. Kyle watched him look up. A change came over Jason's face that he had never seen before, not in all the years he'd known him.

"Yeah," Jason agreed, "maybe you just should have stayed in Texas."

Rick turned his dark scowl to include Jason's angry face, then swept it back across the rolling land that wasn't Texas.

"For two cents, I'd leave this damned place."

Without a thought, Jason was on his feet, his hand in his pocket.

"Here's two cents," was all he said.

Rick was also on his feet and the two young men stood toe to toe, one open hand with two pennies in its palm between them. Jason's hand was steady. Kyle could see the pulse beating in his friend's neck, but the hand didn't shake. There was a sudden hush under the fly and around the cook fire. Every eye was on them and not a muscle moved. Everyone was waiting, but no one said a word.

Kyle held his breath. He could see Toby watching, calculating whether this would end in a fist fight. From the look on the crew's faces, Rick Howard would have a lot of takers if it did.

Rick seemed to be getting the same idea. With a sneer for Jason and for all of La Conquistadora, he took the two cents, then turned to pack his gear and haul freight.

Jason became a one-man receiving line. Every cowboy lined up to shake his hand and clap him on the back. Old Joe nodded at him and winked. Even Toby smiled with approval when he shook his hand.

"Good work, Jason," he said. "I'm proud to have you on my crew."

His friend stood an inch taller than he had that morning.

"All right, Jase!" Kyle pummeled and hugged his childhood friend, just like on the football field. "You showed that son of a bitch. I could hardly have done it better myself!"

"You couldn't have done it any better, asshole. It was perfect."

"Sure I could have," Kyle assured him.

Chapter 3 — Water and Rain

THE DUST HUNG IN the air all day now, a fine haze that wouldn't clear, and by noon the whole basin shimmered with it. The dust worked into everything: the creases of their necks, the corners of their eyes, the grit that crunched between their teeth at every meal. Underfoot, the grass crackled like old paper. La Conquistadora's spring green was fading out in many places, and in some pastures it was nearly gone altogether. The great ranch was a business that ran on cattle, and the only thing that made thousands of cattle possible was plenty of rain and lots of good grass. The ranges of La Conquistadora could produce the grass, that had been proven decade after decade, but it could not grow a single blade without the rains. Thus far the rains had been tantalizingly fickle: a shower here and one there, enough to keep things growing and a little bit of green showing, but not enough to let Degarrin relax and rest easy. The summer grass crop had simply not yet been made, to say nothing of the acres upon acres of grass that had to be waving across La Conquistadora's miles by late autumn. If that crop failed to materialize before the first freeze, the ranch and its hungry herds would not be able to make it through the long winter that was coming closer with each passing day.

Toby began to look a little worried and Degarrin's temper started to fray a little around the edges. Louisa told him not to worry and reminded him that it had always rained before, that it would rain this time, too. Degarrin reminded her of the fifties, when it hadn't rained at all. Toby took to checking the western horizon after every string change, hat pushed back, squinting into the glare. Everybody, from the boss to the hoodlum, began to watch the sky. And the sky was beautiful, a high-crested ocean of the purest and clearest blue, with billowing fluffy clouds that often grew and multiplied into truly awesome thunderheads by afternoon. But then the evening came and the clouds went to bed. Sometimes they rose early the next morning to regroup and marshal their efforts for rain, and sometimes they didn't. Some days it was as though regrouping was just too much effort. On those days the clouds dispersed and spent the day free-floating about their sky, casting shadows, long and short, across the land below.

"As long as those clouds stay around, sooner or later it's got to rain," Degarrin told Louisa, who nodded. "I'm hoping for sooner."

"I am, too," she told him.

They were quiet for a moment. Then Degarrin said, without looking at her, "The Stillmores called again last week."

Louisa's hand paused on the arm of her chair. "And?"

"And nothing. They wanted the quarterly numbers. They always want the quarterly numbers." He stared out at the sky as though the clouds owed him something. "They don't understand what a drought costs, Louisa. They've never stood in a pasture and watched the grass die. They see numbers on a page and they make decisions from a thousand miles away, and they have no idea what any of it means." He stopped himself. He had said more than he intended. "It'll rain," he said, quieter. "It always does."

Louisa didn't answer. She picked up her sewing and the needle found its rhythm, and neither of them spoke of the Stillmores again.

Around the campfire, Toby explained to his crew.

"If those clouds will keep hanging around, eventually we'll get a good rain out of this. But if they float out of here or just dry up, we could be looking at a drought."

Everybody kept on watching the sky.

Finally, one day, the clouds had had enough of caprice and fickleness. As all the weather prophets had predicted, eventually it rained. As was becoming customary, the evening sky had shown promise but had offered no guarantee of rain. Degarrin and Louisa went to bed discouraged and fell asleep in the same state.

The prayers of Louisa and Rufina, and of probably every person on the ranch from dedicated skeptic to true believer, were answered. Sometime in the night, and all over La Conquistadora, without the fanfare of either lightning or of thunder, the clouds simply opened and let their rain begin to fall. Louisa was awakened by the dearest, most welcome sound on any ranch, anywhere: rainfall on the roof. She lay perfectly still, thankful and beaming in the darkness. The curtain at the open window billowed in and touched the foot of the bed, and the room had gone cold in the way that only a thick-walled adobe room goes cold, not a chill but an absence of the day's stored heat, as though the walls had finally let go of whatever warmth the sun had put into them. The smell of it reached her through the open window: the wet earth, the sage, the sharp green scent of grass remembering how to grow.

"Do you hear it?" Degarrin asked.

"Yes, I hear it. It sounds like heaven."

In response, Degarrin slipped his hand over hers and they lay together, holding hands in their bed, and listened to the rain patter down upon their roof.

The rain lasted for two solid days, only it wasn't just rain. The back of the drought, if it had been planning to be drought, was broken by two days of nonstop, full-fledged storm. The wind blew and torrents fell in sheets. The storm was universal, enveloping not just La Conquistadora but half the state as well. The creeks and draws came down with gusto and in more than a few places jumped their banks and spread out across the flats.

Degarrin was stranded at headquarters. There was a lot of mud and water between the wagon and him. Being stuck at home with Louisa, watching the creek rise and listening to the rain fall, suited him just fine. Rain was La Conquistadora's lifeblood and he would always welcome it. Occasionally Louisa would take the umbrella she had unearthed from the depths of some closet for just such an occasion, and together they would brave the elements to walk down and inspect the creek's rising condition. The rain drummed steadily on the umbrella's taut canvas and ran off its edges in a curtain that closed them in together.

"This is beginning to put me in mind of the flood of 1916," Degarrin commented on the second day.

"I've been thinking the same thing," Louisa answered, her eyes never leaving the red river that was rushing past.

They were standing at the corner of the back stables, where the creek commenced its wide bend around the headquarters. The top rung of the pig pen and the dull red of the sty's roof could be seen above the equally red water that ebbed and flowed about it.

"Now, we put that pig pen way up above the high-water line so that wouldn't happen," Degarrin said.

"Yes, but someone forgot to tell the creek it wasn't supposed to come up so high," Louisa answered. "I'm just glad the pigs got out in time and didn't drown."

Degarrin just laughed.

"Those pigs would have to work mighty hard to get drowned. The only time they go near their pen is if somebody's there to feed them. The rest of the time they're out snuffling around, looking for handouts."

Right on cue, the pig herd came waddling from behind the barn.

"Well, good morning," Louisa greeted them. "I'm glad to see you all."

The pigs squealed and grunted happily in response. Louisa was one of their chief sources of handouts. They were always happy to see her.

"Well, I've got better things to do than stand here in the rain, exchanging pleasantries with pigs," Degarrin said, not at all sure that he had much of anything to do and certain there was not any place he could go. He was marooned by high water and roads so wet they could bog a saddle blanket, let alone an Oldsmobile.

"What better things do you have to do?" Louisa asked mischievously, glancing slyly up at him from under the umbrella they shared.

Sliding his arm around her, Degarrin took one last look at his waterlogged kingdom.

"I'll think of something," he said.

Pigs forgotten, they turned and headed for the house.

• • •

Kyle and Jason had put in a long, hard day and were dead asleep in their tent when the rain began to fall. Their awareness of the change in the weather was not quite so blissful as some. They were roused from their slumbers by the impromptu stream that was cutting its course through their tent, the water shockingly cold against their bare feet and rising fast. From the depths of their soggy bedrolls, they learned the sad lesson that there was apparently more to hoisting a tepee than just hoisting it. Apparently the lay of the land merited at least passing consideration, with an eye toward such mundane matters as drainage.

"Damn it," Jason's voice came plaintively from the darkness. "I'm soaking wet."

"Me, too," Kyle was equally dejected.

The two boys continued to lie in the midst of their interior stream, discouraged and with dampened spirits.

"Well, at least it's raining," Kyle ventured.

"Yeah, it's raining all right," Jason agreed.

Those who knew how and where to pitch their tents to accommodate inclement weather slept warm and dry at night. Those who did not, lived and slept under the fly. Kyle and Jason joined the fly dwellers, where they slept a little damp until Joe Ruiz, a barrel-chested man with a black mustache and forearms like fence posts, dried out their bedrolls by draping them near his stoked-up fire. The wagon was shut down for the duration. Neither Toby nor Degarrin were big believers in heroics. This was the land of mañana, and in the midst of a storm, tomorrow would be soon enough.

As time lagged slowly on around the little camp, the air thick with woodsmoke and the smell of wet canvas, decks of cards, Joe's battered old guitar, and a warehouse supply of lies were brought out to pass the time. Rain pooled in the sagging middle of the fly and had to be poked up with a stick every hour or it would come down on whoever sat underneath.

By the third afternoon, the collective state of personal hygiene under the fly had reached a point where even the horses might have had cause for complaint. Cowboys are not, by nature, overly particular about cleanliness when they are in the field, but three days of rain and woodsmoke and close quarters had produced a ripeness that was becoming general knowledge. Larry McIntire was the first one to decide he had had enough.

Without saying anything to anyone, Larry dug a bar of soap out of his war bag, ducked out from under the fly, and walked off into the rain. He walked past the hoodlum wagon and past the woodpile and kept right on going, out across the flat and into the downpour until the camp behind him was nothing but a gray smudge in the rain. He figured he had gone far enough that nobody would see him or hear him or bother him, and he was wrong on all three counts, but he didn't know that yet.

Back under the fly, the card game went on for a little while longer before George Price looked up from his hand and cocked his head to one side.

"You hear that?" he asked.

Everybody listened. Through the steady drum of the rain on the canvas, there was something else, a low, broken sound coming from somewhere out on the flat, rising and falling and rising again.

"That sounds like a cow in trouble," Toby said, and got to his feet. Nobody argued with that assessment, because it did sound like a cow in trouble, and a cow in trouble in this kind of weather could mean real problems. One by one, the crew filed out from under the fly and followed the sound through the rain, Toby in the lead and everybody else stringing along behind in the general spirit of having absolutely nothing better to do.

What they found, about a hundred yards from camp in a little swale where the rain had pooled up around his ankles, was not a cow. It was Larry McIntire, stripped down to nothing but his cowboy boots (because a man will walk barefoot through a lot of things, but a cow camp in the rain is not one of them) lathered head to toe in soap and singing at the top of his lungs with his eyes closed and his face turned up to the sky. He was obviously having the time of his life out there, and just as obviously had not the faintest idea that the entire crew of La Conquistadora was standing in the rain about twenty feet away, watching him do it.

George, as was his custom, was the first to offer an opinion. "I believe," he said, keeping his voice low enough that Larry could not hear him over his own performance, "that is the palest cowboy I have ever seen."

Sam Cook tilted his head and gave the matter some thought. "He's not that pale," Sam said. "It's just the contrast."

"With what?" George wanted to know.

"With the boots."

That was when Jason lost it. The laugh burst out of him before he could help it, loud enough to carry through the rain, and Larry's eyes flew open. For one frozen moment, Larry McIntire stood there in the New Mexico rain, buck naked and covered in soap, wearing nothing but his boots, and stared at the assembled crew of La Conquistadora, who stared right back at him. Nobody moved and nobody spoke and the rain just kept on falling.

Toby looked at Larry for a long moment, then shook his head and turned around and walked back to camp without a word.

Larry stood out there in the rain for a little while longer, rinsing himself off and coming to terms with the situation, before he finally walked back to camp, dripping wet and more than a little red in the face but grinning in spite of himself.

"I didn't think anybody could hear me," he said.

"Larry," George told him, "I'm pretty sure they could hear you in Clauson."

Even so, time limped past, and everyone was delighted when the fourth day dawned with some sun shining through the clouds. Today they could get out of camp and get some work done. The crew was in fine fettle as they saddled up to get back to cowboying.

Chapter 4 — Sophie and Amy

SOPHIE HAD BEEN MARRIED to Joe Carpenter for a long time now, going on twenty years. Throughout each one of those years some things had remained constant and never changing. One was Joe's love for Sophie. He still adored her, had never wavered in his belief that she was a rare and special woman and that he was a lucky man. Another constant in Sophie's life was her nagging feeling that Joe deserved more from her than he got, that she never really loved him enough, because Joe Carpenter was a very good man who had taken only the very best care of her. Joe would have been surprised at Sophie's assessment. She knew that much. She could feel it in the way he looked at her sometimes, as though she still mesmerized him after all these years. She still attracted him, that she knew, and it had never waned. But Joe was a rare and special man, himself. He was very busy, wheeling and dealing and living his life. Sophie suspected that one of the reasons he found her so irresistible was because she was so elusive. She never gave him the faintest reason to doubt her, she was always where she was supposed to be, and yet she knew she had a windlike quality about her that he could sense but not quite hold. Joe had long since come to terms with his marriage. Sophie had, too. He took care of her as best he could, gave her whatever space she seemed to need, and just hoped she would stay. Life carried a tinge of magic when she was around, and lots of fun things happened, and Sophie knew he would have been content to leave it at that forever.

Only Sophie knew that Adam Connor resided in her house, as well as she, her husband, and her son. He took up no room at all, but he was everywhere, still a ghost rider through her heart and through her mind. She had tried to exorcise him from her life, because he did not deserve to hold such a spot. She had felt quite confident that one day she would realize with a start that she had not thought of him in days, or months, or maybe even years. It had been twenty-three years now, since that day in La Conquistadora's office, and he still crossed her mind every day, a dozen times, at least. Sophie was amazed that his hold on her had been so very strong. She had never heard of such a thing. She had read the articles in the grocery store magazines for women that confidently assured her a woman could get over any man alive in six months, five years at the absolute outside. Well, such was not the case, at least not for Sophie Degarrin Carpenter.

Sophie had carried on with her life. She had her son, raised him and had come to love her husband in a warm and rather wonderful way. It had taken years, and when it came, it came so quietly she almost missed it: a morning she woke and realized she had laughed at something Joe said the night before, really laughed, and the surprise of it had brought tears to her eyes. Joe had rescued her. He did not know it, but she did, and she never forgot it. Sophie made sure she paid that debt back, every day, a thousand times over, and she made Joe Carpenter a happy man. A delightful by-product of all this was that between them, they had produced and raised a terrific son who was a tribute to them both.

Sophie had done all that she could and she had given all that she had. If Adam Connor refused to go away, that was just the way it was. There was nothing more that she could do. Besides, she had grown accustomed to his presence. Sometimes he was a comfort, and always he was her companion.

There was one other constant, quieter than Adam and steadier than Joe: La Conquistadora itself. The ranch had been there before Sophie was born and it had always been there when she came back: the same light on the mesas, the same smell of sage through the car windows as she drove in, the same creak of the screen door at Casa Blanca. Even in the years when she could not bring herself to visit, she had carried it inside her like a compass point, the fixed thing by which she oriented everything else. Her father was part of that fixedness. She could not imagine the ranch without him any more than she could imagine it without the sky. But lately there had been a weight in her mother's voice on the telephone, a care in the choosing of words that Louisa did not usually trouble with. It was nothing Sophie could point to. It was only a shade, a shadow, the kind of thing a daughter hears and a stranger never would.

Sophie had never given up her joy in horses or denied herself the great delight she took in riding. A really good gallop on a really good horse was still the best way she knew to send the blues and remorse to perdition. The Carpenter house was both large and nice. The nicest thing about it was that it was across the river in the knolls of Loma Linda. Loma Linda, like all of Carrolton, had started out as open range. Unlike Carrolton proper, Loma Linda had become fields and orchards and had stayed fields and orchards, which is why the little Carpenter clan resided there. Everybody liked it. Sophie had room to see and breathe and keep her mini remuda of two or three horses. Kyle had had space to roam and run and grow up. Loma Linda, in Carrolton, New Mexico, was a good place to call home.

Sophie had learned English equitation from her mother, a product of the Virginia hunt country. But western was the style and the rule on La Conquistadora, as on every other ranch in the west. As a result, Sophie's prowess at English riding did not develop until after her marriage. She wanted to ride, she needed to ride, but she didn't want any reminders of La Conquistadora. Sophie switched styles and became a champion.

The Carpenter house was full of trophies, silver bowls and trays, and boxes of ribbons that Sophie, and later Kyle, had won. Even now, if there was a show going on over at the Carrolton Horse Arena, and the mood hit her, Sophie might saddle up of a Saturday morning and ride over to blow the competition away. She was a natural.

Early one morning, while the son of the house was off cowboying on a place called La Conquistadora, the lady of the house was out inspecting her own kingdom. It promised to be a beautiful day. The stable smelled the way it always did, hay and leather and the sweet warm breath of horses, and Sophie stood in it the way other women stood in kitchens, entirely at home. The sky held a scattering of puffy white clouds that by evening might help create a spectacular sunset.

Meanwhile, sun glistened on the bright hues of the trumpets and hollyhocks that Sophie had long ago planted all around the stable. It was a perfect morning for a ride. Even if it hadn't been, Sophie would have been down at the corral, saying good morning to her horses.

Jerry Clyde got tapped this morning. He had not had a good run in a few days and needed to be put over a few fences as well. There was no point in letting him get rusty and go soft because Kyle wasn't there to ride him. Sophie slipped the bridle on Jerry Clyde and led him out the gate and over to the tack room door. She was busily brushing him and discussing the day with him when she was interrupted by the crunch of a car turning into her gravel driveway.

Sophie was surprised to look up and see Amy Jeffers in her little white Mustang pulling in.

Amy rolled down the window.

"Hi, Sophie," she said, a little sheepishly.

"Hi, Amy," Sophie replied, genuinely and happily. She had always liked Amy. She was a sweet, pretty girl and an excellent rider.

"Are you still speaking to me?" Amy asked.

"Of course. Why wouldn't I be?"

"I broke up with your son."

"I expect he'll live." Then, with a speculative glance at Amy's slightly worn expression, Sophie hazarded a comment. "Perhaps it's just a passing thing?"

Amy grinned.

"Perhaps."

The two ladies smiled at each other.

"I thought you might need some help keeping these guys ridden, with Kyle gone and all."

"I do. Choose your pleasure."

"I'll ride Clyde. I feel like a good run and a whole bunch of fences."

"Good. So does he. I'll take Magic and we'll be the flashiest, loveliest riders to be seen in Carrolton today."

Amy nodded and smiled some more as she took over grooming Jerry Clyde.

Sophie was right about one thing: she and Amy did make a pretty picture as they trotted along the byroads of Loma Linda that morning.

At the hunt field, Amy put Jerry Clyde through his paces with gusto, running the course several times and exhilarating over each fence.

Sophie paused in her cantering of Magic Moment to watch her. Amy rode the way she did, with an abandon that sometimes could border on recklessness. Clyde and Amy were a good team; he sensed her confidence and she knew all about his ability. Each trusted the other to get them around the course. It was an apparently effortless task. In unison and apparent delight, Amy and Jerry Clyde cantered and galloped, changed leads on the fly, and turned and spun. Best of all, they jumped and jumped.

Jerry Clyde's very enthusiasm seemed to proclaim to all that he had come to go fast and jump high. All he needed was a guide and a little direction. In Amy, he found both that morning. She had come for the same reason, and together they were the perfect team.

At last, tired but extremely self-satisfied, the duo came galloping up to Sophie to be told how wonderful they were. She did not disappoint them.

"You two were wonderful! I don't think he has ever done better, Amy! And Jerry Clyde, you traitor! I thought I was the only one you did magic for! Now I see that it's Amy you'll jump your heart out for."

Amy beamed and blushed a little as she reached down to pat her mount's neck and then to hug it. Both horse and rider were glowing and blowing.

"Did we really look good?" she asked, wanting to hear more.

"You certainly did," Sophie confirmed. "I may have to try to lure you into riding him in the fall show for me."

"Won't Kyle want to do that?" Amy asked.

"I don't know," Kyle's mother replied. "I think Kyle may have decided he's outgrown horse shows. He may think it's too sissy a thing for him to do now that he's older, almost grown, you know." Sophie smiled at Amy and added, "Like you."

"I'll never get too grown up to ride in a horse show," Amy declared, appalled at the notion.

"No, you're like me. You'll ride forever if there is a horse around to ride. But boys are different. At some point they decide that riding English is sissy. I think Kyle has been at that point for quite a while and has just been humoring his poor mom. For example, I'm sure he's having a whole lot more fun on the ranch being a cowboy this summer than he ever had wearing a velvet helmet in the show arena."

"Maybe so," Amy answered, "but I'll bet he's the best rider there, thanks to all the hours he's spent on a flat saddle under a velvet hat!"

Sophie considered this.

"Maybe so," she acknowledged. "But at any rate, spoken like a true believer." She didn't specify whether in the riding style or in the rider. "Which brings us back to where we started. You really are welcome to ride Jerry Clyde in the fall show, or in any other if you like. He likes you and you two will do very well. If he didn't like you and know you love it, he would never have poured his heart out the way he did today. He wanted to please you."

"Do you mean it?" Amy asked.

"Sure I mean it, everything I said." Sophie and Amy were riding side by side at a walk, letting horses and riders both cool down. Sophie continued, "The horse needs to be ridden and I've got my hands full with three. You would be helping me out. And Amy," Sophie leaned toward the girl and whispered, "he never goes like that for Kyle."

"Okay," Amy said, "I'd love to ride him some. My horse, Gabriel, is a really nice all-around horse. I love her dearly, but she doesn't go like Jerry Clyde."

"I wouldn't think so," Sophie thought, but did not say out loud, considering Jerry Clyde's horrifying price tag.

Jerry Clyde had been a typical Joe Carpenter indulgence. If his wife wanted something, Joe simply got it for her. A few years back she had wanted a truly great hunter. Enter Jerry Clyde. Exit, more than a few thousand dollars.

"Speaking of Kyle," which they weren't, "do you hear anything from him?" his mother asked, suspecting that love of horses had not been the only motive behind Amy's early morning visit.

"No, I haven't heard from him since school got out," Amy answered dejectedly. The glowing, bubbling girl of moments earlier had disappeared.

"Want to talk about it?" Sophie didn't know if she should be nosing around in her son's love life, but she suspected that if all were left up to him, things could get botched up pretty fast. Besides, the girl obviously wanted to talk about it. Otherwise, she would have stayed at home and slept late instead of dragging herself out of bed so early on this summer morning to appear, unannounced, on Sophie's doorstep.

"Maybe," Amy hedged, not wanting to appear overly anxious.

"We better have lunch at La Cantina, my treat. You can tell me all about it and we'll figure out the best thing to do."

"Good." Amy was very relieved. Like Jerry Clyde, she needed a little guidance, just a little direction.

Sophie took charge. "Let's ride back and feed these guys a little treat for being so good. We have to give Andalusia a little treat, too, of course."

"Of course," Amy agreed. "Otherwise her feelings would be hurt."

"Exactly," Sophie said. "I always apply the parable of the vineyard: he who labors not receives equally with those who labor long and hard."

"That's only fair."

"Yes, at least that seems to be the attitude of those who labor not. Anyway, after we care for the horses, you go on home and change and I'll pick you up at eleven. How does that sound?"

"Perfect. And Mrs. Carpenter ... thanks."

"Mrs. Carpenter? Call me Sophie. You always do. You always have."

"I know. Thanks, Sophie."

"De nada."

There are a few things that never change. Romero was one of them. The plaza was still dusty, the bandstand still needed a coat of paint, and the cottonwoods still made the tiny town an oasis in the desert. Sophie still liked it as well as ever, and that was very well indeed.

As she stepped through the door of La Cantina, she felt that she was home. If you knew where to look, through the dimness, there on the walls in a place or two were a few photographs taken one long-ago summer on La Conquistadora. Sophie knew where to look. There was the chuck wagon and team, and there was the remuda posed in the rope corral and roaming the range for her hungry eyes. All those horses, dead and gone now, filled a space of wall not far from Danny and Adam, grinning and full of life, on their way to an ice cream social. Kyle was there now, her son on her father's ranch, and she wondered what the summer was making of him. The image that caught at Sophie's heart was the one that she always resolved to walk right by without a glance, but never could. It was a scene of Adam and her standing near an empty rope corral with saddles strewn about. They were engaged in earnest conversation, Adam's hand upon her arm. Sophie had absolutely no memory of that moment, but there it was. The girl in the photograph had a face so open, so unguarded, that Sophie barely recognized her. That girl could feel everything, and Sophie could not remember what that was like. A lost event, preserved through light and film, by David Harvey. Sophie had studied that picture a thousand times, maybe more. She wondered what they had spoken of that day, face to face and heart to heart. She hoped that it had been of something wonderful, maybe of love. Sophie hoped that that picture showed one of the happiest moments of her life, but she could not be sure. She just did not know, and she could not remember, try though she did, and always would.

When Juan Soliz saw who his visitors were, he hurried over, delighted to see them.

As always, Sophie ignored the mere hand, and with both her arms gave her lifelong friend a big hug and a bigger smile.

"Amigo mio, it's good to be here," she said.

"It's better to have you here," Juan responded, ever the cavalier. "And you've brought my second favorite girl! Miss Amy, welcome. I have not seen you for a while."

"No," she agreed, "it's been a while. But I'm glad to be back."

"Where would you ladies like to sit? Your pleasure is my command."

"How about the back table by the window? Then we can admire your patio from air-conditioned comfort," Sophie said.

Because this was what Sophie always said, if the day was hot, and because she always sat at the back table by the patio, Juan was leading the way before she could say the words.

He held her chair for her and settled the napkin across her lap, which he did not always do. His hand rested briefly on her shoulder as she sat, a gesture that was fatherly and unlike him. Sophie glanced up, but Juan was already turning to Amy, his smile as bright and warm as ever.

Over hot, greasy tortilla chips and salsa, the best in the state, Amy and Sophie regarded each other.

"I guess I need advice," Amy confided.

"About...?"

"Boys, I guess."

"Anyone in particular?"

"Your son."

"A good choice. He has always been one of my favorites," Sophie commented.

"Mine, too."

"Well," Sophie said, deciding to cut right to the chase, "what happened?"

"He didn't tell you about it?"

"No. Unfortunately, boys past the age of about three often neglect to tell their mothers their innermost personal thoughts. It's a sad oversight, but a fact of life nonetheless."

Amy smiled, but just a little, not at all distracted by Sophie's lightness.

"I guess I just wanted too much of him," she said. "I wanted it all."

Sophie waited. Amy said nothing more for a moment, lost in her thoughts.

"Meaning what?" Sophie prompted her.

"Oh, sorry. When I say all, that's what I mean. I wanted us to get engaged and get married next summer." Amy looked down at her chips. "Everybody's doing it, Sophie. Susie Padilla got engaged in June because her boyfriend's shipping out. It feels like if you wait, you lose them."

Sophie thought wow, but said, "Well, that is quite a lot, isn't it?"

"I guess so. He didn't go for it, anyway."

Sophie thought I would think not, and waited.

"So I broke up with him and started going out with Joel Cannon."

"How was it?" Sophie asked.

"The pits."

Sophie was enough of a mom to be delighted to know that a good-looking doctor's son was the pits compared to her charming offspring. But there were tears in Amy's eyes when she looked up, and Sophie decided it might not be the best moment for a little levity, that it was probably a real good time to get serious instead.

"I can see that talking about getting that serious probably scared him off," Sophie said, stating what even a blind fool could see, but not a seventeen-year-old girl in love.

"But we are serious, Sophie."

"I know that, sweetie. So does Kyle." Which was true. Sophie knew her son truly loved this little girl. It seemed to be a mutual lifelong devotion, with no particular beginning, that had somehow managed to survive and evolve, growing stronger as time went by.

"Well, if he loves me and he knows it's serious, why won't he make it official and marry me?" Amy asked, on the brink of serious tears.

"All right, Amy, I want you to really think about this question before you answer it." Sophie stayed silent for a second and watched Amy, waiting until she had her full attention.

"Okay," Amy nodded and sniffed, but paid attention.

"What would be the advantage of you and Kyle getting married? If you were married to him, would that give you the freedom to do anything you're not already doing?"

There was a long searching look between the girl and the woman, and a moment of pure honesty.

"No," Amy whispered.

Sophie just nodded her head. She had suspected her son and Amy were sleeping together. They were way too tight not to be.

"Amy, sweety," she said, "what possible reason would you have for wanting to get married? What you and Kyle have is already better than ten marriages out of ten."

"What do you mean?" Amy asked, genuinely puzzled. In her lexicon, marriage meant the ultimate happiness and complete fulfillment. When you were married, you had finally arrived. Sophie could see it on her face, the absolute certainty of a girl who had never had a reason to doubt the fairy tale. Sophie had been that certain once. She remembered her own wedding day, a June morning with all the right flowers and all the right words. Joe had looked at her with such open hope that she had wanted desperately to feel it, too. She had smiled for him, the way you smile when you want very badly for something to be true. It had been a good enough smile. Joe had believed it.

"What I mean is this: right now you and Kyle have it all. You have the freedom to be together as little or as much as you want, and as close as you want. But you don't have to worry and struggle with the hassles of just trying to survive from one day to the next. It takes an amazing amount of effort just to keep a roof over your head and food in your stomach. If you are very young, which you and Kyle are, and which you will still be a year from now when you get out of high school, and if you don't have any skills that will earn you any money, just trying to survive can take the fun and the romance right out of life. Love, no matter how sincere and deep it is, doesn't fare too well under those circumstances. It withers up and dies, and in its debris, there is usually a nasty little harvest of bitterness and hate."

Sophie could see the girl was appalled. Her cheerless scenario had no place in Amy's view of the future, and from the look on her face, she felt betrayed. She had come to lunch with Sophie to get some good food and some even better advice. Instead she was getting whopping amounts of ice water poured on her, and she didn't like it one bit.

Sophie watched all Amy's thoughts play across her face with amusement. Growing up was such a pain, Sophie knew. She also knew when enough was enough.

"But not to worry, Amy. Sophie is going to tell you exactly what to do. Just as soon as we tell Juan what kind of great food we want to eat this beautiful day."

Amy was startled to see that Juan was standing by their table, ready to take their order. She had been so absorbed in her thoughts and in Sophie's words that she had been completely unaware of anything else.

"Green enchiladas for me," Sophie announced to no one's surprise, certainly not Juan's.

"Me, too," Amy echoed.

Sophie eyed the girl speculatively and considered a Dos XX beer for both of them. She decided against it. She did not want Amy drunk, and she did not want Amy to decide later that liquor, and not Sophie, had been talking.

When Juan had retreated to his kitchen to cook up a feast for his two star customers, Sophie returned her attention to her audience of one.

"So what am I supposed to do? Exactly," Amy inquired.

Sophie detected just a touch of sarcasm. She ignored it.

"Well, the best course for you and my son to take is to have your cake and eat it, too."

Amy had to admit that did not sound too bad. It sounded a lot better than listening to her parents harp on and on about how young she was, with her whole life in front of her, and how she was ruining that life, and how she would regret whatever she did for the rest of her life. What a bummer. No, the thought of cake and eating it, too, certainly had a better ring to it.

"What do you mean?" she asked.

"I mean, I am very, very fond of you. I would like you to be a part of my family. In fact, I already sort of think of you that way. But I know, in fact I am just certain, that if you force this issue, one of two things will happen. You and he will never get back together, or you will get him to marry you and in just a few years it will all be over. Marriage is a hard row to hoe in the best of circumstances, and life itself is a minefield. You have to have very heavy armor just to stay alive. I could be wrong, but I don't think you and Kyle would make it. He has big dreams and he would start to blame you if things did not go just right. It would all just get to be too much. Pretty quickly you would start to resent him because you were doing everything you could and things still were not working out the way you had planned, the way you had dreamed. That's where the withering picks up speed. The end, with its bitterness and regret, won't be far behind."

Sophie could see that her vision made Amy mad, but it also scared her. There was a ring of truth about it that the girl didn't like, and Sophie suspected she had seen some of what Sophie described happen in the lives of some of her classmates and some of the older kids that she knew. There were tears in Amy's eyes, mostly from anger. This lunch was still not going well.

"But Amy, none of that has to happen," Sophie hastened to reassure her.

"So what should I do?"

"If you and Kyle manage to work things out and get back together, my advice would be this: do not do anything drastic. Keep on dating and keep on having fun. Finish growing up and getting your acts together. Get as ready as you can to take on life and every challenge that it brings. I have every confidence in you and Kyle being able to handle anything that comes your way. But you have to be ready, and you have to get the timing and the sequence right. If you rush it, if you force it, you may very well kill off the whole thing. The goose will be dead, and there won't be any more eggs for you, or for any of the rest of us, to enjoy."

Amy was a little surprised, and she was blushing, just a bit.

"You really do care about me, don't you, Sophie?" she asked in a small voice.

"Of course I do. Amy, sugar, I would love to have you for a daughter-in-law. But I would also like to keep you for a daughter-in-law, and for that you have to wait."

The green enchiladas came. Amy ate mechanically, mulling over Sophie's words. Sophie ate with relish, delighting in every taste. She was glad she wasn't a kid anymore, trying to chart her best course to happiness. All her battles had been fought. Sophie had learned that in the final analysis, most things really didn't matter much, but that good green chile was a gift of the gods that always merited total attention. Sophie kept her eyes and her concentration on her plate. She did not want to encounter Adam's face and smile at the moment. Sophie preferred that any eyes with tears be Amy's. Adam had long since reaped his share.

"So we should just keep doing what we're doing," Amy said.

"If you want to keep him, that's what I suggest."

"Oh, I want to keep him. But first, I guess I have to get him back."

"I don't see that as a big problem. Do you?"

Chapter 5 — Waiting for the Sun

WHILE LIFE WENT ON in Carrolton and Sophie and Amy rode and talked and enjoyed the summer days, life at La Conquistadora continued its watery, and for the most part welcome, pause. Degarrin was in the minority in that he did not exactly welcome the pause, but he was delighted with the water, and for the sake of rain, he would tolerate a hiatus from work. He, and all the crew, rested and waited.

At the wagon, the cowboys continued to spend their days under the wagon fly, the air close and damp under the sagging canvas, listening to the wind blow and the rain fall. Someone was always mending a cinch or oiling a saddle, and the smell of neatsfoot oil and leather mixed with the woodsmoke that never quite cleared.

“This might be the last storm this old rig has to survive,” Toby commented.

His audience, which consisted of the entire crew, looked startled. “What do you mean?” they demanded. “Where are you going to get a new chuck wagon? They don’t even make them anymore, do they?”

“No,” he answered. “I don’t reckon they do. The day of the old chuck wagon has come and gone. But we’re still hanging on. But not for long.” Toby was enjoying the stunned reaction his words produced.

“What do you mean, Toby?” Larry asked for everyone.

“I mean when the work is done this fall, this old wagon is going to be put out to pasture. From then on, the wagon work won’t involve a wagon anymore. We are replacing it with a surplus army truck.”

“I don’t know as I like the sound of that.” Sam spoke the words everyone was thinking.

"Well, Sam, that's because you're way too conservative to be as young as you are."

"No, I'm not," Sam protested. "I just like things to stay the way they are, when they work just fine, and there's no reason to change."

"Well, son, if that's not the very definition of conservative, I don't know what is!" Toby exclaimed. "Not that it matters what any of us think. Degarrin is going to bring this old place and all its heroes, kicking and screaming, into the twentieth century, now that it's two-thirds over. Half the young men who'd have been lining up to cowboy ten years ago are off fighting now, anyway. We're glad to have the ones we've got."

Kyle hadn't heard about this. He set his coffee down and didn't pick it back up. He guessed he was like Sam. The idea of no chuck wagon was an uncomfortable one. He had spent his whole life visiting this wagon. It was central to the realm of magic that was the summer work, and the fall work, too. He did not want to say goodbye to this old friend. He wanted the old chuck wagon to stay, and he wanted his girlfriend to come back.

Jason, not being bound by the deep ties of heritage and tradition, had a healthy curiosity for anything new under the sun.

"So, Toby, fill us all in on this new 'chuck truck,'" he invited.

"It will be overhauled to be a kitchen on wheels. It will do everything this old wagon does. It will be just the same, only better. The truck will carry a lot more supplies, there will be a big built-in gas stove and oven. Everything will be easier on the cook. Why, there will even be a built-in bed, with a mattress."

Joe Ruiz perked up at that.

"This chuck truck and I might get along pretty good," he said, thinking of a big stove and a bed.

Adam was quiet for a moment. Toby's words had come as a shock to him, maybe more than to anyone else. When Adam finally spoke, there was something in his voice that Kyle hadn't heard before.

"It's kind of sad, in a way. When this old wagon goes by the wayside, it will be the end of an era. It is really just a holdover from the open range days. Fences did away with the open range, now an army truck will do away with the wagon. Really, with pickup trucks and horse trailers, you probably don't need any range camp at all. All the work could be done from headquarters and the bunkhouse. You wouldn't even need to bring the remuda out."

Now even Toby looked shocked, to say nothing of the wrangler.

"Well, let's not go quite that far, Adam," he admonished. "Let's just update to something simple, like a new wagon that just happens to be a truck. There will still be a fly, everybody will still sleep on bedrolls."

"Except for me," Joe Ruiz interrupted, much enamored with the thought of his own bed.

"Except for you," Toby agreed with a grin. "Anyway, I have just as many great memories of this old wagon as anybody. I remember sticking noisy little kids' heads through the wagon spokes to teach them a lesson. And I remember how Adam loved to drive the team on moving day. They always ran away. Adam was the only cowboy who loved to drive them when they ran, and they ran away for the first half mile, every time you hitched them up. You could hear that outfit coming a mile off: the team flat out, the pots and pans banging, the whole rig bouncing over the ruts with the dust pouring off it like smoke."

Adam laughed at that, and for a moment he looked like a much younger man. He could still feel the reins burning in his palms and hear old Ignacio hollering from the back, hanging on for dear life. He was turning his coffee cup slowly between his palms, the way men do when their hands need something to hold.

"But the fact of the matter is, boys, those days are long gone. This old wagon has whiskers, and it takes a lot of upkeep. It wasn't designed to be drug around behind some yahoo driving a power wagon too fast. It was meant to go slowly, at a nice sedate trot, which it ain't in years. It won't survive this treatment forever, which it don't have to. We're getting with the modern world next year. All you sentimental types can stop by the wagon shed for years to come and pay your respects to this old chuck wagon, though. If it's like most everything else around here, it will get stored away and kept forever."

Kyle picked up his coffee again. He could see the sense in it; a truck was faster, carried more, and fewer days out meant fewer men on the payroll. He could hear his father saying it was just good business. But the wagon was the last piece of something that had no replacement, and Kyle knew it. He glanced at Adam and saw the older man's shoulders settle.

In the quiet that followed, Toby stared into his coffee. "The wagon's the least of what's changing around here," he said, almost to no one. Then he seemed to catch himself, and whatever he had been about to add stayed behind his teeth. Kyle waited, but Toby just took a drink and let the rain fill the silence. Adam looked at Toby for a moment longer than seemed easy, then turned away.

"I guess our antiquated little encampment, with its nineteenth-century equipment and methods, must look really strange and out of place to those jet fighter pilots that check up on us every few days," Adam said.

Kyle grinned.

"Those guys are just cowboys, too, Adam. Their horses are just a lot faster and they buck higher."

Everybody laughed.

"I guess you're right," Adam agreed.

• • •

That evening, after Joe had cleaned up from supper and the cook fire had burned down to a bed of glowing coals, the crew settled into their bedrolls under the fly and listened to the rain. It had slowed to a steady patter that was almost peaceful, drumming softly on the canvas overhead and dripping from its edges in long, thin streams. The air smelled of woodsmoke and wet earth and the coffee that nobody seemed to want more of but nobody could quite stop drinking.

The talk had been wandering all evening, the way it does when men have nothing to do but sit and wait. It drifted from one subject to another until it found its way, as it sometimes did, to Danny Parks.

"Who was this Danny, anyway?" Sam Cook asked. "I've heard the name a hundred times since I came to this ranch, but nobody ever tells the whole story."

Sam looked at Toby and then at Adam, the way a younger man does when he isn't sure if a subject is off-limits. Toby just nodded.

"Danny was probably the best hand that ever worked this ranch,"

Toby said quietly. "And I've seen my share. He could rope anything that moved and a few things that didn't. He could ride anything with hair on it, and some of them tried their level best to put him in the dirt. None of them ever did."

"From Tennessee," Adam added. "Talked like it, too. He could make you laugh when you didn't think you had one in you." Adam was quiet for a moment. The fire popped and a log settled, sending a brief flare of sparks into the wet air.

"How'd he die?" Jason asked, and immediately wished he could take it back. But Toby answered him, plainly and without drama.

"A rope got tangled around him in the branding pen and a horse dragged him. It happened fast. Nobody could get to him in time." Toby looked into the fire. "He was the finest young man I ever knew."

The quiet that followed was the kind that doesn't invite anyone to fill it. The rain fell on the canvas. Somewhere on the picket line a horse shifted and blew softly through its nose.

"Danny had a saying," Adam said, almost to himself. "He used to tell people, 'It's only tricky if you stay caught.' I never did figure out exactly what he meant by it." He looked into the coals. "I guess I'm still working on it."

Nobody said anything for a while after that. One by one, the cowboys pulled their hats over their eyes or rolled onto their sides, and the camp went quiet.

Jason lay in his bedroll and listened to the rain. Danny Parks. A man he had never met, dead long before Jason was born, and yet present on this ranch in a way that Jason could feel but not explain. Everybody talked about him differently: Toby with respect, Adam with something deeper, Kyle's grandmother with tears. A man who could rope anything and make anybody laugh, and who had died young in the dust of a branding pen with a rope around him. Jason thought about that for a while, and then he didn't think about anything at all, because he was asleep.

The dream came the way dreams do, without warning or permission. Jason was sitting on a fence rail somewhere on the ranch, a place he didn't recognize but that felt familiar, the way places do in dreams. A tall man was leaning against the fence beside him, easy and relaxed, rolling a cigarette with the practiced hands of someone who had done it a thousand times. He wore a battered hat pushed back on his head and his face was friendly, with a lazy grin that seemed to live there permanently. Jason had never seen him before, but he knew who he was. In the dream, that did not seem strange at all.

The man finished rolling his cigarette and looked out across the land for a while. Then he looked at Jason.

"You're having a real good time, aren't you," he said, and his voice had Tennessee in it.

"Yes, sir," Jason answered, because in the dream it seemed like the right thing to say.

The man smiled. "Good. It's a hell of a place." He lit his cigarette and squinted through the smoke. "But don't let it fool you, son. It don't belong to you, and it don't belong to them, either. Never did." He took a long pull on the cigarette and let the smoke drift. "You'll want to stay. Everybody does. Just make sure you leave while the leaving's still yours to do."

Jason didn't understand any of it, and the man didn't seem to expect him to. He just smoked his cigarette and looked out at the land with that easy, unhurried gaze, and after a while he wasn't there anymore, and Jason was awake.

The rain was still falling. The canvas of the fly sagged and dripped above him, and he could hear the slow breathing of the other cowboys in the dark. The dream was already starting to fade, the way dreams always do, but the unease it left behind was not. A man he had never met had told him something, and Jason could not decide whether it had been a warning or just a dream. He lay still for a long time, listening to the rain, and then he turned on his side and went back to sleep.

He never mentioned the dream to anyone.

Chapter 6 — After the Rain

Part 1

Despite everybody's best stories and days remembered, time began to do little more than limp past. On the fourth day, dawn's light broke through the clouds. The rain had come, just when it was needed most, and now it was gone. Now the grass would grow, the range would bloom. In ten days or so, La Conquistadora would be awash in a sea of green. It would be a glorious sight, wonderful to behold. At the moment, though, the return of the sun and blue in the sky was more than enough to put the spring back in every cowboy's step. The crew was in fine fettle as they saddled up. The range was calling, and each and every one of them was ready to answer.

Toby led his riders across the soggy flats toward Walnut Draw, the ground soft and giving underfoot, the air sweet with the smell of wet earth and new grass. The flats were the color of rust where the rain had washed the topsoil bare, and every hoofprint filled with red water before the horse had taken another step. At the far edge of the flat, a small band of pronghorn stood watching them for a long moment, then turned and ran off across the prairie. Overhead, the sky was fast becoming a canopy of blue and white. Walnut Draw had quite a watershed, and could run a big head of water under the right conditions. Three days of nonstop rain, some of it heavy, had met those conditions. Walnut was running high and fast.

Kyle knew the draw was no problem for Toby. The old foreman had spent his career swimming horses across whatever body of water happened to get in his way, be it Walnut, any other creek, and even the river, before the dam was built. Kyle had heard those stories. That old river had been a real beast to get across. It was always hungry. Toby swore it licked its chops when he came around. He just knew its quicksand would have loved to have swallowed him down, and his horse and saddle as well. The dam had tamed the river, and Toby, for one, was damned glad.

Walnut was swimming deep, but from the way Toby sat his horse at the bank, it didn't look too bad to him. Probably not much over the horses' backs.

However, what was cake to Toby could be daunting to others. In fact, all the younger riders looked askance at the flowing red water. Every cowboy knew he was going to cross that draw, one way or the other. Not one of them would have admitted it, but more than a few of them looked a little scared.

"Kyle, is your life passing before your eyes?" Jason asked.

"I thought that was your life I was seeing. None of it looked familiar."

Bob Turner rode up at that moment.

"Have either of you boys ever swam a horse before?" he asked.

"No, sir," they answered in unison.

"Well, boys, it's the easiest thing in the world. Like falling off a log."

Kyle didn't care for the analogy, but let it pass.

Bob took a moment to survey both boys.

"Kyle," he said, "I see you're riding Cochise. He's always struck me as being a little silly, but I guess he can swim. No reason to think he can't, anyway. Jason, I guess Robin Hood can swim, too."

Both boys just looked at him. They hoped he was right.

Bob noticed their tense faces for the first time and laughed.

"Don't worry, boys, it ain't no trick to swim a horse across a little creek. People been doing it forever. First thing you got to do is get off and loosen up your cinch a little bit."

Bob hopped down to demonstrate. The boys followed suit, loosening their cinches just the way Bob did.

"Why are we doing this?" Jason asked Kyle.

"I have no idea."

Jason nodded. He didn't like to be the only one outside the

information loop. As long as Kyle was there with him, he felt better.

Up ahead, Toby had also dismounted and loosened his cinch. Then he tied his hobbles to his saddle horn and took off his spurs and tied them to the saddle, too. There was no sense in risking losing a good pair of spurs. Toby was ready to cross the draw but paused to survey his crew, to make sure they were ready, too.

Kyle and Jason had been watching him closely. They had long since figured out that if there was anything crucial to be learned, they better pick it up by observation. It likely would not occur to anyone to mention it. In unison, the two boys turned their eyes from Toby's actions to Bob Turner's friendly face.

Bob smiled at their anxious looks.

"It wouldn't hurt to do the same thing," he said. "A spur can come off and get lost, so buckle them together and through the hand hole on your saddles. Now, the hobbles part is sort of important. Tie one end of your hobbles to the saddle horn, real good. When you start to cross, get a good grip on those hobbles and don't let go. If your horse starts to thrash around too much or gets in any sort of trouble, you need to get away from him. His legs and hooves are going to be churning pretty good, so be sure and get downstream from him. Your grip on the hobbles will keep you from being swept away by the current. So don't let go."

"We won't," the boys assured him as they hastened to follow his instructions and tried not to dwell on the consequences of getting upstream or letting go of the hobbles.

While they were so engaged, Kyle looked up to see Bob meet Toby's eyes and nod. Adam and every other cowboy had been watching Bob and the boys. No one was going to let their likable young friends ride into the water unprepared.

"Let's go," Toby instructed, and rode into the current.

Like hovering mother hens, Bob and Adam maneuvered themselves into position right behind Kyle and Jason. The rest of the crew seemed to be finding excuses to hang back as well.

Still in wading water, Toby glanced back to check the progress of his followers. There were none.

"What the hell!" Toby exclaimed as he turned back to shore. His horse standing in a foot of swirling red water, Toby faced his sheepish crew and shook his head.

"Okay, nursemaids," he said, "I will personally guarantee that both Kyle and Jason survive this crossing and that neither of them meet with disaster. Bob and Adam and I will see to that. Now, will the rest of you kindly get across the water?"

Everybody grinned and laughed. Jason and Kyle blushed. Still laughing, George Price kicked his horse into the draw and started for the bank. The other cowboys splashed in behind.

"All right," Toby said. "I'll go in first, you kids come along behind. Your horses will follow mine, plus they'll want to get to their friends on the other side. When they start to swim, give them their heads and just let them go. There is nothing to this. Adam, you and Bob come along behind. Let's go."

Robin Hood, with Jason safely on his back, took to the water like a duck. He waded until it wasn't comfortable, then he started to swim. The cold, sand-red water ran over the saddle and up around Jason, almost to his waist. He kept a tight grip on his hobbles and decided this wasn't so bad. In fact, it was kind of fun.

Cochise, carrying Kyle, waded in and kept right on wading. Kyle was keeping a tight eye on Toby and Jason up ahead. They were both swimming now. Cochise was still wading. Kyle wondered when his mount planned to start swimming, like the other horses had.

Cochise just kept walking, even though the water was rising far up his sides. In a moment it would crest his back. The horse just kept raising his head to compensate for the ever-deepening water. He seemed to have no natural aptitude for swimming, and no desire to develop one in a hurry. Kyle was getting more than a little worried. The water was now over his horse's back, the current working to tug him from the saddle. At this rate, he was going to be downstream, all right. Way downstream.

When the only visible manifestation of Cochise was his head, with no neck attached, Adam took charge. He urged his mount, a strong swimmer, alongside Kyle. Bob Turner was right behind him.

"Kyle," Adam commanded, "take a hold of Bob's lariat. It's dallied to his saddle and it will hold you. If you have to abandon ship, let go of the hobbles but keep a tight grip on the lariat. Bob will pick you up. He's on a real good horse. Now, give me your reins. I'm going to try to make that son of a bitch swim."

"Yes, sir," Kyle replied to everything Adam had said, handing over the reins and taking the offered coil of rope.

Seizing Kyle's reins, Adam spurred his mount past Cochise's head, now raised so high water was running in his ears.

"Come on, you sorry son of a bitch!" Adam shouted loud enough for the waterlogged horse to hear.

Cochise was surprised, to say the least, to feel the hand of stern authority on his bit and the voice of command in his ears. The owner of the voice also used a vocabulary familiar to the stubborn horse. It was taken from the same lexicon employed by the bronc buster who had broken him to saddle, years before.

Cochise was not happy with this turn of events. His training and experience with humans inclined him to obey Adam's authority. His stubborn nature made him refuse.

Adam would have none of it.

"Kyle," Adam yelled, "kick the hell out of him! Make your spurs meet in the middle!"

"Yes, sir," Kyle answered and wished he was still wearing his spurs. He could never recall whether he had said the words out loud or not, but he kicked the hell out of Cochise, just as Adam had instructed.

At the same moment, Adam jerked the hell out of the reins, never lessening his verbal assault for even a second.

Cochise was caught off guard by the triple assault. He stumbled and lost his footing on the creek bottom. The horse was now faced with the choice of swimming or drowning.

Adam had just as soon Cochise drowned, and was trying to figure out how to get his head underwater and keep it there. Possibly sensing this, Cochise was suddenly consumed with a born-again aquatic passion. Being dragged posthaste through the current behind Adam, and being driven by Bob Turner on his flank, the horse demonstrated a very credible stroke. Adam continued to drag Cochise along behind him until all three horses and riders were safely on the opposite bank. Only then did he relinquish the reins back to Kyle.

"Well," he said to Kyle, "that's a hell of a way to start the day, isn't it? It got my adrenaline flowing."

"Mine, too," responded a game but slightly white-faced Kyle.

Adam grinned at Kyle and shook his head.

"I've heard of dogs that won't hunt. I guess some horses just won't swim," he said.

"I guess not," Kyle agreed.

Toby was not amused. Kyle could see it in his face: the old foreman had not yet reached the recognition-of-humor phase and likely never would. Kyle knew what vision was playing out in Toby's mind: the drowned body of the boss's only grandchild being swept away down Walnut Draw, while Toby was in charge. Not a pretty picture.

When Adam moseyed up beside him a moment later, Kyle noticed he walked a little carefully on the wet ground, as though the cold water had stiffened something up. It was there and gone, Adam moved past it the way a man moves past something he's used to, and then Kyle watched Toby look at him with relief written all over his face.

"Toby, that horse might look real good as a bag of dog food," Adam commented.

Toby eyed Cochise appraisingly.

"He sure might," he agreed. "Adam," Toby continued, "I really owe you. That could have been a disaster."

"No shit," Adam said, and Kyle caught him glancing over to where he and Jason stood talking.

"There for a minute, I figured you might have been a goner, Kyle," Jason said to his friend. "Did it scare you?"

"Oh, no. Not at all."

"Yeah, you were shitting bricks!" Jason chortled.

Kyle didn't deny it. "You know what I wish?" he asked.

"What?"

"I wish it had been you."

Jason just chortled some more. He was interrupted by Larry McIntire, who suddenly joined their conversation.

"That little episode just now surprised the hell out of me, Kyle. I'd never heard anything about Cochise being a bad river horse. If anyone was going to give us trouble today, I'd have sure thought it would have been Jason's horse. Everybody knows that old Robin Hood nag has a bad river reputation. I'd always heard he couldn't swim at all, but I guess the old boy can after all. Or at least he felt like it this morning. Just another false rumor, I reckon."

"What are you talking about?" Jason demanded to know. "This horse swims just fine!"

"He sure did just now," Larry agreed. "Let's just hope he remembers that this afternoon."

"What do you mean?"

"I mean we're going to have to cross this draw to get back to camp. Only we'll have a big herd of cattle with us to make even more trouble."

With these encouraging words, Larry saw fit to move on, quite delighted with himself.

While Larry and Jason were having this little exchange, Bob Turner checked on Kyle's status.

"I reckon that nag of yours is a little sillier than I thought," he told Kyle with a grin.

"I guess he is," Kyle agreed. "Maybe he just got up on the wrong side of the bed this morning."

"Maybe. Well, boys, we'd better tighten up our cinches again and get ready to ride. It looks like Toby's about to scatter us out."

Raring to go, Kyle filed his morning dip away under the category of "curious adventure" and leapt wholeheartedly into the rest of the morning.

They had been scattered out for maybe an hour, working their sections of the big pasture in the easy warmth of the clearing sky, when the weather turned on them. It came from the southwest without much warning, a dark wall of cloud that boiled up over the mesa rim and crossed the flats faster than a horse could run. Kyle saw it coming and barely had time to pull his hat down tight before it hit. The hail came first, marble-sized and stinging, hammering his hat brim and popping off his horse's rump like gravel flung from a truck. Cochise hunched and turned his hindquarters to it, ears flat, and Kyle bent over the saddle horn and held on. The rain came behind the hail, so thick you couldn't see your horse's ears. A draw that had been bone-dry ten minutes ago was suddenly running bank to bank with red water, cutting Kyle off from the cattle he'd been pushing. There was nothing to do but sit tight and let it pass.

It passed. Five minutes, maybe less, though it felt like an hour, and the cloud moved on to the northeast and the sun came back as if nothing had happened. Kyle straightened up in the saddle, water pouring off his hat brim, and looked around at a landscape that was streaming and steaming in the sudden warmth. His cattle were scattered to hell and gone. Cochise shook himself like a dog and blew hard through his nose. Somewhere off to Kyle's left, he could hear Jason whooping, whether in shock or delight, Kyle couldn't tell. Probably both. That was New Mexico for you. Five minutes ago it had been trying to kill him, and now the sun was out and warm on his back as if nothing had happened at all.

• • •

Larry McIntire rode off to work his section of the pasture in a fine frame of mind. His little seed of doubt about Robin Hood's swimming had been planted and, from the look on Jason's face, was flourishing already. Larry rode happily, chousing and herding off to the roundup ground any and all cattle that crossed his path. He was a good cowboy and a good young man who just happened to enjoy a little practical joke now and then.

Having just sent a couple of pairs on their way, Larry looked around for fresh prey. Off in the distance, grazing by herself, he spotted a lone cow and galloped off to round her up.

The cow was an afflicted one, blinded on her left side by a great and hugely swollen cancerous eye. Suffering this great disadvantage, she kept mostly to herself. Being a cow, and gregarious by nature, she also liked to keep her fellows within scent and within the sight of her one good eye. She was grazing peacefully in her usual way when Larry came riding after her.

As luck would have it, Larry's approach happened to be from the left. The cow, blind on that side, could not see him gallop up. She knew something was there, though, and it was something scary. Something that was running at her, blowing and heaving and making lots of noise. Threatened and frightened, the cow began to run.

Larry and Sugar Baby, his ride that day, gave immediate chase. The cow swung her head from side to side as she ran, trying to get a glimpse of what was after her. She could not see a thing and ran harder still. Larry had a lot of ground to cover that morning and didn't have time to mess around with one silly cow. He touched Sugar Baby with his spurs, a signal to switch on the afterburners. Sugar delivered a burst of speed that put horse and rider side by side with the cow in a handful of strides.

Now, the cow was truly terrified. Whatever it was, was right beside her.

"Why doesn't this stupid-assed cow just turn? The way she is supposed to?" Larry asked himself. Then he noticed the eye, deformed and clouded over, horribly swollen out from her head.

Larry realized the cow could not see him, running right there beside her. To frighten her into turning away from him and toward the roundup ground, Larry began to whoop and holler.

By these actions, Larry certainly succeeded in further scaring the already terrified animal. In one last frantic effort to see her assailant, the cow swung and twisted her head hard to the left, hoping her right eye could finally get a look at this thing beside her.

Such was not to be. Larry and Sugar Baby were a good team. They had positioned themselves in tight formation with the cow, determined to drive her right where they wanted her. They were as close as they could get. Certainly close enough to make contact with an overly large, extended eye.

The cow had put a lot of muscle into that final swing of the head. When she made contact with Larry's Levi-clad leg, it was the eye that gave way. With a sickening splat, the eye burst open, like an egg slammed against a wall. It splattered across Larry's leg and onto Sugar Baby's side. What had once been an eye was now an oozing mass of corruption with unidentifiable lumps and running pus. The sight was horrifying, but the accompanying stench was even worse.

The pain for the cow had been blinding. She stumbled, brought to her knees in agony, before she managed to make her escape to a thicket of brush not too far away.

Larry never noticed what happened to the cow. He was busy puking. And puking. And then puking some more. His life had not been a sheltered one, but there was nothing in his history to prepare him for the up-close-and-personal experience he had just had with the cancer-eyed cow.

"Maybe today's not going to be so good after all," he thought between heaves.

• • •

Jason rode away from the crossing on Walnut Draw in a worried state of mind. He was pretty sure that Kyle had been in some real danger a little while earlier; he could still see Adam's face when he'd grabbed the reins, and that wasn't a man playing around. It was very possible that Kyle had been in a tricky enough situation that he could have even drowned. It was a very unsettling thought. Added to that was Larry's comment concerning Robin Hood's swimming prowess. He might have just been teasing, then again, maybe he wasn't.

What if this horse really isn't a swimmer? he wondered. Maybe he did okay this morning just because there were other horses crossing the creek and he didn't want to get left behind. When it was time to cross Walnut again, Robin Hood might get crazy and do something even more stupid than Cochise did with Kyle.

Jason worried with himself in this manner for quite a while, automatically watching for cattle and rounding them up as he went. The day that had started out with such promise was well on its way to ruin. Jason morosely rode on, doing his job and worrying about his future. It took him a while to notice that the grass he had been crossing had given way to a large sandy stretch of ground.

The sand was still damp from its recent washing, its top layer swept away by the torrents of rain that had fallen in the last few days. Taking more of an interest now, Jason noticed the scattering of large rocks that seemed to lie with some purpose across the sand.

"I'll bet those are tepee rings!" he exclaimed. "Or rather, I'll bet they used to be tepee rings," he corrected himself. "This must be an old Indian camp, and a pretty good-sized one from the looks of it."

Jason looked around in delight. His bleak mood was blown away by the thought of Indians having ridden and walked exactly where he was riding now. Having read his share of science fiction, he wondered if they might not still be here, camping and hunting buffalo in a parallel time warp, as unaware of him as he was of them. Jason looked about him and tried to imagine the Indian encampment he might be riding through. Perhaps it was filled with women and children, hunters and warriors. Perhaps there were horses grazing nearby, and maybe dogs lay panting in the heat while all the camp's residents, human and animal alike, rejoiced in the recent rain. All the dust was laid and their world was fresh and clean again. Soon the grass would be lush and green and the buffalo would grow fat and lazy. It would be a good winter, with plenty of meat.

Jason grinned and then he laughed.

"Farewell, fellow travelers across time and this special piece of earth. I hope you have good hunting and an easy winter. I have hunting of my own to do."

Jason liked the thought that he might be sharing La Conquistadora with others who had come before him. Then it occurred to him that he might be sharing it with those who did not yet even exist. He liked that thought even better.

The thought settled into something quieter then, a recognition, barely formed, that the ranch itself might not always be here in this form. These plains had already outlived one people. They would outlive another. The land didn't care who rode across it. The land just went on.

With a light heart, he turned Robin Hood back toward the grassy plains to continue their cattle hunt.

Perhaps it was just a lucky glance, or a stray glint of sunlight that caught his attention, but right in front of him, practically at Robin Hood's feet, Jason saw the most perfect arrowhead. It was not a small one, either. Beautiful, and sparkling clean, Jason's arrowhead lay on the damp sand's surface, like a gift waiting to be picked.

"I feel lucky today!" Jason said as he hopped down from his

saddle. He had never found an arrowhead or anything else of any note before. High with excitement, he knelt and turned it over in his fingers, the flint cool and smooth, the edges still sharp after God only knew how many centuries in the dirt. He held it for a long moment before he snapped it safely away in his shirt pocket.

Back on Robin Hood's back and ready to ride, all Jason's earlier worries were long forgotten. Pausing, he looked once more across the sandy flat with its scattered stones.

"Thank you," he said out loud to whoever might be listening, and rode away.

Part 2

If Jason's mind was at rest, Toby's was not. He was busily working a stretch of pasture not too distant from the sandy flat where Jason had lingered for a moment. Lingering was not on Toby's mind. Neither was hunting for arrowheads, which was a pity, because he rode right over a real find or two, uncovered by the recent rain. They would have to wait for another day, perhaps another century, perhaps forever.

A couple of things weighed on Toby's mind as he rode along under the vast blue sky and breathed the fresh morning air. One was the fact that the work had been delayed by the rain. He was delighted with the rain. He just wasn't so thrilled with the expense of having a full crew of cowboys lying up around the chuck wagon costing money for three days. He would just have to push everyone a little harder to make up for it. As if enough time had not already been wasted, they were coming up on the Clauson Rodeo weekend. It was an old tradition to let the crew off early on Saturday afternoon and not expect them back at the wagon until Sunday evening. That was one tradition it would be just as well to do away with, in Toby's opinion. As far as he was concerned, the rodeo break just represented two more wasted days, and it wasn't even fun anymore. It used to be fun, back when Louisa had her ice cream social on Saturday afternoon before the rodeo. After all the foolishness over Adam and Sophie, there had never been any more ice cream socials. Toby guessed the heart had just gone out of it for Louisa. Now, there was almost no one left that even remembered that yearly summer party.

Toby had not really thought about Louisa's party for years, he guessed. Remembering those old days, his tanned and leathery face cracked a smile. Despite his determination to maintain a bleak outlook on such a glorious day, memories of those younger days widened the reluctant smile and even put a twinkle in his eye. He even chuckled as he thought of the three girls that had rampaged across these same lands that last summer, and the summers before as well. He had never admitted it to them or to anyone else, but his daughter, and Sophie Degarrin, and Christine had been among the best hands he had ever had.

Thinking of his daughter caused Toby to shake his head in exasperation. Kitten had produced a daughter that was as wild as the wind and as headstrong as a Missouri mule was purported to be. Where his granddaughter, Tammy, had acquired her nature, Toby was at a loss to know, but that was because he was blessed with a parent's memory. Toby's tame reconstruction of his daughter's rather wild and woolly past bore little resemblance to reality. What Kitten had achieved in Tammy was actually a basic replication of herself. It took great determination on Toby's part to fail to see this fact. However, Toby was a man blessed with great determination.

Basically on autopilot, horse and rider gathered every animal in sight, and quite a few that they had to go looking for. A covey of quail burst from a clump of cholla as he passed, the whir of their wings so close and sudden that even Toby's old horse spooked sideways for a step before settling back to business. All the while, Toby continued to dwell on other matters. The plight and reckless career of Tammy was now foremost in his mind. The girl was as cute as a button. Toby was quite sure there were any number of things his granddaughter should be putting her mind to learning to help her become a proper young lady. Instead, she had taken up rodeo riding, not merely with parental permission but with their avid encouragement as well. Tammy was utterly devoid of fear and was possessed of total faith in herself and her pet horse, Maybe Baby. This, combined with an addiction to adrenaline, was a scary but winning combination in the rodeo world. Tammy and Maybe Baby's greatest thrills came from breakneck speed and hairpin turns. As a result, Tammy spent most of her time as the reigning queen of some event or another.

Barrel racing was Tammy and Maybe Baby's best event. They could race straight at a barrel, spin around it, and race on to the next one, faster than anyone else. When running that cloverleaf pattern, no one wore such a look of pure devilish delight as Tammy. Tammy and Maybe Baby rarely lost at barrel racing, and they always scared her grandfather, Toby, to the brink of death and brought her mother, Kitten, to her feet screaming and cheering.

Toby rode on, gathering cattle with consummate skill but only half a mind. With the other half, he dwelled gloomily on the shortcomings of children, both actual and grand. It had been typical but totally thoughtless of Kitten to raise her child to be a daredevil, he concluded, more than a little peeved. While Kitten did the cheerleading and reveling, there he was, left to do the worrying for everyone. Kitten and Tammy certainly weren't wasting any energy on it, that was for sure.

Toby decided Degarrin was a lucky man. He guessed Sophie had turned out just fine, after all. Her offspring appeared to be normal, too. Kyle didn't seem to create any problems, except for nearly getting drowned that morning. Toby decided that incident didn't really count, though, because Kyle hadn't drowned, or even been swept away, and because Degarrin hadn't even had to worry about it. No! As usual, it was Toby who got to worry. And the kid wasn't even related to him!

Toby was settling down into a fine state of dejection. He was pretty sure somebody's grandchild, probably his own, would be the death of him. In this gloomy state of mind, he realized, with a certainty, that in a couple of days' time, at the Clauson Rodeo, he would very likely witness Tammy's demise before his very eyes.

This bleak scenario was abruptly interrupted as a jackrabbit jumped right from beneath Toby's horse. Rider, horse, and rabbit were all equally startled. The rabbit jumped one way, the horse whirled and leapt another. In a direct line of communication from brain to muscle, Toby's body effortlessly went with the horse, then collected the animal up and went riding on. Toby wasted exactly no thought or effort on the rabbit incident. Through it all, he remained firmly and righteously focused on Tammy's reckless horsing around.

• • •

If Toby chose to dwell on the dark side that beautiful day, he did so in solitary splendor. Even Kyle didn't feel like complaining. His day had gotten off to an unusual start and had maintained its unique flavor. Cochise did not recover well from his waterlogged creek crossing and stayed skittish all morning, which was actually quite all right with Kyle. It made for a little excitement. Cochise just refused to settle down. He stayed up on his toes and chewed on the bit. He bolted, or rather tried to. He shied wildly at all creatures, real or imagined. Kyle decided that Bob Turner was right: Cochise was definitely a silly ride, but not a boring one.

Then Cochise performed a feat that ranked him among the truly bizarre of the horse world. Kyle and he had been working some fairly rough country and had gathered quite a few head of cattle despite Cochise's antics. They had worked their way up into the benches and breaks above the prairie that composed most of the Upper Walnut pasture. The rough stuff had to be worked, too, and that's what the two were doing, with considerable success. The cattle up there sometimes got missed and might not see a human or a horse for a year or two, or more. As a result, they were pretty wild and woolly.

One such creature, a crazy-acting dry cow that should have gone to market long ago, decided she wanted nothing to do with Kyle and Cochise. When they gave chase, she gave flight. Actual flight. With horse and rider right on her tail, determined to turn her and drive her from her isolated home, the cow raced right for the edge of the rimrock. While Kyle braced for a screeching, dirt-flying halt, the cow did not. She never even broke stride as she jumped off the rimrock and into the empty air beyond, and neither did Cochise. As they left solid ground for vacant space, Kyle's stomach dropped into his boots and the world went weightless. It occurred to Kyle that this just didn't seem to be his day. Maybe he just should have stayed at home in Carrolton.

Kyle could not believe Cochise was actually going to jump off the rimrock. When he had done just that, Kyle could not believe Cochise actually had jumped off the rimrock. When Kyle looked down, there was nothing below him, only air. He was once again stricken with disbelief.

"I cannot believe this!" he thought. "I am going to die today, all because I rode the wrong horse. There are millions of horses in the world that know not to jump into thin air and that know how to swim. Only I would end up with the one animal that knows neither."

The cow hit the ground first, and not well, either. The impact knocked her flat and the momentum rolled her over and down the hillside into some brush and rocks. Stunned, and with the wind knocked out of her, it took the cow a few minutes to recover. It helped that she was crazy, anyway. Recent events had not been all that abnormal for her, and she was soon able to pull herself together and stagger off, unimpeded by further human intervention.

The Kyle and Cochise team fared a little better. At least Cochise managed to land on all fours and somewhat balanced. Fortunately there were no washed-out ravines or gullies, and no large, life-threatening boulders in their path. Otherwise, it might have been curtains. As it was, horse and rider skidded down the steep, muddy hillside on Cochise's butt with his front legs stretched straight out in front. Their descent was not unlike that of a really bad skier.

It occurred to Kyle that he should simply step off the horse's back and send Cochise on to meet his fate, alone. His next realization was that his rubber legs were not responding well enough to even lift him in his stirrups, let alone support him if he reached the ground. He stayed where he was. He and Cochise had started this thing together and he guessed they would end it the same way.

When Cochise finally quit sliding, he just sat there on his butt, in the mud. His rubbery legs were not working too well, either.

He and Kyle were still just sitting there when Adam raced up, on the double. Cochise looked whipped. He looked like he just might not ever bother to get up again. Kyle's dazed blue eyes looked at Adam from a face that was whiter than he imagined flesh could get and still be living.

Both horse and boy turned their heads and looked at Adam, but that was all. Adam looked back. It did not appear that either one was seriously hurt, just shell-shocked. Finally, Adam broke the silence.

"Are you all right?" he asked cautiously.

Kyle regarded him thoughtfully from Cochise's still-sitting back. After serious consideration, he spoke.

"I don't think this is a very good horse," he said.

Adam burst out laughing, and once started, he could not stop. As he roared with laughter, some of the color began to return to Kyle's blanched face and his eyes took on a hint of their usual sparkle.

"Why do you say that?" Adam was finally able to gasp.

"It's just something I've come to realize."

The laughter was threatening to make a comeback, and Adam could only nod.

The color returned to Kyle's face. Crawling off Cochise's back, he figured it was time to see if either he or his horse could stand.

Adam took charge.

"Tell you what, Kyle. You and dog food there take a little breather while I go up and get your cattle. Then we'll start down to the roundup. It's been quite a day already, and it's not even ten o'clock."

Kyle had no problem with that plan. He was just glad to get a little break.

A little while later, after Adam had returned with Kyle's gather and it had been thrown in with Adam's efforts for the morning, the two cowboys drove their cattle finds down to the roundup ground. Finally something was going pretty well for Kyle. The cattle were cooperative and did not require a lot of herding. For the most part, Adam and Kyle were able to ride along in tandem and even converse a little.

"Have you had a good summer, other than today?" Adam asked Kyle.

"Oh, yes, sir. It's really been great! Even today hasn't been so bad, just really weird."

"I'm glad you're having a good time. Jason seems to be getting a kick out of it, too."

"For sure," Kyle agreed with a laugh. "Jason is having the time of his life. So am I, which is funny. I didn't really expect to like it so much. Even though old Juan said we would love it, that it would be the best of times."

"Juan Soliz, right?"

"Yes, sir. Do you remember him?"

"Sure. He was a great guy and a real good cowboy. I rode a lot with him, years ago."

"I know. He has pictures hanging in his cafe of La Conquistadora and all the cowboys from back then. You are in some of them, Adam. Sometimes, Momma and I will go there to eat and old Juan will come over and tell us one of his stories from the good old days. He loves to do that. And Momma will smile and laugh and be real nice about it, but then after he goes back to the kitchen she'll just kind of sit there, looking at those pictures and not say much. I guess they take her back to when she was a kid. But I don't really like it when she does that."

"Why?" Adam asked.

"Because she seems so gone, like she might not ever come all the way back. So I start cutting up and acting silly. You know, to distract her. If I can get her laughing, then she's okay."

"You're a good kid, Kyle. Do you and your momma go to Juan's cafe very often?"

"Quite a bit. Especially if my dad's out of town. We used to take Amy with us a lot. That was always fun." Kyle's tone had become a little wistful.

"And who is Amy?" Adam asked obligingly.

"She's my girlfriend. Or rather, I guess she was my girlfriend would be more accurate."

"That doesn't sound too promising."

"No. At the moment things don't look so good."

Adam waited. He hated to pry, but being human and curious, he hoped Kyle would continue.

Kyle looked over at him with a sad smile and gave a sort of hopeless shrug.

"She wanted to get super serious. I mean, it wasn't like we weren't super serious anyway. But she wanted to make it officially serious. That scared me to death. I mean, what is the matter with that girl? We aren't even out of high school, for crying out loud!"

"What happened?" Adam asked.

"She dumped me."

"Oh."

"Then she took up with some creep doctor's son. That's the main reason I came up here this summer. If Amy and I hadn't broken up, I probably would have stayed in Carrolton. In fact, if I had stayed at home, we would have been back together by now. Which is why Jason thought it would be such a great idea for him and me to come up here and play cowboy."

"Oh."

"I've been thinking about calling her up, though. I don't talk about it much, but I really miss her a lot. Jason can't stand to hear about it.

He thinks I'm pussy whipped, which I probably am."

Without even being aware of it, Kyle had begun to grin.

"Sounds like love to me," Adam said. Something had moved him, though what exactly Kyle wasn't sure.

"Does she care as much about you as you do about her?"

"Sure, that's why she wanted to get promised."

"Promised?" Adam asked, totally at sea.

"Yeah. That's where I'm supposed to get her this microscopic diamond ring and we promise that someday we'll get engaged and might even actually get married sometime. Isn't that the stupidest thing you've ever heard of?"

"It sounds kind of redundant," Adam hazarded.

"Yeah. It's stupid and redundant. I guess I'll have to do it, though."

"You sound like you really love this girl, Kyle." Adam seemed a little surprised, as though he had assumed Kyle was just caught up in the throes of puppy love. Maybe not, though.

"Oh, yeah. I love her all right. There's no question about that. That's not the issue. The issue is, I don't want to get married. There is absolutely no reason that I can see for getting hitched and trying to be an old married couple when you are seventeen or eighteen years old. We can't even take care of ourselves, let alone each other."

"That's a very good point, it seems to me," Adam had to agree.

"Yeah, it's a good point all right. But I imagine I'll end up doing whatever she wants. I mean, I can't get along without her."

"What do you mean?" Adam asked.

"Well, I had this vague idea that maybe we had outgrown each other and that's why we broke up. I thought my feelings might cool off and just kind of go away this summer if I didn't see her for a while. So Jase and I came here to be cowboys. I've had a great time. But nothing has changed." Kyle rode in silence for a few moments, his expression very tense.

"I miss her more than ever," he continued. "I wish I didn't. My life would be a lot easier if I didn't. But the fact is, I feel like half of me is missing. The half that finishes my sentences for me and thinks the same thoughts I do. We can just look at each other across a room and burst out laughing. Sometimes it seems like we don't even need to talk anymore."

"You had better call her, Kyle. If you have something that special, try not to lose it. I think what you are describing must be very rare. Something like that doesn't come along very often in a whole lifetime, maybe only once." Adam's hand tightened on the rein for just a moment, no ring on it, Kyle noticed, not even a pale line where one might have been. "When it does come along, I guess it's like a rodeo bronc: just ride it till it comes undone or the whistle blows."

Kyle smiled at Adam.

"Thanks, Adam. I'll call her and see what happens."

Adam smiled back, and for just a moment there was something behind his eyes that Kyle recognized but could not name. It was the same look he had seen in his mother's face at La Cantina, sitting in front of those old photographs. Gone, like she might not ever come all the way back.

Then it passed, and Adam was himself again.

• • •

That evening, back at camp, Kyle couldn't sit still. Adam's words kept turning over in his mind, when it does come along, just ride it till it comes undone or the whistle blows, and by the time Joe called supper, Kyle had made up his mind. He would ride to headquarters and call Amy.

He left Jason at the wagon without much explanation and made the ride alone. The evening light was going long and golden across the flats, the shadows of the mesas stretching out across the land like dark fingers. Headquarters was quiet when he rode in, the corrals empty, the saddle shed closed up. Louisa and Degarrin were in the sitting room and seemed pleased to see him, if a little surprised.

"I just need to use the phone, Grandmother," Kyle said. "If that's all right."

"Of course, sweetheart. You know where it is."

Kyle stood in the dim hallway with the receiver in his hand and his heart going faster than he would have liked. He dialed Amy's number from memory, the way he always had.

It rang three times. Then her mother's voice, cool and pleasant.

"Jeffers residence."

"Hello, Mrs. Jeffers. It's Kyle Carpenter. May I speak to Amy, please?"

There was a pause, barely there, just a fraction of a second, but Kyle heard it.

"I'm sorry, Kyle. Amy's not home this evening. She's out with Joel."

Kyle stood very still. Something hot moved through his chest and up into his jaw, and for a moment the dim hallway and the phone and all of it seemed very far away.

"I see," he said. His voice came out flat and steady, which surprised him. "Well. Don't bother telling her I called."

He hung up the phone carefully, the way you do when what you really want to do is put it through the wall. He stood there for a moment with his hand still on the receiver, and then he turned and walked through the sitting room and out the portal door without stopping to say goodnight.

Louisa, who had heard none of the conversation but had seen the look on her grandson's face as he passed, exchanged a glance with her husband but said nothing.

Kyle rode back to the wagon in the dark with the stars coming out above him and a hard, bitter knot in his chest. To hell with her. To hell with her and Joel Cannon and Mrs. Jeffers and the whole damned town of Carrolton. He had ridden all the way out here and worked until his hands bled and missed her every single day, and she was out with that son of a bitch. All right. Fine. He was done.

By the time he unsaddled in the dark, the anger had gone cold and settled into something heavier. Jason looked up from where he sat on his bedroll.

"You okay?" he asked.

"Yeah," Kyle said. "Fine."

Jason knew that tone. He left his friend alone.

Kyle crawled into his bedroll and stared up at the stars and told himself he didn't care. He told himself that for a long time before he fell asleep.

Part 3

Adam and Kyle were not the only ones who felt like it was time to get themselves and the fruits of their morning's labors down to the roundup ground. Jason was headed that way, too. So were Toby, and George Price, Sam Cook, and all the other hands as well. Larry was riding for the same destination, but he was encountering more problems than the others. His injured cow was causing him no end of grief. Larry had long since wished he had never seen her. When he had recovered from his attack and the stench from his splattered Levi's had dissipated to a barely bearable level, Larry had resigned himself to his fate. Saddling up, he rode off to look for the injured cow. Finding her had not been easy, but it had been cake compared to driving her and trying to keep her with his little herd. Larry was not in a sunny mood when he was finally able to join the growing drive.

"Nice you could make it, Larry," George greeted him. "What the hell did you do to that poor cow?" George surveyed the ruptured cow with morbid curiosity. "Man, she stinks!" George screwed up his face in distaste. Then, noticing Larry's aroma, he exclaimed, "So do you! Yuck! This is the grossest thing I've ever seen or smelled!"

Larry surveyed him sourly. "You should have been there. Believe me, what you're seeing and smelling now is nothing compared to what I got to experience."

For once, George had nothing to say and no good advice to offer. He was just glad that Larry had met up with the cancer-eyed cow, and not himself.

Jason, however, was clearly continuing to have a great day. He had found cows and calves everywhere all morning and had sent them all down to the roundup with expert dispatch. His personal contribution to the size of the drive had been enormous. He was having a wonderful time; the day had turned breathtaking before his very eyes. The remaining clouds had turned to high-flung banks of white, floating freely in a pure blue sky. The day was warm and pleasant, far from July's usual stifling heat. The air and even the sunlight seemed soft. Without quite knowing it, Jason was experiencing a rare and wonderful day, one that would linger forever, just on the edge of his consciousness, reminding him that sometimes there are moments of magic.

Even Larry couldn't dent a day like that.

When Jason joined up with the other riders, Larry promptly sidled up to him.

"Hey, Jason," he said, "I sure hope that horse of yours remembers he knows how to swim when we get back to Walnut Creek. He sure surprised me this morning, when he was actually able to get across it! It must have just been some kind of a lucky fluke. I know I've heard that horse can't swim a lick."

"Well, Larry, I feel lucky today. Robin Hood and I could swim the Nile today. We are not worried about Walnut Creek, which has most likely run down by now, anyway. But I'll tell you what, I sure hope it's still running high enough for you to wash some of that stinking mess off of you. What is that, anyway? If you don't mind, Robin Hood and I are just going to go and get a little upwind of you!"

Larry could not remember having a worse day.

Jason could not remember a better one. A smile of contentment still lit his face as he fell in beside Kyle for a moment, before finding a more useful spot along the edge of the drive. Taking a moment to observe the expanse of the noisy, red-and-white herd that he and the other cowboys were pushing along in the direction of camp, he realized how very large it was.

"This is a really big gather, Kyle," he said. "It's going to be a bitch to brand all these calves."

"I know. I've been thinking the same thing. But maybe we'll get a chance to do some roping. That's one of the good things about a real big branding; there's plenty of roping to go around."

"Yeah, that's true. I hadn't thought about it that way. I'd just been thinking about what a pain in the ass it was going to be wrestling calves in the mud all afternoon." Changing the subject, Jason added, "Hey, Kyle, look what I found."

Proudly, he pulled his perfect arrowhead out of his pants pocket and showed it to his friend. Then a sudden doubt hit him.

"I can keep it, can't I? I mean, I don't have to turn it in or anything, do I?"

Kyle promptly seized this opportunity to hassle his best friend.

"No, you don't get to keep it. You have to turn it in to my grandfather. It belongs to La Conquistadora. Granddaddy will probably give it to me. I'll make up some really good story about how I found it, and tell it to anyone that will listen."

Watching Jason's outrage at these dire words was too much for Kyle. He could not quite hide his grin as he watched his friend's face fall.

Jason was much incensed when he finally noticed his friend's barely hidden grin and the wicked gleam in his eyes.

"Asshole!" he exclaimed, and promptly leaned over to give Kyle a good punch in the ribs.

Just as promptly, Kyle nudged Cochise just out of reach and laughed delightedly.

"I still think you should give me that arrowhead, though. I've been having a rough day."

"Tough. I hope it gets rougher."

Toby trotted past the two boys on his way to his steering position at the front of the herd. Still feeling a little crabby, he took time to growl at Kyle and Jason, which caused his mood to improve markedly.

"You boys spread out and quit sitting around gossiping like a bunch of old ladies. We've got work to do."

The boys were in far too good a mood to be affected by any odd kicks in Toby's gait. Instead, they each made a face and saluted his retreating back, but they did spread out and get to work. It would not have occurred to either of them not to do exactly whatever Toby directed.

The drive was going very well, and Even Toby's mood seemed to lift as he surveyed the results of his crew's work. The morning's gather had been a very large one. Toby could immediately see how hard every one of his cowboys had worked. The Jeffers boy had brought in more cattle than anyone, quiet as you please. Toby noted it, the way he noted everything. The land ridden that morning had obviously been worked very well. He had no doubt that the pasture behind them was as clean of cattle as horses and men could make it.

Just about the same time Toby decided that all was right with the world, the friendly fighter jets from Holloman Air Force Base decided to drop by for a visit. Grounded by all the recent rainy weather, they had not been out to check on their range-riding buddies for a few days. What the hotshot young aviators considered "dropping by" was actually more like plummeting by, from a great altitude to ground level in just a few seconds. Feeling their oats, the two pilots, who were only a few years older than Kyle and Jason, decided to put on a little show for their earthbound friends. So they came in very low, just about hat level, or so it seemed, and barrel-rolled across the top of La Conquistadora's prime Hereford herd. This marvel of aviation was then surpassed only by their breathtaking ascent, spiraling straight up and out of sight into the wild blue yonder.

Kyle knew exactly how this would play out. That evening, Degarrin would call the base commander, and the pilots of the United States Air Force would once more be advised not to strafe cattle herds and buzz cowboys. As usual, the pilots would assure their commanding officers that such a thing was unconscionable and certainly not something they would do. After all, they would hasten to add, they had all grown up watching Rawhide, and John Wayne was their idol. They all loved cowboys, and Red River was their favorite movie.

"No doubt," the brass would respond, as they always did.

Before that evening lecture could take place, there were problems to be dealt with under the morning sun.

When the jets came roaring in, every living creature, human or animal, was first startled and then terrified. The lives of cows and cowboys are relatively tranquil, at least when on the range; their existence modeled more on the nineteenth century than on the twentieth. It is not in the normal course of events to have the technology and mindset of the modern day crash noisily, and without warning, into their slow-moving world.

Even Adam, who had done his time at war, or maybe especially he for that very reason, instinctively cringed and ducked. All the cattle, and every horse and rider, did the same. The roar and scream of the jet engines was apocalyptic. Animal instinct, barely suppressed in the humans but rampant in the cattle, took over. The flight was on. It had been before living memory, if ever, that there had been a stampede on La Conquistadora. They had one now. When the jets shot skyward, spiraling away into oblivion, the cattle began to run. They had no particular destination in mind; they only wanted to get away, from what they did not even know.

Close to six hundred head had been gathered that morning, and now every one of them was mindlessly running. At first they ran out of fear, but then they ran just to be running. Each animal ran because it was a fine summer day, and because the sun was out and it had rained. The prairie was washed with a flow of Hereford red and white that poured out across its every bend and fold, carried by the thunder of over two thousand hooves. Above the rumble of those many hooves could be heard the clicking of hundreds of horns colliding.

In one great collective action, La Conquistadora's cowboys moved to gallop right alongside that churning sea of red. They rode hell-bent for leather because it was their job to turn that herd and save the drive. But they also raced so recklessly because it was like a step back in time to the cowboy days of old. To the days when a man on horseback was the freest man on earth, to the cowboy hero that had captured the world's imagination then and had held it forever after. Never again in their lives would these cowboys be given this chance. Stampedes involving hundreds of animals did not happen in this day and age, not even in the movies. Throwing care and caution to the winds, each man rode his hardest and his best because he was a cowboy and that was his job, but also because it was dangerous and it was fun, and because this day would never come again.

Kyle and Cochise threw themselves headlong into the scramble. The ground shook beneath them and the dust rose thick enough to taste. They were flying. Brush and cactus were jumped with neither pause nor thought. Obstacles too large for leaping were dodged and left behind. Kyle gave it to Cochise and luck to keep them free from holes and broken legs. On they raced, to gain the lead and turn the herd. Sometimes their landings were on spots of bare and slippery mud and the horse and rider slipped and slid, almost falling before they were able to regain their balance and their traction.

Kyle called to his mount, shouting him on.

"Come on, Cochise! Come on! Go! Go! Go!"

Cochise did not need Kyle's urgings. He was as caught up in the moment as was the boy on his back. Nothing could have slowed or turned his course.

The same was true for Jason and Robin Hood and for every other horse and rider. Even Adam, who thought that he had done it all, and Toby, who had long believed that La Conquistadora held no new surprises for him, and even old Bob Turner, who had spent a lifetime riding every range that he could find, answered the stampede's call with a young man's abandon, holding and leaving nothing in reserve. The hearts and hooves of all beat in rhythm to the drumming of the runaway herd.

Whether any rider's efforts or heroics that day helped bring order out of chaos was doubtful. A herd of running cattle will tire and slow eventually, no matter how much they excite each other on. The same is true of horses and men. About all that can be truly said of that wild dash is that the cowboys had stayed with their herd and stood ready when its race dropped from a run to a trot and finally to a heaving, blowing, worn-out walk.

While the cattle might have been tuckered out and settled down, the same could not be said for the riders who had charged along in their wake and draft. Their spirits were still in full flight and would not flag for some time to come. Even when calmer thoughts had returned, and in the distant, duller days to come, memories of this summer morning would bring a fleeting lift to every soul that had ridden its ride.

Kyle rode up to Jason.

"Jason," he said, "now that was better than getting laid. Not many things are, but that definitely topped it. Not by a whole lot, mind you, but by enough."

Jason stored that bit of knowledge away for future use. Such a yardstick might come in handy someday.

Toby was still riding pilot at the head of the herd, where he had managed to stay throughout the stampede. This was the major reason that the drive had ended up closer to, rather than farther from, Walnut Creek when all the running was finally done.

Adam cantered up the outside to check in with Toby and make certain that everything was all right with the wagon boss. Mutually reassured, Toby asked his longtime friend to reconnoiter the herd and crew. He wanted to be equally sure that everyone and everything was also safe and accounted for.

Making his circuit a few minutes later, Adam slowed down to greet Kyle.

"It was out of sight!" Kyle assured him.

Adam smiled his agreement. "I guess the base commander will be hearing from your granddad tonight," he commented.

"No doubt," Kyle agreed. "You know, Adam," he continued, "I've been thinking about it and there's a lot to be said for a jet fighter plane."

"Like what?" Adam asked, his interest piqued.

"Like Vietnam would look a lot better from one of those than from a rice paddy."

"I see your point," Adam agreed. "By the way," he added before cantering away, "I've ridden lots of rodeos in Canada. Things look really nice from Calgary, too."

Kyle watched Adam's retreating back with a smile. Calgary probably was a real nice place, he thought. Remembering his conversation with Jason about the possibility of getting tapped to do a little roping in the branding pen that afternoon, Kyle decided to ease back to the drag and do a little practicing. This would be a good opportunity. Thanks to the rain, for once he could get in his illicit loops without having to pay the price in eaten dust.

At the back of the herd, moving along the little dogies, Kyle found Bob Turner.

"Hi, Bob."

"Kyle." Thoroughly engaged in rolling a cigarette, Bob only nodded his acknowledgment of Kyle's arrival. Rolling your own, while riding horseback and holding the reins, was no mean trick. After half a century of practice, Bob had reduced it to an art form. It was only for a moment that he had to rely on two hands. Once the tobacco had been tapped out of its little cloth pouch and into the wrapper, held dished and waiting by only the tips of three expert fingers, the performance became a one-handed wonder. Up to the lips for a few quick licks of the tongue, a flick of the fingers here, a little swipe of pressure there, and all of a sudden Bob Turner was lighting up.

Kyle had seen Bob perform this ritual many times. The most memorable, though, had happened a few years earlier. It was in the autumn and the air was crisp, with a little bite to it. Degarrin wanted a group of bulls rounded up and put into a trap for some reason or another. It was a routine sort of task, not a major endeavor at all. Kyle and his mother just happened to be visiting for a few days, and Sophie decided it might just be fun to join in the project. She had not ridden La Conquistadora's range with any real purpose for a long, long time. It would be fun, and it would also be a nice experience for her son. Kyle, needless to say, had been thrilled. He remembered being just about beside himself with excitement, but determined not to show it. After all, he didn't want people to think he was just some dude, out from town for the day!

Kyle remembered that day as clearly as this morning's breakfast. He couldn't really say why, unless it was because of his mother. He had never before seen her cast in a role so purely from her youth. He knew, of course, that she was an excellent rider, but he had always thought of her in terms of show rings or hunt field courses. He was totally unprepared for how completely at home, and right, she was in a Levi jacket, riding western style across the rolling open range with an old cowboy. It had flashed through his mind that this, and not their plush Carrolton world, was the proper setting for his mom. He had watched in fascination as Bob Turner expertly rolled a cigarette and then, with the chivalry of an aged courtier, offered it to Sophie. Kyle could not recall ever having felt a deeper burst of love and admiration for his mother than when she accepted the offered gift with pleasure and then smoked it with grace. Sophie had waited while Bob rolled one for himself. She had graciously leaned toward the old man when he lit a match and offered her a light. Then the two had ridden along together, companionably smoking and sharing the moment.

It had been a tiny incident, but one that had struck Kyle forcibly and had stayed preserved in his memory with crystal clarity. It had obviously been an innate courtesy with Bob Turner to offer a lady a cigarette if he were going to smoke one himself. While Kyle had never asked her, he suspected that his mother had not particularly relished the idea of smoking the lowest grade of tobacco and floor sweepings rolled up in paper and sealed with an old-timer's spit. He believed Bob's innate courtesy was matched by his mother's. But then again, maybe not. With his mom, you just never knew. It was equally possible that she had an earthy side that had accepted the home-rolled cigarette without even registering it, let alone missing a beat. With Sophie, his mother, you just never knew. Although he had spent his whole life with her and guessed he knew her better than anyone on earth, Kyle could never quite figure his mother out. For him, that morning ride across this huge land with Bob Turner and a home-rolled smoke had somehow captured, in a quick-freeze snapshot, a lot of whatever it was that made Sophie, Sophie.

"That was a hell of a ride, wasn't it?" Bob Turner interrupted Kyle's contemplations.

"It sure was!" Kyle agreed.

"Have you ever done anything like that before?"

"Never! But I'd do it again in a minute."

"Yeah," Bob chuckled, "I'm an old man and ought to know better, but I would, too."

"Bob, you've been doing this all your life, haven't you?"

"What, riding in stampedes and acting like a fool?"

Kyle laughed. "No," he said. "What I mean is, you've always been a cowboy, haven't you? This is what you have always done, isn't it? It's your profession."

"I don't know as I'd call it much of a profession, son, but yeah, it's all I've ever done. For more than about fifty years or so, I reckon."

"It's a great way to live, isn't it, Bob? All this space and freedom. I can't explain how much I love it. I should have started coming here and riding with the wagon every summer a long time ago. I just never dreamed it would be so great. It's like being an eagle, free to soar and fly whenever, wherever you want."

Bob Turner rode in silence for a moment, thinking. The old man was turning something over in his mind, something he'd been carrying a long time.

"It's been a good life, Kyle, and I always had a good time. Even so, cowboying ain't something I'd recommend too much of."

"Why not?" Kyle demanded. "It seems so great, perfect in fact!"

"That's the problem, son. That's just exactly how it seems. This life is all freedom and abandon. Freedom to always come and go, no real bosses, no one ordering you around, and if they do, you just pack your gear and go, 'cause there are lots of big outfits and one of them always needs a hand; all this sky and open land; a horizon so far away you can never reach it. I know, because I've tried. That far horizon is like the pot of gold at the end of the rainbow; you can never quite get there."

"So what's wrong with that?" Kyle demanded again. "It sounds great to me. Where do I sign up?"

Bob grinned at his indignant young friend.

"Kyle, take a good look at me," he said. "I'm near seventy years old. You're seventeen. We are doing the exact same job for just about the same pay. The only difference between us is that I'm a whole lot older and worn out, and I might be a little better at it than you, but probably not much. I guess what I'm trying to say is this, and I've never tried to say it before, so it might not come out just right: be careful with this life. Being a real cowboy, one that really works cattle and rides the range, that knows horses and cattle better than people and likes them better, too, can be mighty addictive. If this life really gets a hold of you, gets a real good grip on you, you can't let it go. You can't ever get free."

"Bob!" Kyle interrupted. "You make it sound terrible! Like it's worse than drugs! And it's not! It's a good life. Being a cowboy doesn't hurt anyone. Look at you, you're a great person and you've had a good life."

"This life is okay for lots of people, Kyle, and it's been fine for me. But it's not for everyone. You're the only person I ever told this to, Kyle. But you need to be careful. Being a cowboy is fun for now, but don't get hooked on it. You're a real smart boy. You'd make a great cowhand, but you'd make a better doctor or lawyer. You need to go on to college, and do real good, too. Then get on out there and make something of yourself. You will always be a cowboy, Kyle. This summer has made you one. You're the real deal now, not the city-slicker, drugstore kind. Now you got to go and be more. Make us all proud, son."

"You're serious, aren't you, Bob?" Kyle asked, strangely touched.

"As a heart attack. You've had your summer, now get on with your life. You can always come back for a visit. La Conquistadora ain't going nowhere, and there'll always be horses that need riding and cattle to be driven. There's always room for a good flanker."

"I guess you're right," Kyle said halfheartedly. He hated to bid his dream farewell.

"Of course I'm right. Here, I'll tell you a story. I saw a book once about the early days on the Texas range, when it was still open, and there weren't any fences. The book talked about this fellow from somewhere back east. He was an artist and he wanted to paint pictures and make statues and things of life on the frontier. He came out to Texas to get a look at everything firsthand, then he figured he'd go home and do his art. The book said he was a real talented artist, that he might could have been great, really famous and all."

"What happened to him?" Kyle asked.

"Well, he got out to Texas and some outfit or another hired him on. He started cowboying on that old open range and he fell in love with it. This old boy was plumb fascinated with the life. He took photographs of every single thing he saw, figuring that they would help him with his artwork. This old boy did go back east to be an artist. But he kept coming back. He just could not stay off that open range. All that freedom, that open sky, and those endless miles of grass that went forever, just got a hold on that fellow that he couldn't let go of."

"Did he ever really become an artist?" Kyle asked.

"No, not really. He did a little work, but not too much. That book said something that's always stayed with me. It talked about how the artist kept thinking that just real soon, he would go back east and get started. But he kept putting it off, until finally his fingers began to stiffen up. After a while, they got so bad he couldn't even hold a paintbrush. It was too late then, for him to be the artist he might have been. I guess he just made his dreams wait too long."

Kyle did not like Bob's story very much. It had a bleakness he did not care for. The cowboy was America's mythic hero; his life was the stuff of legend. Kyle was right in the midst of experiencing that life firsthand, and had found it perfect. He was not interested in hearing about any dark undertow, but he was also curious.

"Bob," he asked carefully, not wanting to seem rude, "has this been a bad life for you? Do you figure you missed out on anything much because of it?"

"No, I guess not, not really anyway. I suppose you could even say this was my dream. But I didn't have no special talent and I didn't have no education to speak of. You could say my prospects was limited. But it's different for you, Kyle, and it was different for that artist fellow. You've got a whole lot going for you. You've got prospects, and you oughtn't to throw them away."

They rode along in silence for a while, Kyle turning over in his mind all that Bob had said. He recognized an act of affection and concern when he saw it. He looked at the rugged, weather-beaten old cowboy beside him and smiled.

"Thanks, Bob. I'd never thought of it that way."

Bob just nodded. He had been wanting to say his piece to his young friend for a long time. Now he had.

Everyone had been a little worried about getting the herd across Walnut Creek. They need not have wasted their energy. Just as Jason had predicted, the creek had run down and was not running more than a couple of feet of water when the drive and its herders arrived. The crossing proved to be routine and uneventful, even anticlimactic. The only person disappointed was Larry; he had been hoping for water high enough to wash cow eye and pus off his jeans. He would just have to wait for camp.

The cowboys were happy to have the creek crossing safely behind them and the wagon camp not so far ahead. It had been an eventful morning, and a little break would be more than welcome.

The final leg of the journey to camp found Kyle and Jason riding drag, throwing practice loops at the calves who tiredly and forlornly straggled there. Their skills had improved and they were roping with some success. Being fond of both boys, Adam moseyed back to join them. The boys were glad to see him, having long since stopped being embarrassed by his presence, and always welcomed his roping tips. They were critiqued, advised, and shown how to do it for a while.

Jason suddenly remembered something he had been wanting to ask Adam.

"Adam, how come we all got off and loosened our cinches this morning, before we swam the creek?"

"If a horse is cinched up tight when he's swimming, he can't breathe. He'll go under and drown. Except for Cochise, of course. He'll go under and drown anyway."

The boys grinned at that remark, but Kyle was looking worried.

"I never knew that, Adam."

"Yeah, that's the kind of thing people forget to mention. Generally speaking, the first time a cowboy hears about it is right after he drowns his first horse. Why, Kyle? You drowned any horses I haven't heard about?"

"Just about!"

"What do you mean?" Adam asked.

"When we were working the Redondo pasture the other day, Jason and I decided to swim our horses in the dirt tank that's up on the north end. You know, the tank with the really deep end?"

"Yes, I know the tank."

"Well, I rode in first. My horse started to swim and then just sank like a rock. He hit bottom and bounced back up and somehow managed to get to the bank and stagger up out of there. We decided it might not be a real good day for swimming."

"Geez, Kyle, you could have drowned that horse!" Jason exclaimed.

"You are one lucky boy," Adam said.

"No shit!" Kyle agreed, imagining his grandfather's reaction to a killed horse.

By the time lunch and a break rolled around, La Conquistadora's crew was ready for it. They were tired. The day had reached its typical hot, high temperature by noon, only now it was mixed with a fair amount of humidity as evaporation began taking back the rain that had fallen. While by Houston reckoning the day was balmy, by desert standards La Conquistadora languished under a sweltering blanket of steam that sucked the energy right out of everyone.

Dutch-oven-baked pot roast with potatoes, carrots, and onions, cooked up to perfection and smothered in thick delicious gravy, was not appreciated. The food was steaming hot, but so were the cowboys, and they already felt like they were smothering. More of the same for lunch was not appealing.

Larry, who had found a change of pants, was once more socially acceptable, but his mood had not been as easily changed.

"I wish I had a cold beer," he announced.

Visions of icy cold beer in a frosted mug, or in a bottle, or even in a can from a lukewarm six-pack, danced through every cowboy's head.

"I wish I had a lot of cold beers," Sam Cook agreed wistfully, speaking for every man present.

Everyone just sat there, under the fly, in the stifling heat, and dejectedly contemplated what they did not have. Even George Price was at a loss for words and had no unsolicited advice to offer.

They scarcely noticed, and hardly cared, when Miss Louisa's pale salmon-colored Oldsmobile pulled into camp. Out hopped Louisa and Annie Lloyd, all fresh and chipper from their nice air-conditioned ride across the ranch. Neither woman had spent the majority of her life on La Conquistadora with its inhabitants not to have learned a few things. They knew that, after the forced hiatus of the rain, both Toby and Degarrin would be pushing their men hard to make up for lost time and work. They had also felt the climbing temperature and humidity all morning and were well aware that tempers and discomfort levels were likely to be rising, too, keeping pace right alongside. This, they knew, would be a good day for a treat.

Watching their wives head for the trunk of the car, Degarrin and Toby lumbered to their feet. They knew their wives as well as their wives knew them. Based on this knowledge and lots of past experience, both men were hopeful that some kind of goodies were about to be produced from that Oldsmobile's open trunk.

"We'd better go help," they decided.

Sure enough, waiting in the trunk was a load for each of them to heft. Degarrin lifted the big barrel-like thermos that weighed a ton and sloshed wonderfully with the sound of ice and lemonade. Toby grabbed up the remaining ice chest. Then, on pure spontaneous instinct, he paused to kiss his wife. He kissed her right there, in front of God and everybody, but mostly cowboys. He knew when he saw that ice chest that she had brought him sherbet. He was delighted to see her and the sherbet, but mostly he was glad he had had the great foresight and wisdom to marry her long ago. Otherwise, this might have been just another hot and humid day.

The gloomy mood that had settled over the camp shot up like an elevator when Louisa and Annie and their offering arrived. The lemonade turned out to be pink and floating with ice, and there was plenty of what looked to be vanilla ice cream for everyone.

"We brought you all a present today, just some little treats, but we knew you might need a lift. So, come and get it," Louisa announced.

No one needed to be invited twice. In record time, a line had formed and then dispersed as cowboys filled their cups and bowls.

Kyle, and everyone else, dug in. There was just nothing like a mouthful of cold vanilla ice cream to cool you down on a hot summer day.

First Kyle's taste buds, and then his face, registered a shocked surprise that was mirrored in Jason's face, and in the other cowboys' faces, too.

Kyle swallowed enough to speak.

"This is pineapple sherbet," he announced the now obvious.

"It sure is!" Toby agreed with relish.

"Pineapple sherbet is Toby's favorite. He just loves to eat a bowl after working hard on a hot day. I knew it would really hit the spot today," Annie explained.

Degarrin paused in his eating long enough to chuckle and reminisce. "I remember the first time Annie brought pineapple sherbet out to the wagon. It was a day just like this; hotter than blazes and everybody just ready to get into a bad mood. Then here came Annie with what we thought was vanilla ice cream. We all dug in. We were all stunned and pretty disappointed, too, when we got that first taste. We hadn't expected pineapple sherbet, and we didn't like it much."

"Is that right, sir?" Jason asked, thinking much the same thing.

"Yes," Degarrin answered. "Then we all figured out, about the same time, that pineapple sherbet was what we had. In fact, it was all we had. It was either that or nothing. Right then, every man on that crew learned to love that sherbet, and we've been eating it ever since."

That afternoon, Kyle and Jason, and all the other cowboys of La Conquistadora, shared a moment of revelation when they, too, discovered that pineapple sherbet, under certain circumstances, really could just hit the spot.

That afternoon, as the branding work went on and on, Kyle was proved correct; there was plenty of roping to go around. Degarrin liked to keep an afternoon's work down to about a hundred and fifty calves; that afternoon there were two hundred and fifty or more to be branded. It was too many, like working a double shift. Degarrin wasn't too concerned about the crew being overworked. After all, they had been lying around camp for the last three days, on company time. He was concerned about the cattle, though. He hated to keep the cows and calves stirred up any longer than absolutely necessary. That was why he liked a smaller, more manageable-sized branding. He wanted the work done smoothly and quickly, with no confusion and no wasted time or effort. Keeping mother cows and their calves penned up and stirred up was a fine way to make dogies. Degarrin and Toby's mission was to get La Conquistadora's prized Herefords in off the range and right back out onto it as quickly and efficiently as possible.

This day had been an anomaly from the start. Everything had been a little, or a lot, off center all day long. The trend continued into the afternoon as calf after calf was heeled and dragged from the herd to be flanked and marked. It seemed to take forever to make a dent, but finally the branded calves began to outnumber the unbranded ones. Progress was being made; it was just slow going.

Everybody was tired, Kyle and Jason especially so. They had worked hard all morning and had flanked calves all afternoon. Wrestling calves was not an easy task; it took a lot of muscle and energy. While both boys were loath to admit it, the day had taken its toll and was beginning to pall.

Toby could see their energy flag and Kyle knew it was time for a change. Sure enough, Sam and Larry had been roping for quite a while, methodically heeling calf after calf. Degarrin had spent the afternoon castrating, Toby vaccinating. Adam had roped for the first hour and then had switched off and was now running the branding iron that stamped La Conquistadora's famous crown on the left ribs of all its cattle.

When Toby switched them in, both Kyle and Jason were delighted; this was their chance to shine. They were also nervous. It might also be their chance to screw up royally. Having the whole crew standing idly and critically by while he tried to rope a single calf was one of Kyle's nightmares, and it was a nightmare that could be on the brink of becoming reality. Kyle hoped not. He really hoped not; his day had already had enough kinks in it.

Jason had no such qualms. His day had been super so far, and he had no doubt it would continue in the same manner. Jason was also unplagued by the presence and observation of two grandparents and numerous other people who had known him from pre-birth to present. All Jason had to do was have fun and rope calves. Kyle, on the other hand, had to deliver up to expectation, and expectations tended to run pretty high.

Billy Bonney was the horse Kyle had chosen from his string for the afternoon work. Billy, unlike his namesake, was a nice, mild-mannered fellow, just about as far as possible from outlaw status. Billy Bonney was calm of nature and always did fine as a roping horse.

The boys' practice and Adam's coaching paid off; they both did fine, having far more difficulty finding an unbranded calf in the constantly moving and shifting herd than in catching him.

Kyle and Billy Bonney were doing themselves proud. Kyle took his time and had to concentrate, but his quarterback's eye stood him in good stead. He seldom missed. Degarrin and Louisa, and Toby and Annie, and Adam were all as proud as punch, but true to character, tried not to show it. Kyle's day was looking up.

Kyle neatly heeled a little heifer and had just turned Billy to drag her toward the flankers when his day returned to its previous course. The calf was just a baby and thoroughly confused. Its mama was a first-calf heifer and wasn't much better off. The baby began to bellow and its not-too-bright mother rushed to the rescue. For all her efforts, the best that the young cow managed to achieve was the hopeless tangling of both herself and her calf in the rope that was tied to Kyle's saddle on Billy Bonney's back.

Kyle saw it happening and felt the rope go tight in the wrong way. He knew what a tangle looked like. He also knew, from his grandparents' stories, what a tangle could do.

Then everything happened at once.

Louisa's scream tore the air.

"No! Oh, my God, no! Not again!"

With impossible speed, three men simply materialized at that taut rope and three equally razor-sharp knife blades slashed down. It was Adam's blade that sliced through the lariat and cut Kyle free. It could just as well have been Toby's or Degarrin's. Perhaps it was Adam's because he was younger and maybe just a fraction quicker or stronger.

"Take my rope off Blue and finish up," Degarrin told his grandson, giving him an affectionate slap on the thigh. "I've got to go and talk to your grandmother."

"Yes, sir," Kyle said. Something major had just happened, he knew, but it had all transpired so quickly he wasn't quite sure what it had all been about.

• • •

Degarrin let himself out of the corral and strode around Louisa's car to her door, which was still partway open. His wife was laid back against the car seat, pale and shaken. Her hands were gripping the edge of the seat and her knuckles were white. For a moment she had not seen Kyle at all; she had seen Danny, and the rope, and the terrible stillness that came after.

Annie was no better off.

Louisa just looked at her husband.

He watched her with a questioning look, wondering if she was going to faint. He had never seen his wife faint, and it occurred to him that this could be the day.

"I thought it was going to be Danny all over again," she told him, a little weakly.

"I know, but you needn't have worried. We've talked about it; you know I always have a knife ready. I've always promised that will never again happen if I'm anywhere near." Then he grinned at her. "Or apparently, if Toby or Adam are anywhere in the vicinity!"

The color had returned to Louisa's face and she mustered a smile.

"Louisa," he said simply, "you can rest assured that whatever it may look like, if Kyle is in any potential danger, I'm watching double close. And apparently everybody else is, too. He is probably safer up there roping than anywhere else in the branding pen. He probably doesn't even know that he was in any particular danger, and I told him to get my lariat and finish up, so that he never will. We don't want him to be scared, Louisa."

"No, I know we don't," Louisa agreed. She managed a little laugh. It was a bit shaky, but it was a laugh. "Don't worry, honey. Annie and I won't carry on over it. We'll pretend it was no big deal. Actually, because of you, and Toby, and Adam, I guess it really wasn't a big deal, was it?"

"No," Degarrin grinned at her, "it was no big deal. Just another day at the wagon."

• • •

Back in the branding pen, the work had started up again. Adam and Toby stood out of the way, catching their breath and letting their pulse rates return to normal.

Toby watched Kyle rope a calf and commented to Adam, "I'll be glad when this day is over. That boy's luck has got to be close to running out."

Adam could only agree.

Chapter 7 — Rodeo Day

IT WAS RODEO DAY. The afternoon was hot and white along the horizon, without a breath of wind. By four o'clock that Saturday afternoon, the wagon camp was deserted. Everybody had headed for headquarters to get all slicked down and shined up for the big evening ahead.

The bunkhouse popped with activity and well before suppertime, headquarters was devoid of cowboys. The single shower had run nonstop for an hour, somebody's radio was playing through the thin plaster walls, and the smell of aftershave and boot polish had replaced the usual smell of horse sweat and tobacco. Except for Kyle and Jason. They got ready for the big night at Casa Blanca, showering in their own personal bathrooms and luxuriating in thick terry towels, the likes of which they had not seen since they had last visited the big house. They would have supper with Kyle's grandparents and then go to town in Kyle's Camaro for the rodeo and dance.

The boys were as shiny as new dimes when they arrived in Degarrin's little sitting room, wearing the Levi's and shirts Rufina had starched and pressed for them. She liked these two kids and wanted them to be the handsomest boys at the dance. With her help, they were.

Louisa greeted her guests warmly when they appeared at the door. "Come in, come right in," she said. "You both look so handsome! Rufina will be so proud! She wanted you to just look perfect, and I must say you do. Are you looking forward to tonight?"

"Yes, ma'am." Both boys assured her.

"Are you boys having a good time this summer?" Degarrin asked.

Again Kyle and Jason answered, "Yes, sir," in unison.

"Mr. Degarrin, I'm having the absolute time of my life." Jason hurried to assure him. "I can't thank you enough for letting me come up here with Kyle and do this. I just hope we can come again next year."

His grandfather didn't answer right away. Kyle watched the hard lines of his face ease, just barely, the closest thing to being moved that Degarrin would allow himself in company.

"I hope so too, Jason. You have turned into a real good hand. We've been lucky to have you both here this summer."

Kyle heard it, I hope so too, and something in the way his grandfather said it caught and held. Not of course or count on it. Just I hope so. It was probably nothing. It was the kind of thing you wouldn't notice unless you were already listening for something you couldn't name.

Louisa and Degarrin smiled fondly at the boys as Rufina summoned them to the dining room by sounding the dinner chimes.

When everyone was seated at the dining room table, the candles lit and the room warm with the smell of roasted meat, Rufina brought in a standing prime rib with a flourish. The candlelight caught the sideboard and the golden eagle mounted above the doorway and stopped there, leaving the corners of the room in darkness. The silver bell sat beside Louisa's plate where it had always sat, small and worn smooth from years and years of her hand.

"Wow, Rufina, that looks great!" Kyle exclaimed. "And Rufina, so do our clothes. Thanks so much for getting them ready for us."

"Yes, ma'am." Jason seconded his friend. "Thank you. If it had been left to us, Kyle and I probably would have looked like we had just crawled out of our bedrolls."

"I know, Señor Jason. That is why I got everything ready for you. I wanted you to look your best."

Kyle caught his grandmother's expression, the faintest lift of an eyebrow, a private amusement she kept to herself. If it had come down to it, she was perfectly capable of pressing and starching and getting the boys presentable. She was just glad it hadn't come down to it.

"Will you and Mr. Degarrin be going to the rodeo tonight?" Jason asked.

"No," Louisa answered. "We old folks will just stay home and nest. You kids will have to bring back a full report, though."

"I guess this rodeo is quite a tradition, isn't it?" Kyle asked.

"It is," Degarrin answered. "I think this rodeo has been going on for sixty years or more. I know the ranch has always called time out for it. By the time I got here, it was already set that the cowboys got Saturday night off and weren't expected back at the wagon until Sunday night."

"Years ago, we used to have a big ice cream social out on the lawn on Saturday afternoon before the rodeo," Louisa said. "Everybody on the ranch was invited, and we would invite a few other people as special guests. It was quite a party." She spoke a little wistfully, with just the faintest hint of melancholy in her voice.

"Yes, it was," Degarrin agreed in much the same tone.

"Why did you quit having it?" Kyle asked curiously.

"Oh, I don't know," Louisa answered vaguely. "I suppose it just fell by the wayside somehow, and never got taken up again."

Something passed between his grandparents, not a look, exactly, but a quality of shared silence that shut everything else out for just a moment.

Jason had been eating his tossed green salad with gusto and tasting a serving of fresh fruit salad with equal enthusiasm.

"You don't realize how much you miss salad and fresh fruit until you don't get them for a while," he said.

"I know," Louisa said with a laugh. "Everyone that has ever spent a while out with the wagon says the same thing. That's why I had Rufina put them both on the menu tonight. And Kyle, she fixed her fabulous calabacitas just for you, too."

"Yes, I know, and I really appreciate it. So far, I've just about eaten my weight in it," Kyle replied, as he took another mouthful of the wonderful corn, squash, and green chile dish.

"Hey, Jason," he said, suddenly remembering something, "show Grandmother your arrowhead." Turning to his grandmother, he continued, "Jason found this really great arrowhead on the sand flats a few days ago. Show it to her, Jason."

Jason had brought along his find for just such a showing and pulled it from his shirt pocket for Louisa's inspection.

Taking it in her hand, Louisa turned the arrowhead over and examined each side carefully. Looking up, she smiled at Jason. "What a beautiful point," she said. "It is absolutely perfect! It reminds me of Danny's spear point."

Jason was a little confused.

"Of what, ma'am?" he asked.

"Here, I'll show you," Louisa said, rising from the table and going to the fireplace mantle. She returned with the great spear point that Danny had given her at that last ice cream social so many years ago.

"Wow," Jason breathed, holding the spear point in his hand and examining it carefully. "This is something else!" he said. "My arrowhead is nothing compared to this."

"Yes, it is!" Louisa exclaimed. "They are equally wonderful. They are both absolutely perfect, and perfect is as rare as hen's teeth. You treasure your arrowhead, always, Jason. I'm glad it was found by you." With a warm smile, she returned Jason's treasure to him.

After another admiring look, Jason handed the spear point back to Louisa.

"Was this found here on La Conquistadora?" he asked.

"Yes, it was," Louisa answered. "It was found here years ago, by a young cowboy named Danny. He gave it to me, and it has been there on the mantle ever since that day. It is one of my most prized possessions."

Kyle watched his grandmother turn the spear point in her fingers before setting it back on the mantle. He had seen it there his whole life, had always known it as part of the house, like the fireplace itself. He had never thought to ask where it came from. Now he watched the care with which she placed it back in its spot, centering it just so, and understood that he had been looking at something precious without ever quite seeing it.

"Would you like to have my arrowhead to sit beside it?" Jason asked.

Kyle looked at him as if he were crazy, and Jason wondered if he was.

Louisa was very much touched by the offer, and his grandfather was studying Jason with a look Kyle had never seen on him before, something between amusement and wonder, as though he had seen this before.

"No, no, Jason," Louisa laughed. "This arrowhead is your special find. You keep it and enjoy it, but if you ever get tired of it or don't want it anymore, well, remember me. Okay?"

"Okay." Jason agreed, secretly relieved, and wondering what had possessed him to try and give his arrowhead away.

Louisa smiled at both his sweet offer and his obvious relief. Kyle saw it, too, the way his grandmother looked at Jason, the warmth in it, a recognition that went deeper than the evening's pleasantries. Just like Kyle, just like Danny. Something about this boy had reminded her of someone, and Kyle could only suppose it was himself.

"Hey, Gramma," Kyle interrupted her thoughts.

Arching an eyebrow in his direction, Louisa gave Kyle a skeptical look. They both knew from years of experience that he only called her Gramma and used a wheedling tone of voice when he wanted something.

Seeing her response, Kyle burst out laughing.

"Really, Gramma," he said, "you shouldn't be so suspicious! What I want isn't all that bad!"

"Tell me what you want and then I'll decide how bad it is, or isn't."

"I was just wondering if I could invite Momma and Daddy up for the last day of the wagon work, and my girlfriend, of course." Casting his grandfather a mischievous glance, he continued, "I'm pretty sure Granddaddy is going to let me finish up the summer work by letting me rope on Teddy Blue the last day."

"Oh yes, I'm sure I'm going to do that," Degarrin said cheerfully, leaving no doubt in anyone's mind that that would also be the day there would be snowballs in hell.

"I think that is a wonderful idea, Kyle! Of course we'll invite them to come up. Won't that be nice, Mike?" she asked her husband.

"Sure," Degarrin gamely agreed. His grandfather was working something over behind that agreeable expression, trying to picture Louisa, Sophie, his son-in-law, and himself all cozily chatting with

Adam Connor over lunch at the wagon. Obviously, his grandmother had not thought this thing through.

Kyle didn't think much of it himself. He was still thinking solely in terms of a pleasant little house party.

"Kyle," Louisa asked, a little puzzled, "I didn't think you had a girlfriend at the moment?"

"Well, I'm just about to get her back. She's been hearing about La Conquistadora for forever. I figure she'll never be able to pass up a chance to come here and see it all, but it's a package deal. If she wants to come up here, she has to take me, too."

Jason spoke up. "Oh, Amy will take you back. There's no doubt of that."

"Why do you say that?" Louisa asked curiously.

"Because she always does," Jason said simply.

That seemed to answer that. Louisa nodded. "We certainly wouldn't want to stand in the way of the inevitable. By all means, Kyle, call your mother and Amy and tell them we will be waiting for them all, with bells on," Louisa said merrily.

"Well, if you're going to do any calling around, make it fast," Jason advised. "We have a big rodeo and dance to get to."

Kyle had to acknowledge the truth of his friend's words. Finishing up their supper in a hurry, the boys asked to be excused. Louisa sent them on their way, telling Kyle to let her know if their invitations were accepted or not.

• • •

Jason didn't feel like listening to the great Kyle and Amy makeup scene, which was just as well. He knew Kyle would throw him out of the room before he called Amy. Jason decided to save his friend the bother.

"I'll wait for you out here on the porch," he said, "but hurry it up, Kyle, okay? I'd like to get to town before the whole rodeo is over."

"Not to worry," Kyle assured him. "This won't take a minute, and if it does, the Camaro will make it up in no time."

"Yeah, well, if you're not out here in fifteen minutes, I'm leaving without you."

"How're you planning to do that when I've got the keys?"

"I'll hot-wire it."

"You know how to hot-wire a car?" Kyle asked, mildly concerned.

"Do you?" Jason hedged.

"Yeah, Skeeter showed me, just before he got arrested."

"Kyle, has it escaped your attention that you and I have all the same hood friends?"

"Did Skeeter show you how to hot-wire a car?" Kyle demanded to know, highly indignant.

"Of course."

"He told me I was the only one he had shown that little trick to!"

"Well, he told me the same thing, so now we know he's a liar as well as a thief." Consulting his watch, Jason announced it was now only thirteen minutes to hot-wiring time.

"Oh, keep your shirt on. I'll be right back," Kyle assured him.

Jason watched his friend disappear into the house before allowing a delighted grin to spread across his face. So, he mused, old Skeeter did know how to hot-wire a car and had shown Kyle how to do it. He would have to get Kyle to show him how to do that. You never know; he just might want to take up an exciting career in grand theft auto someday. Jason settled into a heavy wooden deck chair to wait for Kyle and enjoy the portal's cool shade.

• • •

With one eye on the clock, Kyle picked up the phone, set it down, and picked it up again. The last time he had called this number, her mother had told him Amy was out with Joel Cannon, and he had hung up and ridden back to the wagon in the dark, telling himself he was done. He wasn't done. His mouth was dry and his hand was not entirely steady. He dialed Amy's number from memory.

"Hello," she answered on the first ring.

That could be a good sign, Kyle thought. It was Saturday night, after all; maybe she didn't have a date. But then again, it was early on a Saturday night. Maybe she was getting ready for a date.

"Hello?" Amy said again, a little impatiently.

"Amy, this is Kyle."

Three hundred miles away, Amy sank down on her bed. Kyle could hear the silence change, that particular quality of quiet that meant she had been waiting for this call, even if she hadn't known it.

"Are you busy, Amy?"

"No, I'm not busy."

"You don't have a date with that son of a bitch?"

"No, I don't have a date."

"Are you going out with anybody?"

Amy began to smile. Kyle could hear it. "Are we playing twenty questions?" she teased.

"I miss you real bad, Amy. I can't stand thinking about you being with some other guy. Especially that son of a bitch, Joel Cannon."

"I quit seeing him, and I'm not going out with anybody else," Amy calmed him down.

"What about you?" she asked. "What kind of mischief have you been getting into?"

"Me? I'm out here with the cows! There's no trouble for me to get into!"

"Are you having fun?"

"Yeah, actually I am. Jason and I are having a blast, but I sure do miss you a lot. It would be perfect except for that."

"I miss you, too, Kyle."

"Do you still love me?" he asked.

"Of course."

"Did you ever stop?"

"No."

"I love you, Amy."

"I love you, too, Kyle. I always have."

Kyle leaned back against the wall and just grinned.

"Listen, Amy, I want you to come up here for the end of the summer work. That's not too long from now. My mom and dad will be coming up here, and I want you to come, too. You'll love it; this place is really great."

"Oh, Kyle, that sounds like fun! Will it be okay with your mom?"

"Sure, I'm gonna call her right now. I'll ask her to call you and the two of you can get it all worked out. Listen, baby, I gotta go. I love you. Don't let that son of a bitch anywhere near you, okay?"

"Okay, I love you, too." Amy was laughing. Kyle always made her laugh.

"Hey, Amy, you want my ring back?"

"Of course I want your ring back! Some little underclassman trollop will be trying to seduce you away if I don't have it."

"I'll give it to you when you get here. I really have to go, baby. I'll see you in a few days."

"Okay. Bye-bye, Kyle."

"Bye, baby."

"You'll come, won't you, Momma?" he asked worriedly.

"Of course I'll come. And I'll bring your daddy and Amy with me. It will be a lot of fun for everyone. Are you happy to be back with Amy?"

"Yes, I really am, Momma. I just miss her so much when she's not around. You know?"

"Yes, I know. That's why you should keep her around."

When Kyle hung up the phone, he was still smiling. He had a great mom, a great girlfriend, and he hadn't heard his Camaro start up, so he supposed he still had his car and his best friend.

• • •

Jason, still slouched in the deck chair, looked up to greet his friend. "Well," he said, "I see the great romance is back on."

"How do you know?"

"'Cause you're grinning like a fool and you're lit up like a sparkler on the Fourth of July."

Kyle ignored this response. "How come you're not hot-wiring my car?" he asked instead.

"You still got ninety seconds."

"Well, then, come on. Let's not waste them."

Boot heels clicking, the boys strode down the portal toward the waiting Camaro, pausing only long enough to inform Louisa that Kyle's invitations had been accepted, and to say good night.

• • •

By the time the boys reached the outskirts of Clauson, twilight was falling. To the west flared the spectacular sunset that was a routine, daily occurrence. Even so, the boys could not help commenting on its beauty. The clouds across the horizon and up the sky were streaked in oranges and pinks of every shade, their shadows and ripples painted in purple from deep to light.

"Look at that sunset, Jason," Kyle said, a touch of wonder in his voice.

"Yeah, pretty incredible, isn't it? Even better than usual. Makes you wish you had a camera, doesn't it?"

"I've tried taking pictures of them. It never seems to do justice to it all, somehow," Kyle commented.

Jason watched the panorama spread before them for a moment, taking in the vastness of the colored sky as the evening's production unfolded. "You don't get these sunsets anywhere but in the West," he mused. "I've got a cousin that went to college at St. John's in Santa Fe. He said that every evening up till past Thanksgiving, all the eastern kids would drift outside a little before sundown and just sit there and watch the sunsets. Every night they did that, and they'd stay outside, just watching until it was dark and there wasn't anything else to see. Then everyone would come back the next night and do it all again."

"Is that right?" Kyle asked. "I never thought about going to college and not being able to get a decent sunset."

"Well, old son, there ain't no sunsets and there ain't no green chile at Harvard. Or at the University of Virginia," Jason added as an afterthought.

Kyle grinned. "Then I guess I'd better go to Stanford."

"You better plan on taking your own green chile, then."

"I thought you could ship me a case or two when you're a student at the Carrolton Community College."

"Not me, Ace. There won't be any care packages from me. I'm going to be at Rice, where you can't get a decent sunset and the Mexican food is only half-assed, but you can get to be a hell of an engineer."

"I thought that was Georgia Tech," Kyle said.

They were quiet for a moment.

"You hear about Mark Hadley?" Jason asked. Mark had been a year ahead of them at Carrolton. His draft notice came in July.

Kyle nodded. He turned the Camaro into the dirt parking lot of the rodeo arena.

Darkness was starting its descent. It would not be long before the bright lights of the arena would stand as beacons on the prairie, guiding lights to anyone who might be lost. The possibility of a lost rodeo-goer was remote, but should it occur, the glaring lights stood ready, marking the spot for all comers.

Up in the worn and wooden bleachers, Kyle and Jason quickly found their La Conquistadora compadres, all of whom were looking their best, and some of whom were well on their way to an alcoholic haze.

"Evening, boys," Bob Turner greeted them. "Would you boys care to join us in a beer?" he asked as he handed each a can.

"Sure," the boys grinned. Each popped a top and settled back to watch the show.

The show started with the grand entrance, which by Clauson standards was grand indeed. It consisted of a great string of riders, many of them teenage girls in skin-tight shiny pants with equally flashy blouses, covered in as many sequins as possible. Crowning all this splendor there was usually a color-coordinated cowboy hat in red, blue, green, purple, or just about any other color imaginable. The grand entrance was like a royal procession, serpentining across the arena floor, with flags and banners and bright colors flashing and glowing under the lights. It was a moment of excitement and magic for all who rode in it and for those who watched it, as well.

Despite their studied nonchalance, Kyle and Jason and La Conquistadora's cowboys were caught up, as well. When the lights went out and the colors were posted under the spotlight's glare, those of La Conquistadora rose in unison with the crowd, hats over hearts, to the Star-Spangled Banner.

• • •

Tammy Ryan was one teenage girl who hadn't bothered to ride in the splendid procession. At fifteen, she had already ridden in a multitude of grand entrances and had long since lost her enthusiasm for them. She wasn't wearing skin-tight shiny pants, and she did not own a green cowboy hat. Tammy wore a pair of Levi's and a white snap-button shirt because they were comfortable and she liked them. Her boots were scuffed and could have used some polish and elbow grease. They were not likely to get it, though, at least not from Tammy. She didn't wear a cowboy hat, or any hat at all. Her long dark hair was parted in the center and fell down nearly to her elbows. A barrette on either side of her head held this thick mane back out of her eyes and out of her way. Tammy was not a dress-up-and-play, once-a-year cowgirl. She was a fierce competitor. She had not come to this rodeo, or any other, to look good and maybe catch an eye or two. She had come to win.

Instead of posturing and posing under the lights, she stood stroking and talking to her horse and best friend, Maybe Baby. Her grandfather, Toby Lloyd, was keeping her company.

"Maybe Baby, we'll win tonight."

"Is that a question or a statement?" Toby asked.

"It's a statement," his granddaughter said with an infectious grin.

Toby didn't doubt it and couldn't help but grin back. He always meant to be stern and grandfatherly with her, but he never could quite manage it. He thought all this rodeo business was dangerous doings for this young girl, but he doubted she was even aware of his feelings.

"Don't worry about me, Granddaddy. Baby and I know what we're doing, and we take good care of each other, too. Don't we, Baby?" she asked her mount as she petted his nose. He seemed to agree. "We always come through, and in record time for the most part."

Toby had to admit that this was true. These two rarely lost. He just nodded and checked the cinch on his granddaughter's saddle for the third time in ten minutes. She and the horse would be taking some tight turns. Toby didn't want anything coming loose.

Tammy knew his concern with cinches was an act of love. She just smiled and didn't say a word.

• • •

Out in the arena, the lights had come back up with the final bars of the national anthem, and the procession had receded out the gate and into the darkness. Fanfare and flourishes played out, it was time for the show to begin.

Up in the stands, the cowboys that had come from La Conquistadora, from other spreads, and from living rooms, dance halls, beer joints, and drugstores all delightedly passed judgment on everything they saw. By the time Adam arrived, Kyle and Jason and the rest of the crew had already critiqued their way through saddle bronc riding and were well into the bareback bronc category. Bulls were coming up.

"Say, Adam," Jason asked, "how come you never took up this bronc or bull riding stuff?"

"Staying alive roping calves is pretty easy. It gets a little harder riding bulls," he answered.

Kyle grinned at him. "I'll bet that's the truth all right!"

"It is, indeed." Adam gave Kyle an answering smile. "I like working with a partner, too. Lots of guys will tell you they don't rope calves because they don't want to be stuck hauling a horse around with them everywhere they go. But I like that aspect of it. I've always had super horses. My horses have always been as big a part of my success as I've ever been. I've always owed a lot to my rides, and I've liked them a lot, too. As a matter of fact, lots of times they've been nicer and friendlier than a lot of the folks I've run into out on the circuit. They are generally glad to see me and usually said hello of a morning. Not all people can be counted on for that."

There was a general murmur of agreement with this sentiment and with the feeling that horses could be counted on for better friendship than quite a few people.

"I don't know, Adam," Larry said. "I'd have thought the buckle bunnies would keep you pretty good company."

"Had a wife or two who thought so," Adam said easily. "Turns out being married to a rodeo champ sounds a lot better than it is. They tend to figure that out pretty quick."

Nobody pressed it. Adam's tone was light enough, but something in it closed the door, and the conversation moved on.

When the bull riding was over and the calf roping commenced, Adam could only shake his head at missed throws and slow times. Some of the contestants showed promise, though, and a couple made Kyle think Adam might be glad he'd be retired from the lists when they hit their stride in the not-too-distant future. Someday, somebody out there would give him a real run for his money, and Kyle suspected Adam knew it.

Everyone perked up when a pickup drove into the arena with three fifty-gallon barrels in its bed and began dropping them off in a cloverleaf pattern.

"Hey," George Price said, "looks like it's about time for some barrel racing. Let's see what Toby's granddaughter can do."

"I've seen her ride," Adam said. "When she's hot, she's hot, and I've never seen her when she wasn't."

Maybe Baby and Tammy were fifth up, a pretty good position to draw, far enough back to judge the competition a little, but still early enough to intimidate and shut down quite a bit of the field.

Tammy heard her name crackle over the loudspeakers. They were up. She winked at her grandfather and went to work. Tammy saw no point in wasting time; neither did Maybe Baby. They raced for the first barrel and were in a dead run before they even broke the electronic beam to start their time.

Toby caught his breath, and so did everyone else watching from the stands. He wanted to close his eyes, but he couldn't. It was too pretty not to watch. Tammy and her horse could well have been Reckless and Fearless, and that night, in a little town on the prairie, under the stars and a moon that were dimmed by the glow of the arena lights, they danced a perfect ballet. Three times they dashed straight at the barrel that barred their path, spinning around it only at the last possible second, then racing on before gravity had time to realize it had been defeated. Photographs of Maybe Baby and Tammy rounding a barrel showed them leaning so far over that it seemed they simply had to fall. They never did; they just flew on.

When the two came off the last barrel and began the mad romp for home, they were moving in record time. But that wasn't enough for either horse or rider. It wasn't enough for the crowd, either; with a roar it came to its feet, screaming and cheering for more.

Kyle was on his feet with the rest of them. He had never seen anything like it: the girl and the horse moving as one thing, leaning into those turns at angles that defied everything he understood about staying on a horse. Beside him, Jason had stopped breathing altogether.

Totally focused and scarcely aware of the noise, Tammy and Baby delivered. In one smooth reflex action, Tammy's hand came up to snatch the quirt from where it had been gripped between her teeth, waiting for this last moment. Stretched out over his neck, her voice in his listening ears, Tammy began to bang Baby's flank with her quirt, screaming, "Run, Baby, run!"

Maybe Baby had been waiting for this signal and flipped on the afterburners. Racing for home and flashing across the timing beam, horse and rider were a vision of straining grace with bared teeth and flying manes.

Once across the beam, their skidding and dirt-spraying halt was as spectacular as their ride had been. The crowd and Toby were up and howling. Tammy was hugging her horse's neck and grinning when the announcer broke through the noise.

"Ladies and gentlemen, that's a record! I don't know how this little girl and that horse keep making them and breaking them, but they do! You may be looking at the finest barrel racer in the world!"

Still grinning and hugging Maybe Baby's neck, Tammy whispered to him, "We knew that, didn't we?"

Having only recently been introduced to the complexities of horseback riding, Jason had awesome respect for the feat he had just observed a little slip of a girl perform.

"Kyle," he said, "can you ride like that?"

"Nope," Kyle promptly responded. "Come on, let's go tell her and Toby how impressed we are. That's only neighborly. Want to come along, Adam?"

Adam, having watched each boy down a couple of beers, nodded his head.

"I reckon I'd better."

The three found Toby and Tammy out behind the chutes. Toby was leaning against a horse trailer, visiting with his daughter, Kitten. Kitten had been up in the stands leading the cheering during Tammy's ride. She liked to be high enough to see the whole pattern. At the moment, both father and daughter watched Tammy with unabashed pride and devotion. She was walking Maybe Baby up and down a long line of parked pickup trucks and trailers, making sure he was good and cooled out before loading him up to return to his little meadow on the edge of town.

"She's got a rare talent," Toby conceded to his daughter.

"Yes," she agreed, "she does, and she'll do fine, too. Tammy is much calmer and more disciplined than I ever was."

Toby had to grin. "That's putting it mildly."

Kitten just smiled and watched her gifted child. She had no regrets.

"It would have been better if all that talent had been for something useful, like the piano or something," Toby said mournfully.

Kitten burst out laughing. "Her choice of talents is just fine. Two or three schools have already called to talk about scholarships, and she's only going to be a junior. You just watch, Daddy, Tammy and Maybe Baby are going to go to college together. Somebody in this family will manage to get educated yet, even if it's only the horse!"

Toby was still smiling. He always got a kick out of Kitten, now that he didn't have to worry about raising her.

"I'd like that. They'd look kind of cute in a cap and gown, wouldn't they?"

"Sure," she agreed, "but we might have to special-order Baby's."

Adam and the boys strolled up, putting an end to their plans for Maybe Baby's academic career.

"Evening, folks." Adam said, tipping his hat to Kitten and shaking hands with Toby. "That was as fine a ride as any I've seen," he said without preamble.

"She's really got it, doesn't she, Adam?" Kitten said. It was a statement of fact as much as a question.

"She's got it."

"I have got to tell you that I have never seen anything like that girl's ride!" Jason enthused.

"Hi. I'm Kitten, 'that girl's mom,'" Kitten said, putting out her hand, "and you must be Jason. I've heard a lot about you." Her smile was as full of mischief as ever.

"Nothing good, I bet," Jason said, shaking her hand.

"Oh, lots of good! Lots of good!"

"I think he's all cooled off now." Tammy and her beloved horse rejoined the little group.

"Hi, Adam," she said, a little shyly.

"Hello, Tammy," he responded. "That was a champion ride."

"Thanks. It was mostly Baby, though. He's a great horse."

"He has a great rider," Jason spoke up, surprising everyone, even himself.

"Tammy, you know who Kyle is, of course," her mother said, "and this is his friend, Jason. They're both working on the ranch this summer."

"Hi," Tammy smiled at both boys, "and thank you, Jason."

"How come we haven't seen you out riding at the ranch?" Jason asked.

"Oh, Granddaddy would never let me do any riding there! He just barely lets me near the place. Granddaddy and Mr. Degarrin don't cotton to girls riding and working around cowboys, at all. I think it all goes back to my mother's wild youth."

"Nonsense," Kitten filled the dangerous pause. "I was always the picture of decorum. All tales have been wildly exaggerated."

Jason spoke up again, and Kyle could hear just a trace of unsteadiness in his voice. "Maybe Toby would make an exception just once. The last roundup is in just a few days. Maybe you and your mom could come out at least for lunch and the branding."

"Yes, maybe we could." Kitten chimed right in, tossing her dad a teasing glance. "What do you think, Toby? Could you make one little exception?"

"Oh, all right, all right. You can even come early and help work the herd. If you can get someone to loan you a horse."

"I'll loan you a horse," all three cowboys hastened to assure the ladies.

The deal was struck and the date was made.

Walking back to the stands, Kyle and Adam looked at Jason. He shrugged.

"What can I say? I'm in love."

Chapter 8 — After the Rodeo

THAT NIGHT AFTER THE rodeo, Adam woke up deep in the night. Snug in his bedroll under the wagon fly, he shifted around until he could gaze up into the starry sky and lose himself in thought.

The summer work was just about over. In only a few more days the final drive would be made and the last calf branded. It had all been fun, but Adam's hiatus was also near its end. When he passed through the gateway out of La Conquistadora, it would be to rejoin the world of rodeo, where the roping and riding were ultra-competitive and not much fun anymore. This summer he had come to know that he much preferred the genuine thing to the high-dollar hype played out night after night in crowded but still lonely arenas.

The circuit had been good to him, though. He would never say otherwise. It had given him a life when La Conquistadora had taken his away: a purpose, a direction, somewhere to put all that energy that might otherwise have turned in on itself. He had been good at it, too. Better than good. There were men out there who were stronger, and some who were quicker, but Adam could read a calf the way a man reads a letter from home, and he could throw a loop with such lazy perfection that it seemed to land of its own accord. The horses had helped. He had always had great partners, animals that understood him and trusted him and ran their hearts out when he asked. The championships had come, and the money, and a kind of fame that sat comfortably enough on a man who had never sought it.

But the road was long. Longer than anyone who hadn't driven it could know. There were the good nights, a clean run, a fast time, a crowd on its feet, and there were the thousand ordinary nights between them. Motel rooms in Cheyenne and Pendleton and Calgary and towns so small they barely had names. The company of men who understood horses and hard work, good men for the most part, fine companions over a beer and decent enough friends. But when the last beer was finished and the last story told, there was always the quiet hour before sleep, and that was where Sophie lived.

She was not an obsession. Adam had never been the brooding kind, and he did not pretend that his leaving had been anything other than his own choice. But in those still moments, when the day's noise had fallen away and there was nothing between him and his thoughts, she was simply there, not the nineteen-year-old girl, exactly, because he had let that image go a long time ago, or believed he had. What came to him instead were the small things that had no business surviving twenty-three years: the sound of her laugh carrying across a rope corral, the way she had taken an apple slice from his fingers on Indian Rock Mesa, sitting close enough that their shoulders touched. The taste of that apple had once been so vivid he could close his eyes and be there. Even now, lying under the same stars and on the same land, the memory came easily, though it arrived without the ache it used to carry. It was just a thing that had been.

He had tried to make a life. He had married twice, good women both, and he had entered into each one honestly and with real hope. But he was never quite all the way there, and they both knew it before he did. The road had been part of it, but it was more than that. The divorces had been quiet, without bitterness, and he wished them both well. He just hadn't had enough of himself to give.

A coyote called from somewhere out on the mesa, and a second one answered from farther off, the two voices finding each other across the dark.

Danny would have had something to say about all of it. Danny had always had something to say, and it was usually worth hearing. "It's only tricky if you stay caught," he had told Adam once, in that easy Tennessee voice of his. Well, Adam had stayed caught. Twenty-three years, and he had never gotten free. But he had not frozen the way he suspected Sophie had; he knew enough from Degarrin's careful words and Louisa's careful silences to guess what those years had cost her.

Adam had kept moving. The road was his choice, and he had ridden it hard and well. Moving wasn't the same as arriving, but it was not nothing. It was a life lived out loud, not a life endured in silence. If Danny could see him now, Adam liked to think the big Tennessean would nod and allow that it had been all right. Not perfect, maybe. But all right.

But, all in all, Adam knew he really could not complain about a thing. The same high-dollar hype had brought him fame and wealth. It had lifted him from obscurity on La Conquistadora and had taken him all around the nation, and some of the world, as well. Now, after all the years, it had allowed him to return, as something of a hero, to those same endless, changeless ranges. Rodeo had been more than good to Adam Connor.

But the competition was young, and strong, and determined. All his knowledge and experience might not be enough next season. It had just barely been enough last year.

Moving to get a better view of the Big Dipper, Adam winced in pain. This summer had shown him another thing, as well: the Battle of the Bulge was still taking its toll, and with worse and worse results. The freezing his feet had taken in that bloody and hopeless mess had stayed on through all these years, to haunt and hurt him more and more. The pain had teased him all summer, but these last few days it had mounted steadily, as was its custom.

His knees were not much better, if he was honest about it. Twenty-some years of leaving a running horse and hitting the ground to throw and tie a calf will take a toll on any man's joints. His right shoulder had a way of seizing up in the cold that it hadn't had ten years ago. The body kept a ledger, and Adam's carried a long accounting: every hard ride, every cold night, every season spent pushing past what the doctors told him he should. But every summer he came back here, and the land and the work healed what the road had broken. It had been that way since the first time, after the war, when Degarrin had put him on a horse and sent him out across those empty miles. The sky and the grass and the work had done the rest. They always did.

By the standard measure of Adam's life, this had been an easy summer. There had been no vaults from horseback and races to throw and tie a calf, no marathon drives to the next rodeo. But still his feet rebelled and refused to stay free of pain. The plain truth was that his poor old hooves very likely would not even take another day on the La Conquistadora range, let alone another year on the professional rodeo circuit. The war had broken his feet and the road had worn down the rest of him, but this was the one place that had always put him back together.

Maybe it was time to hang up his lariat. He could leave that world simply and without fanfare, just as he had entered it so long ago. He could go to the little ranch he'd bought a few years back. It lay only a short way out from Santa Fe and was a lovely place. Adam had always planned to run some cattle there, maybe even some La Conquistadora Herefords. In the summertime, he might put on a roping camp and charge outrageous prices that people would line up to pay.

He lay still and listened to the night sounds of the camp: the fire ticking down, a horse shifting on the picket line, the low murmur of someone talking in his sleep. This was the last summer of the wagon, Toby had said. Adam wondered if it would be the last summer of more than that. He had sensed things, a weariness in Degarrin that went deeper than age, the Stillmores' silence growing louder with each passing year, the deferred repairs that a younger Degarrin would never have tolerated. The wagon was going. If a man could read the signs, it might not be the only thing.

Adam smiled in the darkness. He had been roaming for too long; it might be time to settle down. This summer had shown him that. It had reawakened all the fundamental elements that had made him Adam Connor in the first place. He had come to feel that it was time to return to the order and cadence of a life determined by the season and the sky.

Not giving up. Arriving. There was a difference, and Adam had finally learned it. The road had been good to him, but the road was for younger men with younger feet and hearts that hadn't yet learned what they were missing. The ranch outside Santa Fe was waiting, his, the way La Conquistadora had been his once, not by ownership but by belonging. He would run his cattle and teach his camps and sit on his own portal in the evenings and watch the light change over the

Jemez. He would not be lonely. He had been lonely enough for one lifetime, and the difference between being alone and being lonely was something he had come, at last, to understand.

Somewhere in the camp, a horse stamped and blew softly. The stars were thick and close overhead, the Milky Way a bright river across the darkness, and the air smelled of sage and woodsmoke and the cooling earth. Adam closed his eyes. The pain in his feet was there, as it always was, but it was an old companion by now, and he was too tired to argue with it tonight.

Sleep, when it came, came gently.

Chapter 9 — Summer's End

Part 1

Sophie and Joe Carpenter loaded up Sophie's Lincoln Continental and drove to the Jeffers house to pick up Amy. Their trek to La Conquistadora had begun. The sky ahead of them was clear and blue and endless. Tomorrow was the last day of the roundup and branding work, another summer nearly done.

Amy was excited and a little nervous about seeing Kyle after almost a whole summer apart. Sophie could see it in the girl's quick, restless hands and the way she kept shifting in her seat. He had sounded so familiar and so comfortable on the telephone, Amy said, but still, she would be relieved to get past their first meeting and get back to being the steady pair they were supposed to be.

Sophie was a bundle of nerves herself, although it was only noticeable to someone who knew her very, very well and was fine-tuned to her frequency. The prospect of seeing Adam again, after a whole separate lifetime, had her in a well-concealed state of turmoil. She told herself that she didn't know if she wanted to see him again or not. What she knew was that she had to see him again, if only to finally say goodbye.

Joe Carpenter, of course, was perfectly aware of Sophie's mood; she could tell by the careful, attentive way he drove, by the lightness he kept injecting into the conversation, by the way he never once glanced at her with worry even though she knew it was there. No one knew her better or was more finely tuned to her frequency. Over the years he had pieced together the story of Adam and Sophie from things her parents had mentioned and from the way Sophie had never even said a word about the man's very existence or about that long-past summer when she had left La Conquistadora and never truly returned. Sophie knew that Joe understood what that summer's ending must have done to her. She knew he knew it had left her a brokenhearted and armored girl, and that she had never really recovered all the way. His heart went out to her, she could feel it in every small, steady kindness, but she also knew, with equal certainty, that he was glad every day that Adam had lost.

Joe wanted this to be as perfect a day as possible; there was just no telling what tomorrow might bring. It was a perfect day, because he made it one. Joe adroitly distracted and entertained his passengers with stories of his adventures wheeling and dealing in the oil patch. When the atmosphere inside the Continental had lightened and brightened a bit, he skillfully shifted the topic of conversation over to horses, riding, and Kyle. On this common ground of fascination, the rest of the trip took care of itself.

Her husband's sterling traits were not lost on Sophie. She had expected to have a bad day and had had a wonderful one instead. Sophie knew that she was blessed, that this day was typical of Joe. Giving her happy or nearly happy days was what he had done their whole marriage.

Later that day, back in her old home, Sophie stood close against her husband and put her arms around his neck.

"I love you, Joe. I really do. Thank you for this day."

Joe kissed her nose and grinned.

"You're very welcome, ma'am. And thank you for being my lovely bride all these years."

"I try to be a good wife, Joe."

"I know, and you are. You are the very best thing that ever happened to me, Sophie. You'll never know how much I love you."

Sophie knew that what her husband said was true. She was deeply adored, far better than she probably deserved. Looking into his clear eyes, she was touched and deeply moved.

"You're perfect, Joe. You always have been."

Holding her tight, Joe returned Sophie's gaze, look for look.

"Almost," he agreed, "but I just can't seem to make that last yard."

Sophie turned her cheek to rest it on his shoulder.

"I wish I could," he murmured into the quiet.

• • •

The next morning found the Degarrins, Carpenters, and Amy gathered around the dining room table, partaking of Rufina's cooking with varying degrees of enthusiasm. Amy ate very little, as she was still half-asleep and was clearly appalled that there were civilized people that actually sat down to a full meal at six o'clock in the morning. Sophie watched the girl's progress with quiet amusement: the sleepy shoving of food around her plate, the fascinated stare as Degarrin downed serious amounts of scrambled eggs and bacon. Joe was doing the same. Louisa was doing the same, only in a more dainty manner. Glancing up, Amy caught Sophie's eye and got a quick wink. Sophie hadn't made much of a dent in her breakfast, either. Apparently it was okay not to be ravenous at dawn.

"Amy, would you like more bacon? Eggs?" Degarrin asked, already armed with a serving fork to dish up her slightest need.

"Oh, no, sir! I'm just fine. Thank you, though," Amy replied after a startled second.

Joe Carpenter interceded on her behalf. "I think Amy is one of those people whose appetite doesn't quite wake up until about ten a.m. Right, Amy?" he asked her with a friendly smile.

"I'm afraid you're about right. Usually by the time I get hungry, there's nothing left to eat!"

"I know what you mean," Sophie commented. "I've gotten the same way. I'm not much hungry at the crack of dawn, either."

"You used to always eat big breakfasts when you were growing up," Louisa interjected.

"I know," Sophie agreed. "But I think that had as much to do with the fact that supper had been served twelve hours earlier as with anything. You can work up quite an appetite, even sleeping, in twelve hours."

"You couldn't snack?" Amy asked, even more appalled.

"Well, you could," Sophie admitted. "There was always something good to eat down in the kitchen. But that meant you had to go outside and all the way down the portal to get there. Then you probably would have to defend your actions against Rufina. If she heard you, she would come out of her room and demand to know what you were doing prowling around in her kitchen. It was usually less bother to just go hungry. Isn't that right, Rufina?" Sophie asked as the lifelong cook and housekeeper came in with a bread basket full of more toast.

"That's right," Rufina promptly agreed. "I am the only reason you were not as fat as a killing hog. But do I get any thanks?"

"Certainly not," Sophie promptly assured her. "It would just go to your head."

Rufina was spared the indignity of responding by the ringing of the telephone. The telephone was in the linen closet just off the dining room, where it had been installed some forty-plus years before. Rufina, armed with her toast basket, went to answer it. She was back in a moment to inform Degarrin that Toby was on the phone. Then she was gone, taking her toast with her, before it ever made it to the table.

"I hope you don't need toast, Joe," Sophie commented to her husband.

"I hope so, too," he agreed.

Degarrin emerged from the linen closet. "That was Toby," he announced, a fact that everyone already knew. "Adam called last night and said the doctor had cleared him to come back to the ranch today. Somebody needs to pick him up in town. Annie can't because Tammy's here to visit the wagon, and Annie wants to go with her."

"There's no need for any change in plans," Louisa said smoothly. "Someone can drive in to pick him up this afternoon after the branding is finished."

"Is something the matter with Adam?" Sophie asked.

The room went still. Sophie felt her parents' eyes meet hers, and for an instant the three of them were locked in something old and unresolved. It was the first time since the summer of 1946 that the three of them, together, had even mentioned Adam's name.

Degarrin stepped into the breach. "His feet are still giving him trouble. After the Battle of the Bulge, you know."

Sophie knew.

"It got bad enough he had to go to the doctor a couple of days ago."

"Then it must have been pretty bad," Sophie said.

"Yes, I think so, too," Degarrin agreed. "Kyle and the boys have been carrying his share. They've managed."

Then Sophie startled even herself. She didn't quite know where her next words even came from. Maybe they had been held captive in this room for twenty years, just waiting to be spoken.

"I will go for Adam," Sophie said.

"Then I'll go with you," Louisa pleasantly rearranged her plans.

"I think you had better take Amy to the wagon. It's all new to her, you know," Sophie said in an equally pleasant manner, smiling at Amy.

"Oh, I don't need to be there. Amy will be in good hands with Mike and Joe. Besides, once Kyle sees Amy, it won't matter who else is around," Louisa assured her daughter lightly.

Sophie's response was a flat statement, brooking no argument. "You are not going to town with me to pick up Adam, Mother." Her gaze was equally flat and completely devoid of waver.

Sophie could see her mother's anger, the tightening around her mouth, the color rising, but she could also see the calculation. One look at her child and Louisa decided this ancient battle might not be worth fighting again.

Joe interceded. "I think the best thing for everyone involved would be for Sophie to drive into town and see Adam. That will free the rest of us to go to the wagon and have a great time. Amy, I think you will really like it. Maybe you'll even get to see Kyle do a little roping. What do you say, Degarrin? Any chance of that? I'm sure he's spent the summer back in the drags, practicing."

"I'm sure you're right about that," Degarrin agreed, clearly relieved to have Joe break the tension. "We might just see what he can do, this last day out."

"Well. All right. I guess that is settled." Louisa's voice was all crisp and cold, as though to say, I wash my hands of this. She immediately set about planning the upcoming day with Amy, with never another glance or word for her daughter.

Leaving the dining room, Sophie looked up at Joe, more than a little of worry and confusion in her eyes.

"Thank you, Joe," she said.

He gave her a hard hug. "It has to happen someday," he said.

• • •

Later that morning, Joe and Louisa sat together on a bedroll under the wagon's fly, sharing a peaceful moment and a cup of coffee. Far off in the distance, a slight haze of dust floated in the morning air over the final drive. Joe sat and tried to absorb and record all the distance and the space, but most of all the hugeness of the sky and the pure clarity of the light as it played across the mesas and the prairie.

"This is such a lovely place, Louisa," he said. "Some great artist should come here and capture it."

"Well, yes. That would be nice. We did have photographers one summer."

"Yes, I know," he said. "I've seen the pictures."

Joe was quiet for a moment. He had been studying the ranch all morning with a businessman's eye; he couldn't help it. "This is quite an operation to keep going," he said.

"It always has been," Louisa answered lightly.

"I mean the capital side of it. The fencing I saw coming in needs work, and the equipment is getting long in the tooth. You don't run a place this size on love alone." He wasn't prying, not exactly. He was just the kind of man who noticed the numbers. "The Stillmores, they're still committed to all this?"

Louisa's expression did not change. "Would you like more coffee, Joe?" she asked, and reached for the pot.

"Why did you let her go?" Louisa asked, unable to hold the words back.

"Because she wanted to go so badly. I've never stood in the way of anything she wanted, and certainly not anything she wanted badly. Anyway, I couldn't have stopped her. Besides, trying to stop Sophie has too high a price, but you know that. Losing her is not a price I'm willing to pay, unless I have no choice at all." To soften the sting of his words, Joe turned and smiled at Louisa. "It was part of the deal, you know."

"What do you mean?"

"I mean your daughter, for me at least, is fabulous. I love her more after all these years than I did when I first met her, and it was more than I could contain then. When I got Sophie to marry me, I knew what I was getting. And I was damned glad to get it anyway I could."

"And what exactly were you getting?" Louisa asked, not sure she wanted to know.

"I'm surprised you have to ask. I got a rare and wonderful woman who was madly in love with someone else. Sophie still overcompensates for that every day, and as a result, she has made my life and our son's life quite wonderful."

"Oh, surely that's not true," Louisa protested. "That was all nearly twenty-five years ago! Surely Sophie got over Adam Connor years ago. She seems happy, and she has such a nice life with you and Kyle. Don't you think?"

"Well, you tell me," Joe said. He was turning his coffee cup between his hands, the way Kyle did when he was working something over. "What happened to the sparkle and the joy I see in all those photographs, but that I have never seen more than an occasional shadow of in her? It's there to be seen in all the photos and stories of her childhood, until that summer's end. One of my great goals has always been to give that back to her. But I've never been able to."

Louisa hated to have all her carefully constructed illusions about Sophie stripped away. She wanted to believe that she and Degarrin had been right, that everything had turned out for the best. But that was a hard story to buy. She knew that when her daughter had left La Conquistadora's office that day in 1946, she had never really come back.

"Maybe you're right," she sadly told Joe.

"You know I'm right. She never got over him. That's the way it is when you're obsessed. I know. That's how I am with Sophie." Joe grinned at Louisa and shrugged. "What can I say? There's nothing you can do about an obsession. So tell me about Adam. No one ever mentions him, you know. Not you, not Degarrin, and never Sophie. Is he a nice guy?"

"Oh, yes. He's a very nice guy," Louisa said unhappily. "I hate to have to admit that, but he is."

"Was he as wild for Sophie as she was for him?"

"Oh, yes," Louisa said, even more unhappily.

"Is he still obsessed?"

"Oh, yes. I imagine so. There's no reason for me to hope otherwise."

"Then we might have a problem."

Louisa just nodded and gazed across the grass that went on and on to the horizon.

• • •

While her family was busy assessing her life, Sophie was busy getting on with living it. When the Casa Blanca entourage left headquarters, headed for the wagon, Sophie headed into town. Leaving headquarters, she climbed to her mother's "top of the world." Way off to the north, you could see forever, just like her mother said. Sophie was in no hurry this morning and took time to admire the view. After a while, she had crossed the high plateau and dropped down off the rimrock to the great flat below. Sophie pressed her Lincoln steadily on across that great empty prairie toward La Conquistadora's outside fence, seven or eight miles away.

Well, Sophie thought, unless the fates intervene in the next hour or so, I'm going to come face to face with Adam for the first time in twenty-three years. It seemed only natural that she would be inundated with memories during this final journey to her first and only true love. She drove on, half in fear and half in anticipation, waiting to be swamped by all the feelings and happenings of long ago. All around her were the triggers to a cascade of nostalgia. These were the plains and the trails that she and Adam had ridden either together or in each other's thoughts. Yonder were the hills that had held them and sometimes hidden them. She was completely surrounded by the land that had been their land. She passed the turnoff to Indian Rock Mesa and waited for it: the taste of the apple, his fingers, the sage on the wind that afternoon. The images came, but flat and distant, like a photograph of a photograph. She crossed a dry wash and waited again, for the shock of cold water, for his laughter, for anything at all. But no flood of memories came; apparently there would be no bittersweet heartbreak this morning.

Instead, her hands felt heavy on the wheel. The mesas passed, the light played across the prairie, and none of it touched her. She was sorry she had opted to make this journey, sorry she was going to encounter her ancient icon and have to pierce the veil of fantasy and see the god of old as also merely worn out and tired and less than she remembered. Sophie thought about not going into town after all. It would be a simple matter to just turn around and send someone else. But she had fought too hard to make this trip; to abandon it now would only make people think it mattered more than it did.

Sophie squared her shoulders and drove on. Passing through the locked gate, she entered the real world and left the protected realm of La Conquistadora far behind. Before so very long, her Lincoln glided into Clauson. The quiet little town seemed even smaller and less significant than it ever had before. The storefronts along the main street were shuttered for Sunday, and the morning light fell flat and empty on the pavement. How odd it seemed that once, when she was young, driving to this little wide spot in the road for ice, vaccine, and now and then ice cream, had been pure unadulterated adventure. Sophie could recall it as clearly as a crystal bell, but she could no longer feel any of it at all.

With no trouble, Sophie found Bell Street and Grandma Connor's little house. Inside was the great love of her life, a love that after lasting some twenty-three years had turned to dust in just one hour's drive. Sophie had assumed such a strong emotion would have had more stamina. Feeling mostly sad, but also very tired and very old, she opened the white picket gate and walked up the old sidewalk between beds of pinks and sweet William to confront the ancient past.

Sophie knocked on the door and waited, wishing her heart

wouldn't pound so. She forcefully reminded herself of who she was: a beautiful, cool, and aloof woman with a powerful reputation for being in control and casually indifferent to just about everything. These thoughts spun through her head, and they were completely accurate in describing the woman she had been these last twenty years and more. The only problem was that Sophie couldn't recall the woman she had been for all those years, or even a minute ago.

Sophie was stunned and more than a little distraught. How could she have been reduced to a quaking mess of jitters so quickly? Where had all that brittle, enameled composure she was known for gone? For a fleeting second, Sophie seriously thought of bolting. Then, catching herself up sharply, she drew her scattered self together and inward and upward. Taking a long, deep breath, Sophie knocked on the door, and stood her ground.

The door opened, and there he was, half dressed, barefoot, a blue plaid snap-button shirt hanging open over bare skin. He hadn't been expecting her. Sophie knew Adam well enough to know that if he had thought for one minute that anyone other than a member of the roundup crew awaited him on the other side of that door, he would never have opened it in his casually clothed state. In Adam's eyes, a female of any make and vintage merited properly combed hair and tucked-in shirttails at the very least. Bare feet were not even to be considered.

If Sophie was quakingly standing her ground, Adam was entirely taken aback. There was a stunned pause on his part, a hopeful one on Sophie's that was very quickly on its way to defensive haughtiness. Adam had not become world champion calf roper without having split-second reaction time; before the transformation could occur, he sprang into action.

"Sophie, girl! I thought I was dreaming for a second there, and it was the best dream I'd ever had. Come in this house. Don't even think about leaving!" Adam reached out and took her hand, propelling her into the house before she had time to think about it. Holding her hand firmly, he reached past her and shut the door.

At his touch, all the years fell away and the world snapped back into place for Sophie. He was still her Adam. She could see it in his eyes, that same glow that had burned there all that long-lost summer.

The light in Adam's eyes was mirrored in Sophie's face; she could feel it, the warmth flooding back into places that had been cold for longer than she could remember. Looking down at her, Adam saw it too, and Sophie knew he did, because the same incandescence was in his. She had never seen that look on anyone's face but Adam's, and she knew with sudden certainty that Adam had never seen it on anyone's but hers. The world ceased to exist, except for the little old-fashioned house on Bell Street where time flowed backward and Adam and Sophie were taken back across the years to the best of times.

"Ah, Sophie. Sophie, love," Adam whispered, almost groaned. They were standing so close together in Mrs. Connor's dim little living room that they were almost breathing the same air.

Sophie felt like she couldn't breathe at all. I've never swooned, she thought. I don't even know what a swoon is, but I wonder if I'm about to do it.

She need not have worried. Adam was there to catch her if she fell. Sophie could feel his need to drink in her face with his eyes and absorb the feel of her body with his. She could feel the wanting in his arms, the way he held her as though he would never let her go.

"Oh, Sophie, girl." His words were just an anguished breath. He kissed the palm of the hand he still held captive, then pressed it to his cheek before releasing it. His two strong arms slid around Sophie and held tight the girl he had loved for so long. Sophie could feel how good it was for him to have her back; she could feel it in every line of his body.

"Sophie, I've missed you all my life." Adam's words were just a murmur, a breath against her soft blond hair.

"You should never have let me go."

"I know. I've never stopped regretting it. That one thing was the mistake of my life."

"Of mine, too."

Sophie's arms were tight around Adam now. She felt the smooth hardness of his bare flesh and was glad that he had not gotten around to snapping his shirt before she showed up. She relaxed against him, and it crossed her mind that she could happily stay there for a thousand years.

Adam came to himself a little bit and decided crushing Sophie so close might be jumping the gun a little bit. This wasn't some floozy girl at a rodeo dance.

"Let's sit down on my poor old momma's sofa for a minute. We need to talk a little."

Sophie was agreeable. The sofa looked comfortable and inviting, but she couldn't imagine what there was to talk about.

They sat close together and held hands, totally swept away and awash in the strong currents of reunion and hope restored. Adam still could not quite believe his good fortune, Sophie could see it in his face, the same disbelief she felt, that out of the blue, the fates had delivered them right back to each other.

"Sophie, I've always wanted to tell you I'm sorry I let them drive me off. It was the worst mistake I've ever made. If I could go back and do it again, I'd have walked out of there with you and never looked back."

"Why didn't you? I would have gone anywhere with you and it would have been perfect. The last thing I ever would have done was look back."

"I know. Sophie, you are one of a kind. I know that now, but I didn't understand it then. Then I was so stupid, but I thought I was so wise. I thought I knew what was best for you and for me. I didn't think I could take you away from your family and away from La Conquistadora. I loved you so much. I didn't see how I could ask you to leave all those things behind and ruin your life, to take a chance on me."

"Keeping those things and losing you is what ruined my life. I would have rather taken the chance."

"Sophie, Sophie, don't say that. You've had a good life, haven't you? It hasn't really been ruined, has it?"

Sophie thought about her answer for a long moment. She thought about her long marriage and the life that had come with it. It had been a good life, she had to admit.

"No, not altogether," she finally answered. "These recent years have been good years. But it hasn't been what it could have been, what it should have been. And the first many years were very, very bad."

"What do you mean? This guy you married wasn't mean to you, was he?"

Sophie laughed. "Oh, no. Quite the contrary. What I mean is that I couldn't seem to feel anything for years and years. It was like there was something dead inside of me, or frozen. It was like I went through the motions of emotion but never really felt them."

Part 2

"Even now, lots of times, I don't quite connect. Except with Kyle; I love my son with all my heart and all my soul. I would never do to him what my parents did to me. I'll let him live his life and make his own choices, then if he falls I'll just try to be there and help break the impact."

"Like I said, Sophie, you are one of a kind." Adam squeezed her hand even harder, as though that pressure could stop the tide of tears behind his eyes.

Sophie continued, caught in the need to finally voice her story. "The worst thing was that I could think back and remember the girl I was before that summer. I could remember being vibrant and full of life. Even before I met you, I loved life. It was a great adventure, and I reveled in living it to the fullest. Every day was a new day, full of promise. It just got better after you came. Then you were gone and I just felt totally dead inside. I thought, 'Well, after all, this is what a broken heart is all about.' I always figured, even in the worst of it, that eventually the hurt would go away and all my feelings would come back. But they never did, Adam, not even now. Well, maybe now, now this minute. Now that you're here."

"I think I know what you mean," Adam said. "I've never really felt a lot since then. I've certainly never been in love or anything close to it. I guess I never even expected to. I just put all my energy into calf roping. If you had been with me, I'd have never been any good at it. I would never have made champion. I would have put all my energy into you. But I would rather have had you, Sophie."

"Well, I didn't have anything else to put my energy into. I guess I should have been a calf roper," Sophie said, a little tartly.

Adam grinned. "I wish you had. We would have met up on the circuit, and I'd have never let you go."

Then Adam gave her the kiss that had been hanging between them all the while, just waiting. Sophie returned it with all her heart, and lying back on his mother's worn sofa, they were kids again.

After a while, Sophie opened her eyes and looked into the face above her. It was still the handsomest face she had ever seen. The hard-muscled body lying beside her and over her felt so good and so familiar, still.

"Adam?" she said softly, almost whimsically.

He opened his eyes and returned her thoughtful gaze.

"Adam, you know, we never made love."

"I know."

"I wish we'd made love, back then."

"I wish we had, too."

There was a long pause of kisses and silence.

"Sophie?"

"Hm?"

"We could make love now."

"I'm married now."

"But you weren't then. And we should have done it then. We could do it for them. Come on, baby. Let's go in the bedroom."

Inside the bedroom door, Sophie paused. The bed was inviting her, was waiting for her, but still she paused.

"Adam, wait."

Holding her close against his heart, he waited. Sophie could feel her hand trembling where it rested against his chest.

Tiredly resting her forehead against his chest, Sophie sighed. She could feel herself slightly shaking her head, and she could feel Adam feel it, too.

"I can't do this," she finally said. "I just can't do this to my husband."

Adam sighed, too. There were tears in Sophie's eyes and on her cheeks, and she could feel them, hot, against his bare skin.

"I love you with all my heart," Sophie said. "You are the one love of my life. You always will be, nothing can ever change that. But... my love for you made me crazy, and his love for me made me sane. I can't repay that debt this way."

Sophie and Adam stood in that bedroom, both in tears, locked in each other's arms, with Joe Carpenter and more than twenty years between them.

"Jesus, Sophie," Adam cried, "what can we do?"

"I don't think there is anything we can do," she answered.

Sophie could feel the moment pass, the one chance slipping away as surely as it had that distant summer day. She had just lost Adam for a second time, and he had lost her, and they both knew it.

"There, it's done. We've finally said goodbye," Sophie said.

"No. We haven't said goodbye at all," Adam protested. "All we've done is put the past to rest, and it's been a long time coming. What we've really done is just said our first hellos in a long, long time. And that was way past due, as well. Anyway, I'm glad you're back."

"Oh, Adam, that is so sweet, but this is the end of the road, isn't it?"

"Are you dead, Sophie?"

Sophie smiled. "No."

"Well, neither am I, and the end of the road is nowhere in sight. We just survived a hairpin turn, but now we are in the clear."

"How can you say that?" Sophie asked, truly puzzled.

"Because I don't see the world in black and white, right or wrong. I've seen the end of the road and felt the onslaught of beyond hope."

"In the war?"

"In the war," he answered, "and this isn't it. Sophie, there is clear sailing from here on. I'm alive and you're alive and we still have each other, as much today as on any day we ever lived. I'm sorry we can't be together. I'd marry you today if I could. Remember that, Sophie," Adam's voice rasped with intensity. "Anytime, anywhere, just say the word."

Sophie smiled again, only this time it reached her eyes and lingered there. "Someday you might want those words back. There might come a day when I say the word, only then you won't want me back."

Now it was Adam's turn to look truly puzzled. "I'm not playing a game, Sophie. There will never be a day I won't miss you and want you with me. You are my missing other half."

"And you, mine," Sophie's voice choked on her tears.

"Don't cry, sweetheart. Just hear me. I've loved you every day for twenty-three years. Every morning, every night, every mile of road between here and wherever I happened to be. It never went away, Sophie. It was there when I woke up and it was there when I closed my eyes and it never once wasn't there. That's not going to change.

Not ever." Adam grew silent and then said very softly, "I hope it's been the same for you."

"Oh, Adam, it has been. It always has been!" Sophie could hardly speak. She found that being choked with emotion was more than just a phrase. "I've never known how to say it before, but that is just exactly how it's been for me. It was just always there. I just couldn't seem to go on anymore. That's why I married Joe."

"You did the right thing, sweetheart. You waited as long as you could. I should have come for you, but I didn't. You went on and lived your life, and that's what life is for. By the way, I love your son, too. I'm awfully glad you had him."

"I love him, too. He is great, isn't he?" Sophie said.

"He sure is, Sophie. You know, in a funny way, I kind of think of him as my son, too."

"Why is that?" Sophie asked.

"I guess because I would have wanted any child of mine to have had the same mom as Kyle has."

"Oh, Adam," Sophie started to cry again. "You just break my heart, you know that?"

"Yeah, that's me. Just an old sweetie."

"Well, you are," Sophie gurgled a watery laugh.

"You know what I missed most, all those years on the road, Sophie?"

"What?"

"That look you used to get. The one where your whole face would light up, like the world was the funniest place and you were the only one who knew why. I'd give just about anything to see that come back."

"See what I mean?" Sophie asked.

"What?" Adam asked. "Now you've really lost me."

"I mean you just keep surprising me, Adam Connor. You always did."

"Only when I'm around you, baby. You bring out the best in me."

For a long moment, Sophie and Adam smiled into each other's shining eyes, and then for an even longer moment they held each other tightly.

Eventually Adam spoke. "I guess we'd better get you home."

"I guess so," Sophie agreed.

Stepping away from her, Adam's eyes were quiet and serious.

"Remember, Sophie. Just remember," he said.

"I will, Adam. I will never forget."

• • •

Adam drove the Lincoln and Sophie back to La Conquistadora through a warm and perfect summer day. It was a weekday, and once out of town there was no traffic at all. The highway, and all the land as well, seemed empty of every soul except for Adam and Sophie. There was no one to note their passage as they slipped through an abandoned world, first up and over the steep hills and then down through the once-treacherous narrows. Their passage was as a knife through water, marked only by the turquoise sky and the sandstone mesas.

Driving down the lane into headquarters at La Conquistadora, Sophie suggested they stop for a moment.

"Before we go on to the wagon, let's stop for a minute and say hello to Danny."

Adam smiled at her. "Do you do that, too?"

Sophie just nodded. "I know he's not really buried in the orchard. But it feels like he's there, and lots of times I think he is."

"I think so, too," Adam agreed as he parked the car at the west gate to Casa Blanca. "I made peace with your parents for several reasons," he continued after a pause, "mainly to have news of you and to be able to visit the ranch, but also to come and visit Danny. I've had some good talks with him, too."

"What does he tell you?" Sophie asked.

Adam looked a little sheepish. "Well...," he hesitated.

"What?" Sophie insisted. "Tell me."

"Well, he told me how to be a world champion calf roper, for one thing."

"What do you mean?" Sophie asked out of curiosity, not out of any doubt at all.

"Danny was the absolute best. Whether it was riding, roping, whatever... he was a natural. You just can't imagine it, Sophie. I'd never seen anything like it then, and I've never seen anything like it since. Danny was just a natural; he was truly one of a kind. Well, anyway, pretty soon after I hit the rodeo circuit, I started getting a little publicity and a little bit of reputation. You know, I was pretty good but not quite real good. After I'd been at it for a few years, I bumped into your dad at the state fair in Albuquerque. By then I was winning pretty regularly and you were married to somebody else, so your daddy decided it might be safe to act like he knew me. Enough water had gone under the bridge that he invited me to stop by La Conquistadora if I was ever in this neck of the woods. I flat jumped at the chance. I knew I'd hear all about how you were doing, and I'd get to visit the ranch, too. I didn't just stop by the next time I was in the neighborhood; I made a special trip from Albuquerque a few days later, just so I could spend a couple of hours at La Conquistadora."

"Was Momma nice to you?" Sophie wanted to know.

"Well, she didn't exactly get out the good china, but she was okay. Although I do think she thought Degarrin had lost his mind to invite me."

Sophie just grinned. She could well imagine her mother's delight in playing hostess to Adam Connor.

"Anyway," Adam continued, "your mother actually allowed me into Casa Blanca for coffee and a little visit. As I was leaving, I asked her if I could stop by the orchard and visit Danny for a minute. I think that's the only reason I was ever invited back."

"Probably so," mused Sophie. "I always wondered if Momma might not have been just a little bit in love with Danny."

"Maybe so. I know that she certainly appreciated it that I'd remembered him. Anyway, I went in the orchard and sat on the stone bench beside his memorial. I remember it was a very warm, sunny day, so it felt good to sit in that shady place for a little bit. Your mother had planted lots of roses and flowers all around, so it smelled good, too. It was quiet and very peaceful."

Sophie nodded. "Danny's marker is still the floral showpiece of all her gardening efforts," she said.

"Well, I sat there for a while and thought about Danny and that summer. Then I just started talking to him. I told him I was trying to make my mark as a calf roper on the rodeo circuit. He thought that was pretty funny and wanted to know why. I told him I wanted to impress a girl, that if I were rich and famous maybe I could get Sophie Degarrin back."

"Oh, Adam."

Adam grinned at her. "It's true, you know. Anyway," he continued, "Danny thought that was a decent reason. Then I told him the trouble I was having. The trouble was, I wasn't good enough. I told him I was good but that if I had just a smidgen of his talent, I would be great. I told Danny I wished I were him."

"Danny really thought that was funny. 'I wish you were, too,' he said. 'Then I'd be the one that was alive and worried about how to catch a calf.'"

"That kind of stopped me cold. Which really gave Danny a good chuckle. 'Never mind,' he said. 'Never mind. There's nothing much to roping a calf, hopping off a horse and running and tying that calf up, real quick. Unless it's hopping off the damned horse. Sometimes getting loose from a horse can be a little bit of a trick.'"

"I had tears in my eyes, sitting on that bench listening to Danny. All my troubles seemed so small. 'Never mind,' Danny told me again. He sounded suddenly tired, as though he'd had enough. 'Never mind,' he said, 'it will come to you. There's no big deal to roping a calf.' Then he just faded away and was gone."

"That night I dreamed of Danny, and he showed me all the tricks to roping a calf."

"And you became the world champion calf roper," Sophie said softly.

"Yep, me and Danny did."

"You know, Adam, this must be the most emotional day of my life. You'd have thought I would have run out of tears by now," Sophie sniffed, wiping her eyes with a disintegrating, soggy tissue.

"Me, too," Adam concurred, handing her his own damp handkerchief.

Sophie snapped a few cuttings from the trumpet vines that grew all along and over the orchard wall. She and Adam laid the bright green branches with their rich, deep orange trumpets at the foot of Danny's marker. The two stood, unconsciously holding hands, lost in the past with their missing friend. The air was warm and sweet with the scent of Louisa's roses, and the afternoon light came down through the cottonwoods in long soft columns. The trumpet vines along the wall stirred once, though no breeze touched them. Sophie saw the grace of nonchalance as Danny, on horseback, whirled and spun his way through working the herd and riding his endless range. She glanced at Adam and saw that his eyes were somewhere far away, too, back in the bunkhouse mirror, she guessed, getting ready for the ice cream social, Danny's devil-may-care grin right beside his own.

Finally, Sophie touched the stone, warmed by the sun, and said farewell. Adam paused at the newer marker beside Danny's and touched it, too.

"My dear friend, Danny, take good, good care. We will come again, often, to remember you."

Still hand in hand, Adam and Sophie slowly walked back to the waiting Lincoln. They stood and took one long last look around the empty headquarters that silent summer afternoon. Then, without a further word, they got into the waiting car. It was time to go to the wagon, one more time.

• • •

Earlier that day, the wagon had served as a busy stage. It had first been the setting for a heart-to-heart between Louisa and Joe Carpenter, and had then seen the reunion of Amy and Kyle and the reacquainting of Jason and Tammy.

Of these encounters, Kyle's and Amy's was the sweetest. When Kyle rode into camp that morning to change mounts for working the herd, he was as nervous as a cat. His stomach's flutterings felt like a thousand butterflies were batting about inside it, all trying to find a way out at once.

"I sure hope I don't throw up," he told Jason as they loped up from the herd.

"I can't believe you," his best buddy said disgustedly. "How you can get yourself all worked up over seeing Amy Jeffers is beyond me. I mean, you've seen that girl nearly every day since birth. I don't see how either one of you can manage to work up any excitement after all this time. Looks to me like you'd both be sick to death of each other and of the big romance by now. Just the way I am. You ought to look around for somebody new."

"Bullshit," Kyle said cheerfully. "You'd jump on Amy yourself quick enough if I wasn't in the way."

"Yeah, right. Just like oil jumps on water." Jason noticed just in time that his old friend was about to take offense and start heatedly defending his back-again girlfriend. "Oh, calm down, Kyle," he hastily said. "You know I like Amy. She's okay. But you forget, I've been tripping over her just about every day of my life, too. It's a little hard for me to get too thrilled over her, that's all."

"Yeah, but you'll be able to get yourself pretty thrilled if your little Tammy shows up."

Jason blushed. "Yeah," he said. "I might be."

"Yeah, you will be. I'm going to think it's pretty funny watching you write letters and pay long-distance phone bills and drive all over the damn place to rodeos. Amy and I are going to sit back and laugh our asses off."

Jason ignored his friend's teasing. He just grinned and kept on loping.

All the ladies, Louisa, Kitten, Amy, and Tammy, walked out to meet the two boys as they rode into camp. Amy felt a sudden sensation that they were all somehow caught up in a far-away and distant time and were held there breathless and waiting for the men to come back after a hard and long campaign. For a moment, in that catch in time, she felt the tremor in her heart and the sudden shyness and bounding pride and joy known to every waiting woman who had ever existed as she watched him gallop home.

"Kyle!"

He noticed that her voice was different, breathless and husky for a moment. Pulling his horse to a stop, Kyle smiled down into her upturned face.

"Amy." Without thought, he sprang down and gave her a crushing hug. "I'll kiss you later, when we haven't got such an audience," he whispered in her ear.

Amy laughed and kissed him anyway.

A little embarrassed, but as happy as he had ever been, Kyle slid his arm around her and held her tightly for a second more.

"Come on," he said. "I've got to change horses and get back out to the herd. Gramma, did you bring a saddle for Amy?" Kyle asked Louisa.

"But of course. I brought my very own, complete with quick-set stirrups. You can have Amy saddled up in no time."

"Thanks, Gramma. I owe you."

"You always do. Here's your dad now, with the saddle."

Joe walked up carrying a fancy, beautifully carved saddle that Degarrin had made for Louisa years ago.

"Thanks, Daddy." Kyle stepped to meet his father. He shook his father's hand and took the saddle in one movement.

"Kyle," his father said, shaking the offered hand. "Did you have a good summer?"

"Super, Daddy. It's been just super."

"Good," Joe smiled as he watched his handsome son.

But Kyle scarcely heard him.

"Come on, we've got to hustle." Kyle stripped the saddle blanket off his horse. Then, slipping the bridle off in one quick gesture, he turned to Amy. "Come on," he said. "Let's go."

"She might need this," Joe Carpenter commented, holding out Louisa's bridle to Amy.

"Yes," she laughed, "I sure might."

When Kyle and Amy reached the rope corral, Toby already had his best horse saddled for Tammy. Jason might have invited her, but Toby was in charge. Tammy winked at Jason as she mounted up.

"Let's ride!" Tammy said.

"Let's ride!" Jason agreed.

Watching them gallop off, all Amy and Kyle could do was laugh. Tammy and Jason might remember them when they reached the herd, or they might not.

Serious for just a second, Kyle watched Amy's beautiful profile for a moment.

"I missed you, Amy. I'm awfully glad you're back."

Amy turned to him with a radiant smile that lit her eyes and made them shine like stars.

"Me, too," she told him, and then continued, "I love you so much, Kyle, that if you ever leave me, I'm going with you."

Kyle just laughed and shook his head. "It's a deal," he said.

• • •

Over lunch and into the afternoon, Louisa Degarrin watched the full-blown flower of Kyle's and Amy's romance and the tentative budding of possibilities for Jason and Tammy. She only watched in idle curiosity. Kyle and Amy were entirely too young, she thought, whereas she knew Jason and Tammy were entirely inappropriate. Louisa had dealt too many hands and played too many cards trying to manage other people's hearts. They just would not be managed. Today had certainly proven that, she thought. Years ago, she had gone to the wall and practically destroyed her relationship with her only child to save the girl from worthless Adam Connor. Now, after all this time, after oceans and rivers of water under a solid rock bridge, where was that girl now?

"Somewhere off with that worthless man, I suppose," Louisa answered her own question. "I give up," she thought. "Let her do what she wants. I suppose she will, anyway."

Louisa told herself she was glad to be out of the game. But even so, she kept a keen eye trained on the distant road winding out across the prairie. She hoped to see a white Lincoln there, carrying home her wayward child. Some games were hard to leave, and there were some that could not be left at all.

• • •

When the white Lincoln finally did arrive, it was as though all of La Conquistadora let out its breath in a sigh of deep relief. Degarrin asked Toby to call time-out in the branding pen. Even though the work was nearly done, it was time to take a break. It was time to welcome his daughter back to the fold, and it was time to turn his lariat and Teddy Blue over to his grandson. It was time for Kyle to finish up the last roping of the summer work, and it was time for Sophie to watch what her son could do.

In those last moments inside the Lincoln's glassy sanctuary, with way too many eyes watching them, Adam grabbed Sophie's hand one last time. He held it hard in his and looked at her just as hard.

"Remember, Sophie," he said. "Anytime, anywhere. Just say the word. I'll turn this car around and take you out of here right this second if you want me to."

Sophie grasped his hand and held it just as hard, torn for a moment. She looked at this old familiar scene and at the branding pen with all her family and all her memories.

"I'll remember. Always."

With these last words and one last longing look at her old love, Sophie opened the door and stepped out into La Conquistadora.

Standing beside Sophie's car, Adam watched her trim, straight back as she walked away from him toward the branding corral. Sophie did not look back, but she knew he was watching; she could feel his eyes on her the way she always had. Adam squared his shoulders and put his Stetson firmly on his head. She heard him pause, and she knew, without turning, that he was looking out across her father's kingdom, sweeping those restless eyes from horizon to horizon, across the waving green pastures to the mesas and back again. It was the most beautiful place he had ever seen. It always had been.

Joe Carpenter walked to meet his wife. Halting where they met, he gave her a long and searching look. It was the same look he always greeted her with. Joe Carpenter always checked to make sure Sophie was okay. He smiled at what he saw.

"Sophie. You're back."

"That I am," she said.

"I'm so glad," Joe said simply, and gave her a mighty hug. Looking into her eyes, his smile grew all the more. "Do you know what else is back?" he asked her.

"What?"

"The sparkle in your eyes. You look eighteen."

Sophie just laughed. "You helped put it there," she said. "You're a real good man, Joe Carpenter. Today, I feel eighteen."

Joe was no fool. He knew very well when not to push it, when to let a sleeping dog lie. With his arm still firmly around his wife, he said, "When last I checked, Kyle was mounting up on Teddy Blue to finish up the roping. Your daddy's going to let him finish up a star today, I guess."

"My, my! I guess so, if he gave him Blue! I've only ridden Teddy Blue a handful of times myself."

"Well, let's go and see what our boy can do."

With her husband's arm around her, Sophie and Joe walked together through the afternoon heat to watch their son under the timeless turquoise sky. In the pen, Kyle sat Teddy Blue like he had been born to it, his loop already building, and Sophie could see in the set of his shoulders and the steadiness of his hands everything this summer had made of him. At the fence, Louisa watched her daughter's face and saw something she had not seen in twenty-three years: the girl from the photographs, open and shining. She had not kept them apart. She had only delayed the reckoning, and raised its price. Somewhere behind them, she knew, Adam was watching, too.

• • •

The guests left that afternoon. Sophie rode back to Carrolton with her husband and her sparkle, and Adam drove north toward Santa Fe. The crew scattered to bunkhouse and town. By evening, the headquarters was quiet.

Degarrin found Louisa on the portal, in her chair, watching the last color drain from the sky.

He sat down beside her and was quiet for a long time.

"The Stillmores have found a buyer," he said.

Louisa's hands went still in her lap. She did not look at him.

"When?" she asked.

"They've been talking since spring. I didn't want to say anything until it was certain." He paused. "It's certain now."

"What will happen to us?"

"The new people will want their own man. That's how it works." He looked at his hands, the same hands that had branded a hundred thousand calves, mended a thousand miles of fence, held the reins of horses whose names he still remembered. "We'll have until spring."

Louisa reached over and took his hand. They sat together in the gathering dark, listening to the creek and the last of the swallows, two old people at the end of a long and good life on a place that had never been theirs, not in the way that mattered, the way of the deed and the dollar, the way that had always belonged to people a thousand miles away who had never stood in a pasture and watched the grass die.

Out beyond the corrals and the empty branding pen and the wagon shed where the old chuck wagon sat in its final dark, the range stretched away to the mesas under the first stars. The grass was thick and green from the summer rains, and it would be thick and green next summer, too. The monsoon would come. The creeks would run. The light would pour down in the long afternoons and the mockingbird would sing its stolen songs in the orchard. La Conquistadora had been here before the Degarrins, before the Stillmores, before the people who had chipped their arrowheads on those sandy flats. It would be here long after all of them were gone. The land did not grieve. The land did not remember. The land simply went on, beautiful and indifferent and unconquered, exactly as it had for millennia. That was its nature. That was its name.

The only thing that had ever changed it was the weather.

Author's Note

This novel grew out of a place I knew.

My grandfather managed a cattle ranch in northeastern New Mexico – a land grant property of more than a quarter million acres, old enough that the adobe walls of its headquarters had been standing since before the Civil War. He ran it for over twenty years. My family lived in the orbit of that ranch, and I grew up absorbing its rhythms, its people, and its particular combination of beauty and hardship.

The ranch in this novel is not that ranch, and the people in it are not those people. But the country is the same country. The work is the same work. The way the sky looks before a storm, the sound a lariat makes when it catches, the smell of a branding pen on a hot afternoon – I did not have to look any of that up. I knew it the way you know the rooms of a house you grew up in, by feel, in the dark.

The characters are my own invention. But the world they move through, I borrowed. I borrowed it from the men and women I watched and listened to as a girl – cowboys and cooks and ranch wives and my own family, none of whom knew they were being studied by someone who would one day try to put them on a page. Whatever truth lives in these pages, it came from them. Whatever I got wrong is mine.

I should have read a book about how to write a book before I wrote a book. But I had a story, and it wouldn't leave me alone, and eventually the only thing left to do was tell it.

I hope it was worth the wait.

Acknowledgments

A novel may have one name on the cover, but it does not get there alone.

Chris Greer believed in this story when it was sitting in a drawer not doing anyone any good. He read it, understood what it was trying to be, and then did the considerable work of helping it become that thing. He edited with care and without ego, built a publishing house around it, and never once let me settle for less than the book deserved. Every writer should be so lucky. I wasn't looking for a partner in this, but I found one, and the book you are holding exists because of him.

My grandfather ran a great ranch in New Mexico for more than two decades, and in doing so he gave me the world this novel lives in. My grandmother kept the headquarters and held everything together in the way that ranch women do — which is to say, completely, and with very little credit. My parents raised me in that country, on horseback and in dust, and never once suggested I might want to be somewhere else. My brother grew up in the same country and loved it the same way. Everything I know about that life, I learned from the people I am related to.

The cowboys, the cooks, the wagon bosses, the ranch wives, and the foremen I grew up around — I watched all of you more carefully than you realized. You are in these pages whether you know it or not, and I thank you for being worth writing about.

And to the land itself — the mesas and the Canadian breaks and the big empty sky — I did my best. You were always the hardest character to get right.

www.ingramcontent.com/pod-product-compliance
Lightning Source LLC
LaVergne TN
LVHW041103080826
845145LV00007B/1674

* 9 7 8 1 9 7 2 1 9 4 0 6 5 *